In March All Grays Open

A Novel

Luke J. Kosmas

Book cover art by Sabrina Kosmas.

Dedicated to my parents, John and Teresa,
and my friend, Josh Walsh.

Special thanks to Bethany Sousa for encouraging me to write,
to Jim Girdlestone for your invaluable wisdom and guidance,
and to my editor, Kerri Miller.

Many thanks to all my family and friends who've encouraged,
read, and steered this story into something better
than it would be without.

Contents

February 23rd

His feet inched down the darkened hallway, nothing but a hand on the wall to guide until he reached the bathroom. After a few more blind steps, David's hand entered an opening in the black, fidgeting a few seconds over the switch until the bathroom light flicked on.

David's hair flattened over his ears and neck under the showerhead. His body welcomed the warmth, the water offering the closest thing to comfort he had felt in the past eight, sleepless hours. His mind began to finally slow, the thoughts plaguing him falling along with the drops from his head. Standing became difficult, his tired body eager for a break already. He slowly sat, reaching to plug the bathtub drain as the water rained over his skin.

The mirrors clouded as steam escaped through the sliding shower door he'd left ajar. The heat would eventually bring him to a sweat, but he had to combat the frigid morning. Winter had but a month remaining; nevertheless, it multiplied its harshness in the weeks before spring.

David only meant to rest his eyes, yet his chest was completely submerged, body beginning to slide and sink. The water almost made it up to his nose, but this was not what woke him from his unexpected slumber. He flinched awake, sending a wave through the shower door, splashing onto the tile floor. From down the hallway, the ringing continued to scream to add to the chaos. Seeing the tub was inches from overflowing, he quickly unplugged the drain.

His panic at the obnoxious ring was brief, remembering that he was the only one home; the high pitch would not fail to carry throughout a house even as vast as theirs. For this morning, he'd chosen the most disruptive sound he could find, paranoid that his typical alarm might not wake him. Finding reassurance in the fact that his carriers were out, he curled and tucked his knees into his chest as the water drained.

Towel wrapped around his waist, he trudged back down the hall. 6:31 a.m. He silenced the maddening melody and tossed his towel on the bed, adding to the disorganization of where he'd fought to sleep. Had David known he would have given up on sleep and risen out of bed early, he may have never set the alarm to begin. His restless, kicking feet had disrobed the queen-sized mattress in the night.

For some time, David's carriers had offered to buy him a king-sized bed, pressing him up until his Fifteenth year in anticipation of his growth spurt to come. He'd insisted that the king would be too large, and neither of David's carriers was all that tall anyway. He now wondered if such a large bed would have allowed him to sleep better last night. He looked around his room for his backpack, admitting that a king bed would not have bettered the sleep for a single five-foot-nine Potential.

The thin-rimmed glasses sat on the nightstand beside his bed. His vision was not miserable, mostly needing the pair for reading. Whether tasked to read for school or choosing a novel or comic book from his corner shelf, it was just enough to keep them on at all times.

Putting his glasses on brought the picture to clarity. The painting hung above his guitar, depicting an abstract combination of outer space and his home city, Bellark. It was the only addition to the wall, other than the three-foot-wide contration vent that lined the bottom. He had not yet hung any other decorations since he had recently moved rooms, taking what used to be his sister's after she left for university in November. It was furthest from his carriers.

Zipping his jeans, David glanced again at the guitar, certain if he picked it up the strumming would not stop. He'd learned the instrument fairly quickly and could already tune it by ear. His best friend Jensen had pointed out that most beginners do not learn that skill after only playing for three months. Still, David saw himself as any other novice. It was purely a love for the sound that kept him at it each day. The only person David truly compared himself was to himself, had he discovered the instrument sooner, often wondering how skilled he might have become had he not waited to begin once his relationship with Olivia ended.

The quiet of the living room would be productive, he thought, reviewing for the Empirical Scholastic Exam, or ESE. The room was spacious and grand as the white pearl walls vaulted high above. The matching pearl couch and chairs complimented the wide transparent coffee table. As far back as David could recall, his father and mother only purchased the most extravagant, often cycling out furniture every couple of years. This pattern of frequent purchase finally came to an end when David began secondary school. He never asked why, assuming that his carriers had finally found the furniture set worth keeping.

Normally, the house would bustle with family performing their morning routines, including his sister Penelope. Now, with her living in a different city and his carriers out early for work—David's father had a rare early meeting downtown, and more unusual, his mother had accompanied him—the only sound in the silence of the titanic living room was David's pant leg rubbing speedily against the chair.

The nerves from the night had doubled soon after he removed his materials from his backpack. He read aloud a formula from the study guide, "X equals negative b, plus or minus . . ." This one he felt comfortable with, maybe even confident.

Moving on to the next equation, his body grew warm under the hoodie. There were many different symbols, letters, and numbers to register, and the large, odd geometric shape did not bring it to clarity. His mind balked at his attempt to sort and order all on the pages. Before the anguish could grow, David skipped the practice equation, wishful that it would not appear on the exam more than once. *I'm pretty sure the professor never spent more than a day covering this*, he thought.

Despite the shower and quick bathtub nap, he did not feel close to rested or awake. Red circles trapped his eyes inside, visible even under his glasses. A few blemishes had emerged in the night as well, marring his usually smooth cheeks and forehead under the still-wet hair, which would eventually dry into brown waves.

A honk interrupted.

David strutted out the front door for his driveway, running a finger through the front patio waterfall just as he did each morning. Shortly after moving in several years ago, his carriers decided to purchase a six-foot-tall fountain to distinguish their front yard. Before adding the stone fountain, their property appeared almost exactly like all the others in the neighborhood, each house nearly a mirror reflection of the other; a similar pattern decided the front lawn grass. That was David's father's only complaint about living in these suburbs, the difficulty to set oneself apart, but he was satisfied with the security and quiet the neighborhood of northwest Bellark offered.

Further north was a forest that stretched to the next city, more than a four-hour drive away, where Penelope attended university. East, after the surrounding woods cleared, was a desert, until the next city appeared. The west would offer a blue ocean horizon if it was a clear day and one lived high enough to see over other homes and buildings; David's family did, but today he could only smell the salty ocean breeze in the February chill. He squinted toward the coast, struggling to find the waters through the overcast.

"Hey," he said, stepping into the truck.

"I don't think you've ever come out this quick," Jensen said lightheartedly.

Picking up David was a part of the normal routine, even walking to school together before Jensen received his license. That began when they befriended one another in their Tenth year. David had just moved to Bellark with his family, and it was his first day of primary school in the new area. Jensen made a joke in class, asking the teacher if he could be contrated rather than take the quiz everyone was dreading. The class erupted in laughter. The teacher had been writing on the whiteboard, and when she turned around, the first person she saw laughing was David. The rest of the class zipped to a silence in fear of the easily displeased woman. David did not catch the cue.

"Do you think you're funny for making that joke? Looks like you're the only one laughing," she blurted angrily to David.

He was never much of a talker in social settings but found the courage to give a simple, yet rebellious reply. *"Yes."* The class was shocked not only by David's answer but also by the fact that he took responsibility for Jensen's attempt. David figured the joke was not meant to disrespect the teacher as much as it was intended to give the class a laugh.

"Well, go be funny in detention," the teacher said.

Surprised that the new student was taking the blame, Jensen rose from his chair. *"Wait! It wasn't him who made the contration joke."* He lowered his eyes in apology. *"It was me."*

"Well, you can join him then." The teacher pointed to the door. *"He is new to our school."*

"Guess we're in this together," Jensen said to David as the two walked to the detention room. *"Looks like I've got to get your back now."* The two were inseparable since.

Jensen backed out of the driveway as David creaked out another yawn. It took an effort to think about and respond to Jensen's previous comment; he was correct. David was seldom ready by the time Jensen arrived, usually still rushing to collect his school supplies. Rarely was he the one to wait, much less have time to study.

"I got ready pretty fast," David finally responded. "Took a pass on breakfast, which sped things up."

"No breakfast?" Jensen said concerned.

"Wasn't hungry."

"You look tired, man. Should have eaten something."

"I hardly slept," said David. "Breakfast wouldn't have made a difference."

"You gotta stay positive. You've studied and done all you can."

A new thought overtook David, his mind like a leaf stolen by the wind. *I should just skip the ESE. Graduate and just try again later.* Throughout the recent weeks, he never failed to grow sick at the thought of failing the exam. *At least in post-secondary schooling, I get more time to prepare.* David dreaded that scenario more, however. The idea of having to continue further education that was not university level was humiliating. Another doubt rushed through: *How can I make my carriers proud? Penelope scored a perfect 10.* This pattern continued, his mind wandering in every direction that his insecurities tugged.

David sought to distract himself by looking out the window, watching the passing houses, businesses, and other structures on their usual route. Their normal vibrancy was muted, however. The sun was hidden behind the clouds, as it had been for most of the month. Most Bellark February's were similar to this year's, and the clouds never seemed in any rush to leave. The residents considered it a decent day if the sun climbed its entire self through the clouds more than twice. Still, even under the gloom, David had to admit that northwest Bellark was impressive. The area had developed in so little time.

After the secession, and once the depression and technological stall had ended, Bellark had experienced explosive growth. It was not the only prosperous city; most of the nation had been rebuilding busily. During reconstruction, the government had managed to accomplish its goals while pleasing the majority of the people. David felt brief excitement, acknowledging he would be able to vote soon and bring his opinion to bear on the nation's future after reaching his Eighteenth year. *Just a few more days.*

The two pulled into the student parking lot. Glenn Haven Secondary School was architecturally superior in every aspect, layered of variant colored brick. It was four stories high and resembled a university with different greens climbing up the sides of the building. The school offered a premier education compared to its counterparts elsewhere in the city, preparing students most thoroughly for the ESE and future university education.

"You know they make the Prep ESEs harder, right?" It was as if Jensen had heard David's unspoken worries. "You'll be fine." Only students younger than Seventeen take the Preparatory ESE each year. David had failed three of the PESEs in primary school but had passed each one in secondary, though just barely.

"Yeah, I know." He tensely wiped his palms on his jeans.

They remained inside the truck under the parking lot overhang. The two had some minutes to spare, and Jensen did not want to sit in the classroom longer than needed. The ESE was enduring and lengthy, and the daunting recollection of the preparatory exams was enough to rid any eagerness.

A natural for academics, Jensen was not too nervous for himself, the type of student to not take notes or even turn in all his assigned homework. His grades naturally suffered, but these reports did not accurately reflect his intelligence. He had the photographic memory most Potentials envied, scoring two 9's and an 8 on the last three PESEs. David scored one 5 and two 6's.

He made sure to not communicate his completely candid thoughts to David, even with body language. Though Jensen's belief in his friend possibly failing was minuscule, David may still latch on to any of Jensen's small doubt and make it his own. "You ready, man?" He said optimistically.

David hopped out of the truck. When Jensen caught up to him under the entrance, David read the school sign: "Haven Glenn School Secondary?" There was a sly smirk on his face.

If Jensen did not respect him enough already, he admired David all the more for the well-timed joke. David had confided his learning disability that first day they met in primary school. Just as when he declined Jensen's offer to write the detention essay for him, David took every opportunity to overcome his dyslexia, even if sometimes that meant making himself the punchline.

This new, odd confidence did not manifest from David's certainty that he would pass the ESE, nor could he guarantee that his dyslexia and anxiety would be completely manageable during the entire length of the exam. Rather, the peace came from knowing all was not lost if he were to fail. At worst, there would be a year postponement before he began university. He thought to himself: *Much better to get set back a year and live.*

*

"Your ESE is five hours long," said the head proctor. "You have three hours for the first section. You will take a half-hour lunch and continue your exam at noon. The last section of your exam must be completed by two o'clock. During the exam and lunch break, you may talk to no one.

"The Empirical Scholastic Exam plays a key role in your future academic career by determining which universities you will be eligible to attend, so try your best. The highest possible score is 10, and the lowest is 1. Scoring a 5 or higher is passing and scoring a 4 or lower is failing. Also, I imagine you all know this, but I'm legally required to explain." He looked around the room. "Scoring a 4 or lower allows for a Pote, yourselves, to qualify for a contration. Whether you can be contrated then depends on your carriers' income. Because you are all attending this school, it's safe to assume they're doing just fine. Anyone who fails this exam will most likely find him or herself at a post-secondary school for a retake opportunity next year."

The classroom was full of other students, all Seventeenth-year Potentials, spaced four feet apart across five rows of wooden desks. They had all begun their final year of secondary school in November for the new academic year; students were arranged accordingly, none reaching their Eighteenth years until after the February Closing that followed the ESE. David and Jensen were on opposite sides, but the curvature of their shared row allowed them to see one another.

"You may begin," said the proctor.

David opened his exam book, bubbling in his first answer after a few minutes. The quiet scribbling of pencils filled the empty air, along with the turning of exam book pages and the occasional cough or sneeze.

The first two hours passed. Thus far, David was

maintaining a consistent pace within the allotted time frame. While he did read and answer more slowly as he exerted the extra effort to comprehend the letters and words, there remained a poise that allowed a rare momentum. Jensen glanced up to check on his friend, assured by David's unbreakable concentration to the booklet in front.

"Thirty minutes remaining," the proctor announced.

It was almost time for lunch. David was eager, a growing hunger crawling throughout his empty stomach. The consequences of refusing to eat breakfast on top of the sleep deprivation began to take hold during the last leg of the first section. There was an added delay to each remaining question, but nothing that would prove detrimental to his personal goal, he thought.

The proctor glanced at the timer on his desk. "Put your pencils down. That is time."

David dropped his pencil and scanned over the answer sheet. Thirteen unanswered—one shy of his goal. The hunger had stifled him more than anticipated. Though slightly disappointed, he felt reassured by his performance on the ones he did complete. Not even on the PESEs did he feel so engaged.

Gathered in the cafeteria, students tried to keep their chewing quiet in the uncomfortable silence. David took no mind, however, inhaling his food like a vacuum so that any nearby student took notice. One made a quiet comment when a chaperone drifted far enough away, but David only nodded, too focused on his lunch to listen. He gathered it was something sarcastic about how obnoxiously he was eating.

Jensen was chuckling under his breath, having watched from a few tables away as he ate his sandwich. Being physically bigger than David, Jensen was usually the one to finish his food first. However, he knew not even he could devour his lunch as fast as David in that moment.

The students returned to the classroom and waited for the proctor's next direction. As soon as all were seated, he gave the command. Heads once again leaned forward and down, knowing there was no margin to grow lax. The gravity of this exam was apparent to all. No matter how exhausted any student felt, their future depended upon this performance. Nevertheless, though they felt the weight of societal and familial pressure to attend a prestigious university and build a prosperous career, each student knew their stresses were not as severe as those taking the ESE in other secondary schools outside the northwest.

The mathematics portion of the ESE was the second and final section. This was David's least favorite, a disinterest bordering on disdain for the subject. With reading and writing, he at least found himself engaged with much of the content. The same went for other homework or projects if assigned an interesting book with a fair amount of time to finish. Mathematics, on the other hand, was a persistent gnawing at his brain.

He knew he could not rush these equations, beginning with an even slower, careful focus than what he began in the morning. The first equations were familiar, a few similar to what he had studied the previous night. *I can do this.* The first twenty minutes went much as the first section had. If this kind of momentum continued, he thought he might, by some miracle, score a 7.

Confident, he turned the page in victory once more.

His breath paused as if halting his lungs would allow his brain to work better. After rubbing his eyes, he again stared down to bring the characters into anything resembling an order or grouping. The letters, numbers, and symbols were moving and disappearing, but more alarming was his inability to calm his rising heartbeat. He blinked a few times and opened his eyes wide as he read, any effort to combat the intruding anxiety. *I didn't study enough for this.* It was the same geometric shape that his eyes had try to ignore that morning and every other time he'd seen it in the study guide.

Skipping the equation, he almost tore the page from the panicked turn. There it was again, a similar order of letters and shapes, but entirely different. *Twice? We hardly spent one day on it in class.* His heart rate was quicker than the rapid movement of his eyes. The symbols on the paper were shaking as if there was a tremor beneath.

"Thirty minutes remaining."

It was far beyond him to grasp how the time had soared. David turned the page once more, feeling the added pressure to complete the remaining equations in half the time he would usually spend. "No way." The words escaped him sneakily, but the neighboring students were able to hear, some even turning to take notice of David's lifeless face as he stared at yet another equation similar to the two he'd skipped.

Another page flipped.

Why can't I just . . . He rarely cursed his learning disability, yet he couldn't help himself in this situation, the bitter negativity poisoning what mental focus he had left. His hand was writing with a frenzied, schizophrenic will of its own. While the remaining equations were nowhere near as difficult as the three that had blindsided him, the damage was done. David could no longer put forth his best against the ticking clock. Each beat of its cold, mechanical heart seemed to mock him, each one an insult for falling behind.

He glanced up for Jensen. He was already finished and looking at David, all of his thoughts now focused on his hope that he would end well. But Jensen had an idea of how it was unfolding from David's untamable, shaking leg.

"Five minutes remaining."

David was the only one left with an open exam atop his desk, and he had twenty-one questions unmarked. *What a lie. Whoever said the practice exams were easier is full of it.* Just about all his fortitude forsaken, he answered only one more.

"That is time," said the head proctor. "All pencils down. A faculty member will come by and collect your exams. You may be released once all are collected. Because today was your ESE, you all may leave school early."

The two friends exited the classroom last. David's paranoia rose as he overheard other students discussing how effortless the ESE had been as if intentionally shining a spotlight of shame on him. His mouth set in a grim line as they left the building.

Jensen broke the silence. "How'd you do?" he asked

carefully. He had his suspicions but was more concerned with freeing David from his head.

David's spirit was low. "Well, I was the last one to finish."

"You finished?"

"No. I had twenty left on the last section."

Jensen took a moment to respond. "Well, what about the first section?"

"Ehh. Not too bad. I think I did okay. I feel like I may have done better there than I did on the practice exams. It was only after lunch when it went south."

"Well, at least you've got that going for you."

"I butchered the math portion." David stopped walking. "The only way I would have done decent on it with that many unanswered is if I got . . ." He stopped to think. "I don't even know. I'm not a math guy, apparently." The two were just before Jensen's truck. They could hear light drops of rain tapping the overhang. The scent of the wet asphalt hinted that the rain had arrived sometime earlier.

"I'm sorry, man," Jensen said. "Who knows . . . Maybe you did alright on the ones you did answer?"

David's eyes went to the ground, following a thin stream that fell from an overhang gap and trailed down the slight slope of the lot. "It'd be a miracle."

Jensen looked in the back of his truck; he'd almost forgotten what was inside. He hadn't bothered bringing it up to David the night before since his mind was busy enough.

He looked up as Jensen began walking around. "What's up?"

"Check in the back," Jensen said, grinning. There, lying in the truck bed were two fishing poles. Next to them were a tackle box and a cooler. "You up for it?" He said more pressingly, "I figured it would be good for us to do something fun and relax after the ESE. Plus, we're out of school early."

"Nod Meadow? But it's raining."

"When did that stop you?" Jensen hopped into the driver's seat, knowing what David would choose.

The traffic was not as grueling as usual since they were

released from school early. The frequent sightings of corporations, digital billboards, and freeway junctions increased as they neared downtown, but keeping on the southbound 125 mostly kept them out of stop and go traffic. There was a bit of a slowdown as they merged for the junction to take Highway 38 east, but the road soon became their own once they left the city walls for the open valley beside the northern mountainside. Before the highway continued into the desert that grows more barren, the boys turned to ascend the hillside, rising and winding through pine trees.

Though there were closer lakes and ponds, they enjoyed traveling to Nod because it was deserted more often than not, following the incline dirt road that meets a dead-end at arrival. Only a handful of cabins were scattered across the foothill countryside, helping to aid the seclusion. Jensen's grandfather Sam first took him there when he was a toddler, and after he and David became friends, the invite was his forever. Once Jensen received his driver's license and truck, the two boys had gone as often as they could get away.

When they reached the meadow, the rain had ceased entirely, a few sunrays emerging through the thick gray. The temperature dropped with the new elevation, but the meadow always seemed to feel just right despite the chill. The beams illuminated the faint green grass, one ray, in particular, kissing the surface of the lake for a quiet glimmer. Many trees surrounded the meadow itself as if they were its sworn protectors. Unlike most of the plants and flowers that disappeared in the winter, the pine trees stood strong.

What was unique, however, even for the boys before they accepted the strange phenomena, was how a few determined others bore their green as well. Among those resilient few were the six fruit trees perched near the meadow entrance. Jensen and David strolled through the grass to check on their first greeters. However, the usual introduction instead brought a solemn surprise. It was a colder winter, but this did not soften the blow for the boys. Three trees slumped, their bases yellow and white.

"Wow," Jensen said. "Just when you thought they could suffer through anything."

"Have you seen this before?" David set the tackle box down to feel the wilting leaf of one.

"Yeah. Not in a long while though. Before you ever came here, there were seven. That winter got only one though. Not three."

Despite the unsettling discovery, they gathered the last few hanging apples from the dead trees. David was just as confounded as Jensen when he first learned the mystery of how these still bore fruit through the season, but he eventually came to accept it. *But even they can only fight so much.*

The other fighter that endured and held on to but a few of its last season's leaves was the large maple tree beyond the lake. David likely would have never checked on it to begin if it were not for discovering the dead fruit trees, but his eyes went to the maple, curious if it met its end as well. *Turn away.* His head snapped reflexively away from the distant tree, positioning his body to behold the rest of the meadow instead.

David's heart began to steady. The concern of his impending exam grade, along with the recent maple tree distress, dissipated with each minute he kept his gaze across the lake. His only interest now was to cast his line into the rippling body of water.

The two settled in their accustomed spots and began. David may not have had the highest test scores, but he could outfish anybody. The amount he reeled in continually baffled Jensen, though he had a general idea to explain David's success. They dropped their lines in at the same time and used the same bait. However, David had an unrivaled patience, able to sit still in one spot longer than his friend. Jensen would arise and walk around more frequently, especially if there was no action from his fishing pole, taking greater delight in the outing than in the sport itself. It was David who had the true heart of a fisherman.

David stared out into the water intently as if trying to make eye contact, but unable to find a pair to meet. He was thinking about the life dwelling below the lake's surface: the algae, the fish, and even the insects that rested on top. He meandered further down another one of his typical silent rabbit trails, wondering how many fish were swimming and how many remained in their eggs. *What does it take to hatch? Time? Strength? Maybe each fish is guaranteed to.*

David's eyes jumped to his line as it tightened and pulled down the rod tip to the water. His arm shot out, bringing the pole to grip with both hands. Lifting and yanking, he braced himself for resistance as he reeled. There was no strength to come against his, however. Disappointed, he spun in a few more rotations to confirm. "I don't know where she is now, but she definitely took a nibble at it," he announced to Jensen, perched twenty feet away.

Though feeling a minor loss, these were the moments that motivated David most. Not one for traditional ball sports, this was his game, the kind that brought out his competitor. He anticipated the next activity from his line, expecting immediate action, but there was none.

David kept his focus glued to the rod for a long while, but after thirty minutes, his eyes went beyond the pole and line. Even with the task in front, he could not help the glance, though he did not wish it. His eyes were set on the maple tree once more, unable to take them away like the sudden reflex that brought them there. Fist tightening to rod, but not as a reaction to a bite, he knew it was inevitable to come to the unsettling memory.

Olivia's first and only time at Nod was with him and Jensen last summer. She said she had never been fishing, so he invited her to join, though without consulting Jensen. Although frustrated and protective of their private spot at first, Jensen ended up having a great time with the two. He even gave his official approval of their relationship by driving some distance to hike through the mountainside and leave the couple alone.

David turned the rest of his body toward the tree, like pushing a rotting tooth. Though the pain grew, he could not remove his sight. *You made the right choice.* The decision's toll was incalculable, which became all too real when Olivia severed contact, and her family moved out of Bellark. Since their split, time tried to heal, but it seemed whenever he returned to Nod Meadow, it was as if blood dripped from an old wound.

On several occasions, David almost asked Jensen if they

could search for a new fishing site. But he knew no other area measured up half as well to the isolation, beauty, and peace of Nod. Of course, David was sure Jensen would accommodate his request if he were entirely honest with his conflict, but he felt it would be selfish to remove Jensen from the lifelong fishing getaway, especially since David's decision about Olivia had nothing to do with him. However, had Jensen known it was under the maple tree David and Olivia first gave themselves to one another, he would have never asked David to come to the meadow again.

Knowing this, he'd never confessed it to Jensen, instead claiming that their first time was at Olivia's house. As long as they remained friends, and for every time they would venture to Nod, David felt he had no choice but to blot out the difficulty. Thankfully, in a strange sense, he could still find the purity in the meadow. It just took time to adjust, and it was imperative he kept his sight away from the maple tree.

"David!" Jensen yelled.

The pole was bent nearly to the point of snapping, forming a narrow arch. He leaped for it, yanking it upward to secure the hook into his new rival. Confident this was not a mere nibble, David put his methodology to work. He lowered and raised his rod when appropriate. He loosed the line and reeled it back in. After a few minutes, a drop of sweat rolled down his nose. "Not this time," he said, remembering the ESE. In one dynamic motion, he yanked up on the rod once more and gave a mighty reel. The fish broke the water's surface and fell to the shoreline flopping, almost triumphantly as if it knew what fish it was.

"Of course you get that one!" Jensen ran toward him.

David laughed. All attention returned to the thrill of the game, the maple tree now submerged somewhere deep in his subconscious. Nothing could erase his grin. *That fish must have lived a decade in this lake.* He looked down in satisfaction at the beastly calico catfish, pleased that he may have nabbed the largest in the water.

"I swear, man. Either I must be cursed or the fish just like you more."

"Yeah, I guess they do." David could not lie to himself or Jensen. It had been his greatest catch.

They neared their neighborhood. The sky was almost dark, a muffled twilight lingering by a hair. The two boys could still feel the ecstasy from their outing, especially David. Jensen said enthusiastically, "We're going to have to cook that fish up soon."

"Absolutely."

"Now, if only there were a holiday or some day of celebration coming up. You know . . . Give us a good reason." David read his cards immediately. Both chuckled. "Oh, come on! You didn't think I would forget?" He punched David's arm. "Okay, I know I forgot last year, but that's because I had food poisoning that day. I was living beside the toilet."

David laughed. "I know. I told you I wasn't mad."

Jensen said, "Anyway, back to what I was trying to say. Your Eighteenth is coming up in like what? Three days? Four?"

David said, "Four."

"Okay, then in four days! We'll fry her up for your first bite of life."

"Sounds good," said David, but his new thought tamed and reined in his laughter. For most, it was a commemorative occasion, reaching life, but David felt there would likely be no kind of celebration with his family. Recently, he began to wonder more, as he was now, what would become of him if his carriers were not wealthy. As the last few years passed, their divide had seemed to grow wider.

The most extended conversation David had with his carriers in the past year was when they encouraged his decision with Olivia. However, after she moved away to cement the end of their relationship, his carriers checked out once again, though his mother not as quickly. During that time near the tail end of last summer, he and his mother actually went out to dinner, just the two of them; the first time since his Fifteenth year. Despite the laughs and memories shared that night, there had not been a time since.

David had rarely questioned the Contration Department in his years, other than the occasional, minor suspicion. In the last year, however, he'd cast any quiet skepticism far and away. Most people agreed that it was right and just. And the nation was prospering, much more so than the surrounding countries, especially the South. Still, he could not rid himself of the unease as he pondered his coming Eighteenth.

"Jensen." David's voice had shrunken.

The sudden change let him know this conversation was not heading toward another laugh. "What's up?"

"What if I fail my exam?"

"Didn't we already talk about this sort of? Post-secondary school, right? But that's crazy unlikely."

"I know. But it's possible." David leaned forward in his seat, his belly churning. "We find out tomorrow."

Jensen always sought to reassure David when he could, but he was finding it difficult to give an easing answer. He wished David's high from the meadow had lasted longer, at least until they got inside to meet with his grandfather.

"What if my carriers were poor?"

"What do you mean?" said Jensen.

"Do you think they'd have me contrated?"

Jensen's eyebrows rose. "Do I think they'd have you contrated? David, you shouldn't even be asking that. It doesn't matter. You don't qualify."

"I know. I just wonder. You know?"

"Yeah, I guess. But you don't need to wonder," said Jensen. "Look, I know your relationship with your carriers is bad, but don't let your head go there. You're safe. You're fine. All you should be worrying about is the first thing you're gonna do when your Eighteenth comes around. Okay?" Jensen nudged him. David forced a smile to appease his friend.

It was dark when they arrived. A new moon had passed days ago, but the scant crescent moon could not do much to disrobe the cloak of black on the night. Jensen's house was similar to David's in its design; however, it lacked the front yard waterfall.

Jensen lived with his grandfather a couple of blocks down, about a ten-minute walk for David. A porch light illuminated the front patio like most the houses in the neighborhood, though David knew when he finally walks home, he'll stroll up to a house barren of light.

Parked on the driveway was a company truck belonging to Jensen's grandfather, Sam. On both sides was the graphic and name, '*Lloyd Electric.*' Though Sam had acquired great wealth from his company, he still enjoyed working hands-on in the field to pass the time. He had earned enough money to retire, but he enjoyed the work, even the unpredictable kind that comes with customer service. Sam was well respected by his customers, providing affordable rates for those who had a below-average income.

Having struggled to find a career that satisfied him after serving in the military during the secession, Sam eventually decided to leverage the electrical engineering experience he'd gained during his time of service. The business had grown steadily in the decades since, especially after the depression and technological stall. Jensen worked with him on occasion, and though a natural, he did not have a passion for it. Working with his grandfather was only a means to gain experience and some extra money.

"Hey there, fellas!" Sam rose from his chair to greet the boys walking through the front.

"Hey, Gramps," said Jensen

There was not much resemblance between him and his grandfather. Jensen's six-foot-two height and sturdy build would cause one to wonder if there was a blood relation between the two. The only hint of their relationship was the faint scatter of freckles beneath their eyes. Perhaps if Sam were young, he'd share the same auburn hair as Jensen, but his was now streaked with gray, though he'd retained a strong hairline.

Sam's face was much more rugged than Jensen's. Old age did play a role, but Jensen had soft, attractive features. David couldn't miss how many second glances he received from girls at school, though Jensen would never admit it. The year before,

19

Jensen would often turn the subject on David, claiming the girls were instead staring at him, jealous of his girlfriend, Olivia. However, after she moved away, these girls did not make any overtures with David as he had predicted. This did not bother David, however. Truthfully, he was still trying to recover after Olivia's move, and the fact of the matter in David's head: Jensen was better looking.

"How's it going, Sam?" David shook his hand, delighted to see the cheery old man. Unlike his house, Sam had the same furniture for many years since David first started visiting. He was a simple man, content with what functioned well. If the couch was comfortable, there was no reason to purchase a new one, even if there was a side tear or two. He mainly took residence in northwest Bellark to provide Jensen with safety and the best educational opportunities.

"Well, I can't complain. Just trying to keep warm and keep from turning blue," Sam said. "What about you boys? What'd you guys do today?"

"We just got back from Nod. David caught a huge catfish!"

"Did you? I guess it's fair to say you're making us dinner tonight, then?" Sam patted David's back.

"Nope," Jensen said. "We're saving it for his Eighteenth."

"That's right! That's right around the corner!" said Sam. "Yeah, yeah. Save the fish for then. What else will you do?"

"Umm, I'm not too sure. We'll figure something out," David said.

"Well, if you don't figure something out, I'm going to make you help an old man with tending his garden. I need to put some mulch down."

Jensen said quickly, "We'll figure out something to do. You're on your own with that, Grandpa."

"I know, I know," he said, chuckling. "I'm just trying to give David some motivation to get on it! You're about to become a living being. You have to celebrate."

"Don't worry. I'll buy cigars for us or something." David smoked an invisible one with his fingers.

"Now we're talking!" Sam said.

David sat on one of the living room chairs while Jensen and Sam went to the kitchen to pour drinks. He was thankful to have them in his life, more of a family to him than his carriers or sister. With them, he could be honest and confide his grief following the breakup with Olivia. Though they never advocated for his decision, they provided the best support and counsel they could offer.

David gave his attention to the television. The previous commercial had ended, replaced by a chipper voice. "Hello and welcome to Bellark Tonight! I'm Diane Culver, and tonight we have a special treat for those tuning in to our program. As promised, we've brought in the Chief of Bellark's Contration Department, Salvador Goode!"

Sam and Jensen quickened in the kitchen and came to the couch. Interviews with Salvador Goode had become more frequent lately. He was usually selected to speak on behalf of the CD because of his eloquence and history with the department. The year before, he had received an honorary award from the president for his dedication and achievements as Chief of the BCD.

Salvador Goode sat straight in his chair as the camera zoomed. Though around his Fortieth year, his handsome, youthful features threw him back a decade. He wore a black jacket, scarlet tie over a white shirt, and black slacks. The wide-angle showed his dress shoes were polished to a mirror shine.

David had not always anticipated these occasions with Salvador Goode. Once, he'd agreed with Jensen that the man was uncomfortably dominant, his demeanor and tone laced with a thread of arrogance. While Goode had never grown on Jensen, David's opinion changed over time. David would not claim to be a fan of Goode, but he would acknowledge that he better understood the reason for the Chief's advocacy. Salvador's faith in the system was so great that it seemed to fall on and over others until they, in turn, gained the same confidence.

Now, Jensen had to be tactful with his critiques of the Chief ever since he and David got in a heated argument late last year. Sam, on the other hand, had little to say about Salvador Goode or the system in general.

"Thank you for being here with us this evening, Chief Goode," Diane said, crossing her legs and resting her folded hands atop her knee.

"Thank you for having me again." Salvador's smooth baritone was almost hypnotic.

"It's been a few months since you last interviewed with us, but once again our president has asked you to provide clarification and insight as to the purpose of the CD, especially with these recent protests."

"Absolutely." Salvador leaned forward in his chair.

"First, would you mind providing our viewers with a general description of the Contration Department?"

"I'd be happy to. You know, these protesters are really saying some interesting things." The corner of his mouth quirked up. "False information should never be deemed 'truth' just because it's screamed or spoken through a megaphone."

He took a breath. "To begin, I'll briefly talk about the Closing that occurs at the end of each month, since it's around the corner." He cleared his throat, "Each month, Potes selected for contration, those Seventeen and younger, are transferred to a designated contration facility. We have different facilities for different age groups, and the chosen Potential will go to the appropriate facility. Usually with a Closing as big as February's, since it is the month of the ESE and updated score releases, we tend to need all facilities, even sometimes our older ones if there's a lot of traffic.

"Now, the decision to contrate a Pote is entirely up to the carriers. There are, however, two conditions for an approved contration. The first requirement is fairly straightforward: the annual household income of the Potential's carriers must be below thirty bancos. For the second condition, the Potential must have failed the annual Empirical Scholastic Exam, whether preparatory or official. Let it be noted; this exam score is only applied as the second condition once she or he begins primary school in their Fifth year. Before this age stage, the carriers can contrate a

Second to Fourth-year Potential solely based on income. Once taken to a facility, the selected Pote receives a painless euthanasia. They depart moments after."

David finally swallowed the ball of air that had been building.

"Thank you, Chief Goode," said Diane. "Now, I think most of the public understands what goes on, but a minority of the people have been asking why contration is necessary in the first place. Our younger viewers, who did not see the secession, or live through the depression and its aftermath, might benefit from a thorough explanation. I think the tension lies mostly in passion versus facts."

"Yes, yes!" he said eagerly. "I could not agree more about the disparity between facts and subjective intuition, or passion, as you call it. Essentially, to clearly identify what is 'true' and what is 'false' and explain the reason for the CD, we must address three main points: why we do it, the justification, and the overall benefit from the institution.

"The official Contration Department, as we know it now, came to be with the re-establishing of our nation. Our country was experiencing a severe economic depression that almost led to our collapse before the secession. After conducting studies, we were able to see a direct correlation between adverse socioeconomic outcomes and a specific type of individual: one who belonged to the impoverished or criminal demographic of the country.

"More often than not, these individuals lacked honest, sustainable jobs because of insufficient academic performance during their youth. In addition, they often came from financially unstable households. Not only was the unemployed not able to produce an income, but they also devastated their immediate families with their need for financial resources and support. Seeking this support prohibited the unemployed person's family, mainly carriers, from saving, retiring, and ultimately securing the latter parts of their lives. The family eventually cannot support their child because they cannot support themselves, and an overwhelming percentage of these noncontributors resorts to a life

23

of crime, poverty, or both.

"Following the secession divide, our leaders knew we needed a solution to the destructive trend that almost consumed us completely. Contrations were nothing new, most people familiar with the classical procedure. However, we acknowledged *that* method of contration limited the extent of good such a philosophy could accomplish. Thus, we had the impetus for the modern Contration Department, which legalized contrations through the end of the Seventeenth year. Its purpose is to prevent crime, poverty, and burden to society and carriers alike."

"This guy has got his spiel memorized," Jensen said scathingly.

A knot formed in David's stomach. The Chief's explanation had not yet reassured him as he was hoping it would. Even a month ago, David would likely have found peace from hearing Salvador speak. He could not help but return to the harrowing memory of his ESE performance earlier. *Why should failing qualify me?* Yet he knew in all fairness that he could not object to the logic here; otherwise, he would have to object to the whole, and this would unleash a monstrous unfolding of uncertainty and regret. The words of the protesters could not win out. *Listen to the Chief. You have to.*

Salvador said, "And as for the *how* we can go about this process. We knew we had to develop a fair and ethical system. Our new leaders rightly concluded that we cannot kill a living human being with legal status. It is inhumane, and the preservation of human life is of utmost importance. This then provoked a valid question: When does a human actually begin life and receive this status?

"After some of our greatest physiologists and philosophers conducted extensive scientific and metaphysical research, the federal cabinet concluded that life begins once the being is fully developed, when the self enters fullness and personhood. Before that fullness, or personhood, these beings are merely 'Potentials,' one who has the potential to exist in complete personhood. The last stages of development take place in the brain, and this organ does not finish developing until one is well into their mid-

24

Twenties; thus, our research team unanimously agreed that this is the climax of complete human development. However, because our country needed to rebuild our military as well, we made a minor compromise. Because a person of Eighteen has enough physical and mental capacity to operate in our nation's military, the Eighteenth year is when one enters his or her life."

Diane lifted the pen in her hand. "Excuse me while I interrupt you really fast."

"Oh, it's fine. Someone had to stop me from ranting." Salvador flashed a wide smile. It was strangely and uncomfortably held for too long as if a person out of frame was lifting the corners of his lips by threads.

"Tell me if I'm wrong, but for our viewers at home, the first eighteen years of a Pote is more or less a trial period to see whether that individual can contribute to society by operating in relative independence?"

"Regarding the ESE? Yes," Salvador said. "The income of the Potential's carriers is independent of any effort the Pote can put forth. The Empirical Scholastic Exam is in the Potential's hands. It would be unfair to isolate the trajectory of success strictly to the carriers' income. This is why there are two requirements for contration. We must give the Pote the opportunity to demonstrate their value, because determination and ability can overcome any economic setback. Not only does the ESE operate as a factor for a contration, but it also sets up the Pote for university education and career."

Salvador clasped his hands on his lap. "And in all of this, the department finds it imperative to emphasize that the institution operates in a fashion that values human life, as well as our society and individual choices. As soon as the Potential passes the Eighteenth year and becomes legally alive, it is our nation's conviction not to allow any contration."

Salvador swallowed a big gulp of his water and set the glass on the table between him and Diane. "Now, as for the last point we need to address," he said. "I want to first begin by saying I think we can all agree that the CD is not the first vision for any society. You see, I wish everyone in our nation labored with their

25

entire being and contributed. I wish every person would avoid crime for a life of integrity. It would be quite ideal if carriers were not financially burdened to provide for a son or daughter who refuses to consider the ramifications of apathy. However, I acknowledge this world is far from perfect; not all of us want to accept the single greatest invitation—becoming the best you can be.

"Since the beginning of the modernized Contration Department, this nation saw a rapid decrease in unemployment. We continue to see thriving businesses with the unemployment rate at the lowest ever recorded in our nation's history, even before the split. Since *our* CD, our crime rate has dropped dramatically; our streets have never been safer. Parents of adult children can financially invest in their own lives, and retirement plans have doubled in the past ten years!

"I am a believer in our country. I believe the carriers' decision whether to contrate their child—" Salvador abruptly stopped to find the word he meant to say, "—their Potential—is one of the most sacred choices we as a people should and must guard. It requires exceptional strength to set aside one's personal feelings in favor of the greater good. Let the proof be in the pudding; the current thriving state of our great nation is the testament."

Diane had to take a moment to process it all. "Well, Chief Goode. Thanks again for joining us and thank you for providing the public with this helpful insight into the Contration Department. It was an absolute pleasure to have you take time out of your busy Closing schedule to spend some time with us."

"No, it was all my pleasure! See you again next month, Diane?" Salvador closed with the same charm he'd entered the interview.

Before Diane could respond, Sam turned off the television. He placed the remote back on the table a bit aggressively. "Well, I think that's enough television for one night. David, are you going to have dinner with us?"

Dinner? The word distressed him more than his morning alarm, remembering that Penelope was coming home from her university tonight. She'd insisted on cooking dinner for the family since her classes were canceled for the following two days; the dread ruined any appetite he might have had. There had been enough experiences with these family dinners to imagine the evening's narrative. His carriers had admonished him to be at the house by 6:30 sharp. He checked the clock: 6:36 p.m.

"I'm sorry. I can't. I forgot that I have a family dinner," David said. "Thanks though."

"You know you're always welcome," said Sam.

David left up the street, strolling at a relatively slow pace on the uphill. He figured that since he was already late, there was no point in hurrying and saving no more than an extra few minutes. And these were now precious minutes he did not have to spend with his family.

*

Salvador Goode quickly departed the studio shortly after the interview. A man of manners, he made sure to give every thanks and farewell to the higher-ups: Diane Culver, the producer, and the director. They were not insulted by his hasty exit, knowing it was the last week of February.

The Chief was able to rest his eyes, not having the responsibility of driving back to headquarters, though it was only fifteen minutes away. He would not claim fatigue, but the Vice Chief knew he needed relief of any duty she could carry out, despite Salvador's initial pushback to drive himself. Delaney Abbot was approaching her ninth year of partnering with Salvador Goode and her seventh year as the Vice.

Every year was the same, every February the same with the updated ESE and PESE scores. Salvador received as much rest as Bellark received sunshine during this late season. With most department employees laboring over the final details of tomorrow's Closing, Delaney had offered to escort the Chief herself. Of course, he suggested she retire for the day, recognizing that she too had invested more than eighty hours of work that week. Politely and stubbornly, she declined.

Their vehicle was an ant among many, towered over by the colossal infrastructures of downtown Bellark. They had two of the nation's seven tallest buildings in their city alone. Salvador opened his eyes and looked out the window into the artificially lit street. "Well, another one done."

"I didn't think you were awake," Delaney said.

"I had a coffee right before the interview," he yawned. "It's torturous when your eyes want to quit, but your brain won't let 'em."

"I still don't understand why they scheduled you for the interview the night before the Closing." Delaney shook her head, her blonde hair unmoving in her tightly wound bun. "What do they think we're doing this week? Sitting in vans, listening to music until 10 p.m. tomorrow?"

"It's because of the protesters. Someone has to be the voice of reason. Disapproval has grown since last year."

"Yes, but by how much? 4.2 percent. It'll drop down again like it always does. Up and down, up and down. The president doesn't need to go into a panic every time this happens."

Salvador rubbed his eyes. "It's not panic. She simply sees the value in reeducating. They're aging out, the generation that saw what almost happened to us. Their votes will have to be sustained by the emerging demographic. Plus, 4.2 is the largest spike we've seen."

"I suppose. But why you? As if you don't have enough on your plate already."

"Well, they do it for a reason." Salvador smiled. "Didn't you listen to me? Smooth as butter, Abbot."

"Dear god," she snickered despite her restraint. "Now I don't feel bad for you anymore. You're driving your cocky-self next time."

"Not if I give you the order."

Delaney now belted out a laugh. "An order? Please. You have way too much dignity. You'd fall asleep at the wheel first."

Salvador needed a good laugh. He probably needed it more than the shuteye. Although he hadn't seen much rest as of late, the Chief could steal a few hours here and there. A laugh, however—he had not had one like that all month. Another reason why he had kept Delaney Abbot in her position for so long.

"Maybe next time we'll get Adán to fill in," he said.

"I have a feeling he would love the camera, maybe even more than you," she said sarcastically.

"More than me? Are others still even made with more conceit than myself?" Salvador poked back. "Adán knows his stuff, even if the kid does frown more than he breathes."

"I wouldn't put him on camera. He's as inviting as a contration van."

"A little bit of experience could ease him. He only graduated the academy three years ago," Salvador said.

"I'm not sure if the kind of experience he's getting really warms the heart. The only thing I could imagine him feeling in any of this is sadness since you didn't bring him with you tonight. But I guess if he wants to be you one day, even he has to do some grunt work. Not even titles can free you from sweat. Look at us."

"Yes, look at us," Salvador said. "But it's what he wants. Just like we did."

"Just like you," Delaney corrected. "I never want to be Chief. Keep me behind the scenes. I like what I do, and I'm good at what I do. That's why you keep me around."

"You're right."

"You even promoted me quicker than you did your mini-me." Delaney brought the car to a stop at a red light. "You really like him, don't you?"

Salvador turned her way. "Luis Adán is dedicated. We all have reasons. I have mine, you have yours, and he has his. He deserved the promotion. The department knew it too. Even if other officers were bitter, jealousy only self-condemns and confirms his competency."

Delaney slowly accelerated at the green light. "The moon labors not to eclipse Mars, but the Sun."

"Exactly. Where'd you get that from?"

"After this Closing, you need to start reading some books, Chief."

Before Salvador again shut his eyes, he reeled through his history in the CD: his training at the academy, his first day as an officer, and the monumental occasion when he became the youngest Chief to serve the National Contration Department. In his academy application essay, he did not fail to share that after his wife died, he contrated his Potential to dedicate himself to the department, much of what drove his determination.

When he ascended to the highest rank, the first year was pure extravagance from all the federal approval and accolades. But once things settled down, he found himself right where he'd been before the CD. Empty and grieved, Salvador was ready to quit and renounce all titles and notoriety. No amount of reports of a strengthening economy or propaganda about the ever-prospering country, especially the city of Bellark, could cause his late wife to arise from the ash she'd become.

The Bellark CD was conducting interviews for those who had just graduated from the academy. He chose to complete his short time as the Chief with as much dignity as possible and be present for the interviews. Afterward, he would submit his official resignation.

Salvador began to imagine his release from the department, wondering what he would do or where he should travel to discover what he longed for. Then Delaney Abbot had entered the room, her blonde hair wound and tied in the same bun she wore today. Salvador was not one to be blindsided by appearance, even with her emerald eyes. The series of questions began, and by his absent body language alone, she had no grip on his interest.

Anyone could state a personal opinion of the Contration Department that runs parallel with its ethos. *For the good of the nation. For the virtue of choice. To protect our people.* That's how the interview began, and the platitudes failed to spark Salvador's interest. His perception of the young woman never shifted because of a measured tone, extensive vocabulary, or wit, all of which she had.

"But why you?" Salvador hoped to hear something original and make the time go by.

30

Had she never gone off script to share her own experience, Salvador would have never promoted her as he did. Had Delaney never been honest about her own contration, the procedure that she claimed to have saved her life, that day with the department would have been Salvador's last.

*

Hoping for a stealthy entrance, David cautiously closed the door. After setting his backpack down beside the living room chair, he stopped at the family portrait perched on the wall. It was all four of them. The smile on his toddler face inside the frame was real, he remembered. The melancholy seldom hit him as recent years had numbed.

He studied his carriers in the photo. His father provided a reluctant smile to the photographer, his teeth bunkered behind a closed mouth. That stoicism only dissipated when he expressed affection for Penelope. David inherited his dark brown hair and eyes, but his father was without glasses.

His mother, on the other hand, did not hesitate to display her radiant smile. It was rare, but when it did show, it was infectious. He wished his mother smiled more like she had when he was young; the prescribed medication seemed not to have the effect the doctors had hoped to combat her depression. Day to day, David forced himself to remember the earlier years lest any positive regard for her diminish entirely.

Penelope did not have her mother's blonde hair, taking her father's like David, but she did share her mother's blue eyes, though Penelope's were a bit brighter. Since her youth, Penelope was aware of her princess appearance as if the mirror first praised her before anyone else. Later, puberty worked in her favor as well. Every now and again, some boys in school uttered inappropriate comments about her womanly figure. One time, David had finally stood up for his sister after an older boy walked up and grabbed Penelope from behind. David shoved him, sending the boy to the asphalt, but David left that interaction with a bloodied nose and a swollen lip. That same evening, Penelope lashed out on David for

31

sneaking into her bathroom cabinet. He'd been searching for cotton balls to dab the wounds on his face.

His attention broke from the picture. "And that's what I was saying to all the other girls in our class," Penelope said, giggling from the kitchen. "You can't just get the passing grade by flirting with them. Not every professor is like that."

"You're saying some fall for that?" their mother said.

"Come on, Mom. Cute girls, young professors. I mean . . . Really, even older ones love the attention."

"Well, I'm happy to hear things are going well. And making it to the top of your class so quickly!"

David stepped into the dining room next to the kitchen, going unnoticed. Penelope was fixing dinner over the stove. David's carriers sat on the kitchen counter barstools facing their daughter, their backs turned as well.

"You seem to have found your way quite well at the university," David's father said. "We could not be more proud."

David took a deep breath and walked forward. "Hey. Hi, Penelope."

She turned around. "Oh, hi, David! You're finally here." There was a hint of passive aggression. "It's past 6:30. Thankfully, the noodles needed to cook a little longer. Else we would have been waiting."

David bit his tongue.

His mother turned. "Hi, David." She forced a smile in hopes of calming the animosity between the two siblings. She hated conflict. Her approach was to usually dodge or change the subject, unlike David's father, who typically took Penelope's side.

"You're a little late, aren't you?" his father said.

"I'm sorry," said David. "I got hung up at Jensen's."

David's mother interrupted with artificial enthusiasm. "Well, your sister has prepared a delicious meal for us before she goes back to university tomorrow."

"Yep," Penelope said, following her mother's lead. "Pesto and lemon chicken pasta. Dad's favorite!"

His father turned around. "David, why don't you set the rest of the dinner table as your sister brings out the food?"

David nodded. Despite their meager relationship, he never had trouble doing what his father asked. He was never late completing his chores and sometimes went beyond, taking a chore from his sister if she forgot. In fact, his father's voice had guided David most in navigating the end of his relationship with Olivia. Unfortunately, his father's negligence failed to change afterward.

Dinner was just as David had predicted. He pushed food around on his plate while Penelope and his carriers continued to catch up on his sister's life. David did not share about his day despite his mother's disingenuous efforts to include him every ten minutes. He presumed catching a fish was nothing in comparison, and he certainly had no intention of telling them in Penelope's presence how he fared on the ESE.

Penelope continued. "So he walked up from the other side of the room and said to me, 'Hey, I know I'm no scholar, but I feel like we can help each other out if we're partners. I know you have the best grade of all of us, but you might enjoy my company.'"

"He did not!" David's mother became giddy. "How did he know you're at the top of your class?"

David's father quickly answered, "A guy can find out more than you think if he develops an eye for someone."

Penelope closed her eyes, flattered. "At first I was a little thrown off, but the more I think about it, the sweeter it seems to be."

"Most guys hate admitting that a girl is smarter than him," their father said with a quiet chuckle, keeping his teeth concealed.

"Was that it?" his mother went on. "Just partners for your biochemistry class?"

Penelope stayed silent for a few seconds as her cheeks eventually rose. "No. He asked me out on a date." She let down her composure. "He's taking me out Friday night!"

"Oh, my goodness! We're going to have to meet this boy."

David's father shrugged, "It's their first date. We'll have to see if Penelope decides to keep him around after." He sipped his red wine. "This guy's digging for gold right now. That's not easy. We'll see if he strikes."

At that comment, David had it. He glanced at Penelope and saw she was eating each of their father's words with more gusto than the food on her plate. *We have that much in common. Neither of us likes your cooking.* He could not help but let his mind wander to her ESE score. Thinking of her perfect 10 sent David's resentment to the peak. He tossed his napkin on the plate and sat up from his slouch. "Dad. Mom." The chuckling subsided. "May I be excused?"

David's mother could feel his unease. "David, you've hardly said a word."

"What do you want me to say?"

His father spoke before anyone else could. "For starters, maybe you can thank Penelope for making dinner. She did after all drive from her school to see her family."

"Thank you, Penelope," said David unconvincingly.

Penelope tried fronting compassion, but the inauthenticity was a nail on a chalkboard. "David, I know we aren't the closest, but can't you be a little more positive, maybe even grateful? How often do we get to have dinner as a family?"

David took a final sip and slammed his cup on the table, abandoning any semblance of patience. "This is not a family dinner!" He shot up from his chair. "This never was going to be a family dinner. They never are! From the start, this was going to be a dinner where you shared all your recent news and accomplishments with Mom and Dad, while I did my best to eat your dried-out chicken!"

Even his father was speechless at that.

David started to pace away. "Oh, and by the way, I took my ESE today." He turned angrily. "I probably didn't even pass, but don't worry. This means I won't go to as great of a university like Penelope, so nobody has to worry about her being outshone by her kid brother. While I'm at post-secondary school to pass that bullshit exam, her stories will be just as great as they always are."

Without looking back, he stormed off up the stairs. The

table was left silent. David's carriers exchanged a glance, while Penelope kept her eyes on her pacing brother. Uncertainty crept on his mother's face, but his father seemed to show little to no expression.

David lay in bed staring at the ceiling. With the weak moon, hardly a speck of light crept through the slits of the blinds. He was wide-eyed thinking about the dinner. After an hour or so, he had finally calmed a bit, losing himself in the memory of his trip to Nod earlier that day. It was soon after he saw himself reeling in the catfish when he drifted.

February 24th

Indie rock softly vibrated the truck speakers as the sprinkling scattered from the overcast sky, the sun unfortunately not having any fight for this morning either. Having not yet spoken, David stared out the window, watching the passings through the streams of water gliding along the glass.

Finally, Jensen said, "Dinner not go so well?"

David rubbed his eyes. "No, not exactly."

"What happened?"

He took a deep breath. "Well, I told Penelope her dinner sucked."

"You what? You said that to her face?"

"Yep. In front of my mom and dad too." David paused. "I didn't actually say that it sucked. I just said her chicken was overcooked."

"At least we know she can fail at something."

Despite himself, David grinned. "I lost my cool, man. I yelled at my carriers and pretty much called them out for being obsessed with Penelope."

"What'd they say?"

"They didn't," said David. "They didn't have anything to say back. I said what I wanted, and then I went to my room. I think I left them speechless."

"Well, that makes sense. I mean, how many times have

36

you yelled at them?"

"None. Never," David said firmly. "I stayed up for a while last night, wondering. I know I'm not the smartest, especially compared to my sister, but I just don't know what I did, or didn't do for it all to turn out this way. Makes me care less about how long post-secondary schooling will take. I just need a good exam score to have something to show them."

"No. No, David." Jensen became disarmingly stern. "That score won't be for them. They don't deserve you as a son if some bullshit score determines their pride."

David tried forcing a grin to set himself at ease, finding himself rather uncomfortable now that they were talking about his carriers in this way. "That's what I called it last night. The score," he said nervously, not sure how else to respond.

Jensen's seriousness did not lessen. "When I found out my dad left me, I promised myself I wouldn't let his decision bring me down. It's just not worth it. I'm sick of seeing and hearing how much your family drags you. I mean, they could all learn something from you on how to be decent. A good person. Even Penelope with all her smarts."

David could only nod, tongue caught and glossy-eyed. He had never heard Jensen speak about his family so candidly. While Jensen did occasionally give hints of disapproval of his carriers, it was never in such a straightforward manner.

"And her lack of cooking skill?" David finally managed to say.

Jensen then chuckled. "Sure. And her lack of cooking skill."

Often, David would remain closed-off when he didn't want to hear a strong opinion, just as he avoided discussing his relationship with Olivia to Jensen during their last month together. However, in this instance, David needed and appreciated the honesty. "Thanks, man."

Jensen reached across and patted David's chest. "Just speaking the truth."

David found himself much more relieved as the day went on, almost even reaching a point of optimism. Despite knowing his carriers would receive his ESE score later this afternoon, his earlier yearning to know had lessened. Jensen was right, he thought. *I'm a good person. That will take me somewhere.*

With only a few minutes left in his final class, David sat, fading in and out as he fought to pay attention to the biology professor. He shared the class with Jensen and had the extra benefit of being able to sit next to one another. Jensen, on the other hand, was entirely captivated by the lecture.

"The brain is a complex organ," the professor continued, putting back on the thick-rimmed glasses he'd just wiped clean. "Believe it or not, students, although you are thinking and listening to everything I say, that which is registering what you see and hear is not fully developed. Though it is far along, your brain has not yet reached its completion. With that said, you are incomplete. And incomplete is not yet living."

Jensen's face scrunched and he lifted his hand. The professor called on him. "I listened to the Chief of the Bellark CD last night. He was in an interview."

"As did I. Chief Salvador Goode," said the professor.

"Yes. Well, I have a question," said Jensen. "Why do we choose to let the brain's development determine when a person is alive?"

The professor was thrown off by the accusatory tone. "I thought you said you watched the segment last night? Leading physiologists have performed the research and—"

"I know that," Jensen interrupted. "What I mean is . . . What is implied by 'complete development'?"

"Hmm, I guess the message was not as explicit for Potes as I thought." The professor scratched his chin. "As I said, incomplete is not yet living. Complete body and brain development allow for optimum human sentience to form identity and engage the reality we exist in. Without such, you or any other Potential cannot yet fully and properly exist in this reality and world."

"What does sentience mean?"

The professor wore a proud grin. "Exactly my point. Sentience is the ability to perceive and experience your reality, or a simpler word, your *world*; all that you see, hear, smell, and so forth. Put even simpler regarding this exchange: A complete brain allows a true experience, and a true experience is personhood."

"Why didn't you just say it like that?"

"I didn't think I had to water down science. One day, you'll understand it all at personhood."

Jensen ignored the jab. "Well, you're right. Goode did not say it as you *simply* put it. I agree though. That message should be implied even if he never said it word for word."

"So, you agree?" The professor crossed his arms in triumph.

"Sure," said Jensen. "At least, I agree that's what the Chief believes. It's an interesting thought process to give life to whoever can perceive *completely*."

"One that many agree with."

"That's what I hear." Jensen exchanged a glance at David first, looking as if he were about to step off a ledge. "How old are you, professor?"

"Excuse me?"

"Pardon me if that was rude." Jensen's voice softened, but the directness remained. "I imagine Sixty or nearing Sixty-Five, since you've said you'll retire in a couple of years?"

"First of all, that question is mildly inappropriate, and second, my age should have no place in this class session and limited lecture time."

"I'm sorry. I don't mean to be rude, and I know my question was a bit forward, but I promise it's related to the discussion."

The professor said reluctantly, "Okay, go on."

"Thank you. I don't exactly need to know your age, but that would have been my starting point." He leaned forward to rest his forearms on the desk. "If at any point, whether in their Sixties or Seventies or some other age, if a person begins to lose brain capacity or cognitive function, shouldn't that then revert them to the status of a Pote?"

"Absolutely not." The professor shook his head emphatically. "No. You need to slow down and rewind before coming to a farfetched conclusion."

"Farfetched? How?"

"The answer is in your conclusion. You begin by admitting complete brain development has already taken place. The argument is cinched from the start. You cannot take away personhood once it has been attained. It is nonsensical for a being to go from life to death when what is alive has already been determined decades prior."

"Wait, wait, wait. You just said it's not even necessarily about that. What about sentience, experience, and all that?"

"Mr. Lloyd, I do not have that much time. We really should move on from this question; otherwise, I expect we'll just be running in circles. It is the law of our nation—"

"Yeah, well, what if that law changes?" Jensen brought all students to listen who may have drifted. "What if down the line a retired biology professor gets brain damage or dementia—or worse, what if the poor man gets into a terrible accident and finds himself in a coma for a year or two, or more? I can't imagine he would have any reality to perceive. Your sentience, identity, or whatever you want to call it, wouldn't have anything to even weigh in on the matter. Sentience is life, right? Well, what if our law has you gassed up one day just like the thousands of Potes who will be gassed tonight? The law's changed before."

The whole class was silent, several heads looking back and forth between the forward Potential and the professor.

He cleared his throat. "Mr. Lloyd."

"Yes."

"Is it fair to say that I have an advanced degree in human biology and you are just a student?"

"Yes, but that wasn't my quest—"

The professor cut him off. "Is it fair to say that the nation's best physiologists have conducted much research and study into this matter, and they may just have a more accurate grasp on human development than a Potential like yourself in his Seventeenth year?"

"Well, maybe. I guess, but that still doesn't answer my—"

Cutting him off once more, the professor looked to the

clock. "Okay, class, we are out of time. We'll pick up where we left off tomorrow. Remember, your carriers should have received your ESE scores today."

The final bell rang. Jensen shot up from his desk, not having any items to put away since he never took notes. His strides were long and fast as he left for the classroom exit, while David and the other students scrambled to gather their belongings.

"Can you believe that?" Jensen said, waiting outside the class when David emerged. "He never answered my question. Anyone must be able to get an M.D., Ph.D., or whatever.D these days. Doesn't seem to matter anymore."

"Where'd that come from?"

"I don't know," said Jensen. "It just came to me. If classroom sizes are going to drop after every Closing, all I'm asking is to know why. Degree my ass. Why don't they just contrate us all?" He saw David struggle to look up from the floor. "I'm sorry. I just don't always get it. This Contration Department. It makes sense, and it doesn't. I'm sick of them telling us what's true without explaining it; *truly* explaining it. I wasn't trying to make you—"

"No, it's okay," he said. "I know you were only trying to figure it out. It's what you do." He put his backpack on and walked. Jensen followed, already regretting his last words.

The professor shouted from the classroom, "Be off the streets before the ten o'clock curfew tonight! Unless of course, you feel like getting contrated. And no taping off your vents!"

The nearby students gave an appreciative chuckle as they knew no gas would enter through their vents. Though they all lived in the northwest garden of wealth, it was the law for every bedroom to have the appropriate ventilation. David tried to hold back but accidentally allowed a shy grin. The only one who did not laugh was Jensen.

The rain had finally stopped by the time Jensen pulled up to David's driveway. Like the afternoon before, the sun generously donated some light through a few openings in the clouds.

"Angels coming down to earth," David said. "At least,

that's what my mom used to say. She said that's what her mom used to say to her too." He continued fascinated. "As a kid, I wondered if instead, it was an angel going up. You know? Like the clouds opening to let it, or him or her, back in. But that's when I was little and didn't quite get the light only comes from the sun. I would argue with my mom that if something were brighter, it could part the clouds and go up."

Jensen repeated the strange sentences in his head. "To join the sun?"

"Sure. Or join whatever. I guess I never got that far."

"Well, if something was that bright, shouldn't we want it to stay here with us?"

"Good point." David's eyes followed the iridescent orange and yellow streams. "Unless its going up helps us out."

Jensen nodded, though not yet wholly understanding. He had on many occasions found himself lost when David spoke in this abstract manner. For that reason, he recommended David should write lyrics to go with playing his guitar. Insecure about his singing voice, David typically resisted the advice.

"I guess it's time to see the damage." David opened the truck door.

"Are your carriers even home?"

"No, they don't usually get home until later today," said David. "But they always leave our home computer on with no password. It'll be easy to see my score."

"You think it'll be awkward from last night, once you see them?"

"I guess we'll see." David stopped walking. "Actually, yeah, it will." He walked further from the truck. "But I'm sure me scoring a 10 will make them forget all about last night." Jensen laughed as he backed out, giving a honk as he drove down the street.

As he approached the front door, David felt around his pockets. Sighing, he remembered he'd forgotten to grab his keys from his desk that morning in his rush to avoid seeing Penelope or his carriers.

He tried the door to test his fortune, but it was locked.

Like many times before, he strolled to the side of the house and opened the gate. Walking through the backyard, he passed the pool, spa, and outdoor barbecue set. The last time he and his family spent time outside together was far from memory. He lifted the back-patio mat and grabbed the spare key.

Trudging back through the side yard, David's heard from beneath the window above. The voices were all too familiar, yet this did not take away the surprise. Confused by why his carriers were home so early, he stopped walking and listened in from below.

"I don't know. It just doesn't seem real," she said.

His father spoke. "Honey, what did you honestly expect? Did you think he was going to score a 10 or 9, or even an 8 or 7 for that matter? I was hoping at best for a 6."

David's stomach dropped. He prepared himself for this moment and had even found peace earlier that day, but now all of his previous thoughts of rejection and disapproval returned like dirt thrown into the air, only to fall back onto his face.

"We've talked about this for some time now," his father said.

"I know. It's just . . ."

"It's for the best."

When David's mother did not respond, he continued to the front door with head down, trying to accept his failing ESE score. Unable to stomach a confrontation, he went straight up the stairs and into his bedroom. He lay flat on his back, chest exhaling and collapsing.

Hours passed, and David had not yet gone downstairs. He'd thought by now he might have gathered the courage to discuss his exam score, but remembering the dinner incident last night, his body felt strapped to the mattress. Another hour passed. Lifting against the cruel gravity, he finally crept out of his room to take a shower, being as inconspicuous as possible. There was no going unheard, however, after David dropped the bottle of body wash for a couple of clanks atop the bathtub surface.

David sped out from the bathroom and down the hall quicker than he entered, slipping on a pair of flannel pajama bottoms and a white T-shirt to warm against the evening chill. The house heater was barely fighting back. He looked at his guitar as he sat on his bed and realized that it had been more than a day since he last played. Pressingly, he jumped up and grabbed it.

One string plucked; a few more for a chord strummed. Before long, a song played. He could feel his body loosening.

After playing for an hour, David glanced over at a pen on his desk. He removed a notebook from his backpack and tore out a piece, but this did not rid the hesitance as hoped. He closed his eyes and visualized the scene from earlier: the light emerging from the cluttered sky, the peace and commentary born again. He lifted his eyes slowly as if the picture might escape if opened too fast. The pen began to mark the paper one stroke at a time. It was a steady and progressive process as if the appearance of each letter was like peeling a fruit from its shell.

David was staring at the completed message in disbelief. He had recited it several times over until the lyrics were committed to memory, yet he was afraid to play and be heard. Not wanting his carriers or anyone else to stumble across the new piece, David protectively folded the paper and slid it into the pocket of his flannel bottoms.

I should at least record some chords . . . Maybe even sing the words quietly. David reached for his cell phone and removed it from the charger. There were two missed calls from Jensen. He almost declined to return the video call, but he decided to record the audio on his phone after.

It was close to 9:12 p.m. The ringing over the line seemed it was almost at its end. David imagined Jensen might be asleep. The most recent call was from forty minutes ago. David had not thought it through when he first dialed Jensen's number. He was now relieved, but not because he was uncomfortable discussing the afternoon's events with Jensen. Rather, David was simply uncertain whether he had the will or the strength to revisit that moment. It took everything from him—the blow of hearing about his failing ESE, and most immediately, the creation of his first written song.

"Connecting," his phone announced. An instant later,

44

Jensen's face filled the screen. David made the compromise just as quickly as Jensen greeted him. One story would be enough, he resolved, deciding to tell of his song the next day.

"They never actually said you failed?" Jensen asked after David explained how he heard the news.

"No, but it was pretty much implied," David said. "They're going to send me to post-secondary school. He said, 'It's for the best.'"

Jensen lightly chewed on the inside of his lip, looking above the camera frame in thought. "Well, it beats trying to find a job without a degree, right? At least you can still apply for universities after post-secondary."

This did not encourage David much. "I guess. I really don't want to take that exam again. Plus, I'll graduate university a year behind—if I can even keep up then."

"Yeah, but really . . . Look at the benefit here. If you can nail your ESE in a year, you can get accepted into a good university. Imagine if you barely passed this year's. That would have closed you off to most universities anyway. An added year only means added points to your score next year. Right?"

As David tried forcing a nod, Sam's face appeared to dominate the entire screen. "Hey there, David! You make any plans for your Eighteenth yet? Or will you be helping me with my garden?"

Realizing he still had not planned anything, he improvised. "Yes, umm. Jensen and I are going fishing."

"Again? You boys can't get enough. At Nod?"

Going with David's lead, Jensen responded. "Of course at Nod."

"All righty then. The weather channel said it should be getting a little chilly here in the next week, so go prepared. Go warm."

Jensen rolled his eyes. "We will."

"I'm sorry, boys. I know you'll be fine. I'm just a little older than you young bucks. You kiddos are a lot warmer blooded than me! Speaking of old and aging, I need to get my beauty sleep. I'll see you soon!" Sam waved and left the frame.

45

"So, we're fishing it looks like?" said Jensen.

David answered, "Looks like it."

"Awesome. Well, I'm going to get to bed too, man. Get some rest tonight. Try not to worry. Here's another incentive to look at all this glass-half-full. It'll just be an extra year of not having to work full-time after you graduate university."

"Yeah? Then how about we trade scores?"

"Ahh, there you go." Jensen pointed into the camera. "A little wit from you. I like it. You're going to need that for next year's exam." He yawned. "Well, guess it's time to hit the sack here . . . But seriously. Try not to stress too hard on this. You'll be fine."

"I guess so." David caught the yawn. "Stay off the streets tonight."

Jensen shook his head before the call ended.

Before David settled and flicked the light switch, he glanced at the vent lining the wall. Now in the dark, he wondered for the first time how many bedrooms in Bellark, how many bedrooms in the country would receive the gas. *It's a shame*, he thought, saddened that most Potentials would not have an opportunity to attend post-secondary school. *Hypocrite.* The word flashed in his head, forcing David's eyes open as if there were fire under them.

David tried to distract himself with pleasant memories, beginning with Nod and the fishing trip from the day before. It had the opposite effect, however. Next occupying the screen of his mind was the maple tree. He saw Olivia, her eyes looking into his as they did that day. The only difference was that her ambers were full of pity. It was not there before, but he could not force another image to take its place. Before long, he was revisiting each moment they had from the beginning. Though tireless, eventually, he fell asleep.

February 25th

It was if two thumbs pressed over his eyelids. In the small slit available, he could see nothing but pitch dark. *Are my eyes still closed?* His mind was fogged, making it difficult to focus on any given thought. He tried blinking in hopes of quickening his sight, but to no avail, blackness kept his vision.

"Hello?" a raspy voice said from the dark.

David froze, frightened.

The voice called out again, "What's going on?"

Someone's in my room. David tried kicking his legs and moving his body more vigorously, but his efforts met opposition.

He heard another voice. A different one. "Where am I?" It cried. "Get me out of this!"

Suddenly, lights flashed above to invade every corner, making the prior darkness more desirable in the first blinding seconds. It was a white room with tiled floors, much like a hospital but without windows to the outside. David frantically turned his head back and forth to examine the foreign place in which he was bound.

There were eight beds in two rows of four. Strapped to one was David, and the bodies of seven other boys lay bound atop the others. The overhead lights continued to pulsate and beat downward, leaving no space for a shadow to dwell other than beneath the beds. David was across from the entry door, which had a square window at head level. At the far end of the room was

47

a large metal hatch in the middle of the wall, no larger than a widescreen television. David looked at his imprisoned body, one strap across his chest and the other across his legs, clothed in the same flannel pajama bottoms and white T-shirt he'd fallen asleep in.

The Potential beside him clattered, "What's going on?"

Another called out, "I shouldn't be here! This is a mistake!"

The one on the far end, closest to the metal door said in a commanding whisper, "You guys need to shut up!" He had black hair, slightly blemished skin, and a masculine build that lent authority to his words. He fidgeted under his chest strap, seemingly loose or faulty compared to the binding ones across David.

The boy beside David said frantically, "Do you know what's going on?"

"Didn't I just tell you to shut up?" the boy with black hair hissed. "These lights just turned back on, which means we don't have much time."

Another said, "What are you talking about? Do you know where we are?"

"Everybody needs to shut up the hell and keep your voices down!" the black-haired again ordered.

All sense came to David. But a sorted mind did not rid his fear, ushering it forward all the more instead. "Listen to him," said David, trying to keep at ease. "We're at a contration facility." Many thoughts raced and intertwined in his head. *How am I here? This is impossible.* In a moment, however, these fled. While he was entirely lost and horrified as to why he was in this room, he was more certain he needed to get out.

The boys fell silent at David's grave tone. The one next to him grew pale. A large, weighty boy continued to struggle to free himself, sweat pouring from his forehead. Another with dark skin lay diagonally from David; he kept motionless, though awake. There remained only three boys across their beds with eyes still shut.

The awakened halted their attempts at liberation and

perked their heads up, alarmed. Outside, voices drew close from beyond the room. Two men. The words muffled from the other side, but David could hear the conversation slip under the door crack. "They caught whoever took out our power?"

"That's what I heard," the other man said.

"He definitely knew what he was doing. Shut us down for a little while. Even the backup generator."

"This facility is so old. Anyone could have done it. Boss is still going to get roasted for this." The man chuckled. "At least we still get paid for these extra hours."

All looked to the boy with black hair for some direction. He mouthed, "Shh," and closed his eyes. The others followed his lead.

Should I just shout and tell the men I'm not supposed to be here? Uncertain, David closed his eyes while hoping the Potential across from him would awaken; he was closest to the entry door.

One of the facility workers entered. David couldn't help peeking with one slitted eye. The man appeared in faded black pants, almost a charcoal color, and a white scrub shirt. On his belt was a rectangular device that resembled a cell phone. He pushed a cart, carrying eight syringes with a translucent purple liquid inside each. Wheeling it into the gap between the two rows of beds, he stopped between David and the Potential across from him.

He picked up a syringe.

David's heart thumped harder when the worker stepped toward the boy. *Wake up!* David looked over to see if black-hair had made any progress. Already successful with unbinding the chest, he fiercely but silently tugged at the leg strap. David glanced back to the facility worker to see if there was still time, but the needle had already sunk into the boy's arm as the man slowly pushed the liquid into the vein. Nauseated, David watched.

The man wheeled the corpse through the gap between rows, making his way toward the metal door. Before the worker could see, the boy with black hair had thrown the chest strap back over his torso and gone still.

The worker continued with the bed to the end of the

room. After undoing the straps, he opened the hatch, lined the bed up with the opening, and pushed the sliding plastic bed cover. The body slid into the hatch before the metal door shut behind. With a push of a button, flames consumed everything through the tinted window: the plastic mattress cover and the Potential.

David shut his eyes when the man turned, wheeling the bed to its original position. He brought the cart to the foot of David, reaching for another syringe. Again, David opened his eyes for a small window. Needle in hand, the man crept toward him. *I need to say something!* But in the corner of his eye, the boy with black hair silently rose out of his bed, having fully freed himself. Despite all fear and uncertainty, David kept still, placing his faith in someone he did not know to execute a plan that he had not agreed to, acting as if he was, in fact, a Potential selected for contration.

The man grabbed David to expose the underside of his forearm. In the cold grip of latex gloves, David's regret and panic screamed at him for choosing to lie still. The worker hovered the needle above his arm, looking for a vein. David opened his eyes for a larger window, desperate to find his help. *Where'd he go?* Quick as a blink, the needle pierced.

"Stop!" David yelled before the man could push the liquid. Startled, he let go of the syringe, almost tripping as he took a step back. He was speechless as he made eye contact with the awakened Potential. David raised his head upright, breathing heavily. The other awakened Potentials watched. "You have it all wrong. I'm not supposed to—"

Slam!

The boy with black hair crashed the metal tray to the man's head, sending the remaining syringes to the tile floor. He went down to the ground with them, yelping in pain. The man reached down for the electronic device on his belt, but before he could grab it, the black-haired delivered two more blows, knocking him out.

Quickly, he unbuckled David. "We gotta go."

David looked at the others imprisoned to their beds. "What about them?"

"Please, let us out of this," one pled.

The boy with black hair shook his head. "We don't have time."

"We have to let them out," David said unwavering, removing the needle from his arm. He swung his legs over the side and stood. David did not wait for any further negotiation as he undid the straps of the Potential with the buzzcut next to him. Reluctant, David's rescuer followed his lead and helped free another.

With four of them standing, David approached the silent boy who lay diagonally from him. Being freed from the straps brought him no words either. He stood, shorter than the others, an unthreatening presence. His thick curly hair rose only a couple of inches. If David had waited any longer, his confusion over this boy's lack of speech and action would have gone nowhere.

David walked up to one still sedated, aggressively shaking and patting the sleeping body. The buzzcut tried waking the other unconscious Potential similarly, while the black-haired cautiously peered through the door's window. "The hallway is empty," he said. "Let's go."

"What about these guys?" asked the buzzcut.

"They aren't waking up, so we gotta go. This may be our only chance while the hallway is empty."

Dissatisfied, David started to unbuckle the straps of one. The others followed David's lead and unbound the second of the sedated Potentials. The black-haired grew more impatient. "What are you doing? They're out cold. We need to go!"

David paced to the door and said, "We have to leave them with some kind of chance." Each added effort of aid seemed to further enmesh David with the group, every strap undone binding him more tightly to them instead; there was presently no thought of how he could establish that he was not one of them. Turning to the man face-down on the tile, David spotted a card key attached to his belt. He went over quickly, reaching for the key.

The black-haired had an idea of his own, spotting one of the syringes that landed where his foot was. "Each of us needs to

51

take one," he said, picking it up off the tile. "We saw what it can do." Two of them took his advice, but the silent boy stared blankly, making no movement toward the needles.

Hesitantly, David followed the order and grabbed the one he'd pulled from his arm. *But I won't kill anybody.*

The black-haired said, "Okay, none of us knows where we are exactly. We have to keep moving and get out of this building. As of right now, no one here knows about us. I think. If we can be quick and quiet, we can maybe get outta here."

"Then what?" said the buzzcut.

"Then we'll make another plan."

"When do we use this?" The heavy-set boy held up his syringe.

"When you need to."

David was catching his breath. "Will they still kill us? Now that we're awake?"

The black-haired looked out. "Probably." He reached out his hand to David. "Let me get that key. I'll lead us out." David dug into his flannel pocket and handed it over without reluctance.

The five slipped out of the room one by one, the black-haired in front. At the far end of the hall were an elevator and a sign with a left arrow: '*Stairs.*' There were other rooms in the hallway. Ten total. The boys crouched to keep below all other windows.

David held the rear of the line but soon halted beneath the window of the door across from their room. Any attempt to dismiss his curiosity lost. He slowly raised his head and peered through the glass. His stomach once again met the earlier nausea at what he saw. David lowered his head to gather himself, turning to the others who continued through the hallway, unaware that he had fallen behind. Despite wanting to catch up with the new cohort ahead, he found himself unmoving.

He rose once more for the window. The room was identical, another two rows of four beds each. However, it was seven girls instead who occupied them. David looked to the empty bed that moments ago held the girl who just became ash. Now, the worker was above another. Before David could think to panic, the man stuck her with the purple. This worker seemed faster on his feet than the other, hastily pushing the second bed toward the metal hatch. David stood, frantically thinking if there was anything he could or ought to do.

One of the other boys finally turned around to discover David had stalled. "What are you doing?"

There's no way, David thought. To sacrifice the welfare of the group of boys to execute a rescue he had never anticipated was impractical. The boys crouching down the hallway had a realistic chance of escape, not the drug-induced girls. As he took a step toward the boys, he could not help the final glance into the room. At once, his feet became stone, and his eyes slaves. In the bed opposite the door, the same position in which David himself awoke, a girl's body struggled.

She tried breaking free of the straps as the worker slid the contrated Potential through the hatch. But no amount of flexing or pushing would unbind. All strength depleted, she looked toward the door, causing her pupils to dilate in dark brown irises after seeing David. The shutting of the metal hatch and the activated incinerator snapped her head back for a moment. She turned to David again, a drop of sweat running from her forehead to cheek, mixing with a tear along the way.

His stomach sunk, her plea one of haunting semblance. "Give me the key," David said to the other boys waiting on him.

"Why?" The black-haired demanded sharply. "We can't stop."

"A girl in this room is awake! Just like us. We need to get her out!"

Black hair followed the others hesitantly, but last to come was the silent boy. "Are any of those guys in there?" said the buzzcut.

David said, "Just one."

The boy with black hair looked at David. "Okay," he said displeased. He held up the syringe. "We'll go in there and stick one of these in him. There's five of us, so we'll be able to overpower him if he gives us any trouble."

53

"We don't need to kill him," David insisted. "He'll see we each have a needle."

"We can just knock him out like the other guy if we need to," said the buzzcut.

Black hair rolled his eyes. "Fine."

David slid the card key into the door, hoping it would unlock. Inside the slit sounded a quiet click. David turned the handle and felt more adrenaline than relief as the door wedged open. All the boys funneled inside with syringes in hand, not wasting a moment of their surprise. The worker stood stunned next to the incinerator as the boys poured in. The boy with black hair rushed the man and slammed him against the wall, bringing the needle to his neck.

David locked the door from the inside. "Get them out."

Four girls were awake, and two were still unconscious. David approached the girl he first saw through the window. She watched him dependently with her dark eyes. "We have to free the rest," she said confidently, without inhibition, as if the earlier fear of death never had its home in her. David could only nod. Even with life at stake, he could not find words. The odd, thwarting familiarity when they first met eyes had not left.

The other boys were slow in comparison, but they managed to free the other three girls. One with ruby red hair promptly and quietly expressed her gratitude. The other two girls seemed unable to speak as they stared at the metal hatch, almost hypnotized by both their fear and relief.

David walked to the two unconscious girls. "They wouldn't wake up?"

"No. We tried," said the heavy boy.

David started to undo one of their straps. "We'll leave them with a chance, just like we did for the other guys."

The boy with black hair kept the man pinned to the wall. When his attention diverted to check the status of the others, the man quietly reached down for the device on his belt. Just as he pressed a finger on top, the black-haired turned to discover the man's now-obvious action. Before he could act, the facility speakers alarmed immediately, a screaming pitch ringing

54

throughout the entire building.

"What was that?" the boy with black hair yelled, unnerved by the ringing alarm.

The worker said, "You Potes should have stayed in your beds. It was going to be peaceful."

His eyes widened. "Peaceful? Like this!" He jammed the needle into the center of his neck. A second later, the man fell dead. His corpse sat upright against the wall, some blood seeping from his neck down his scrubs, staining the shirt down the middle like a wet, red tie.

David's heart skipped. "Wha . . . Why'd you do that?"

"You didn't have to kill him!" said the brown-eyed girl whom David unbound, sharing in his horror.

"This guy just ratted us out." He pointed an accusatory finger at David. "You wanted him alive, and now look! His only goal was to have us all contrated. From now on, I'm doing this my way. If you want to follow me, feel free, but I'm not putting my ass on the line like this anymore." There was a silence, but none, including David, thought to leave on their own.

It was a conflicting dilemma; a man was now dead because of an escape David had contributed. The scope of the situation had just grown well beyond whether he should or should not be at the facility. Regardless, it seemed that David chose his allegiance as soon as he allowed the boy with black hair to save his life.

A voice blared from the intercom, "Alert! We have escaped Potentials in room 35B. Security personnel: Attend to and stop them by all means necessary."

"We have to go," said the redheaded girl.

The black-haired glanced around and spotted a pair of scissors on top of the cart. "Grab what you can," he said, taking the scissors. The girls grabbed syringes, seeing that the boys each had one. The redhead leaned over the body of the deceased man and wrenched a wallet out of his back pocket. She looked up at David and immediately stopped as if it were his decision. He nodded.

The group charged out of the room and ran down the

hall toward the elevator. In much more of a hurry than their earlier crawl, no one ducked their heads or crouched. They caught quick glimpses through the other room windows of several Potentials struggling and screaming at the tops of their lungs. It seemed the ventilation drug had completely worn off on all. Nevertheless, the facility workers in each room doggedly tried to complete the contrations.

The intercom spoke again. "All facility employees currently working: Carry out your contrations. Security personnel: Continue pursuing the escaped Potentials."

The group neared the elevator but came to an abrupt halt as they heard it ding. The elevator doors opened to reveal two men in black, each holding a transparent rifle-like weapon.

"Run!" one girl yelled, turning left to the staircase. The entire group pivoted before the elevator doors could finish opening. They heard a shout and pounding feet as the two guards emerged and gave chase. The boy with black hair opened the staircase door for the others.

David was still holding the rear. As he neared the door, one of the guards fired at him. It missed by a mere two inches, but it hit a different target. The overweight boy collapsed to the ground, limp and motionless with a purple bullet dart in his spine. David jumped over the body, regretful but sure that there was no hope for him. The black-haired went through last after David and slammed the door. Multiple rifle darts collided into the door, striking like hail on a car. David was shocked to see him emerge last, especially since he had reached the door first.

"Those aren't real guns," David said, panting. "They shoot out a dart of that purple stuff they were trying to contrate us with."

Black-haired gripped the door handle. "Go down the stairs with everybody else."

"What about you?" David said lost.

"Go. I have a plan."

David took the stairs two at a time to catch up with the rest. Halfway down, he saw that the others had just made it to the bottom from the third floor where they'd started. He looked up to check on the boy with black hair. Before David could spot him, the door opened, and one of the security guards barged through. The guard spotted David and aimed. Swiftly, the black-haired, who had been standing hidden behind the open door, jammed a syringe through the guard's neck. The rifle fell from his nerveless hands, clanking against the stair rail to the bottom floor. The man dropped just like it but was spared the plummet, coming to rest beside the door instead.

The buzzcut boy ran forward and grabbed the rifle that fell to their floor. "The triggers jammed!" he announced, struggling while taking aim. Defeated, he dropped the weapon to the ground.

The other guard followed in to take his shot at the Potential with black hair. The boy dodged, then rushed the guard and led with a blow to the face, forcing him to drop the rifle. His sizable build gave him an edge fighting the equally sized guard. After exchanging punches, the man began losing footing against the more fervent and resilient boy until his back hit the railing. Pressing the advantage, the boy with black hair surged forward, and suddenly a body was falling through the air. Two of the girls screamed as the group pressed back against the wall just in time to avoid being crushed. With a sickening thump, the man's body hit the ground floor beside the broken rifle.

"Did he get you?" the brown-eyed girl called out.

He held out his shirt, a hole in it next to his ribcage. "I got lucky," he said, picking up the strange weapon.

David waited, and the two hurried down the stairs to join the others. The group followed behind the black-haired as he led to the bottom floor exit, while David maintained his preferred position in the back. Directly in front of David was a girl about the same height as him, with sandy blonde hair. He could not yet see or remember her face from the room, but she ran sluggishly, arms crossed over her large hoodie above her stomach.

The boy with black hair reached for the exit door. Catching him by surprise, the door opened from the other side. The new guard was equally staggered to so suddenly come face-to-face with the escapees. He raised his rifle and shot as quickly as possible without taking precise aim at anyone in particular. The dart soared past the shoulder of the leader and hit one of the girls behind. With duel-like response, the black-haired shot the guard in the chest. Both the girl and the guard fell limply to the ground together.

The girl with brown eyes leaned down, bringing her hand to the other girl's neck. "She's dead." The others seemed to trust the diagnosis as did David. She, the girl whom David unbound, appeared to have the most trepidation as she kneeled and kept her fingers against the other girl's neck. The contrated girl never spasmed like the man beside her or the heavy-set boy above; her dart was square in the chest.

None could fully comprehend all the chaos since they awoke, but all were certain this girl breathed her last on the dusty ground, and if they weren't careful, they might as well. The boy with black hair grabbed the guard's rifle and looked at the others, unsure. Deciding, he walked to David and handed him the weapon.

David looked over the gun, afraid of the seemingly unalterable act of taking it, then glanced at the contrated Potential. Just then, a sickening wave of insecurity came. *I can't kill anybody. If I do . . .*

"Let me take it instead," said the buzzcut. The black-haired turned and glared at him, but he wasn't rattled in the least. "Trust me. I probably know how to shoot this better than you. Unless you grew up hunting."

David didn't hesitate and handed the rifle over. *It makes more sense for one of them to take it.*

"Okay, okay, it's settled," said the black-haired. "If you're gonna be shooting, stay in back."

After the black-haired checked for clearance, the group made their way through the exit door. They found themselves in the front parking lot of the contration facility. It was almost too vacant, like walking into a theater mid-show only to find the screen blank and audience missing. Each of them prepared for some confrontation, but the only opposition was the frigid wind and the gnawing asphalt under their bare or sock-covered feet.

"They weren't ready for this," said the redheaded girl. "If we woke up, then every other kid must have too. Any other guard that comes for us would be leaving other Potes inside fighting to escape."

"Well then, let's use it to our advantage," said the black-haired. "We gotta move fast."

The building was four stories high and close to fifty yards wide. The exact color was difficult to determine in the early morning darkness. It could have been brown, dark blue, or black. On the bottom floor was the front entrance with two glass doors, through which leaked a bit of light. They saw that there were no other buildings nearby nor lights other than those on the facility property. The only other sign of civilization was a two-lane highway. Their sense of direction and location were nebulous, but one fact was clear: They were not inside the city of Bellark.

The parking lot was almost vacant. Only five white vans, a truck, three sedans, and a black SUV occupied the asphalt. The group ran toward the vehicles.

The boy with black hair pulled the stolen pair of scissors from his pocket. "Watch my back," he directed the buzzcut. He plunged the two blades into one of the back tires of a van, then repeated the action with the other rear tire. "Giving us some insurance." He continued puncturing the back tires of every vehicle except for the black SUV. The blow of air rushing out of the tires whistled through the lot.

David held position next to the other armed boy, who trained his rifle at the building entrance. Walking toward the SUV, the black-haired flipped his gun as he approached the driver's side. He angled the butt of the rifle and struck the window, but the glass remained intact. He went to strike the window again but stopped. The redheaded girl opened the unlocked passenger door before he could commit.

The others clambered inside as David remained outside to keep an extra pair of eyes scanning the area. Almost everyone was safely inside the SUV by the time the ignition rang.

The buzzcut entered before David without giving warning. Before he could fully sit back, the buzzcut jerked and fell out onto the asphalt. A bullet dart stuck like a flag from his back. David jolted his head back toward the building. Fifty yards away, one of the guards limped out of the exit door from the stairwell as a rifle aimed their way. Immediately, David fell to the ground. Grabbing the gun next to the dead Potential, he quickly rolled under the SUV for cover. *How'd the guard survive the fall? Must be that other rifle that fell too. I thought it was jammed.*

"Get in!" the redhead pled to David through the ajar door.

David adjusted his body, extending and raising the weapon. Even beneath the vehicle, there was a large enough opening for him to take aim. The man kept limping through the parking lot. *Not a high enough fall.* The man's disorientation seemed to impair his judgment to seek cover or take another good aim, shooting haphazardly around the SUV and missing. David contemplated whether to fire but realized he needed to board the SUV by any means necessary. *It's him or me. Him or them.* David never paused to think about his lack of glasses.

Missed.

Before David could shoot again, he heard the boy with black hair. "I've got him." The other rifle was barely visible from beneath the SUV, only the barrel extending out the driver's window. David squinted and aimed. Two more darts shot from the SUV at the same time. The guard gave one last groan before collapsing. David was unsure if it was his that landed, but the other confirmed. "You got him. Get in!"

He jumped out from under. The others had left the front passenger seat open for David as if he was entitled to it. The SUV reversed quickly just as more security personnel rushed through the entrance doors. The boy slammed the SUV into drive and floored it, the tires screeching as he jetted for the highway. The guards scrambled and loaded into the other vehicles.

"They're coming after us," the blonde girl with the large hoodie said, her voice cracking.

Black hair checked the rearview mirror. "They won't get far." He took a right turn onto the highway. None of them had any idea where they were or which way they were now going, but nobody questioned his judgment. Their eyes were fixed on the vans pursuing from behind.

The redhead said, "They're slowing down."

"I know," said the black-haired.

After speeding no more than a hundred yards, the back tires of each van, truck, and sedan had been chewed and spat out by the road. Clouds of sparks flew behind two of the vans, glowing in the predawn shadow. The SUV trekked down the highway in the darkness, the headlights of the trailing vehicles quickly growing faint. The more distance they put between them and their pursuers, the more each escapee's panic slowly quieted.

The cold of the early morning still grew inside their skin despite the car heater's efforts. While their bodies came down from adrenaline, there was no coming peace or ease. The paramount question finally dawned in their minds, though none could yet voice it. *Why am I here?*

David's mind was spinning. *What did I just do? This is not right. I shouldn't be here. How is this happening?* His pulse was ready to jump out from his skin. The initial instinct to survive and protect the others had kept the confusion at bay. However, it would no longer be silent. *There must have been some mistake. I am not qualified for contration.* There seemed no rational explanation for why he was in the vehicle, why he was just forced to kill a man, or why he'd awoke in the facility at all. He turned first to see the boy with black hair, then fully around to get a glimpse of every face, shadowed as they were from the night. Six had evaded contration, including him. All of their eyes met his. Fear, to be sure. But under their fear was relief, one that provided David a refuge from the questions that assaulted him. *They're safe.*

"We're alive," the girl with brown eyes said in the silence.

The black-haired balked. "No, we aren't. Not yet."

*

The Chief of Bellark's CD received a phone call late in the night reporting the escape of six Potentials from the facility off of Highway 38. He hurried to the facility with a few handpicked officers from the department. With him of course were Delaney Abbot—she had answered Salvador's call after one ring—and Luis Adán, the promising officer Salvador had arranged to shadow him.

On the drive, they saw one vehicle traveling the opposite direction on the highway, but it didn't match the description of the one the Potentials had hijacked. The recent report also told that the escapees fled opposite from the city. A helicopter was sent to scout the highway eastward.

After arriving at the facility, Salvador waved several of his officers off to investigate for clues, while he strode through the entrance; those accompanying him struggled to keep pace. Despite the situation's urgency, he had managed to don freshly pressed slacks, dress shirt, and jacket. Professionalism was never to be neglected, regardless of the circumstances. As they approached the facility manager's office, the manager opened the door and walked out to greet them. Fear was painted across his face and sweat already soaked the back of his shirt.

"How long has it been since they escaped?" Salvador said without preamble.

Intimidated, the manager said, "Almost two hours ago."

"You sent men after them?"

"Yes, Sir, but we were only able to send one vehicle."

"Why is that?" Salvador said tempered.

"They slashed the tires on all the other vehicles. My car was the only one parked in the back." The manager had difficulty looking up from the floor.

"Did it catch up to them?"

"No, not yet. It's pursuing in the direction they were last seen driving."

Salvador's face grew graver. "And that was away from the city?"

"Yes, Sir."

"Tell your men to drive faster." Salvador turned to Delaney, thinking over their strategy. "The helicopter should gain on them quick."

Luis Adán had been standing to Salvador's left, opposite

Delaney. He stood shorter than the average man but had a thick build. There was a layer of fat over every muscle of his body, but he was not to be mistaken for out of shape. What he lacked in height was made up by his build. His hair was slicked back, with a hairline at the dawn of recession. His attire resembled Salvador's, but Luis also wore a tie. It was the one item Salvador had forgotten.

He listened to every one of Salvador's words and observed his every movement and expression, ready to respond to anything. Presently, his sole desire was to advance the CD, but if asked, he would admit to dreaming of one day becoming chief of a department. For now, however, his concern was to track down the escaped Potentials.

Luis had an enduring allegiance to the Contration Department. He'd grown up with an identical twin brother in a poorer family, and in their Sixteenth year, their carriers had threatened contration—assuming they failed the ESE—if they did not work part-time jobs. The motivated type, Luis knew he could accomplish his carriers' commission of working thirty hours a week. However, his twin brother Joseph did not have the same attitude; their similarities as twins were limited to their appearance. Joseph managed no more than ten hours of work a month and often missed certain classes. He was usually preoccupied with both his club and school baseball teams. Their father too had a deep love for baseball; he'd played as shortstop years ago in secondary school.

In the end, Joseph failed his final ESE but had already signed to a minor league baseball team. Seven months after reaching their Eighteenth, while Luis was attending university to become a lawyer, Joseph broke his collarbone in a base-sliding collision during a game. Yet their father believed enough medical treatment could heal his favored son and resurrect the baseball career they both desperately desired. The physicians said if there were any chance of healing, it would come at the cost of extensive surgery. Though all the family savings were exhausted on several surgery attempts, Joseph never returned to his former glory, and now in financial debt, Luis' carriers could no longer support his

63

education with the little money they gave in the first place.

Forced to attend a less-renowned university, Luis would never forget the robbery of his dream to become a lawyer. Never should such an injustice happen to anyone, he believed. Then began his journey with the Contration Department. During Luis' first year in the CD Academy, before he officially severed himself from his family, Joseph dared to ask him for money. Luis bluntly told him, *"You deserve my money just as much as you deserve your life."*

Having gathered his thoughts, Salvador addressed the facility manager. "Well, due to your incompetence, I have already ordered the department to pursue the Potes. Fortunately for your position, they are driving into nowhere." He frowned. "You said six escaped?"

"Three males, three females," Luis said as the manager paused. The manager spoke slowly and dragged on his sentences. He'd quickly wearied of it just as Salvador and Delaney had. Even Delaney could not deny the natural chemistry of working alongside Luis.

"I want a profile on each one," Salvador ordered. "Give them to my Vice. This is Delaney Abbot."

"Yes, Sir," the manager said, signaling with his eyes to one of his aides standing nearby. The worker raced off to retrieve the profiles.

"Chief Goode, would you like to take this conversation into a more comfortable setting?" The manager gestured toward his office door.

Salvador did not answer but walked into the room. Delaney and Luis followed as the manager held the door open, while two other men of Salvador's cohort waited outside the office. The office was dark and subdued compared to the rest of the facility, the lights dimmed to just enough brightness to read by. There were two seats in front of the desk. Salvador and Delaney took those as the manager settled in the chair behind. Luis stood behind his boss and pulled out his cell phone to take notes.

"Please, tell me how six Potes were able to escape from this facility," Salvador said patronizingly.

The manager cleared his throat. "As you know, our electrical system was tampered with, which disabled the power for a couple hours. It's an old facility, and the backup generator was faulty. Must not have been given maintenance for some time. I was only recently posted at this facility. A difficult scenario to predict."

Luis caught every detail of the testimony, including the mysterious young Potential who inconveniently and improbably sabotaged the facility's power in the night. By the time they had restored power, the effects of the anesthesia had worn off the escapees.

"Security camera footage reveals a planned and strategized escape by the group who are now at large," the manager said. "In their escape, four of our men were killed."

"At their hands?" Delaney leaned forward, awestruck.

"Yes. We were not able to stop them because the rest of our personnel were preoccupied with the other Potes awakening in every room."

"Who is this Potential that turned off the power?" Salvador demanded. "Where did he come from?"

"We do not know." The manager reached over and turned the security monitor around to face Salvador. The live feed showed a sullen-faced young man slumped in a chair, arms bound behind his back. "He has not said anything. He refuses to speak."

Salvador rose from his chair, jaw clenched. "He'll speak to me." He turned to the door. "Take me to him."

The manager led the Chief to the custody room, which was much like a contration room without the beds or incinerator. The boy stared down at the glossy metal table in front of him, while two guards stood next to the exit, monitoring his actions. Salvador took the seat across the table from the Potential, with Delaney and Luis standing at attention some feet behind.

The handcuffed Potential did not react nor pay attention to anyone in the room, continuing to stare broodingly at the table as Salvador studied him. "You've caused some trouble for us," he said calmly. The boy kept silent, but the Chief could see that he was thinking. "Pretty smart not bringing any identification with

65

you."

The boy recognized the voice and racked his brain to remember where he had heard it. After a few moments, the recollection hit. He looked up to the man across the table, vividly recalling the interview of Salvador Goode that was broadcast to the nation —the broadcast he'd watched with his grandfather and his best friend, David.

"What you've done is wrong," said Jensen.

Salvador smirked. "So that's why you're here, huh? Why you did all that you did?" With no answer, Salvador went on, "At least you're a straight shooter. Well, it would seem that you know who I am since you're accusing me of some 'wrong.' Now, how about you tell me who you are?"

His eyes remained fixed on Salvador's, face devoid of expression. "Jensen."

"Jensen," Salvador said, studying the Potential. Behind, Delaney nodded mutely to her Chief, not knowing his next course of action but providing her tacit support for whatever it was. Luis' arms crossed in wait.

Salvador leaned back. "It is apparent that you did what you did because you disagree with this system and what we do. You aren't the only one." His eyes rose, pupils just below his eyelids, as if looking for information inside his head. "Unfortunately, I am not here to defend or explain. I've done that plenty and something tells me you have heard it already."

Jensen held his stare.

"What I want to know is, why did you come to this facility to perform this act of sabotage? There are others in Bellark."

"I followed one of your vans to this one," Jensen answered. "I waited in the city during the night until I found one to follow. The van I chose happened to come here."

Salvador's suspicion grew. Jensen's eyes bounced from Salvador to Luis, to Delaney and back to Salvador, not once breaking the stoicism he had managed to maintain since beginning the conversation. Each was carefully scrutinizing his every word and action.

"Very well," Salvador said skeptically. "How did you know what you were doing with the power?"

"Does it matter? Experience."

Salvador grew weary of Jensen's attitude. "You think you're doing good for the world, don't you? Are you trying to be some vigilante on the side of right? This nation is a democracy. Our people believe this is right." He gestured at the facility around them.

Jensen took a few seconds. "The people don't know very much."

The door opened. One of the personnel handed Delaney a folder. Jensen watched the blonde woman open the folder and skim its contents through her rectangular glasses before handing it to Salvador. "The profiles on the Potentials, Sir."

The Chief opened the folder then glanced up at Jensen and angled the contents away so he couldn't catch a glimpse. There was a two-minute silence in the room as he reviewed each profile. He cleared his throat and set the contents on the table. It lay open, but Jensen did not peer down to read. Salvador pushed the folder a little closer. "Because of your actions, six Potes escaped our facility."

Jensen's neutrality cracked. "Some escaped?"

"Yes, some escaped," Salvador said, noting Jensen's change of tone. "And in their escape, four of our employees were killed. This leads me to my next question. Did you know any of these?" He nudged the folder even closer. "I think perhaps a relationship with one of them provoked your actions tonight."

"No," Jensen returned sternly, still not looking at the profiles in front of him.

"What were your hopes in coming here tonight? Was your goal to free all them?"

"I wanted to make your jobs difficult."

"Sounds like a suicide mission," Salvador said, chuckling. "You didn't plan too well for an escape."

"I guess not."

Salvador's irritation heightened a little more. Though his forbearance had grown thin, his respect for Jensen had risen as

67

well. Salvador had always enjoyed a challenge and was never one to shrink from a confrontation. "What's your last name, Jensen?"

He considered the repercussions of revealing his last name. Sooner or later, the department would excavate all his information, and the punishment would remain the same, he knew. "Lloyd."

Salvador gave no immediate response. He collapsed his hands together and allowed his thumbs to fidget against one another. His thought process deviated from the question he had planned to ask. "Whom do you live with?"

Jensen was confused by the question. He did not see the relevance to the matter at hand but didn't mind answering. "My grandfather."

"No carriers?"

"No."

Salvador scratched his chin. "They leave you?"

"Not my mom."

"Where is she now?" Salvador shot out before Jensen could finish his last word.

"Why are you asking me these questions? If you're trying to find other people guilty for what I did, you won't. No one else was involved. I'm the only one responsible. My grandfather has no idea where I am right now. I promise you that."

Salvador was still processing the information. Delaney too found Salvador's approach a bit confounding. Luis grew anxious in the back, restless to apprehend the escaped Potentials, not to learn about the saboteur's upbringing. However, Delaney gave Salvador the benefit of the doubt, hoping that his questions would advance the investigation.

Salvador again slid the contents closer to Jensen. The push was gentle as his aggression reined in "I want you to look at the profiles of each of these Potes."

Jensen grabbed the folder. Inside was a picture of a smiling redheaded girl with a general description. He found the photo ironic, imagining she did not once wear that smile in the facility. Going through the next four profiles did not take away the grief he had been trying to conceal, yet there was a satisfaction knowing the stranger faces were free.

He turned to the last profile.

Jensen made sure to show no variance. He scrutinized the picture and read the description slowly, maintaining consistency with how he'd read the other five. But his heart became a jazz snare as realization lifted him from the mourning he'd been sitting in. The Chief, Vice, and stalky officer had not once removed their eyes from him. He raised his head to Salvador after reading the last sentence of David's bio: *Enters Eighteenth Year February 27th*.

"Recognize any of these faces?" asked Salvador.

"I don't."

Delaney spoke up. "None, huh? Maybe you've seen one of these Potentials at some point? Passing through a grocery store, maybe?"

The Vice seemed even more skeptical than the Chief and almost as suspicious as the shorter man now jotting notes on his cell phone. Luis' lightning-quick hands aroused some uncertainty, causing Jensen to wonder if he'd somehow exposed himself or David. "No. Never seen any of them."

Salvador stood and said briskly, "Well, Jensen. Thank you for cooperating. You will be billed for the property damage done this night and serve one hundred hours of community service to the Contration Department."

Luis was alarmed. "Sir?"

Salvador ignored him. "Is your vehicle nearby?" he asked Jensen.

"Yes," he said, also confused at receiving such a minimal punishment. "My truck's parked a little bit away."

"You will be escorted to your vehicle by one of our officers after your release from custody in an hour or so. Drive directly home and do not intervene in our business again. We will look you up and mail all documents pertaining to your punishment." He picked up the folder and snapped it shut. "I will not be as gracious next time."

Salvador paced out of the room, Luis quick to follow. Delaney hung back for a moment. She and the Potential exchanged a brief, silent stare, and then she exited the room to

69

catch up with the others.

Jensen sat there, astonished, not because the Chief hadn't thrown him into juvenile detention or worse; that would not have mattered. David was alive, and he would have gladly taken any sentence for that to be the truth. A guard unlocked Jensen's handcuffs and gestured for him to follow.

Delaney had almost caught up with Salvador, who'd made some distance down the hall with his quick pace. His intensity had returned. "Sir, what are you doing?" Delaney said, still a few steps behind. "Four men died tonight. I'm still willing to bet he knew a Pote that was here, whether that one escaped or was contrated."

Salvador swung around, halting her stride. "Abbot, you are my Vice, so in fairness I expect you to object to what you deem as unwise. However, this decision is final and irrevocable." Salvador gave no hint of weakness as he turned to Luis. "Adán, I know you're probably navigating in your head how you wish you could take back your insubordination in that room. Good for you—but never again. If you ever question my decisions in front of the accused, it will be your last question in the department."

"Yes, Sir," he said after gathering himself. Salvador continued toward the exit. Luis chewed on every word that had erupted from his Chief's mouth, determined never again to threaten his position or rank. There was no reason but to trust Salvador Goode, the man who had accomplished more for the Bellark CD than any other.

Salvador blew through the doors. "No time to waste," he announced to the officers waiting in the parking lot.

Delaney, however, could not simply forget the matter with Jensen Lloyd. Knowing Salvador, she felt confident she could bring her concerns forth in private at the appropriate hour. But she, like the Chief, focused on the priority of the moment.

*

The sun cracked over the horizon, its top edge not yet masked by the gray lurking above. It was the most frigid morning

70

of the week, likely to frost the SUV windows if the heater had not been blowing. Despite the warmth inside, resting one's hand or cheek against the window would not begin in comfort against the cuttingly cold glass.

The vehicle continued down the two-lane highway. Since they'd left the facility, the few spectacles for observation were the occasional tree or boulder in the uncultivated land, or the neighboring mountains north and south. The valley highway intermittently provided signs telling how many miles they were from Bellark.

However, David could not give any attention to the signs, temperature, or location at that moment. Having just gone to warm his hands in his flannel pockets, he felt a piece of paper over his right thigh. He quickly knew what it was, recalling when he'd slid it in there before bed.

The words had indelibly printed on David's mind. No need to pull it out and reread. It took him back to his bedroom where he'd written it, in northwest Bellark before he'd drifted to sleep just hours ago, which ushered the fear and confusion forward more insistently. He almost spoke the conundrum aloud but felt these people were not the ones to seek counsel. Not only would he not expect answers or clarity, but he did not want to make them feel any sense of inferiority since he knew their carriers legitimately decided theirs contrations.

But it lurked in the desert of his mind, a reality he was not ready to consider, the implications yet unfathomable. It was far from conclusion, more like a loosely formulated notion, the parts not yet taking the shape of the whole but existing nonetheless. *Maybe this was not an accident.* It was like an eruption in the far distance, the exact sound or source impossible to determine. It went off again—*maybe*—faint in the wilderness of thought but patiently beckoning an audience.

"I still don't understand why we're driving back to the city," the blonde girl said. She had a flawless complexion and a rounded nose. Her sandy blonde hair was long and lush down to her shoulder blades. Though not immediately observable beneath her large hoodie and sweat pants, she was slightly plump. By the

71

looks of her skin, she did not need to spend endless days under the sun to achieve her natural tan.

"Because they think we're driving the other way," the boy with black hair repeated.

"Yeah, but it's where their headquarters are."

David sought to ease the disagreeable girl. "It's the only way we can go now." He also figured it was the only way to learn the mystery of the accidental means for awakening in the contration facility, assuming he would discover the answers or deliverance in Bellark.

They'd initially traveled away from the city. After gaining a safe distance from the pursing vans with the slashed tires, the boy with black hair had turned off the paved road. With headlights off, he continued through the dirt about a quarter mile north from the highway, then parked the SUV facing the road. After an anxious five minutes, the group saw another pair of headlights traveling rapidly down the highway, going further and further east. Once safely distanced, the black-haired took the SUV back west, keeping off the highway until they passed the facility by a mile. Though coarse, the dirt was safely drivable.

When they returned to the paved road, the cloud coverage had thinned to barely a sheet, and the sliver of a waxing moon peeked through to illuminate the desert valley. There had only been two instances when the group had to pull off the main road to hide. The first time, they saw one set of lights coming their way. On the second occasion, it was a convoy of three, driving well over the speed limit, almost as fast as the boy with black hair. Since then, there had been no other sightings, though at one point before the passing convoy, they'd heard an indistinct chopping in the distance above.

"I think it's the best move anyway," said the redhead, defending the boy with black hair. She wasn't sure whether her support would embolden or insult him if he had a contrary pride. "I don't think they would expect us to drive into the city. They probably think we wanted to get as far away from Bellark as possible." The black-haired did not respond, but his silence seemed to approve her timid commentary.

The girl with brown eyes said, "Does anyone know where we are? I know the signs say we're headed to Bellark, but have any of you ever been in this area?"

There was a unanimous "no," except from the dark-skinned boy who still had not spoken. He sat in the very back next to the redheaded girl, who had just plunged into thought; though she'd denied any knowledge of their whereabouts, the valley highway, and its geography did have a sense of familiarity. Since she wasn't sure, however, the redhead did not yet want to speak any misleading presumptions.

"I haven't been in this area," said David. "But I've been on this highway. Never gone this far though. All I can say is it eventually takes us to Bellark through the eastern wall."

"Did you check the radio again?" said brown eyes.

David turned the small tuning nob to search for reception. "Still out of reach of any signal it looks like. When we get closer, maybe something will come up."

"We still can't be that far from home," she said wishfully.

"We have no home," the black-haired said cynically. "Plus, we better hope if we ever do get reception, there's nothing said about us."

All eyes kept to the road, attentive for threats as well as anything that could benefit them. David gave his greatest effort to stay focused and serve as an effective copilot, but his mind was a pendulum, swinging back and forth between current survival and doubts related to his contration.

The redhead leaned forward from the back seat and squinted. "Look!" No one could have guessed her voice could rise so loud. "A sign for gas and food. There's got to be a convenience store too."

"Good call," the brown-eyed commended, squinting to read the distant sign. "I can still barely see it."

"Thanks . . ." The redheaded girl trailed off, not having a name to thank. "I'm Rylie, by the way."

The girl in front turned. "I'm Abigail." They shook hands, bringing a shy smile to both. "But my friends call me Abbi."

73

David turned around. Dawn had finally brightened enough to see the faces as they were. It was almost instinctive for him to shift toward her voice, his body demanding to know the name and face. Her hair, eyes, and skin were like a palette of different brown, going from light to dark, beginning with her skin and ending at her curly hair.

Abbi observed the sudden reflex. "What's your name?"

He began to speak but struggled to get the first word out. He cleared his throat. "David. I'm David."

"You were the first one to see me. In the facility," she said.

"Umm, yeah. Yes, I was." David hoped she didn't take much notice of his tongue-trip. The smile she paid him now was night and day compared to when he first saw her through the facility window. Even now, the familiarity, the tension of feeling duty for something not ever attained or experienced grew.

Abbi turned to the blonde girl beside her. "Mia," she answered before Abbi could ask. "My name's Mia." She was not as inviting as the other two girls. Her arms crossed over her stomach, face set toward the window to end any further conversation.

Rylie turned to the silent boy beside her, wearing a white tank top and forest green sweatpants. "What's your name?" she asked.

He released a great yawn, capturing the attention of everyone. It was the most noise he'd made. His eyes studied all those in front. "My name is Bobby." The others guarded any surprised reaction. It all made sense now, especially to David, who'd had his previous frustrations with the boy. Bobby continued speaking slowly, "Thank you all for saving my life."

His lagging, struggling speech, in conjunction with his lack of initiative during the escape, left no doubt in their minds that he had some cognitive or motor impairment. David felt a lump form in his throat as he imagined the circumstance that sent Bobby to the facility.

Abbi's voice softened. "Well, Bobby. You played just as much a part in helping us escape, so thank you." She saw his

74

choice of sleepwear. "Aren't you cold in a tank top? You gotta be freezing."

"Not anymore." Bobby seemed to appreciate the question. "This heater in here is warm. Mom always turns ours up really high at night, so it's not that bad."

The boy with black hair glanced down at the gas gauge; it read less than a quarter tank of fuel remaining. He spoke, relieving Abbi from coming up with an appropriate response after Bobby brought up his mother. "We're almost out of gas." He looked into the rearview mirror at Rylie. "How much further until that gas station?"

"The sign said ten miles," she said, also contrite from Bobby's comment.

"We'll need to fill up before our escape gets broadcast."

"We can get a map too," Abbi said. "See just exactly where we are."

The black-haired spoke to David. "We'll need to hold the clerk up or whoever is there to get the gas. Make sure that facility gun is still loaded."

David stared at him in disbelief. "Huh? No, putting a gun in someone's face will just make us more wanted. You can't seriously plan to threaten an innocent person."

"We can't be more wanted than we already are," he argued back. "They're after our lives as it is. Plus, as long as they listen to us, whoever's there at the station will be fine."

"We'll only be proving their point if we do," said David. "You need to show them you're good. That we're all good. No more violence."

"Proving their point? You trying to say if we behave good, they'll let us off? No. They decided, our carriers decided. It's done. You know what happened to those other kids that didn't make it out like us. They're ash now. All of them. If putting a gun to a man's face keeps me from that, I'll stick them every time."

Rylie interrupted, "We won't need to." She held up the wallet she'd stolen from the facility worker. Abbi reached for it, pulling out a credit card and some cash. "They pay these guys pretty well."

Had Rylie not spoken up, David was ready to confess to the others. He was a word away from demanding to be dropped off along the road. He would figure out the whole mess after walking himself to the gas station to call the department, so long as he disassociated from the other Potentials. Now that the wallet granted a reasonable plan, his alarm dwindled.

While discussing how they would refuel the SUV and purchase a map and other food and drink necessities, only the boy with black hair was strategizing further. He decided it would be premature to share his agenda with the others now. They would object, and independent as he was, he did not want to physically harm any them if he had to hold the SUV in his possession. Also, he'd grudgingly developed a trust for David. Not in the emotional sense, or so he thought. Rather, he felt his life may actually be secure or at the least supported if put in David's hands.

"You never told us your name," David said to him.

"I didn't."

"Well?"

Everyone waited for him attentively. He sighed. "Look. I get you all want to become friends and get to know each other, but not me. We're a procedure that failed, but because we were in that facility, we're written off as dead. And they'll be damned if we don't become that way. The sooner you realize that, you'll realize this kind of chatter is pointless. What is important is living . . . or coming to life. Let's focus on what matters. Not each other's names, but on where we are and where we're going. If we don't figure that out, then we'll be dead forever. And death doesn't remember names."

While disarmed, the blunt comments oddly resonated with most of the group, none finding themselves at odds with his logic. Only one was unsettled by his claim, having already begun wrestling with it even before the Closing. *You're wrong. You're as alive as the people after us.* The words almost left Abbi's lips.

*

Sam poured himself a cup of coffee as part of his morning

routine. He sat in his recliner, warming beneath the living room heater after picking up a book he had been trying to finish for two months. He read through one page and realized he could not recall a single word. The coffee had not yet stimulated his brain for the task.

There was a reluctance to turn on the television. He had progressively grown exhausted of what the news reported. He disagreed with many happenings in the nation, but he rarely vocalized those objections. One person could not change things, he thought. Still not having the energy to read the novel, he turned on the television. On the screen, six faces occupied the morning program. Before he could analyze the faces, the segment transitioned to a woman reporting the story's details.

"Very early this morning, six Potentials escaped from a contration facility outside of Bellark," she said. "In the escape, the Potes murdered four CD employees, and dealt serious head injuries to another."

The screen again displayed the faces and names of the escapees. Sam leaned forward and squinted, his vision not as sharp as usual this early.

"If anyone can identify any of these Potes, please contact authorities immediately. All escaped Potentials are dangerous and must be arrested and taken into custody for the safety of the public."

Sam came to the last young face on the screen just as he was taking another sip of his coffee. His hand slackened, and the brown liquid dropped and expanded on the living room rug like an army of ants emerging from their hill. He rose and walked closer to the television to be sure. "Jensen!"

He ran upstairs to wake his grandson. Turning on the bedroom lights, he jolted his head every which way, only to find the sheets kicked off the bed and Jensen absent. He leaped to the bathroom. Empty. Sam bolted outside to a driveway vacant of his grandson's truck.

*

"What are we doing?" said Mia, brushing her hair from her eyes.

Abbi looked at her. "What do you mean? We're going to fill up on gas and grab a map."

"I know," Mia said. "But after that. After we find a map, where do we go? What will we do?"

The light from the SUV's rear window caused Mia's blonde hair to glow from the back. It looked as though the sun had the strength to absorb the cloud expanse come noon. Perhaps the first day for clear skies was before them.

The boy with black hair was listening intently to Mia. Hers was the most legitimate question he'd heard thus far. He held his tongue to see where the conversation would lead. If he had the opportunity, he would take it, depending on how he gauged the rest.

"She's right," said Abbi. "We'll need another plan after we get gas."

Rylie suggested returning home in hopes of reconciling with their carriers. She guessed their carriers might have a change of heart when they learned of their escape and the horrors of the facility. Bobby was readying to accept the idea, until the others objected, giving no detailed explanations, but bitingly declining the idea. Abbi proposed turning themselves into the authorities in hopes of being shown some form of clemency. This would not happen though. Mia reminded them of the four CD employees who were now dead, an accusation of guilt directed explicitly to the boy with black hair, but he ignored the jab.

The black-haired finally said what had been building since he first hot-wired the vehicle, "I'm going to the North."

"What?" said David. The others all listened, confounded.

"If we can get there, we'll be a lot safer from the CD."

David found himself fully invested, processing the probability of the plan as if it entirely applied to him as well. "Will that work? From where we are, it could take days, even a week to get to the North. Even if we did make it, wouldn't their authorities hand us back over? Their government needs to keep in good standing with ours."

"You want to stay here? Or how about the South?" the boy with black hair said sarcastically.

"Do we have any other options?" Abbi asked, glancing at David. "I think he's right. The North is the only place we have a chance. If we can cross in secret, we may be okay."

David thought to himself, taken aback by Abbi's leaning body in his peripheral. She and the others waited on his answer as if they would only go to the North if he agreed to the proposition. He estimated the outcome if they stayed in their country—most likely apprehension and a completed contration for each of them. The South was out of the question. The boy with black hair was only trying to make a point. David also acknowledged they had one vehicle among the six of them. He would not be shocked if the unnamed boy went to extreme measures to keep the SUV. The ambition of the nameless acquaintance was respectable, but David knew the chances of making it to the North were slim. Even if they did slip through the northern border, the group would most certainly become wanted internationally.

Stop including yourself with them, David! The teetering between new loyalties and self-interest sent him into a dizziness. "Why do we have to be here?" He said aloud, closing his eyes as if that would take him somewhere else. *Should I just tell them? Maybe they'd be happy to drop me off, or even help me out.*

Abbi placed her hand on his shoulder. "None of us should be here, but we are."

David turned to meet her, wondering if she would still show the same pity if she knew his contration was a mistake. Nonetheless, her compassion was just as pure as the dependence in her undertone. He looked at everyone in the second and third row. Behind Mia's exhaustion was fear. Bobby, an innocent confusion with a tinge of anxiety. Rylie, on the other hand, shone with a remnant of hope. David turned to the boy with black hair. He peered down the road as he drove—fear.

David was overwhelmed. "Well," he sighed, "I was so close to reaching my Eighteenth too." He did not know how long his felt union would last, but there seemed no way to yet retract his sense of commitment. *Their lives are important, maybe even more so*

79

than mine. The ESE came to his mind immediately. Next moment, he was thinking of his sister Penelope, along with her noteworthy life, education, and future. *I should be here.* It was not a scream, but nor was it faint in his mind's abyss like before. Instead, it was like a whisper into one ear. *Could I be? Could my carriers?*

Rylie said, "How long until Eighteen?"

David took a second to understand that Rylie directed the question to him. "Two days," he answered, relieved that she'd interrupted before his thoughts could stretch further.

Abbi's head tilted. "Really? I reach my Eighteenth in three days."

Mia let out a flat grunt, the others unsure if it was an ominous chuckle or sob. "Well, it looks like we were the last-minute contrations," she said. "Our carriers could only hold out for so long. I pass my Eighteenth in two days too. February Twenty-Seventh."

Abbi's head rose, sorting through her thoughts. The revelation fell on her like an eroding cliffside, Mia's comment the final drop of water to usher the collapse.

Bobby spoke up, eager to share. "Mine's on February Twenty-Eighth."

Abbi whipped around to him. "That's the same day as mine, Bobby," she said with disarming interest. The others paused to process her unexpected exuberance. "What about you, Rylie? What day does yours fall on?"

The redheaded girl sifted through her head, not to figure out her date but to try and figure Abbi's approach. Her nerves fled after finding ease. "Umm, same as yours. Twenty-Seventh."

"Same as mine or Mia's? Mine's the Twenty-Eighth."

"Oh, yeah. Sorry. I'm on the Twenty-Eighth." Rylie blinked a few times in between. "Brain blanked there for a second."

Another line drawn and connected for Abbi. All were looking at the black-haired, waiting for his response. Abbi's urgency to learn everyone's birthdates was strangely commanding, as well as captivating. "And you?" David probed. "You may not have a name, but you do have an Eighteenth."

The black-haired resisted at first, having no preference for trivial talk, but he realized there was something deeper, perhaps even crucial to Abbi's curiosity. He first assumed she was abdicating the fight for life and prolonging the conversation only to distract from their harrowing circumstance, but now it seemed as if this new acquaintance came to an epiphany. "I pass my Eighteenth tomorrow," he said less suspicious.

Abbi collected her thoughts while running one hand through her hair, finishing at the back of her neck where the curls ended. She was desperate to be certain her proposal was not only worth speaking but logical. "No wonder we were on the same floor and in the same rooms. Mia said it. We're *those* February contrations. You guys, if we can stay on the run long enough until we all reach our Eighteenth year, until life, they can't contrate us."

The comment was not one any of them could have predicted. Everyone in the group, including the boy with black hair, took a long moment, thinking over the idea; he was shocked it hadn't come to him first. With each second that passed, the new proposal seemed more plausible.

"It's the law. You can only contrate a Potential, not a living human being," Abbi added.

"Do you mean stay here, inside the country until we all reach our Eighteenth?" Mia asked. "And then continue our lives like nothing ever happened?"

"That's impossible," the black-haired said. "We can never continue our lives here as if nothing ever happened. Four of their people are dead. We destroyed property and stole a vehicle." He thought a moment. "But our chances of having a life here are stronger than fleeing to the North illegally, I gotta admit. I would get the worst punishment of all of us. The facility had security cameras, but at least I would have another chance. A fair trial even." He glanced in the rearview mirror to Abbi. "Your plan is best. We stay on the run long enough until we all become living."

Abbi acknowledged the unfortunate truth. "We'll have nothing to go back to."

"Having nothing to go back to is a lot better than going

81

back to people that don't want you," the nameless boy said. He regretted the revealing comment immediately.

David was astounded by the idea and the way the Abbi had rallied the others, bringing them to a unanimous agreement in minutes. Not that he'd written her off as helpless, but her resolution was firm, without any self-doubt. Her confidence made him think of Jensen for the first time since escaping the facility. *If only I were like them.* The walls and ceiling closed in, once again plunging him into mental claustrophobia, returning his headspace to the impossible . . . *I am where I'm supposed to be.* The internal attack tried to pin him, but he would not give in. *I'm from the northwest.* He struggled to drown the daunting reality, just as bizarre and unreasonable if he examined it from another angle. *My carriers will come for me.*

The group soon came to an agreement, and a distracted nod from David solidified the plan. Each would continue their evasion of civil authorities until reaching their Eighteenth, traveling wherever necessary to avoid the CD. They didn't discuss, however, whether those who gained living status first would continue traveling with those who remained as Potentials.

Understandably, David was not able to decide as simply. At the very least, the Potentials, himself included, attained living status at Eighteen. It would only be four days total, he reasoned, turning around to look at the last ones to reach life on February Twenty-Eighth. He lingered on Abigail a moment longer.

*

"There it is!" Rylie pointed ahead. Everyone squinted to spot the nearing structure. She felt she recognized the sign reading 'Jack's Gas and Goods,' but Rylie did not want to inspire any falsehood. Their agreed-on task was to attain a map first. She could bring the matter up after, she thought.

The station was entirely vacant of customers in the early morning. In this remote location, there were only two available spots at the single standard gas pump, two nozzles to each side. The teens parked in one. On the opposite side of the convenience store was the fill-up for any semi-trucks, but apparently it was not in high demand either. The station was quite aged, clearly predating the secession.

It was Abbi who had volunteered to pay for the gas, the map, and other essential goods inside, but David did not hesitate to offer to accompany her. They felt the prickling chill of the morning immediately after stepping from the heated vehicle. Their visible breath led in front as they walked toward the store's entrance. Their pajamas could not keep them warm outside for long, yet the morning's briskness was sobering. Being barefoot as well, the ice-like asphalt reminded them of their fresh blisters. The punishment their feet took from the facility's concrete stairwell and asphalt parking lot returned, but neither allowed even a limp, knowing that entering the store barefoot was conspicuous enough.

Mia was first assigned to fill up the SUV since she was sitting closest in the middle row, but after she argued that she would be too slow to hop back inside in case of emergency, Rylie agreed to fill up instead. They switched seats.

David and Abbi entered the store. The interior, too, was run-down. The store appeared as if it had not received a thorough sweeping or dusting in several months. The elderly clerk behind the counter reflected the antiquity of the store. Behind him was an ancient television, decades old. David approached the clerk quickly to keep his bare feet hidden by the counter while Abbi shopped. "Can I put this on number two?" David handed the clerk cash.

"Anything else besides gas?" The elderly man coughed between the words.

David turned around to Abbi. "I can't find a map," she said from down an aisle.

"Do you have any local maps?" David asked the man.

The clerk bent down behind the counter, his body bobbing around as he searched. He finally grabbed something and straightened to set it on the counter. David analyzed the flattened map, which looked as though it had not been consulted in years from the pronounced fold creases and coffee stains. "Great. How much will it cost?"

83

The old clerk let out another raspy cough to clear his voice. "Ehh, you can just have it." He chuckled. "I know where everything 'round here is already. It's easy to find where nothin' is."

"Thank you."

The clerk nodded. "Anything else?"

"We have someone to fill up our car outside. We just need to find a few more things in here," David said. Rylie began to fill the gas tank after David gave a thumbs-up through the window.

The black-haired watched her closely through the side mirror. He was unstoppably fidgety after witnessing the speeding truck zoom by, readying to ignite the engine. Fortunately, because the last truck shot through the highway so quickly, there was no need to abandon the post. *Where'd he come from?* Though relieved that driver brought no issue, the tapping of his fingers over the steering wheel would not stop. *It could be the CD next.* In his mind replayed the vicious roar of the incinerator that had consumed the Potentials just hours ago; he had not realized the method of cremation was still in use. With modern science and recent advancements, as well as voter opinion, he'd expected the bodies, or at least some of its parts, to undergo salvage for another consumer need. That may have been just as excruciating to stomach, he thought. After escaping and seeing their location, he quickly understood; their facility was not like the modern ones constructed in the city, likely lacking the resources for anatomical salvage.

David and Abbi returned to the register to pay for the rest of their items. They'd picked out some water bottles and pretzels. David studied the pretzel bags on the counter, wondering whether they had expired. Judging from the looks of this place, he was not sure if he could trust the old clerk in doing inventory. *But beggars can't be choosers.*

The clerk arose from his chair to ring them up, walking to the register and grabbing the remote control that lay next to it. He pointed it to the old television behind, then began ringing up their items.

Abbi was already staring at the television as the program came into view, but as the clarity increased, she felt as though her legs were sinking into the cracked tile flooring. She discreetly nudged David's side, intentionally holding her breath to help her cause. He shifted his attention from looking out the window back to Abbi. She moved her eyes toward the television. David subtly turned his gaze to follow. The clerk kept his head down, having difficulty scanning one of the items. David's blood shot like bullets. He turned from the television and found a poker face. Abbi saw the sudden response and followed his non-reactive example.

"Shucks," the clerk said. "I'll be right back. I have to check the price of this. It's not ringing up."

"It's okay!" urged David. "We'll be fine without it. We'll just pay for everything else and call it good."

"No, no," the clerk said. "It's no problem for me. It'll just be a minute. I need to kill some time anyway. Most of the truckers, the entire one or two that is. Well, they don't get here for 'nother hour."

Despite David's efforts, the clerk turned around to search for the price. In the process, he glanced at the television and froze. He squinted to make out the image on the screen, then turned to back to the boy and girl, then back to the what the television screen displayed: *"Wanted and At Large: Six Criminal Potentials."* An enlarged image of David's face appeared on the screen next.

As if his decrepit body were merely a costume over a dueling outlaw, with rapid dexterity the clerk reached for and somehow snatched a concealed revolver lying just below the register. He raised it to David just as quick, "Now you two don't move." The old man crept to the phone, fixing his aim on David.

"Stop!" David lifted his hands. "Please stop. This is a mistake. I'm not a contration!"

"Huh?" The old man tilted his head. "Boy, your picture is up there. I think they know what they're sayin'." He placed his hand on the phone.

"No! I promise. My carriers couldn't have!" A vein in David's forehead bulged as he continued his plea. "I'm telling you this was a mistake. This news isn't right." Abbi froze in raising her hands for a brief second, but her confusion from David's claim was shrinking next to her enlarging fear.

The old man switched his scrutiny to Abbi. "Hmm, well what about her? She a mistake too?"

She begged, "Please, sir. Put the gun down, and we'll be on our way."

"No, I'm going to let the CD figure this out." He grabbed the phone and pinned it between shoulder and ear, keeping the gun in one hand and dialing with the other.

Crash!

The clerk only pressed four digits before the glass rained down at the store entrance. Alarmed, he dropped the phone, the cord pulling the base to the floor with it. In his unpredictable swiftness, the old man again shifted his body and aim to the front entrance. Before he could make another move, a purple dart pierced the right side of his chest. Amid the broken glass knelt the boy with black hair, the transparent rifle still aimed. Nearby in the heap of glass was a large, heavy rock that he must have used to provide the opening. David and Abbi rushed to look over the counter at the clerk, unsure what to feel: horrified because a man complying with the law was now dead or liberated because the same. There was no time to work it out. They grabbed the supplies and fled outside.

"I told you we should have held him up from the start!" the nameless boy said as they ran toward the SUV.

The comment quickly triggered David. "Why? So you could kill him right away?"

"Maybe. Or maybe with a gun to his head like I said, we could have tied him up and spared his life. Obviously would have been better than your idea!"

At this, David grabbed him by his long-sleeved shirt and rammed him into the driver's door. "You better not put that on me! I never told you to shoot the guy!"

The boy with black hair retaliated with a swift right hook to his cheek, sending David a few steps. "You might as well have! Son of a bitch, man. You guys should have run as soon as he turned on the TV, not negotiated with him."

"Stop it, you guys!" Abbi stepped in the middle.

David recovered his balance. "You saw?"

"Of course I saw! How long do you think I could wait? When I went to check up, the old man pulled a gun on you. What the hell were you even saying to him?" He said wryly, "'Please, don't kill me! My carriers don't love me, but you should.'"

Abbi looked at David, remembering what he'd said to the clerk. "Was that true? What you said to the man?"

The black-haired studied David. "What's she talking about? What'd you tell the guy?"

"Nothing." He looked to Abbi, his cheek throbbing. "Nothing important right now."

The others fixed their eyes on the debacle. David glanced up and saw their faces perched behind the SUV glass. He figured there was perhaps no longer any reason to withhold from them what he revealed to the clerk. Now, he was an accomplice to a legitimate murder, which established him as a criminal, if not a legitimate contration. There was a clear distinction for David between the justified defensive killing of the facility employee at the parking lot and the tragedy of the clerk. He would tell them eventually, but time was of the essence. "We need to get in the car. We're on the news," he announced for the others to hear. "All of our pictures are being broadcast. We need to find somewhere to go, somewhere to hide. Now."

"What are we gonna do?" Mia asked, panicked as they loaded the SUV. "We can't just drive forever."

"She's right," Abbi said. "It's only a matter of time before someone finds that poor guy." She switched her focus to the matter at hand but did not forget what David had said. Abbi let him know with her suspicious glance that he would have to explain later. If David's claim was a bluff, it was a rather quick one and one so outlandish that it failed to ease the clerk or prevent his death. However, understanding and overcoming her own denial, she kept her sympathy quiet. *He really believes his contration was an accident. Poor guy.*

Abbi was not alone in debating what to share and what

not. Rylie was not one hundred percent sure, but given the recent circumstances, it seemed like the group had no other choice. She was only a young girl when she and her father got sick that one summer, presumably after drinking milk they'd purchased from a gas station. She did not recall how far the station was from her family's summer mountain cabin, nor could she remember if 'Jack's Gas and Goods' was its name, but she felt inclined to speak up on her fragmented faith.

"You guys." Rylie failed to gain an audience at first. "Guys," she said again.

"What?" the boy with black hair said irritably.

"Pass me the map." All heads turned, surprised by her command. David passed it at once. Rylie studied the map as if trying to assemble a puzzle completed once before.

*

"Grandpa!" Jensen barged through the front door. Finding out David was alive encouraged his unwavering speed. Before the two CD officers escorted him to his truck, he was sure they would follow him to his house. However, this was not the case after one officer received a call to pursue the escaped Potentials. He was surprised until he overheard one officer muttering to the other about the pursuit being shorthanded.

He did not once let off the gas, his foot seemingly stuck to the pedal. It was a risky move to pass the gas station on the desolate highway and each one in the city, but he had no time to throw away. To his amazement, he returned home with no adversity other than the truck's gas tank being ounces from empty. Sam scurried down the stairs after hearing his grandson's cry.

"They took him! The CD took him, but he escaped. They're gonna contrate David, Grandpa!"

Sam pulled him under his arms. Jensen squeezed harder as a tear tumbled from his face. For the moment, Sam restrained his own grief, despite its begging for release. "I know, I know. I saw it this morning. I'm so sorry, Son. I saw the news, but

88

thankfully he escaped."

"The news? People know?"

"How else did you find out?" Sam struggled to reason through it. "Where have you been?"

Jensen let go of his grandfather and took a step back, fighting to regain composure. "I woke up last night to go to the bathroom. But I could smell the stench from downstairs. I forgot to take out the trash again." He began his detailed account of the night, while Sam's ears clung to each word.

As Jensen dropped the kitchen trash into the can at the end of the driveway, headlights were moving up the street. Jensen ducked down, remembering the enforced curfew for the night of the Closing. It must have been adults returning from some late outing, he thought.

The van approached at an unusually high speed. He made sure to keep his face and body hidden from sight. It would be no easy explanation if these residents called to report a Potential strolling on the night of the Closing. After the sound of the engine zoomed past, he raised his head to try and figure out, by the car's model and color, which of his neighbors roamed about so late. The vehicle, however, was not one usually seen in these streets. It was a white van, and on the rear was painted a unique logo only on select buildings in Bellark. A crimson shield was the backdrop for a budding seed as a vine shot up into the skeletal outline of a tree.

"I never saw one in our neighborhood, so I ran to follow it," he said to Sam.

Jensen jogged up the street to catch up to the van. After closing the distance, he came to a halt just as the van did. He crouched behind a car some yards back, looking through the rear window. He could not yet figure out why it parked out in front of Mr. and Mrs. Brady's house. He did not know the couple beyond their annual interaction when he was younger. For Halloween, the spirited seniors handed out the largest sized candy bars. He and David made sure to begin each of their Halloween exploits with their home. The couple was just as eager as the two boys, generous to give an extra chocolate bar to the first arrivals. Conveniently, this house of Halloween handouts was across the street from David's.

"Then the guys got out their equipment." Jensen grew solemn. "The two of them pulled out what looked like an ambulance bed and some kind of container that sort of looked like a fire extinguisher, but it wasn't red. I thought either Mr. or Mrs. Brady must have gotten hurt or something. I knew it was a CD van, but I didn't really make sense of it yet."

Jensen crouched behind the car, feeling uncertain. Was the hospital short of ambulances? However, his question changed shape as the men moved away from the Brady property, now wheeling the bed toward David's driveway. Jensen shot up from behind the car. Are his carriers hurt? He only crouched, watching and waiting, like a man who sees a cloud in the distance, unsure if it will bring shade or a storm. The men emerged from the front door ten minutes later with the bed.

David's mother came running out of the house. "No, we can't do this!" she cried, pushing one of the men wheeling the bed. David's father ran out, struggling to get hold of his hysterical wife. In an effort to calm her, he whispered words into her ear that Jensen could not make out from across the street. She gathered no ease, but her body expressed surrender as her husband lead her back inside. "We can't," David's mother said brokenly once more as the front door shut.

The two men from the van continued to wheel the bed down the driveway. Finally, Jensen could identify the body. His hands clenched as they began to shake. Where are they taking him? His questioning led to no answers.

"How did I think the CD could be there for something else? I don't know what I regret more," Jensen said regretfully to Sam. "Not doing anything to stop them, or telling David his carriers would never do such a thing."

The men loaded the unconscious David into the back of the van. Jensen thought about sneaking up on the two men in hopes of snatching his friend, but he still had not yet wrapped his mind around what was happening. 'Is David's mom crying because he's sick or hurt?' The engine ignited and bellowed down the mute street; Jensen's brain seemed to finally start too, no longer wasting another moment as he sprinted down the street, unconcerned whether a neighbor caught the Potential out past curfew. He grabbed his keys from the kitchen counter and ran outside. Hopping in quickly, he started the truck as the van rolled back down the street for each house able to get another look at the sprouting seed logo.

"I followed them all the way, all the way to where they were going. I didn't have a plan. I just went." He choked again. "I wish I hadn't been so stupid and realized it right then. I shouldn't

90

have waited for them to put David in the van. I should have fought off those guys right when they rolled that bed up his driveway."

"Don't blame yourself." Sam placed his hand on Jensen's unsteady shoulder. "You couldn't have known. Who could have? It happened so fast and how would you be able to understand it all? You were hoping for the best."

Jensen shook his head. "My hope got him taken."

He trailed the van into the heart of Bellark. It was graveyard-silent as it always was during a Closing. Most restaurants and establishments shut down even before dinner. The city was cloaked in darkness, only streetlights providing some guidance. The lack of building lights made it difficult for Jensen to follow the van from a safe distance, but he stayed focused. Any physical exhaustion would be impossible for him at this point. Rest was an afterthought.

The van left the city, taking a highway Jensen was quite familiar. They headed east. When making their fishing trips, Jensen and David only stayed on the same road for a few miles until they turned off. There was not much beyond that point; the land became increasingly bleak. The highway was a straight stretch in a valley, both sides surrounded by desert, though the northern hillsides were within a few miles.

"It wasn't a short drive. It took some time to get there, and I just kept going."

Upon nearing the facility, Jensen stopped and parked behind a cluster of boulders. He ran to the front parking lot just in time. Some other men emerged from the entrance and unloaded four bodies from the van, including David's; he had not realized there were others.

"Like I said, I didn't have a plan. My mind jumped to what I knew. After they wheeled David inside, I sprinted to the back of the building and saw their electrical tech, the generator, everything." Jensen looked up from the floor to his grandfather. "I went for it."

There was little exterior lighting, but fortunately, his eyes had adjusted to the night. He tinkered with wires, yanked cords, and did just about all he could to ensure the electrical system would not function. In minutes, the entire facility was pitch black. Jensen continued in the darkness, ripping wires, stomping buttons and switches; anything to ensure the damage was beyond

91

repair. Five minutes after the power went out, some guards arrived and held him at gunpoint. One, in particular, crept behind and took the butt of his rifle to Jensen's head.

"They took me in after that. I was out for a while. Out cold during David's entire escape."

Sam was burning with questions. "What happened after? How did you escape?"

"I didn't. They let me go. He let me go."

"Who?" Sam's voice almost cracked.

"Goode. Salvador Goode."

"Salvador Goode? The Chief?"

"Yeah, him. I don't know why, but he did. All he did was ask me if I knew any of the Potes. I bluffed, and he bought it. At least I think he did. I told him I only went to the facility because I opposed the Contration Department. He let me go with a fine and gave me service hours to the CD."

Sam's shock only heightened. "That's it? He didn't ask what school you went to or what part of the city you're from? He didn't ask you anything that would make it look like you knew one of the kids in the facility? Someone at least had to follow you back."

"No." Jensen shared in his grandfather's confusion. "None of that happened. I was surprised too. They took me to my truck, and then the officers were called off to find David and the others." He tried dismissing the unusual interrogation, but hearing his grandfather's thoughts on the matter caused his uncertainty to return. The two sat silently for a minute.

"We have to help him," said Jensen.

"Yes. Yes, we do." Sam rose swiftly, unlike his usual arthritic rise from the chair. "We'll need to get to him before they do." Sam looked as though his brain were reorganizing itself as he stroked his gray chin stubble. A new hesitation arose. "You know we'll get in trouble for this, don't you, Jensen?"

"Yes," he said.

Sam glanced at the television. "The media has been covering their story all morning. They may have something for us to go off of to find them."

It only took about ten minutes after turning on the television for the program to be interrupted by breaking news. The recent update told of their activity at a remote gas station off of Highway 38, stealing a map and gasoline after murdering the clerk. "The department arrived on the scene not long after the fugitives fled. The testimonial from the trucker, who arrived just minutes after, suggests that the Potentials are now traveling west on the 38," the reporter said.

Jensen's frustration with himself grew with every detail reported. It made complete sense to pass the gas station at first. He was not only frantic to return to his grandpa and share the news but also figured it unwise to test his luck by stopping where a CD vehicle was parked. Never did he bother to look at the driver. The sprouting seed logo on the side door was enough to repel him to the South.

"Let it go," said Sam. "Don't feel bad about not stopping. Any sane person would have done the same."

"What's the plan, then?" Jensen asked, still forgiving himself for the missed opportunity.

"They're headed west toward the city. They're going to have to hide out somewhere. We'll head out to find them."

"You don't think they'll keep on the move?"

Sam said confidently, "I don't think so."

Puzzled, Jensen looked to his grandpa. "Why not?"

"I saw all their info this morning. Best for them to wait on life."

Sam paced upstairs to his room, putting forth more vigor than Jensen had observed in some years. His grandson trailed a step behind. Sam approached the metal safe he had not opened in months and entered the combination. From beneath some notebooks and papers, he pulled out a black case. Jensen watched closely. Never having seen the item, his curiosity was piqued. Sam unzipped the carrier and removed a handgun and a supplementary attachment.

Sam could see the awe and confusion on Jensen. "I haven't had to use it before."

"How long have you had this?" Jensen carefully studied

93

the object for the first time.

"Awhile," Sam said. He held up the slender attachment. "I bought this part from a black market. I got a little leery after they built those new contration facilities inside the city. Haven't been much of a law-abiding citizen for some time, I suppose. I never had one quite like this even in the military." Sam screwed the illegal silencer onto the end of the gun. "Just in case, you know? I have another one in here. Thought it would be a nice gift to pass down to you at the right time."

Sam loaded the two guns with ammunition from their cases. At first, Jensen wanted to ask why his grandfather had purchased silencers for the arms, but he soon realized it was for the exact reason he'd brought them out.

"Why now?" Jensen said. "You've had your thoughts about the Contration Department even before David was involved, didn't you?"

Sam looked up, thinking how to articulate it. "Every person, I think, has a sort of breaking point." Jensen heard his grandfather's solemn shift. "This moment, it seems for me, finally compels belief and action to intersect. Trying to separate the two is like trying to separate salt from sugar once mixed. And that's what happened when they took David. Knowledge is power, but more, knowledge is accountability. What I know is that David is out there, days from life, and other people are trying to stop that."

The two loaded the RV on the side of the house that had sat idle since their camping trip the previous summer. At first, Jensen suggested using his grandfather's company truck to make it appear as if the two were working for the day. That would be their defense if conflict came with the authorities. Sam then told Jensen the plan was not to only save David but also the others, and the RV could hold them all.

"But didn't they murder that clerk? The others could be dangerous."

Sam understood where his grandson was coming. "Yes, maybe they are dangerous. Truth is, anyone can be dangerous, given that someone lifts the gun to them first. No doubt if the clerk were alive still, David or one of the others may be contrated.

94

My best bet—they did it so they could keep on. For all we know, it could have been David who shot him."

Sam backed out the RV as Jensen guided and signaled from outside. Once it reached the street, he hopped in. As they drove, neither of them spoke it, but the thought crossed both their minds. Everything was happening in flashes, and Sam dealt decisions quicker than gambling cards. Nevertheless, they both knew that returning to any ordinary life was cast further away every second they continued down the street.

Sam wrestled with how much he should disclose to his grandson, but he knew they might never have another chance to have this conversation. Jensen had frequently asked when he was a child. He'd felt the more he searched for specifics, the easier it would be to understand why his father had left him. Sam always gave him the same vague answer, and eventually, Jensen quit asking.

Sam cleared his throat. "Son," he said. "As you know, your father left you to me."

Jensen's head lifted, full attention provided.

"It was during a Closing near the end of your second month. Late May. Almost eighteen years now. He wanted to have you contrated right after, right after your mother passed away, but not as many facilities existed back then. He was told to bring you back the following month once the waitlist cleared." Sam's eyebrows furrowed. "After he denied my final plea, I took you off his hands at the facility he meant to have you contrated. I have not spoken to him since."

Jensen leaned his head against the window. "Good."

*

It was just minutes after the Potentials had fled when the semi-truck arrived at Jack's Gas and Goods. The Chief and his convoy rerouted as soon as they received the call, though the police and the media got the news first. It took some time for the CD to backtrack and arrive at the convenience store, so Salvador ordered the helicopter to instead pursue in the direction the trucker reported seeing the hijacked department vehicle.

Upon arrival, Goode and Luis Adán questioned the stout driver for the same account he'd given to the police officers also present. The hijacked SUV was a speck on the horizon when he turned into the parking lot. The trucker was unsure of how the dead clerk met his fate but gave his theories. However, it was all conjecture while they waited for Delaney Abbot to figure out the old security cameras.

"I think I've got it," she said as the picture finally appeared on the old television. "Yep. There we have 'em." Salvador and Luis leaned over both her shoulders. "It's just two of them here."

The Chief opened the folder of all the profiles. "Abigail Rosario and David Kingsley," he said. "They killed the old man?"

"No, I don't think so," said Delaney. "Watch the replay. The dart came from outside. The angle didn't catch the breaking window, but you can see some of the glass falling at the bottom of our picture here. I think the shooter was outside."

Luis was astonished. "He shot after breaking the window. I'm willing to bet on who it was."

"Same here. I don't think these two would have had it in them anyway." Salvador put his finger on Abigail's face on the screen. "She's horrified when the clerk falls. You can see the other kid next to her is spooked too."

"Doesn't matter. They were there," Luis said. "If they hadn't been, then this man would be alive. One holds the gun, the other holds the map, and the other pumps the gas. Each one of them killed the old man."

Delaney said, "We weren't able to identify anyone outside. The exterior security camera seems to be broken or dead. We'll have to take the trucker's word that the stolen SUV was here. Hopefully the Potes didn't split up."

"Perfect," Salvador said, frustrated. "This place is an antique. Why even have an outside camera?" He gathered himself. "How long has it been since they left?"

Delaney said, "Less than an hour, Sir. The chopper should be gaining on them. I sent some of our ground team out as well."

"I can't believe our chopper hasn't found them yet." The exhaustion was catching up to Salvador. Never had there been a contration escape in Bellark since he was promoted to Chief. Attempted escapes were not entirely uncommon in the nation, but the atypical last-ditch effort for a Potential to run away on a Closing never met success. Only once had a selected Potential successfully crossed the North border. However, she fled from a city that already neighbored the North. To the bold escapee's misfortune, that country tossed her back no sooner than she could take another step on the new soil.

The thought fanned Salvador's disbelief. He was not only experiencing his first cat-and-mouse chase, but it was with *six* of them. He found a scrap of reassurance, however; Bellark was a southern city and furthest from the North, excluding the small beach towns to the southwest. "Do we have any new leads on where they're going?"

"They acquired a map of the area from the store," said Luis.

"Smart," Salvador said reluctantly. "They're developing a plan that goes beyond just driving. Abbot, contact the carriers of the Potes and see if you can gather any information on where they might head. We need to find them as soon as possible. Time is ticking. I want them all found and contrated before midnight tonight."

"Why midnight?" Luis slicked back the hair that was starting to fall over his forehead.

Salvador walked toward his vehicle as Delaney and Luis followed. "Because that's when our first Potential passes his Eighteenth. Can't let this old man's murderer come to life."

The Chief gave a strict order to depart immediately, but Delaney stopped in the act of stepping into the vehicle, rushing back into the store. Less than a minute after, she emerged with her forearm over her mouth, sprinting around to the back of the store. She reappeared just as quickly as she had vanished.

"The old clerk never got around to unlocking the bathroom," she said almost nonchalantly as she buckled her seat

97

belt. "I apologize for the holdup. I knew I should never have ordered my steak rare last night."

Salvador was able to give his attention to her now that they were well on the road. "Is it all out of your system?" he asked. "That's why you don't do rare unless you grill it yourself. I don't need you throwing up anymore." He said it in a matter-of-fact manner, but he couldn't hide the undertone of dependency.

Delaney sat in the middle row diagonal from Salvador, who sat in the passenger seat as another officer drove. The nausea had come out of nowhere. She hoped the small pile behind the station was the last of it.

The Vice studied Salvador's fingers, fidgeting over his knees as if there were a keyboard. Delaney had an actual laptop open on her lap, gathering all the names of family members her Chief had requested. In front of her were faces she had never seen, home addresses she had never visited, and phone numbers she would commission other officers to contact. *To what extent will these carriers give information? Will they help at all?* Contrations do not come easy for many carriers, she knew. Asking them about the whereabouts of their Potentials could be salt on a gnarled wound. For other carriers, however, giving such information may come as simple as giving directions.

Delaney glanced up again. Luis was sitting behind Salvador, studying all the notes and details he had jotted on his phone. *Such a wound young man.* She had to admire his tenacity though. Looking again to Salvador, she saw that his hands had finally rested on his knees. She hoped his eyes would follow his fingers' example and shut for even a brief minute. Yet she felt the pressure as if for every brick of burden he took on, she would naturally accept the other. Unfortunately, the Chief still felt the entire weight.

Though the occasion was now inappropriate, it did bring the Vice a bit of sadness that she could not share with Salvador what she'd planned after the night of the Closing, what she put off for several weeks. It would have been a celebratory occasion, especially for him, she felt sure. If the news was brought forth now, however, she feared it would only add to his stresses—and worse, Salvador would most certainly command her to withdraw from the pursuit. *After*, she decided. *My stomach just needs to keep settled. I cannot lie to him again.*

The feeling had seemed strange at first. But with each passing week, the familiarity returned; a remembrance that was almost a ghost of a memory, a haunting that followed like an invisible shadow. However, that was nearly a decade ago, before she joined the Contration Department, before she met Salvador Goode; two people in bondage, each one of them believing they held on to the other's key for comfort and liberation. She placed a hand on her stomach, waiting, almost hoping for movement. Too soon, she knew. Interestingly, there was also a relief.

*

"I think it should be coming up soon," Rylie said, studying the topographical map. They were all a bit thrown off and doubtful to hear Rylie's idea. It was difficult for her to recognize their whereabouts at first, but after the gas station incident, she felt confident enough. She shared of her grandparents' cabin where her family used to stay for vacations, usually in the summer. It was tucked away in the forest up in the foothills north of the highway. After Rylie's father passed away, she and her mother no longer continued the summer tradition.

"Your grandparents still go there?" Abbi asked.

"Not in a while," she said. "My grandfather's driver's license got suspended because of poor eyesight, and my grandmother hates driving. That happened over a year ago."

"You certain your family's cabin is around here?" The unnamed boy was doubtful.

"Certain? No," said Rylie. "But I think there's enough reason to look."

The open desert hardly changed as they continued west. A thin gray veiled the sun hanging atop the sky, but one could look directly to the shielded sun like a cloth-covered flashlight.

Rylie knew there was a prominent landmark to guide her if they were anywhere near the cabin. She remembered a bridge that crossed a river just before her father would turn off. This turn was one of the few highway exits, particularly where the base of the mountain met the highway no more than a half-mile away. It would make for a short distance to the climbing dirt road. Rylie peered intently down the fading yellow divider line to see if she could spot the bridge. The highway was closing in on the base of the mountain. She did not know how long it had been since she took her last breath but hoped her next would be one of relief.

"There it is!" Rylie saw light bounce ahead. "That's definitely it." She glanced down again at the map, then back up to see the river come into view, though it was hardly a sliver from their distance. "Take your next right up here."

The boy with black hair checked the time on the digital clock. "How long will it take?"

"Not too long, I think. Twenty to thirty minutes," Rylie said. "I can't exactly remember."

A sniffle entered the conversation. Mia wiped her eyes with a sleeve. She had not spoken since they fled the gas station. Bobby had spoken more than she in the past hour, though only quietly aloud to himself with no one able to hear his words.

"It's all right. We're almost there," Abbi said reassuringly.

Mia sniffed. "It's not that."

David opened the glove compartment in hopes of finding a tissue for Mia. It was a quick remembrance of where his mother kept tissues in her car. Instead, he found some napkins and handed them to her. She cleared her nose into the coarse paper. At this point, she had no reservation about blowing unrestrained with her roaring nose.

"We're gonna make it, Mia," said Abbi. "We're still alive."

Mia turned to the window. She kept silent.

"It's not about being alive or dead," said the black-haired.

Mia's eyes shifted from the window to him, as did everyone else's.

"Turn right here," Rylie directed. "This is it. You're

going to follow up this road for a while." The SUV went from asphalt to dirt. The initial transition was turbulent from the dips and ripples in the path, but it eventually smoothed. The outside breeze soon blew the behind cloud of dust to invisibility.

David looked to their driver, unsure but curious. "What's it about then?"

"It's not about being alive or dead," he said steadily, and somewhat impatiently. "What's being alive if no one wants you? Mia's not wanted. She, unlike all of you, has accepted why she's here, why we're all here. You can only deny that for so long until it hits you like it's hitting her."

Abbi was unconvinced. "Yeah? Has it hit you? You don't seem worried."

"It hit me before all of you," he said, stone-faced. "Our society likes to tease us. Likes to make us think we have a shot, that we can actually bring something to the table . . . to their table. How many of you studied extra hard before you took the ESE? Not me. I never had a chance. I wasn't gonna buy into that."

"You gave up?" accused David.

"No, you all gave in."

Abbi doubted his confidence. "So, what? On the night of the Closing, you just lay down in your bed waiting for the gas to come through your vents so they could pick you up? Did you ride shotgun to the facility too?"

"You're funny," he scoffed. "Hell no. I knew they were coming for me. That's why I took off last night. I knew my old man wanted me gone as soon as I got home. Didn't speak a word or even acknowledge me. That's all I needed to know. I tried sneaking out. I had a plan to catch a train north. Lo and behold, the bastard was waiting hidden outside my window for just that moment. He tried to stop me, and it broke out into a classic father-son brawl." A lump grew in his throat, but the others could not see. "I overpowered him and ran as fast as I could, to wherever I could. I didn't get more than two miles before the CD got me. It was three hours before curfew, so I'm guessing the old man gave them a tip. If I was smart, I would have left weeks, months before. But even I thought, 'Maybe it won't happen.' I kept that hope for too long."

An echoing silence resounded in the vehicle, loud and intrusive, but no one had the words to quiet it. It was soon interrupted at Mia's next sniffle and nose-blow. Turning to the boy with black hair, only David could see his lip's quiver, unsure if it was from spite or sadness.

Bobby cleared his throat from the back seat. "I'm glad you are all living."

His agitation spiked after having just explained the harrowing account. "Living?" The black-haired looked into the rearview. "If we were living, we wouldn't be where we are now! If we were living, none of us would know each other, and this conversation wouldn't be happening."

Abbi lost her sympathy at his lashing out. "Why are you like this?"

"Why am I realistic?" His sarcasm was cutting, "Well, I don't let myself be fooled, for one. I don't give anyone the power to tell me my worth anymore. Don't feel bad, Mia. I had a moment like yours, but once you realize nobody gives a damn about you, you adjust. I did."

"Don't listen to him, Mia," David said quietly but firmly, protective if the statement bit the others as well. "We're all cared about." No sooner had the words left his mouth did they meet him with whiplash. He wondered how he could assert the statement so instinctively but then doubt its authenticity just as quick.

"Shut up," Mia lightly sobbed. "He's right."

"No. Don't. Don't listen to his ranting," Abbi implored.

After a few seconds, Rylie's quiet voice came next. "You say you've adjusted? I don't believe you. I think you're hurting just as much as Mia. Keeping a strong face doesn't mean you're without pain. It probably means you're just holding on to more."

The boy with black hair could not find a response as quickly.

All conversation stopped for the next twenty minutes. David tried the radio once more for any reception, but only static

102

pricked out of the speakers. Rylie was the most frequent to speak, providing the occasional update on where they were or how many minutes she estimated until they should arrive at the cabin.

They had ascended into the hillsides. The higher they climbed, the more trees, birds, and other wildlife appeared. The many pines provided a natural shielding cover: any helicopter in pursuit would have difficulty spotting the SUV through the thick foliage. There were a few turn-off roads on both the left and right. Rylie mentioned there were other cabins, and even a few permanent homes tucked away beyond the trees.

Eventually, after seeing the occasional roof or fence lining of another person's property, David saw a snug opening in the trees, an uncomfortably slim dirt path that hardly widened further on. "Are there any homes down that way?" Rylie looked where he pointed, trying to recall where the opening led. David had hoped the boy with black hair would slow to better view the narrow road, but he continued on instead, determined to see if the cabin in fact existed.

"No," Rylie finally said. "There's no homes down that way. It's a road though. Our family never drove it for too long since it's a bit rough. It cuts through the trees and only goes deeper into the woods and mountain, from what I can remember."

The nameless boy said, "If this is even the mountain your cabin is on."

"Yes. If it is," said Rylie. She gained more confidence but did not see the worth in trying to convince him at this point.

"We need to remember where that turn is back there," said Abbi. "Even if that path just leads deeper into the woods, it could be a good option. For worst-case." The others agreed.

"Take your next left," Rylie said after another five minutes.

The new path was unexpectedly spacious as if it was intentionally widened for two cars to drive side by side. Only for a short twenty-yard stretch did the road shrink; the vegetation became all-consuming, the long branches like hands at a church service, brushing against the SUV as if it had asked for prayer.

Each set of eyes looked out their respective windows, both admiring and dreading the wilderness surrounding them. No matter how much prettier, it was merely another leg in their exodus.

"There it is," David said pointing, the first to see a lone cabin after emerging into a clearing.

The cabin was a large brown body, the top story windows like the eyes of an old man. The rotting wood underscored the structure's longevity, a remodel a manifest necessity if it was to stand another ten years. Fallen leaves and branches shrouded the porch entirely, alongside the faded green plastic bench. The house was far from a summer magazine cover. But none of them had expected it to be. They were satisfied enough to discover it indeed existed.

Rylie, however, felt a range of emotion as she looked upon her old vacation home. Love and loss, gratitude and sorrow, converged at the site. Two realities, seemingly mutually exclusive, forced to marry. The longing for her father was the greatest it had ever been. Though she'd shed no tears like the hundreds at the funeral for the respected firefighter, having one more minute with her father was more desirable than reaching her Eighteenth year. Another minute with him seemed more likely, she thought. Her father's motto, or more so his conviction when it came to the relationship with his daughter, rang through Rylie's head: *"You first."* Perhaps the effort would turn out to be fruitless, but at the very least, seeking the safety of these new friends united her closer with his memory. *I'll still do what I can for them.*

The real spectacle was the view the cabin commanded. It rested along the rim of the mountain. The trees separated so that one could gaze upon the winter-brown valley with the highway cutting through like a razor to cardboard. The road was slender from their elevation but still well visible. The river journeyed south as far as the eye could see, but the waters appeared frozen from their vantage point. From here, the landscape looked like a calendar picture, not so much a symbol of life or death as they had previously seen it.

They jumped out and headed for the rim first to gauge

their whereabouts. Unbeknownst to David, as he extended his right leg out of the door, the folded paper slid out from his flannel pocket, falling down and beneath the chair. The new surroundings had stolen his attention entirely, just as it had for the others.

After taking a moment to observe the new surroundings, they walked for the cabin's front door. To their left was an attached garage, containing tools as well as the family truck. It was used for any excursions after her family settled in, an efficient vehicle for climbing the mountain with plenty of cab space for passengers in the back. While explaining it to the others, Rylie recalled this was the same old truck she sat in when retrieving the gas station milk that had made her sick.

David asked, "How come your family just left it here?"

"Remember? My grandpa can't drive anymore," said Rylie. "And my mom could barely leave the house, much less come back here after my dad died."

Even after the group crunched the leaves on walking up the wooden porch, this in no way exposed any surface beneath the crumbles. They could feel the wood surface beneath, but nothing more. Most of them kept their feet light as if they believed the wooden porch took the damage rather than just the dead leaves. The boy with black hair, however, treaded forward with no mind to his steps. "It's locked," he said, jiggling the resistant doorknob.

"Of course it is." Rylie shook her head. "Why wouldn't it be? It's old, but it's still our cabin. Step off real quick." She nudged him off the welcome mat hidden beneath the leaves and lifted it. Underneath, lying on top of the cleared wooden surface, was a rusted silver key.

"You don't want anyone to break in, but you put the key in the most typical place?" The nameless boy's face relaxed, almost smiling when he said it.

"Bet it would have fooled you," Abbi said. "You probably would have taken the rifle to a window, like you did with the SUV. If you'd done that, we would have driven through the night with the freezing air."

The snickers followed immediately after. Rylie had the

most resounding of the laughs, the contagious kind that provoked the others further. Even Bobby clearly remembered the scene when the boy had failed to break the SUV window during the escape, only for Rylie to discover the middle door unlocked. David was subtle with his laughter, waiting for the other boy's reaction. David's left cheek still stung from the strike at the gas station—enough for him to now proceed with caution.

The boy finally responded. "Bet you would have gladly froze in the night rather than burn in that facility." This was the first time he had hung the escape over their heads. It was manipulative, to be sure, but most of the others understood that it was a tired reaction.

Like the exterior, the interior appeared as though no one had stepped inside for several years. In the living room were a brown sofa and two old recliners with ripped leather. Across the way was a dining room equipped with a square, chipped wooden table and four wooden chairs, each one a different color and model as if each was picked out at a different time from a different store. Dark beige carpet with frequent tears and stains covered the floor.

Rylie set the key on the stand next to the front door. "Make yourselves at home."

"Will anyone come here?" asked David.

"I hope not," Rylie said. "Unless you invited someone."

Bobby spoke up. "Rylie?"

"Yes, Bobby?" Her ears picked up his urgency like sonar.

"I have to pee."

She relaxed. "Of course you do. The bathroom is down that hall on the right."

The rest found seats in the beaten recliners or couch, layers of dust jumping into the air as the bodies collapsed on top. It only took a couple of minutes before everyone again tasted their thirst. The salted pretzels from earlier seemed to have absorbed all the water they'd drunk. Rylie went on a hunt to see what the cupboards held. To her surprise, there were still some canned goods in the pantry and a case of bottled water.

She struggled to walk the case to the living room, a pack

of thirty-six bottles a heavy load for her tiny frame. "I don't think we've cleared this place out since my grandparents stopped coming. Looks like they left us some stuff." She'd planned to set the case down gently, but it tumbled from her hands gracelessly, her fingers ready for relief at the earliest opportunity. The thud shook the coffee table, but its wobbling legs held. David and the boy with black hair chugged their bottles quick and in unison together.

"We should have enough room for us all to sleep," said Rylie.

"We'll need to keep someone on watch at all times while we're here," the boy with black hair said wiping his mouth. "They're still searching for us."

David nodded. "He's right. We have a pretty good view from this cliffside too."

"We could all take a shift," suggested Abbi.

"Works for me," said Mia.

"Not all of us. Just us." The nameless boy pointed down the hall to where Bobby was still using the restroom. "We can't put him out there."

"Why? He'll want to help," Abbi said. "He'll be fine."

"I know he wants to help. We just can't guarantee he'll be able to."

Abbi challenged him. "All he has to do is stay awake and let us know if anybody is coming."

"Look, I don't know how else to say this. Our lives are in each other's hands right now, except for his. His life is in ours. He seems like a good guy. I just can't put my life in his hands since he's . . ."

"Because what?" Abbi chimed in. "Because he's not as smart as you or me?"

"Exactly," he said. "It's not his fault, but it's the way it is."

After listening and weighing the exchange, David spoke. "I'll do his shift with him. Bobby will go on a watch like the rest of us, and I'll go out with him. I'll take mine after. That work for both of you?"

Abbi and the nameless boy looked at one another and nodded. A flush sounded from down the hallway. Bobby walked back into the living room. "I heard my name," he said. "What's happening?"

David said, "You and I are going to stand guard outside a little later."

Bobby matched his smile. "Great."

The group developed their rotation. Each person would watch outside in two-hour increments, then switch to the next person for their entire stay. The boy with black hair immediately volunteered for the first shift and went outside as soon as their plan was set. Soon after, Mia and Bobby fell asleep in one of the two guest rooms. The cabin master bedroom had the only queen-sized bed, but no one thought to assume it from Rylie.

Rylie and Abbi grabbed cans out of the pantry to see what they could fix for dinner. Their only options were canned beans, chili, and a few varieties of soup. After setting out their choices on the counter, Rylie disappeared for a little while, but her steps from upstairs let the others know she was up to something. She returned ten minutes later, her arms laden with clothing—jackets, sweaters, beanies, shirts, and even a couple pairs of shoes set on top.

"I couldn't find any pants or jeans, but we're pretty stocked with stuff for outside. Not sure if these shoes will fit any of us but take your pick." Rylie laid everything out on the carpet behind the couch. She then opened the downstairs closet next to one of the guest rooms and returned with several blankets.

Abbi and David nestled in their recliners, each taking a blanket and leaving the selection of clothing for later. Rylie soon took the couch, quickly drifting off where she lay. Abbi's eyes were growing heavy too.

"I don't want to sleep very long," she said to David, the only other awake.

He looked over to her. "I'll wake you in a little."

"You aren't tired?" Abbi said. "A lot on your mind, I bet." There was assumption in her sentence, a clear recollection of what David had announced to the clerk at the gas station. But her comments were gentle, avoiding accusation. She felt genuine sympathy, whatever reason David had for arriving at the outlandish conclusion. She had initially figured David's plea to the clerk was a Hail Mary effort of deception. But as she sat on the drive, recalling what he spoke, and how David proclaimed it so quick, urgent, and concise, she began to consider otherwise. "Is it true?" Her drowsiness melted away any filter. "Do you really think you weren't supposed to be contrated?"

"Did you tell the others?" He could not understand why he felt paranoid. Perhaps it was weariness elevating his sensitivity. *Would the others accept or trust me if they knew?*

"No," she yawned. "I've been with you the whole time."

"You're right . . . and you're tired." It was not that David was trying to conceal his thoughts forever. He simply did not have the energy to talk about it right now. Still, sleep was not his main desire, even if the need for it pressed upon him. Instead, he anticipated the first moment of silence to himself. "Later. You need to rest."

Abbi nodded and drifted off soon after. Being honest with herself, she was not ready either, her heart still heavy over her father's decision.

Everyone else joined in slumber, except the boy on patrol outside. David felt his shoulders lower from their tight winding. He could finally process, free of distraction. There was no highway sign to look out for, no department officer to evade, nor were there any other questions to answer from those now asleep. *Why am I here?* The question returned yet again. *I wonder if my carriers are looking for me?*

He glanced at Abigail, asleep in her recliner, yet her body was not entirely still, a few flinches and adjustments every couple of minutes to take David's attention. *She's not at peace yet. Safer here than the facility at least. If I never saw her. . .*

As David wandered deeper into thought, his presumptions shifted. *I'm here, but how far would I have made it without them?* It was Rylie who provided the cabin. It was Abbi who'd realized that life was still within grasp, and as abrasive as the boy with black hair had been, David could not deny his saving efforts, even though the unnamed might have done so reluctantly.

I wonder what their ESE scores are?

David was sure his was the lowest, aside from Bobby's and the nameless boy's, though he admitted to not studying for the exam. *If I ever did leave them, how could I justify it? Most of them would make it further in life than me.* He now wished Abbi had not fallen asleep, suddenly awakened and eager to process his false contration with somebody, and by merit of her silence, she seemed trustworthy.

Abbi's body rustled once more, unlike Rylie who seemed to have continually slept at peace since she first drifted. David looked at the two, unsure of how long either will keep asleep, though it seemed the more restless of them would likely wake up first, just as it was Abbi's open eyes he first met in the facility.

Recalling last summer, David could not yet tell whether his attraction to Abbi was greater than his to Olivia. The realization caused him to feel a bit uneasy, but it soon receded after he admitted that no other girl had come close to rivaling Olivia since the relationship ended. They looked nothing alike, and David had not known many girls of Abbi's ethnicity, but this seemed to draw him in more. Usually, he may place guilt upon himself for admitting that Olivia's appeal was challenged by someone else, especially after the way they'd parted, but he was beginning to feel a sort of permission.

Though Abigail could turn her body and lift her legs in the recliner, this restlessness was almost a similar imprisonment as the binding straps. With both Abbi and Olivia, in their different circumstances, never had he seen such a combination of desperation and hope in one expression. David felt a twinge of regret, wishing he'd had his current mindset last summer.

He recognized that he still could not say he truly knew Abbi. Far from it. Yet David was certain he knew the face; Olivia wore it first. He could not thoroughly understand it now, but keeping with Abbi, as well as the others, steadily lifted the weight from his shoulders that he never quite saw build, though surely felt. A six-month stored breath escaped his lungs like air from an ocean cave.

*

The chili came to a rumbling simmer, but the subtle burnt scent never went beyond the kitchen. Rylie turned off the stove gas burner and pulled a stack of paper bowls from the cabinet. She suggested they ration their food since they would have to make it last for another four days until March arrived. Though the food seemed plentiful now, between six people and three meals a day, it would run out quickly.

Everyone had awoken from their naps and gathered in the living room. The black-haired was outside finishing his watch, a bit warmer after Rylie ran a coat out to him earlier. He had not immediately thrown on the coat or thanked Rylie, but she'd looked out twenty minutes later to find him wearing the extra layer. Rylie grabbed the last hot bowl and walked outside with it, the steam rising in the chill air like candles just blown out. Some yards in front of her was the silhouette of the boy, with the rifle leaning against his shoulder. He perched himself on a rock that overlooked the cliff's edge. Three more feet forward and he would be freefalling. The sun had just set, but the remaining light glowed a burnt orange and purple through the gray.

"It looks a lot better from up here," Rylie said.

He jumped, unaware of her presence. "Don't do that!"

"I'm sorry," she apologized, trying to cover her giggle. "Just looked like you were enjoying the view. I didn't want to disturb anything. Did I scare you?"

"Well, considering people have been out all day trying to kill us, I'm a bit guarded."

"I have dinner here for you." Taken aback, he cradled the bowl she extended to him. "You don't have to be afraid of us," she said as she turned to walk away.

"Huh?"

Rylie stopped. "You don't have to be afraid of us. We're all in this."

The boy was quick to defend. "You think I'm afraid of all you?"

111

"We don't even know your name." She started to walk back to the cabin. "Thanks for keeping us alive."

He loosened his grip and laid the gun on the rock. Eating the food, he continued to look over the landscape. Even with fading skylight, he could make out the highway below. He gazed upon the opposite set of mountains south, wondering what was on the other side and beyond. In that moment all seemed pure, even the idea of the South. For a few minutes, the boy with black hair felt peace. The warmth of the food, the view from the cliffside, and his short conversation with Rylie allowed him to take his first deep breath in a while.

As much as he'd resisted her overtures, his previously choked yearning for this new relationship was beginning to find a foothold. Even with his determined will, the nameless boy could not in his limited strength keep himself locked away from Rylie. Her persistence unsettled him at first, forced to confront what he'd lost. He couldn't help but compare. The two were extraordinarily similar in his mind: the way they spoke and the command in their meekness. It was a strength he admired and envied. Not even a full day passed since he met the redheaded girl, and never had anyone else provoked such a longing for just one more moment with his brother.

The others inside spooned their dinner slowly, trying to savor every bite. The pitiful meal of pretzels from earlier did not compare. No one spoke, only mouths blowing air in an attempt to cool each steaming bite. They were coming to the end of what remained in their bowls, and nobody was entirely full. They were, however, satisfied to know there was something substantial in their stomachs. Physically, any dizziness from earlier had dissipated.

"Thanks, Rylie," Bobby said, a bit of sauce smeared across his chin.

"Canned food has never tasted so good." Mia closed her eyes and allowed herself to feel a fragmented form of bliss.

Rylie said, "It's not necessarily a home-cooked meal, but it gets the job done."

"I'm pretty sure we're all just happy to eat something,"

said Abbi. "It seemed like we were driving on that highway forever. I was beginning to wonder if we were gonna have an actual meal at all today."

"My mom makes the best homemade chili," Bobby said nostalgically. No one had a response. They'd felt removed from their situation in those few minutes as the bowls heated their hands and laps, every bite a distraction, until Bobby's comment brought forth reality once more.

David looked at his half-empty bowl. He had been scooping and swallowing slowly to trick himself into thinking he had more to eat. But hearing Bobby, he extended his bowl. "I'm finished with mine if you want the rest."

"Really?" His innocent face lit up as he quickly reached for it. "Thank you!" Though his renewed joy provided levity to the atmosphere, none could escape the fact that they were hiding out from the CD.

Mia spoke again of the matter. "If we do make it to our Eighteenth, what will we do after? I don't have a home to go back to. Will we even be able to live normally? Get jobs, live somewhere, have medical insurance?"

"I think right now, it's important just to survive," David said, overwhelmed by her all-too-valid concerns.

Mia rose, irritated. "What's surviving if there's nothing to go to after? Okay, I get it. We need to survive. But we need something other than 'survive,' or else it doesn't matter."

She had a slightly waddling stride down the hall to one of the guest rooms. Her steps echoed to the living room, her frustration solidified by the slamming door. The others were taken aback. It was hard to understand her trigger and which words had pulled it. They couldn't hold her outcries against her, however. They did not know the reasoning for her contration or what her specific dynamic with her carriers was. All they could do, all David could do, was give Mia patience. Having realized her question was legitimate, David felt guilty for not thinking through her grievances. But he knew he didn't have a decent answer to give closure to her, the others, or himself.

My contration was not an accident. The assassin thought was

113

followed by panic. David switched it from a declarative statement to a question, his only defense against the attack. *If so, how?* Reframing the thought gave his soul no peace, distress filling his body like a jar under a collapsing sand castle. He desperately wanted to process aloud, suddenly wishing he could talk with Abbi alone. *Can I really trust her?* The thought squeezed through before he again shifted. *What about them?* He glanced at Rylie and Bobby.

The boy with black hair suddenly entered through the front door. "Who's taking the next shift?" His entrance disrupted the quiet and served as a distracting lifeline for David. "Mia, right?"

Abbi said, "Yeah, but she just went to one of the rooms. I can take it for her."

A door from down the hallway swung open, spearing into the wall. Rylie seemed to pay no mind to the dent the doorknob had likely engraved into the cabin. Mia paced out with fire beneath her feet, more aggravated than the minute before. She wiped her faint red eyes. "No, this one's mine." She swiped a coat from the floor, and then snatched the rifle from the black-haired before she hurried out.

"What's up with her?" He took a seat on one of the recliners.

"She's mad. Mad and scared," David said, looking out the window as Mia strode to the cliffside.

"Why wouldn't she be?" said Abbi. "It's crazy. How we're even here."

"You were chosen to be contrated," the boy with black hair replied bluntly. "Just like the rest of us."

"I knew you would say something like that." She stared down at the carpet as if it was the one that had spoken the offense.

David saw the defeat unfold over Abbi. The thought of her or any of these people dying struck a chill up his spine. Though the unnamed boy was back on his nerves, David did not want to see him contrated either. He no longer saw them as mutual survivors, but rather something close to friends.

Soon enough, Bobby had left for the room Mia had just emerged from. When Rylie checked some minutes later, the light to the room was off, but she could hear a quiet snore from the rolled over body. "Doubt we'll be seeing him again for a while," she said, returning to her seat on the couch.

The four in the living room began to discuss what they would eat for breakfast tomorrow morning. Rylie listened instead, seeing the others struggle to keep the subject going as if they knew where the conversation might lead next if they didn't. It was all a façade to avoid speaking their most dominant thoughts. With Mia's recent reaction, she knew the same kind of doubt would overcome the rest of them, even the nameless boy. The surface-level discussion could only numb them for so long. Rylie had been trying to figure out what could combat the rising fear, what could still its tongue before it had the opportunity to speak.

Then the memory came as if it heard her unspoken dilemma. As any usual toddler, Rylie was greatly afraid of the dark, and with most this age, it always took an advocate to help. Her father long complied with his daughter's wishes whenever she called him to her bedside. But one night, after her father attended to yet another cry, he did not begin with a traditional bedtime story.

"What scares you about the dark," he asked tenderly. At first, young Rylie was confused, forced to confront the intricacies of the dark and the distress it provoked. Nevertheless, she reluctantly spilled all of her grievances. *"I can't see anything. And, and someone can be under my bed. Ghosts and monsters too . . . Umm, they only come out at night. And, and . . ."* Strangely, her heart steadied as she went down the list, while her father had kept silent during her long discourse. *"Why would a monster come at night? They wouldn't be able to see all that well either. Monsters ought to be smarter. And ghosts—why would they choose to come out in the dark if that's when I can't see as good?"* Musing, she grabbed her blanket and turned her back from the bedside where her father sat. He gave her a proud kiss on the head, though later saddened that it was the last night she called for him in the night.

A silence kept for another five minutes, each trapped inside their heads after coming to a dead end on the breakfast discussion. Rylie caught David's eyes periodically finding Abbi before they retreated to something else; Rylie figured he had some level of concern or attraction, or both, for her. Keeping his focus to one thing, the boy with black hair tirelessly and aggressively pinched a loose piece of leather from the recliner as the small part of fabric took all the punishment of whatever anger he harbored.

Rylie cleared her throat. "My dad died when I was in my Twelfth year." Each head rose as she continued. "It hit my mom and me hard. I don't have siblings, so the house got lonely too. I was young and didn't entirely understand the importance of school quite yet. I started doing pretty terrible with the Prep ESEs. I didn't care. I missed my dad. That's all I cared about." She had to close her eyes for a moment to steady herself. "He was the only one who had a job. My mom tried finding something, but she wasn't working most the year, bouncing from one job to unemployment, to the next job, and out of work again. We were barely gettin' by. But still . . . I didn't think she could do it. Looks like I was wrong, I guess. Here I am."

The others watched Rylie raise her hand to wipe away a single tear, in shared disbelief as she looked to each of them with a slow nod. Even the boy with black hair gave a silent gulp, quickly leaning his chin down to cover. Rylie's lips curled beneath the freckled cheeks. The smile was not one of denial or inauthenticity, but one of genuineness, an invitation to her listeners. They understood the common language, the kind that speaks of a mutual pain, yet paradoxically becoming the means of comfort. Once again, the darkness around Rylie was not as dreadful as once thought.

Abbi took a sip from her water first. "My mom was never around," she said. "She left not too long after I was born. I don't know why. My dad never brought her up until I asked why I don't look like him. I'm half black from my mom's side, but my dad got the Guatemalan light skin. So, it was just the two of us. I was never 'Daddy's little girl' or anything, but he treated me good, even after he got laid off. I was in my Fifteenth year. He couldn't get much work after, so I had to get a job to help out. At that point, my grades started to sink a bit. I was at the top ten percent of my class too. Passed my first secondary school prep ESE with a 10, but eventually, I had to take more hours. He was out every day looking for a job, so I understood when he asked me for help.

"That changed when I reached my Seventeenth year. He had given up looking and started to drink a lot instead. The search burnt him out. I couldn't stop working though. I had the only money for us on top of his unemployment. My hours were long. Too long. Come the final ESE, I failed. First time ever. During the Closing last night, I thought I would be all right. I mean . . . I was the only one working to help him out." Her head was shaking, entrenched in disbelief. "But here I am."

Rylie, who was sitting on the couch next to Abbi, rested a hand on her back, offering a gentle rub to console. The black-haired looked at the girls, in wonder how the two could be huddling so close. Rylie looked up and met eyes with him. He turned away quickly, keeping his sight to the living room window.

There was a minute's silence. David figured the others were expecting to hear his story, given the boy with black hair had not yet even shared his name. Abbi's eyes found David's repeatedly, waiting. If she had searched for them before this conversation began, she would have succeeded. Now, he knew better, knowing her silent request was a grip shaking his body to spill. He had sat up and leaned forward, elbows resting atop his knees. The room was so quiet the others could hear the sliding of David's clammy hands. Even the nameless boy noted his strange behavior.

Abbi was cautious not to expose David if it would bring no benefit. But still, he needed a release for his own sake. For this reason, Abbi walked the middle of the road, not speaking directly of what she knew of David's confession at the gas station. "What's going on, David?" It was a gentle push.

He did not expect to be called out. "Me?" David said almost offended, scratching one of his arms.

"What'd you mean at the gas station?" She went for it, forgetting any previous delicacy.

David held his composure but inside was rioting. *How could she? How does she want me to answer this? I don't even know for myself!* He understood the spirit of vulnerability was ushering a sort of unison in the room, but the answer to her question was far

117

beyond him. Neither was he certain how the others might respond if they learn he's a false contration. *What if they don't trust me after?* David's mind was about to go up in smoke. His face became hot, his sweat no longer traveling to his hands but through his armpits and soaking the white T-shirt he'd slept in the night before. *I'll just say it. I'll give it to them. I'll be honest as to what I know.* "I failed my ESE," he said. "I have dyslexia, and I failed."

"I'm so sorry," said Rylie, while Abbi thought more critically on what he revealed. "Getting contrated for something that's truly out of your control."

David was undecided whether to confirm her comment. "I was never going to do well on the exam. It's haunted me for years."

"What's your relationship like with your carriers?" Abbi asked directly, picking up on his subtle dodge. "Was it something similar to ours?"

David felt the spotlight just then turn to the burning sun itself. Abbi would not quit with what he felt was now an interrogation. "Umm, my relationship with my carriers. Yeah, to put it plainly—it's not good."

Abbi pressed. "How?"

Give me a break. "My dad and I never really clicked. He loves my older sister, and that's as much affection as he'll give anybody." His voice trembled but continued as the others gave him their attention, even the black-haired. "My mom and I though . . . When I was little, we were close. I think she loved me too. For whatever reason, though, when I got older, she kind of backed off a bit. Not a bit. A lot." David had not noticed his shaking speech had eased to thoughtful reflection. He leaned back in the chair. "It's really strange. To be so close to someone, then seemingly ripped away." He finished with a dry swallow.

The nameless boy broke the empty air. "I know why."

"Huh?" The statement was like a shove to David's back.

"You seem confused still. Your own words surprise you a bit. It's like your shocked that you're here."

David frowned. "How . . . What are you trying to say?"

There was no jest to the way the unnamed boy spoke.

"This might be hard to hear. Your carriers; they thought to contrate you whenever it was that your mom cut out. Actually, no. That doesn't all line up." David's offended glare did not distract his deduction. "Since it's your Seventeenth year, they, or most likely your mom wanted to leave you with some chance to do well on the ESE. Like a last resort."

David said fuming, "You think you can say whatever you want just because you never gave your name? Just because your dad tossed you to the curb, doesn't mean it's the same for everyone. It was impossible. I couldn't have been contrated!"

"Easy man." It was the most sincerity from the black-haired thus far. "What are you trying to say?" Rylie shared in his confusion. Abbi did not have the whole story yet, but David's outburst, though still a shock, was not completely out of left field. The boy with black hair continued. "Why was your contration impossible?"

David threw his hands on his head in regret, wondering if it would have been best to have given the truth from the start. That, or have been more strategic with his words to avoid giving anything away. On top of those layers, he felt guilty for responding to the black-haired with such pretention. He stood up with hands on his hips. "I'm sorry." He gathered how to explain. "I need to be honest with you all."

"What do you mean?" said Rylie. "You have been. We won't hold it against you for getting emotional."

Abbi had anticipated this moment. She did not know exactly how it would flesh out, but once David started speaking, it was only a matter of time until his sudden confession at the gas station received full explanation. She remained quiet, knowing either David would provide immediate disclosure, or it would trickle out following the questions from Rylie and the black-haired.

"No, I mean—I don't think I'm supposed to be here. Or if I am supposed to be here, I don't know how." David looked to the black-haired. "I said it's impossible for my carriers to have contrated me because I don't think I can be here."

"You don't think you could have been contrated?" Rylie

tilted her head.

"Yes, I'm from northwest Bellark. I'm from a wealthy family, one that lives in a typical rich neighborhood." An unexpected relief followed the declaration. "Do you understand what I'm saying? I failed the ESE, but I shouldn't qualify for a contration because of my carriers' income."

Abbi's mouth dropped, dumbfounded. "But how? How are you here if your family's rich?" Her tongue had its own mind. She had honestly assumed David was under an unfortunate case of denial, and she'd probed him to talk so he could receive counsel and perspective as to why he was contrated. It now made perfect sense why he was so uncertain, why he was not able to speak until forced. Her stomach dropped, regretful for thrusting him into the conversation.

"I think there's something else at play for why I'm here, whether a fluke or accident. I'm sorry." David stopped himself. "Each one of you has already been through a lot."

Rylie said swiftly, "We're fine, David. Stop overthinking and tell us. Let's see if we can help you like you've helped us."

The other two found themselves agreeing with Rylie. Back at the facility, even the boy with black hair understood his nature immediately and at the time found David's impulsive altruism aggravating. Now, there was a shared desire to support David in some way.

"So, you think it's an accident because you're rich?" Rylie helped to verbalize. "Excuse me. Because your carriers are rich?"

"Yeah, I think so. Maybe it was a technological glitch with the CD's system. Like a malfunction of which Potential to gas and pick up?" David turned to the black-haired, remembering his comments in the heat of the moment. "Sorry for what I said. It was wrong to slam you like that."

He lifted his head. "You want my advice?" Though he did not address David's apology, the response seemed like a sort of acceptance.

"Yeah," said David.

"Okay." He became almost clinical. "Again, I don't think

this was an accident. I stand by what I said." He said grimly, "Your mom backed away some years ago, right? I think that's when it first came to your carriers." He stroked his chin at the prickling hairs from late puberty. "You said your dad loves your older sister. She in college?"

"Yeah."

"Hmm. I don't know how. I don't when. I don't know the specifics, but I don't think your carriers have money anymore, or not as rich as you thought."

"What? How?" David asked, incredulous.

"Think about it. Your sister's in college. Your relationship with them—messed up for years. They had to make a choice."

Abbi raised the question before David. "A choice?"

"A choice between him and his sister. My guess is money became tight, knocking your carriers below the income line," said the unnamed. "They could only choose one."

Though feeling swept from his internal footing, David could not yet find a place to disagree; the statement was not as ridiculous as it first seemed. The pieces matched up, however awkwardly. Yet he knew there was more to this assumption than just intuition. "How did you think that up?"

"I told you a bit about my life already," the black-haired said, turning from David to Rylie as she leaned forward. "I'm used to fighting. Whether that's taking a beating from my old man or keeping on the run like we are now. It's all the same." Coming back to David, both of them finally blinked together. "My dad was a pretty good stockbroker for some firm. His money scored him a beautiful wife. He isn't too great-looking of a guy. Was she a terrible mom? Generally speaking, no. She was okay at best. Did our laundry and made our lunches for a good while. If there was anything terrible she did, it was leaving me and my bro to my dad. I was in my Thirteenth."

"You have a brother? Older or younger?" Abbi asked.

"Umm, younger, I guess. Well, I had a brother," he said. "Cancer got him. He was diagnosed a year after my mom left."

There was a long pause. "I'm sorry," Rylie said heavily.

"I'm sorry that happened to him."

"Don't be. He suffered through treatments for a while. Most likely escaped this too," he said, pointing a circling finger around the room. "Neither of us liked school, and his medical bills ran through the roof.

"After my brother got sick, my mom would come from wherever she lived to visit him. I never asked, but I think my dad used his money on my brother, yeah to save his life, but . . . One of her complaints was that he was too invested in his work and didn't care about her. This was around the same time he had a couple down years with brokering. Crazy enough, she never said anything about how he mistreated me and my brother." He chuckled wryly. "I bet he thought if he could save his youngest son it would help him win back the girl. I would give him some benefit of the doubt if he never beat on him before the cancer. Little did he know, using the rest of his savings and missing work would not win her back.

"My dad always had a special relationship to the bottle, but after my brother died, after he used all his money for treatments and procedures, after seeing my mom for the last time at the funeral . . . the bastard took it upon himself to marry it. A lot of drunken nights for him, and a lot of bruises for me. After reaching my Seventeenth, I finally realized I was bigger than him. During another scuffle, I took one of his bottles and broke it over his head. He bled all over the kitchen floor. I've gotta hand it to him for not going to the hospital. I can't believe I even offered to drive him. After that, he never laid a hand on me again. He continued to drink and waste the little money he had from selling our old house."

They all turned in alarm after hearing a door shut outside. The relief came just as quick, thankfully. It was Mia, taking refuge in the SUV from the dropping temperature.

The unnamed boy kept his gaze out the window. "It's interesting to see how at one point, someone can seem to value life. My dad was spending thousands to give my brother a fighting chance. Then, here I am, a fully healthy Potential, and he uses the last of his money to coast. He's been unemployed for the past three years. I don't know at which moment he made his decision, but it was definitely before I really knew. Shouda been smarter and ran away sooner. Life is a nonstop series of investments, whether that's time, money, or love. If you throw a rock into water, follow the ripples. What someone will do, act, or choose is right there. The simple rule of deposit. One of the useful things the guy taught me, I guess."

He found David again. "I'm not saying it's for sure, but you need to think, even if hurts. If this was an accident, don't you think you'd have seen something on that TV this morning, explaining your contration was a mistake? Some people are just shitty. My dad and my mom were. It's a world with a lot of bad people. A few good ones, but most will do anything to convince themselves that their right to life is more important than yours."

David's teeth shifted over each other. Though the black-haired lacked nuance and was quite straight shooting, David understood there was never a malicious intent behind all that he shared. It was crippling for David to fathom his carriers did intentionally contrate him, but that would then remove the mystery. Unfortunately, what David might have gained in closure, he lost in peace.

David's confusion quieted, but something else inside spoke, its voice rising with each second until it became a scream. His body eventually came to shake and sway the recliner chair as his breath rushed out through flared nostrils. The kindling despair and anger blinded David from seeing the devastating toll the conversation had on the boy with black hair.

"David?" Abbi said carefully, trying to determine whether his revelation was for better or worse. He didn't respond.

Rylie, on the other hand, kept her attention on the boy with black hair, knowing David needed a moment, or maybe longer. The black-haired's disclosure provided a risky opportunity, but Ryle said boldly anyway, "You wish they had loved you."

The black-haired looked to Rylie suspicious, but her gentle gaze reassured him that the statement was no attack. "Yeah. I guess I do." He breathed deeply, feeling like she had just laid ten blows to his stomach. "How long you been wanting to say that?"

"Since you kept your name from us," said Rylie.

He nodded.

David found a vicarious kind of calm in the nameless boy's admission. All in the room, Mia and Bobby also, had personal woes with their carriers. While David had to wrap his head around a harsh possibility for his circumstance, he did not stand alone. If there was anybody who could empathize, it was each of these new companions. "I'm sorry all that happened to you. To you and your brother," David said, looking to the girls next. "Sounds like both of you had a rough lot too. Sorry for making this all about me."

"Stop saying sorry," the black-haired said sternly. "Yeah, our carriers screwed us, but we at least had some time to accept it. You're just taking it all in now. Stop trying to play hero all the time, and just take a second to be pissed." He said in a low chuckle, "Maybe we all could use some time to be a little pissed, especially now that Red got me to just say what I did."

Rylie smiled first, of course, though the nameless boy kept his head down and never intended to cause her rise. Neither Abbi nor David could keep from perking their cheeks either. "Hey Abbi," she said. "What part of Bellark you from?"

It was the first question of many, as they delved into their ordinary lives. Not speaking of anything related to the CD naturally put a cap on the loaded conversation. Now, the revealed secrets were instead what they did for fun and leisure, or what school they attended.

The conversation progressed organically. Rylie and David discovered that their secondary schools had a longtime rivalry in girls' water polo. The girls poked into David's life and finally got him to share his love for playing the guitar and fishing with his friend, Jensen. Abbi shared that her favorite classes involved medical study, cameras, or film. This continued as the boy with black hair kept to himself; the others well understood that it had taken all his strength to tell of his life earlier. Nonetheless, he listened to their conversation, unexpectedly

124

enjoying the exchange.

Abbi looked at the wall clock above the fireplace. 6:51 p.m. She pointed at it. The boy with black hair followed her finger, as did the others. "Five more hours," she said. "Almost Eighteen."

"Yep," he said, unsure.

Though it was unspoken even hours ago, the consensus went unbroken; the others did not want to force the unnamed boy to stay at the cabin. "If you stay with us, you'll be risking your life," said David first. "If the CD finds us, they'd probably still shoot you or whatever it is they plan. Even if you are alive, they'll assume you're a Potential."

"David's right," Rylie said. "You should leave at twelve. Take that old truck in the garage. I didn't think it would have any gas, but it still had a quarter tank of some old stuff in it when I slipped in and checked. Should still run decent enough."

Abbi was surprised. "When did you check?"

"I'm quiet," Rylie said, smirking. "That can get you to the city. There's some extra cash from the facility guy's wallet to help you fill up or get some food later. Other than that, I guess what's next is your call. Can't imagine you'll want to stay in Bellark for long."

"Wait a second." The black-haired shook his head, lost. "What are you saying? You're just gonna let me take the truck? What if you guys need it?"

"We have the SUV," said Rylie.

He looked at David, who also nodded. The boy with black hair began to shift in his seat as he looked at those surrounding him. At first, they had been strangers; some he even viewed as deadweight in the escape. And yet, he saw their certainty, a consent to prioritize his life's guarantee. All their faces together were an image of trust, both for him and in him. "David," he said. "My name is David Drake."

*

A strong wind commanded billows of clouds to march

125

from the west, small pockets appearing intermittently for the moonlight to shine through. The trees and bushes along the rim surrounding the hideaway cabin quietly danced.

David had been prepared to assume the watch himself, but Bobby woke up right before and joined eagerly. They pulled the SUV up to the cliffside, close under a large pine tree for some level of concealment. He and Bobby lay on the hood where it edged out from under the branch covering, offering an opening beneath the sky above. They were both dressed in the old coats and beanies Rylie set out; otherwise, they would not have lasted outside as long as they did. David mostly kept the watch over the highway while Bobby let himself get lost in the happenings above.

"You really like to look up there, don't you?" David said. "It's because you like space, right?" Bobby had stated a few times how greatly he desired to become an astronaut.

Bobby could not turn away from the temporarily exposed moon. "Yeah."

"Why do you want to go up there so bad?"

"It's beautiful."

"Can't disagree with that, I guess," said David. "It's pretty dangerous up there though. A lot of things have gone wrong with space exploration."

Bobby tore his eyes away from the night sky's enchantment to David. "If all the other astronauts didn't go up because they were scared, where would we be?"

David turned his gaze upward. "Guess you're right there too."

Silence followed the rest of their watch. Bobby took enough delight in counting the stars before the next group of clouds swallowed them. David thought about their exchange, unable to rid the new pity he felt for his new friend, remembering when Bobby had mentioned earlier that he only lived with his mother. *I wonder if she encouraged him about space? No . . . He's here.*

David thought about his own aspirations, if there were any. He did not dream like Bobby, though, never giving career much thought. At most, he imagined himself playing the guitar. Remembering, he reached into his right pocket. It was not panic as much as it was a regretful shrug, knowing the lyric sheet must have gone lost during all the commotion of the day. He'd much rather find a guitar to breathe it all to life.

"Your time is up!" Abbi caused the two boys to flinch. Rylie accompanied her, the two interlocking arms for warmth as they walked over. "We're gonna do what you two are doing and do our watch together. I don't want to spend two hours out here by myself, even with a gun. Rylie's taking hers after, so we're just gonna partner up for both."

"You two are clicking." David handed over the gun. "You know how to use this?"

"Aim and shoot," Abbi said.

"Well, yes," answered David. "But not all guns are that simple. Some you have to cock or do some other things. These dart rifles are pretty straightforward though. Like you said, aim and shoot. Just take it off safety if you mean business."

"Gotcha. Mia's asleep on the couch," Abbi said.

"We'll be sure not to wake her."

Rylie added, "I think she's a heavy sleeper. We made a bit of commotion while packing some bags."

"Packing bags?" asked Bobby.

"There were some duffle bags in the closet. Best to throw some clothes, food, and water just in case, right? A to-go order."

"Sure," said David, impressed. "Smart thinking. What about Drake? He asleep?" It still felt unusual to know his name at last. They tried persuading the black-haired that they didn't mind using the shared first name, but he stressed that he'd been going by Drake for a long time anyway. *"Why?"* they asked. Drake laughed and admitted his first name was much too generic. Whether it was a lie or not, that decided it.

"Not a chance," chuckled Abbi. "Drake's . . . Gosh, still can't believe you guys have the same name. Well, he's reading in one of the rooms. Found a book to keep him entertained. Oh, and he said he wanted to talk to you."

The two boys gave up their coats to the girls before heading inside. They found Mia sound asleep on the beaten-up couch. *Must have been too tired to walk to the guest room,* David thought.

For the first time, she appeared somewhat at peace. He hoped she was finally getting some rest. Of all of them, she probably needed it most now, especially after missing out on the therapeutic living room talk. She was sleeping on her back, chest and stomach under a bundle of blankets.

Bobby said good night and went to the room where he'd napped earlier. David strolled to the end of the hallway to the next bedroom. Beneath the closed door, he could see the light line the bottom. He knocked quietly. "It's me, David." At Drake's grunt of acknowledgment, he pushed the door open. Just as Abbi had said, Drake had a book in hand, sitting upright in the bed with his legs under the covers. Next to his twin bed was another just like it.

David sat on the empty bed. "What you reading?"

Drake lowered the thin book face-down on his lap. "Some little story. It's about a prison escape. Ironic, huh? There were some others in the closet, but this one grabbed me."

"You gonna read that whole thing tonight?"

"Nope. I've already read it before," said Drake. "It was a choice for required reading when I attended private school back in my Twelfth or Thirteenth year. Bet you couldn't have guessed I was in the private system, could ya? Advanced English Lit too. Got yanked from it midway through, though . . . My brother's hospital bills. And well, I started to fail. Anyway. It's a pretty old story, but not too bad a read."

"Why'd you choose it over the others?

"Hope you don't mind if I ruin more of the story for you," he said. "So, the main character guy makes it out of the prison, right?"

"Sure. That's good. Or is he a good guy?"

"Better than most. You can't help but pull for him. That's why it's like you're escaping when he does. The ending's a little vague though. Just read it again."

"What happened?"

"He escapes," Drake said. "But you don't really know where it goes after. You know his plans, where he wants to live, and how he plans to do it. But you're left not knowing if it all happens. I remember hating that, but now, after just reading, I got a new closure."

"And what's that?"

"Even though I don't know what's gonna happen to me, or any of us, I guess I feel a bit empowered."

"Empowered?"

"Yeah, I think so." Drake finally figured out how to say it. "To dream for or imagine a better future than the one I got right now."

David never guessed Drake to be much of a reader, much less enrolled in an advanced literature course at a private school. It was even more curious that David found himself feeling strangely enlightened.

Drake's demeanor changed, humble as he looked at David. "I know I've been kind of a dick." He gave a glance to the book. "You're the main reason why we're all here. I would've left them all at the facility too. Without you, well, they wouldn't be here, and maybe I wouldn't be either."

The directness made David question whether he'd heard right. Still, he found the right words. "They wouldn't be here if you didn't help either," said David, knowing it would be difficult to convince him. "You led us out. *You* freed me from that bed."

"I led no one. They just followed."

"What about me? Why'd you help me when you could have just knocked out that man and left?"

It was rare for Drake to let someone stump him. "I guess I thought it was the right thing to do."

"There you go," said David. "Maybe you're not quite as bad as you put yourself out to be." Drake did not smile as David had hoped, choosing instead to look down to the book on his lap. "So, is that what you wanted to tell me? Why you called me in here?"

"No. I said that spur-of-the-moment," said Drake, closing the book. "You chose to stick with us, even when you thought your contration was a mistake. Again, I'm not so sure it is, but you stayed, thinking that it was. You could have died thinking that."

"But I didn't."

"That still doesn't take away what you did." Drake threw the sheets off, sending the book to the carpet. "I'm staying with you guys. After I pass my Eighteenth, I'm not leaving."

David again doubted his ears. "You're staying with us?"

He nodded. "I'd like to stick around until we all reach our lives. I don't have anything to go back to. Plus, I figured we could all celebrate our Eighteenth together, right?"

"Yeah? Alright then."

Drake rose from the bed and reached for the book on the floor. "I'm gonna go read in the living room. You probably want to get some sleep." He took a couple of steps toward the door. "I saw you earlier. I can tell what I said about your carriers, your contraption . . . It cuts deep. I know. I don't hate my dad any less than I did when I woke up. It's still there. You're the balanced one though, so don't do anything reckless. Probably hypocritical for me to say, because if I saw my ole man right now . . . Eh, it wouldn't be good. But you. Try not to let it get to you. If they didn't want you, forget about them. You're a pretty good guy from what I can tell."

As he almost left the room, David called, "Hey, David."

Drake stopped and turned.

"Thanks for choosing to stay with us. You're a good guy too."

Drake nodded with a rising, hesitant grin. He shut the door before it showed in full.

David settled into the other twin bed, dropping his head to the pillow. Despite the taxing day, it was the earlier living room conversation that depleted him. The recently birthed resentment spiked at unpredictable times after, causing David to curse his carriers, wishing to have never been their son. It was only whenever Olivia returned to his mind when he found himself checked and challenged, forced to ease back from grabbing ahold of any entitlement to condemn, no matter how tempting.

February 26th

The Chief's eyes were bloodshot in the early a.m., veins like tiny red rivers webbing throughout a plain of white. He had not yet seen any sleep since he woke to investigate the facility breakout. Though his desk chair could recline, he kept it upright to collect his thoughts rather than drift off.

The office was well-furnished with a shined wooden desk and leather chair. The walls were a rich russet, but the low, warm light toned down the color. The door to his private restroom was a lighter copper. A thirty-inch monitor sat atop the desk, surrounded by the typical office items and a black remote. The Chief had opened the file of every escaped Potential on his screen. Behind him was a floor-to-ceiling window overlooking downtown Bellark. Only a few other windows from surrounding buildings helped illuminate the night, other working-class men and women compromising a full night's rest.

Salvador had returned to the Bellark CD headquarters around eleven o'clock, along with Delaney Abbot and Luis Adán. Because they had failed to find the escaped Potentials, they returned to reevaluate their strategy. Some patrol vehicles and a helicopter were still on the hunt outside the city. Luis was in his own office speaking with the police department. The situation had evolved, and by Delaney's persistence, Salvador finally conceded to request their aid.

Delaney was sitting across from Salvador. "I do not

131

understand," he said. The weariness lodged a rasp in his throat. "They have nowhere to stay or go. Unless they made it into Bellark before we set up the checkpoint outside the city."

"We set up the checkpoint immediately after their activity at the gas station, along with a perimeter in case they try to enter the walls from a different direction on foot. I don't think they would abandon their only means of transportation. The mountains give us a barrier, so they couldn't go far north. They'd likely have to leave the car for that too. Not many roads, but a good place to hide. I'd say they're either up there, or for whatever reason, headed south."

A knock came. Salvador lifted the remote on his desk and commanded the door to unlock with a click. Luis entered, a renewed confidence in his steps.

"What's the word?" Salvador asked.

"They're in," said Luis as he led into detailing the report he had with the police. The CD would receive their assistance once Salvador decided how the two forces should coordinate. Salvador and Delaney debated the appropriate means of partnership with the police and the number of bodies, vehicles, and additional posts needed. Luis jotted notes as they spoke. Salvador continued to weigh the strategy and alternatives in his head, rotating his chair to stare out the vast window. Neither Delaney nor Luis had brought up the matter since they'd left the facility, but now that the police were involved, a positive move forward, the young officer thought perhaps the Chief would be willing to hear the option.

"Sir," Luis said cautiously with respect. "Perhaps we can again contact Jensen Lloyd to investigate further."

Salvador stared over the city. "Jensen Lloyd?"

"Yes, the one who sabotaged the power at the contration facility."

"I know who he is," Salvador said, turning from the window to Luis. "We will not investigate further with him. He knows nothing."

Confused by Salvador's refusal, Luis' voice rose just a hair. "Sir, he might. What if he lied? Shouldn't we exhaust every lead?"

"If our department were doing the job correctly, if you were *exhausting* your job correctly, we would have found these Potes by now, and you would not be asking about Lloyd. Hear me now, Adán. This is the last time we speak of him. Clear?"

Luis tried to fight his sour tone. "Yes, Sir."

Salvador dismissed Luis and ordered him to communicate the new instructions to the police and to regroup their on-site personnel. However, it was mostly a means to remove Luis from his presence. His questions regarding Jensen Lloyd only provoked Salvador's agitation.

Delaney had seen the Chief wearied before, but never like this. It was as if his entire body became iron. To press forward was to press against himself. She was troubled about where now to search for the Potentials, especially after Salvador again disregarded Luis' appeal. If it were her decision, she would have agreed to investigate Lloyd, but she opted to trust in her Chief. She did, however, have a response in mind. Though there would perhaps be resistance, his current state compelled her.

She delicately and gracefully rose and made her way behind him. Deeply engrossed in the images on his monitor, he had not noticed her presence until her hands gently rested on his shoulders. One hand, fingers glossed in black nail polish, ran underneath his collar and down his chest. Salvador's body was ready, instinctively leaning back into the chair. He resisted, however. "Delaney, not now."

Her stomach took the request quite literally, whatever was inside ready to punch up and out. Salvador was taken aback by how his comment sent her stumbling away, but he gained a degree of understanding as she barged through the private bathroom door. She didn't bother to shut it. From the sound of her heaving, there was no time to consider privacy. Salvador opened the mini refrigerator below his desk, pulled out a water bottle, and went to her aid.

"I thought you got it all out this morning," he said, rubbing her back with a tenderness he could only show in private. There was another flinch from her kneeling body, but nothing

133

came from her now-empty stomach. "Drink this." He cracked open the bottle and placed it into her hand that reached up while her head remained over the bowl. "Whatever bug you got wants to throw up something. Don't drink it too fast."

She took a sip. "Thank you," she said weakly.

"Some steak, huh?"

She wiped her mouth with some toilet paper wrapped around her fingers. "I guess so."

Salvador kept scratching her back, but this did not relieve Delaney as usual. "I know I said I need you, but if you're getting sick. Like sick-sick. Not food poisoning. Then I think it might be best for you to take the rest of the night off. If you feel better after some sleep, then we can speak of you rejoining."

"I think that's the last of it, Sal." It was the name she only used when they were off-duty. "I'll be okay."

"I know you will, but I don't imagine as quickly as you think. Both times it came from nowhere. At inconvenient times, especially just now." He managed a chuckle. "It's like you're pregnant again."

The statement seemed much more an invasion than the jest Salvador intended. Delaney searched for a response, any excuse to correlate her sickness again with a steak she never ate. She could have even shared in his laugh, and he would never have suspected anything. But it was her silence that had him lift his hand from her back. If she threw up again, it might have been from the knots twisting throughout her stomach.

"Delaney?" He first gathered reason before he spoke next. "Are you?"

She knew relief would come, but it would be a vapor next to the dread. Delaney would not have to continue the concealing or prolong a fabrication, but as soon she confessed, the truth would exist for him just as much as it did for her. She'd planned to share it with him after the Closing, but even now, that excitement seemed to have existed for a different person than the one kneeling before the toilet. Every time there was a joy gained, but inevitably, sometimes weeks, sometimes months, that joy became coal when she remembered her first pregnancy and her

134

first contration. So many years ago, yet the old fears, without fail, became the new.

"I am," she said quietly, staring into the bowl.

A few moments after, he put his hand on her back. "Well, that's great news." He was able to smile, but it could not grow beyond a small curl. In seconds it faded into a frown. "Delaney, how long? How long have you been pregnant?"

She realized there was no circling around it. "I was going to share after the Closing, but then this all happened." Delaney stood up, hoping that walking away from the toilet would ease her stomach and bring back her composure. Yet even before she hugged Salvador, her guilt did not allow her to look into his eyes. It was too difficult to hold on to him any longer, not while she held on to the words inside. "I took the test a month and a half ago," she said, releasing Salvador, who'd never fully wrapped his arms around her. "I just wasn't sure. I was scared and didn't know if I was ready to share." Delaney returned to the desk, reaching to pick up her phone and ID.

Salvador turned the restroom light off as he stepped out. He knew she'd just shared much, and typically he would attempt to slow his curiosities to decide how best to respond for her sake. However, he could not help but default to feeling wronged. "Ready? Delaney, these are things you need to tell me." His eyes were unblinking, fastened on her as she looked away. "Is that why you told me you wanted to wait a little while until we tried for one? You were going to keep this a secret?"

Delaney knew he deserved her attention. Turning to him, she nodded slowly. Her heart was aching for the man she loved, but at the same time, she felt justified for withholding.

Salvador went to the wall window, struggling for a response as he overlooked the city. He walked back to her. "We made the other decisions together. This one must be ours too. Together. Isn't this what you want?" He placed his hand on her stomach, convinced he felt slight growth. "Never keep anything like this from me again." The strict order sent caution through Delaney. "This is our child."

That word rarely came from his lips. It should never,

Delaney always thought on the occasions that he slipped. Taking a step back, she pushed his hand off her stomach. "No, Sal. Stop that." He did not see her tears build, a couple ready to peel off. "Sal, this is why, why I kept it from you as long as I did. What if I'm not ready?"

"But you are now." He was on guard.

"What if I wasn't? Like our times before."

"Then we would talk about it like our times before."

"Talk about it. Sure." She crossed her arms. "Talking about it means you trying to convince me until I put my foot down. I almost had to beg you to contrate the last one."

Salvador became unhinged. "Well, then how many until you're ready? Why don't we contrate this one too! For god's sake, Delaney. How many until you're ready? You have your career. You have me! You said you wanted to have one. Your words. After this year, I would retire from the CD and help raise it, and you could continue as Vice."

"I kept it, didn't I?" Running from her eyes were unbroken streams. "I'm telling you now! Like I said, I was going to tell you after the Closing. I thought about contrating it. I did. I thought maybe we could still wait. But I didn't, and now I'm telling you."

"Wait for what?"

Delaney's eyes widened at the interruption. "I don't know! It's a lot, Sal. You know it is. We had our first contrations before we were even together. I was six months pregnant when I got the news then. You think that's easy just to forget?" She rested her hands on her hips and tried to relax.

"Delaney, we've said we could cross that bridge if that were the case again," said Salvador. "That was an entirely different time. Not every Potential is going to threaten your health."

"It's more than just being pregnant, Sal." She took a sleeve to her eyes. "What if I just said I didn't want to have one, and that was that?"

Salvador leaned on his desk to steady himself, now recognizing his rising passion and frustration. "Okay, I think it

136

would be best to talk about this later."

"What if I changed my mind on this one?" she said direct, a subtle provocation as one weakly, but intentionally pokes a bear. "What if I just didn't want it?"

Salvador's brow furrowed as he carefully rehearsed what she'd just spoke. "What are you trying to say?" He walked toward her slowly, keeping his steps soft as if to not frighten a gazelle. "Please, Delaney. Do not say that. I love you, and I'm sorry for the hasty things I just said." He rested a hand on her upper back. "We're both exhausted and not thinking straight. This, you being pregnant, is a good thing. We'll catch these Potes, I'll finish up with the CD, and we can finally get our family started." He hoped his plea would soften her again. "You are what I care about most in this world."

She wiped her eyes again. Salvador reached out and wrapped her in his arms. Delaney leaned her left cheek on his chest. Even in heels, she stood a head shorter. Resting her face against his heart always brought her comfort, joy, or in this instance, closure.

The moment of reconciliation was interrupted by a knock on the office door. Salvador released Delaney and walked for the remote on his desk. She checked herself in the mirror to make sure she looked presentable, though the red surrounding her eyes would take time to fade. Fortunately, the low lighting would help disguise her.

Luis entered with two other CD officers. "Sir, we've been trying to reach your cell phone."

Salvador scanned the desk to find his phone where he'd set it down before running to the restroom. "I'm sorry. Abbot and I were discussing strategy, and I didn't notice it going off."

Luis nodded, yet his skepticism remained as to why Salvador would not have heard the phone vibration right next to him. He had not yet voiced his knowledge to the Chief. For one, he was in no position to bring up the subject, and two, he assumed his Chief and Vice must have wanted to keep their relationship secret if they still had not publicly shared the matter. Luis was mostly impartial of the love affair, so long as it did not hinder the business of the department. He may, however, admit to supporting their relationship on certain days, believing on account of their notoriety, that it might benefit the Bellark CD to some intangible degree. However, at this moment, Luis began to doubt that belief, understanding that Salvador most likely neglected his phone to engage with Abbot. Like everything else, he would keep the matter noted.

"We've received a call from a resident of Bellark county," he said, "living on the outskirts. She claimed to have seen a black SUV trail up the hillsides north of the 38 yesterday afternoon."

"Why are we just getting this call at 1 a.m.?" Salvador asked.

"The lady, she's elderly. She goes to bed early. Woke up and turned on her television when she couldn't go back to sleep. It was the first time she saw the coverage of the Potes, or 'The March Runaways.' It's what they're calling them now. The media's caught on."

"Of course they have. Only a matter of time before people figured all these Potentials are alive in March." Salvador did not hesitate to question the report. "All right, let's go." He grabbed his jacket. "I want as many vehicles and men as we can get. Notify the police to divert most of their force to join us. Do we know what road the lady spoke of?"

*

The sluggish walk to the front door would have remained the same even if David had not splashed the faucet water on to his face. The sleep was deep, but even more, scarce. Abbi, for the briefest of a moment, doubted if he would awaken after calling his name. It was not until she noticed David's still and breathless body when she jumped to his side. She felt relieved at first, but then a bit embarrassed for forcibly shaking him from his sleep.

The outside temperature had taken a dip but was not unbearable. Abbi followed David outside, but while she had her coat on, David walked out clad in his pajamas. "It's chilly," he said, crossing his arms across his chest.

Abbi said, "Rylie's out here. You can take her coat. Though I bet this wakes you up."

"Sure does," he chuckled. "But it doesn't compare to that death grip of yours."

The embarrassment returned, but Abbi squeezed a smile. "I called out your name like ten times, and it looked like you weren't even breathing. You would have freaked out too."

There was a modest glow from the crescent moon, the clouds clearing for what looked like the largest pocket of the night. The stars scattered like shining sand. David imagined Bobby would have loved the sight. In Bellark, the night sky was guarded by the smog and light pollution, especially downtown. Even on the clearest night in Bellark, only a fraction of the stars shone through.

David spoke to Rylie, who was lying on the SUV's hood. "You're free to sleep now."

"You rested?" she said. "Don't go falling asleep on us when you're out here."

"I'm fine. I'll just need your coat," he said, trying to warm himself with his hands. "Go and get some rest. Both of you."

"I'm not tired yet," Abbi said. "I'll stay out with David for a little."

"You will?" he said, surprised.

"Sure." Abbi shrugged. "In case you fall asleep. You're still waking up. I'll pinch you this time if you begin to fade."

Rylie handed David the rifle and coat, giving him a hidden smirk so that Abbi could not see. She went back to the cabin. After a short time, the two opted to sit inside the SUV. Their breath was smoke in the crisp air. David started the SUV to run the heater for a while, but Abbi urged him to preserve the gas after fifteen minutes. They'd used half a tank since the gas station.

"I don't think you could fall asleep if you tried," Abbi said to David. Both leaned back on the chilled leather seats. "Too cold for that."

"You're probably right." He laughed nervously, not knowing what else to say. Speaking with her casually alone seemed to hold more pressure. It was the first time it was just the two of them. No running. No shooting. Nobody else; not even a body to sleep beside them. And no more unspoken barriers after Abbi probed David to share his concerns earlier. Though first overwhelmed by her persistence, he was now relieved to have shared his contration dilemma.

Now, whatever his next words, David burdened himself that they must be worth the girl's intrigue and time. They looked out the windshield over the cliff to the scantly lit valley. She yawned. He did not want to lose the opportunity, saying the first thing to come to mind, "So, you're a brain?"

"Huh?" She turned to David.

"You're smart," he said. "You know, school smart. You said you always did well until you had to get that job."

"Oh. Yeah, I guess so." Abbi was confused why he brought up a seemingly unrelated topic, yet somewhat flattered it concerned her.

"Smart and pretty." He did not think before he spoke, those last words like a hiccup. To talk so forward with a girl was not typical for David. In fact, it was Olivia who'd introduced herself to him before their relationship. He swallowed, instantly regretting the comment. In his periphery, Abbi turned her body his way, elbow resting on the middle divider. After gathering the courage, he met her eyes.

"Is this how you talk to girls?"

His chest tightened, casting his vision out the window to the valley. "I don't know." His heart oscillated between shame and assurance. In one moment, he felt stripped naked; in the next, elevated, as if he were stepping onto a podium to receive an award. Between the two extremes, he couldn't tell whether he was failing or succeeding in his efforts.

"You don't know?"

He couldn't see her grinning. "I don't have the emotional capacity to figure these kinds of things out. I guess."

Abbi said chuckling, "'Emotional capacity'?"

David whipped to her as if her laugh reeled him back. She leaned closer to David, knowing it might make him uncomfortable but also sure it was the right response.

David shook his head. "You're just repeating what I say."

"'Repeating what you say'?"

He laughed, finally. "Okay, I give up. You try giving a girl a compliment, and it somehow gets turned around on you."

"I still can't believe you used the words 'emotional capacity,'" Abbi said, maintaining her jovial tone. "Who says that? Your vocabulary makes you sound like the brain."

"I mean, I like to read here and there. You come across smart words when you read. I know how to use them, just not always spell them."

"That's right," she said, remembering why he had failed his ESE.

"Yep. That's my lot. Everyone's got one though, right?"

David turned again to the dashboard, the response unrelated to their dynamic; his thoughts were once again with his carriers and his contration. Abbi joined in peering down at the valley, aware that a chord was struck. The already shy moon had been overcome again by the next wave of gray.

David glanced left, eastward. "I wonder how far down that facility is. We drove a long way."

"I don't know. I'm glad we got out, though," she said. "You didn't have to."

"Have to?"

"You could have kept going at the facility. If it wasn't my life or the other girls, some of the others still might have lived."

"No, don't say that," he said to Abbi, strict.

"I don't say that for pity. It's the truth." Abbi looked downcast but sure. "Why'd you do it?"

He saw it right there again, Abbi unsure and mournful, just as Olivia once looked to him. "Your eyes. At the facility; they demanded help," he said. "My help."

She did not doubt the simple explanation. It seemed his conviction had more layers than the words told. "I'm grateful for it, David. Really."

He tried heaving the memory to the furthest vacancy as they continued. It helped, the more they spoke of their lives. He

141

hoped his troubled mind went unnoticed, but in time, each sentence became more natural until he forgot about Olivia. David elaborated further on recently picking up the guitar and even confessed he had tried his hand at writing.

"Too bad there's not a guitar for you to play here. It would probably help calm everyone and pass the time," said Abbi.

"I wouldn't mind that."

She smirked. "Well, I guess you could still sing for us acapella."

"Oh. No, no, no. I don't sing in front of people. At least, not yet. I don't even know if I have a good voice."

"Gotta find out sometime."

David shrugged but knew she was right. He felt again for the song in his flannel pocket, hoping the paper would reappear. He thought perhaps the first step was to let someone read his work, but in the pocket was nothing. David was still much too self-conscious to speak the memorized words aloud.

"I mentioned it earlier, but I do like to read." She had asked him what else he enjoyed. "And I guess reading is what first inspires anyone to try their hand at writing too."

"Reader and writer, huh? You must spend a lot of time inside," Abbi said. "Not in a bad way. And I think that's much cooler than just playing video games or something."

He replied quickly to defend himself, "Well, I fish too. Outside." He chuckled nervously. "Of course. Fishing is my go-to sport, I guess. My friend Jensen taught me a while ago. Been making trips pretty frequently for a while now."

"You mentioned him earlier. You guys close?"

"Like brothers," he said solemnly. "His grandfather is like mine too." David winced, disappointed that he had not considered the two much since the escape. "I can't imagine what they're thinking right now. I know this has got to tear Jensen apart. Me being here."

"Sounds like a great friend. I don't think I have one like that."

"We were supposed to go fishing to celebrate my Eighteenth. We go to this place, Nod Meadow. It's a pretty

142

secluded spot with a small lake. Not too far from Bellark, in the country like we are now. That's why I knew of the 38. We'd take it to get to Nod. Far from here though."

"Maybe we can make a stop there if we get close?"

"Sounds good." He grinned after Abbi did. "What about you? What do you like?"

She began where she felt she related most with David. "I probably don't read as often as you, but there's always a deep satisfaction that happens when I do open a book, but honestly, I can't sit still for long. I'm usually content anywhere so long as I'm with good people, but I'll always be the first one to recommend an outing. Thankfully, my friends like the beach." Abbi said sweetly, "Might even bring a book with me." She admitted if she ever was inside for long, it was to study, particularly for her science classes, mostly biology, which she excelled at most. "And on rare occasions, like a rainy day, I could find myself on a couch to watch a movie."

"Sounds like you were cut out for keeping on the go. Traveling or something," David said.

"I agree. That was my plan."

"Yeah? How would you afford it and make it happen?"

Abbi let out a slow breath. "Well, the money would come from doing it, I think." The next ran through her nose. "I've wanted to work in another country or overseas since I was a girl. I know what I'm good at."

"Science." David sat up in his chair, eager to recall. "Or biology. You said you were good at that, right?"

Understanding his genuine interest, Abbi felt encouraged to continue. "I guess so, but there's a specific path I wanted to take. Where both my skills and desires match."

David spoke, this time because she hesitated. "What is it? C'mon, I want to hear about it!"

Finally, a smile fought through, her lips even allowing her teeth an opening. "Okay, okay. I'm sorry. I just haven't talked with anyone about this in a while."

"Stage is yours."

"I love the idea of working with other nations in the

medical field but implementing our practices from here with their own. It might seem strange," she said. "In my biology class last year, our professor showed us a video of a pregnancy delivery. Even though it was kind of graphic, I was captivated."

"I remember those. Definitely intense," he said. "But I wouldn't say strange."

"No, no. I know it isn't. Maybe strange was the wrong word. Other girls have aspirations to enroll in nursing school and deliver Potentials as an occupation. But what I did next might be," she searched to find the word, "unconventional. After watching that video in class, I went home and went on like a ten-hour binge."

"TV binge?"

"Not exactly. There were some videos though." Abbi found his eyes. "I went into full-on research mode. I investigated the science of delivering Potentials. Methodologies, medicine prescribed, everything. I was watching videos of traditional delivery and cesareans . . ." She saw David's confusion. "C-section deliveries. Like surgery. Taking the Potential from the mother's abdomen and uterus. You see . . . That's why I think it would be great to travel to a different country where some people don't have our resources. With the right medicine, equipment, and training of a delivery nurse, do you know how many mothers and Potes I could help save? Actually, I don't think they call them that overseas, but I digress."

Her passion was a current of life, David unwittingly inspired as he let it overtake him. He listened, attentive and intrigued by all her plans to enroll in medical school and later uproot her life for the sake of another people, somewhere. She was certain of which university she would attend, the tuition costs and financial aid. There was not a detail unaccounted; any possible obstacle had a solution. The only unsettled matter was where she would travel afterward, though Abbi said it did not matter. "Need is need. So long as I have the skills and resources, and some people could use either. I only need to make the move."

David meditated further on everything he knew of Abbi and the new information she'd shared. Never had he heard a desire so strong, not even from Jensen. She knew what gave her purpose, having ready the next pages to write out her life. He became uneasy, now understanding her hesitancy before she shared. Neither David nor the others could fully empathize. To have the next chapter planned and outlined, only to have the pages torn out before the next sentence could be written.

"You don't deserve to be here," he said. "You shouldn't be here."

"None of us should be here," Abbi said, thrown off.

"No, we're here because we're not like you." His voice rose slightly, "You're here because of a fluke. Right?"

She sat up straight, shaking her head to herself. "No."

"Yes, it i—"

"Stop that!" she said before David could finish. Her back was straight. "No. I see what you're trying to say. David, don't buy into that."

"You would make it in the real world and do good; you, of all of us. You, of any Potential in Bellark, could travel the world and save lives. While you'd be delivering Potentials, we'd all be struggling just to pass the retake of the ESE, again and again."

"That's nonsense," Abbi protested. "You sound just like them."

David's face scrunched. "Who?"

"The CD, our carriers . . . Everyone. You think I deserve to live over the others because of your idea of what *good* is? Because you think I'm better? Dangerous thinking. It's the same kind that brought my dad to a different conclusion than you. And here I am, on the run." Abbi looked toward the southern mountains. "No matter your idea of good, it'll always be someone else's bad, and their bad will always be someone else's good; and as long as we keep rotating that judge, anyone can end up where we are."

The instinct to defend himself fought hard. *I'm not my carriers.* Considering what he'd just said to Abbi, there was yet no valid response to refute her accusations. Speechless, he stared out the windshield. Abbi added nothing more, leaning her head against the window, closing her eyes to calm down.

"So, you think it, huh?"

Abbi was still wounded. "Think what?"

"You think . . . you think we're alive." David was too timid to meet her eyes.

The statement forced Abbi into a position she did not realize she had put herself. If she spoke immediately, it would have been a drawn-out semantic attempt to validate both her feelings as and the Contration Department she had known for so long. But for the first time, she drew her line. "I do." The chilling window forced her to lift her head. "I think I always have. I'm alive. You are too. Same as those people inside that cabin."

Abbi waited for a response, but David only swallowed. "Look at us," she said, bringing her hand on top of his. She lifted it and brought his hand to his chest. "You feel that? Just like your sister's, your carriers', and the people after us. We're supposed to seriously believe that a single second in time differentiates our heartbeat from theirs? That single moment makes them living?" She studied his face, watching the tears trail down his cheeks onto the borrowed coat.

Abbi couldn't be sure exactly what had struck David, but considering his silence thus far, she figured he was attaching to her words in some way. Admittedly, it was liberating for Abbi to finally articulate the beliefs her soul had stored away for so long. "Whatever you believed before all this is okay. We were born into it, and unlearning is the most difficult. You can't doubt this any longer though. I'm here, and you're here. In this moment, in yesterday's moment, and tomorrow's."

"Abbi," he said, turning to her, face stained with thin streaks. "You're right."

"Good." She squeezed his hand, yet his melancholy persisted. "What's wrong?"

"I—" David's tongue recoiled more quickly than hair lit aflame, his attention stolen by what appeared in the valley. A parade of lights flew from the highway, nearing the river. Above the swarming vehicles, David saw another light, as if the sky had ripped open to birth another moon. It drifted above the horde of vehicles but began to change course.

146

"No," he said. The two bolted out of the SUV to the cliff's edge for a better vantage point. "They found us." David watched the aggressive pack of headlights. "We need to leave right now!"

The two sprinted for the cabin. They barged through the front door, waking up Mia. Soon after, Drake emerged from the hallway after jumping from his bed. Rylie scurried down the stairs next. David and Abbi's heavy breathing and fear braced them for what would follow.

"We gotta go!" said David. "They're coming our way right now. Go and wake up Bobby!"

As if by instinct, Drake was prepared for the next move, grabbing the rifle from David. The girls snatched the bags of food and extra clothing Rylie and Abbi had prepared, while David shook Bobby awake. Within two minutes, the lights in the house were all turned off. The helicopter drew closer, the chopping growing louder as if the blades were slicing the sky to hone its edges.

"That road a couple miles down," said David. "Rylie, you said it leads further into the mountains?"

"Yeah, but I don't know where or how far."

"It's fine. We have nowhere else," David said.

Drake quickly added, "We only have half a tank. If we take it as far up north as the SUV can go, we'll be sitting ducks once it runs out of gas."

"No," Rylie said. "I don't think it goes up. I know it didn't go higher. That's right. It went with the mountain, not against it."

"Up, down, with or against. It doesn't matter," David said more direly. "We'll take wherever it leads."

Mia said, "I don't know about that. They're close. If we leave on the road now, that helicopter will easily find us."

"If we stay here, they'll find us too," Bobby said to everyone's surprise.

Rylie watched the hysteria. She had been wondering when to tell them, continually conflicted on what response the confession would cause. "You guys take the truck," Rylie said.

147

"I'm going to take the SUV down the hill. They don't know we have the truck and will expect all of us to be in the SUV."

"What?" Drake said, "No way. You're coming with us." The others turned to Rylie with immediate disapproval as well.

"No, I'm not," Rylie said. "Listen. I'm only in my Sixteenth year." They dropped speechless and dumbfounded. "My Seventeenth year doesn't even come until June. I lied about my Eighteenth being this month." She continued plainly, knowing the others' shock would allow it. "Prep ESE got me. My mom didn't want to wait as long as I had hoped. I think I was right. The longer I stuck around, the harder it would have been for her."

Abbi was the first to speak against it. "Rylie, it's okay if you're in your Sixteenth year. You don't have to do this! If we leave now, we can outrun them."

"No, you won't be able to. I'm only going on my Seventeenth year. I can't stay on the run for another year after! I planned on telling and leaving after you all made it to Eighteen. Please." Rylie begged, "Let me give you all a chance."

No one could deny the angle from which Rylie appealed. David and Abbi wanted to object further, but they could not bring themselves to prolong it, reading the determination in Rylie. Her eyes were brimming with tears, but behind them was belief.

Drake took the initiative. "Okay, you guys heard her. We gotta go." His certainty derived from nothing else but Rylie's. He felt if he lingered any longer, he might change his mind and take Rylie with them, even if by force.

"The keys are in the truck." Rylie matched his urgency.

In an instant, the cutting blades outside resounded tenfold as if the helicopter had teleported to the cabin. It rose from just beyond the cliff's edge, its uproar sounding in full now that the cliff no longer provided a barrier. The metal beast shone its light through the cabin window. The group sprinted through the side garage door before the light could betray them.

They tossed their bags haphazardly into the truck bed and said their farewells unceremoniously quick. "Good luck," was all David could say. Rylie forced a smile and nodded. Abbi wrapped her arms around her and released just as quick. Drake was the last to bid farewell, "Thanks." She leaned in to kiss him on the cheek. "Goodbye, David Drake." Drake was the last one to get in the truck, taking the passenger seat since David was behind the wheel.

Rylie emerged from the side garage door, giving her cover from the brush beside the garage. She ran to the SUV, keeping close to the trees and avoiding the light from the hovering helicopter. To her fortune, the spotlight remained focused on the cabin interior, providing her a convenient buffer. She finally reached the SUV at the cliff's edge, turning the ignition immediately. It was only seconds before the helicopter turned its spotlight on the reversing vehicle.

The others listened breathlessly in the garage to hear when the helicopter had traveled a safe distance away. Abbi was still collecting herself in the back seat, wiping her eyes with her forearm. The helicopter's roar grew faint. Thankfully, it took one attempt to start the old truck. They left the garage door open, abandoning the refuge they'd had for too brief a time. Driving back down the path they'd come in on, David kept the headlights off despite the darkness and thick brush.

The first ten minutes seemed an eternity of driving, each anxious of the department appearing. The only dialogue exchanged was between David and Drake, discussing how much farther the hidden road might be. Those in the jammed back seat fretted between thoughts of Rylie's life and what would become of their own. But none could find themselves immersed in the same grief as Abigail. Her quiet sobbing would have seemed excessive to David if it weren't for the conversation he had with her before the CD appeared. If they'd all shared in Abbi's newly confessed belief, their tears would account for each moment of each decade since the establishment of the Contration Department.

David wondered if it was wrong that he was not responding like Abbi. *Do I not believe it? Shouldn't I cry as well?* He knew the answer to his questions but was much too fearful to look it in the eye. Unlike Abigail, he and the others were still slaves. David's chains, however, were attached but unlocked, yet he found a desperate safety in the binding.

"There it is." Drake pointed, seeing a slender gap between some brush and trees. David swung the steering wheel over. The rumbling road turned soft as they entered through.

*

"We have the SUV confirmed as our own. They're escaping down the hill," Luis said to Salvador and Delaney. "Our chopper is following it down the mountain. We've got 'em."

They stood behind the blockade set up on Highway 38, fortified at the foot of the mountain on the west side of the Huffman River, just at the end of the bridge. There was another blockade set up half a mile east in order to run down the escapees. Stationed at each post were numerous vehicles and officers from both the contration and police departments. By the number of officers attending the highway, one could imagine the city empty of patrols.

Luis said, "We'll catch them before they can get anywhere."

"Let's hope so," said Delaney.

Half a mile up the mountain, Rylie descended rapidly. She wanted to give as much distance as possible between the others and the helicopter. Leaving the headlights on kept the helicopter directly on her tail. Her heart raced, but hardly for her own sake, desperately hoping her friends would find the mysterious road she remembered. In younger years, her father never took her quite far, stopping at what may have been an eventual dead end. Regardless, even if the path led to nowhere, it was their best chance.

The trees and vegetation cleared as she neared the foot of the mountain. She looked both directions and saw the two blockades lit up from the countless patrols and spotlights. Two pits of fire illuminated both east and west, both directions promising the same fate. One solution remained. Looking west and seeing the river, she turned toward the city.

The stolen vehicle accelerated toward Salvador Goode.

150

"They're not stopping!" He shouted to the officers. They had their rifles pointed at the SUV approaching at full speed. Unlike the dart ones from the facility, these weapons readied lead. Luis Adán was most anxious to fire.

Salvador turned to Delaney, who had remained beside him. Her hand rested atop her handgun holstered on her belt. He became unsure and protective at the sight, looking her up and down, the woman and his Potential. The Chief's next words were impulsive and unprecedented. "Stand clear, Abbot." He drew his gun. "We should have enough support up front."

Delaney's ability for response was crippled. She did not know what she felt more strongly: hurt or belittlement. "Salvador!"

Her Chief was walking for the front line but gave a quick glance back. He raised a gentle hand to her, signaling a cryptic message. While she was not certain of the exact intention, Delaney grasped that the message was nothing short of patronizing. *Stop? Stand Clear? Relax?* Her polished black fingers tightened on her gun as she stepped forward.

Salvador shouted for all to hear, "On my command, take out the vehicle. Aim for the tires and driver!"

Rylie kept her foot on the gas pedal. Taking a deep breath, she turned on the high beams and stomped the pedal to the floor. She made her foot iron in case any obstacle or force would try and sway her to lift it.

Not even a half second after the tires made contact with the bridge, Salvador commanded the officers to fire. The eruption lanced the sky like nails. Multiple bullets penetrated the windshield.

Having excellent accuracy, Luis exhaled and fired.

Rylie felt an impact in her right shoulder. Blood began to run down her arm. She had let out a shriek, yet her leg and foot remained steadfast, applying the totality of her strength to the gas pedal. The bullets were like a rain of fire propelled by a screaming west wind. Rylie kept her head low, fighting to ignore her shoulder. Though it had seemed time slowed since the shooting began, she had reached the middle of the bridge.

Salvador had grown frightened by the durability of the stolen department vehicle. The defensiveness of the behemoth was designed to favor the CD, not its enemies. With the SUV drawing nearer, he estimated that he could shoot just above the dashboard to achieve a fatal penetration. The moment was critical: either he disabled the driver, or the black metal hulk would plow into their line. As he felt for the trigger, he caught a body moving past him, stepping in front of the line. Wearing an unusual confidence, the kind that could only rise once abandoning fear of consequence, Delaney lifted her gun. All officers ceased fire.

The gun's echo silenced Salvador's plea. Whatever word of appeal he yelled failed to fall on her ears, let alone anyone else's. The SUV was a mere thirty yards in front of Delaney.

The bullet chipped past Rylie's left ear, but she didn't even feel the nonfatal wound. It was now time as she understood that in seconds, harm would come to the army of officers. Rylie pulled the steering wheel to the left, next combatting the steel that tried to keep her straight.

The metal guard rail never stood a chance against the plowing force. The bullet-tattered SUV soared through the air, fifty feet down. A cascade flew to the bridge's height after the impact. The large vehicle floated for a few seconds, allowing Luis and the officers to sprint to the bridge's edge to see the spectacle. With the front bumper facing away, no one had a clear vantage point to see through the only non-tinted window.

The SUV began to drink the river from the shattered and pierced windows. Rylie managed to shove the driver's door open and unfastened her seatbelt, then suddenly stopped at the realization. *This is it. Either up there or down here.* The water rushed in quicker now that her door was open, but it was not freezing as she expected. Oddly, it was comfortably warm, almost inviting. Perhaps her body was misreading it from her wounds from the crash, she thought. Maybe it was her imagination. She stopped questioning. *Why disagree with comfort?* The warmth rose quickly from her thighs to her chest. The moonlight above the river's surface dimmed as the SUV sank deeper. Rylie shut her eyes and crouched her head to meet the water with her chin.

"We got them!" Luis announced from the bridge. "Chief!" He expected Salvador to be by him; instead, he was speaking with Delaney Abbot, the dialogue unintelligible from his distance. From what Luis could see, the conversation was grave. The Chief extended his arm and pointed a harsh finger toward the city. Delaney stormed off, angrily stepping into the vehicle they'd arrived in together. Not surprisingly, Luis found himself satisfied with Salvador's decision. Though the chase was a success, neither the Chief nor he could afford any further distractions.

Salvador marched toward Luis. "Send men down there to the river and take care of any Potes who think they can swim. Retrieve all bodies for confirmation."

"Yes, Sir." Luis nodded assuredly.

Salvador joined the rest of the officers at the twisted guardrail where the SUV had crashed through. No struggling swimmers or bodies came to the surface. Salvador's initial assurance faltered, a cramp in a marathon's final stretch.

"They must have struggled with their seat belts," Luis said.

"We'll need to haul the vehicle out of the water. This river is deep." Salvador commanded one of the officers, "Call for a tow truck and divers."

"How long do you think that'll take?" Luis asked.

The Chief strained to remain calm, clenching his fist as a substitute for lashing out at Luis. "Depends on when we can get that truck and those divers."

Salvador felt himself flattening as a coin on a train track, his pressures passing over him one wheel at a time. Despite needing the body count and verification, he was able to find some relief in the fact that it was done. Yet it was the new debt he'd just accrued that he would have to pay. After the harsh manner he'd just spoken to Delaney, it would be difficult to persuade her that his order was out of love or urgency to protect.

After collecting the bodies and writing the report of the pursuit from start to finish, perhaps the more difficult task would begin. Delaney was forgiving, yes. However, this was the first time he'd manipulated her this way, admittedly taking advantage of

153

both his position and their relationship. His stomach twisted, surprised that his thoughts even went to such a place. *She wouldn't.*

*

David almost glided along the unexpectedly flat dirt road, leaning forward over the wheel to see his whereabouts. Thankfully, his eyes were strong enough for the task, easier than reading a small font in a book. His driving was smooth enough to allow those in the back to drift off to sleep eventually. Abbi was the last of the three and probably would never have given in to slumber, but the grieving had left her empty. Drake kept awake.

"You think she's alive?" David said quietly to avoid disturbing the others.

Drake was silent for a moment. "I hope so. But not likely."

David was unsure of the grim conversation starter but continued. "I don't get it."

"Get what?"

"Why she didn't tell us she was Sixteen."

"Probably didn't want us to leave her like her mom did," said Drake. "Makes more sense now. Why she was so committed to help. There was never a chance for her."

"It's too bad."

"All of this is too bad."

David looked stumped. "Did she get grouped with us by accident? How do they organize contrations? I thought it was by years, or at least by birth month?"

"At this point do you really expect the CD to have any consistency?" Drake sneered, but David knew it was not toward him. "Everything with them is always changing, always being rewritten. A new circumstance, a new situation, and before we know it, a new law, until another situation changes that. Why Rylie was grouped with us, I'll never know, but she was there for the same reason."

David's teeth ground one another until a yawn opened his mouth to stop the aggravation.

"We can swap driving if you get tired."

"Maybe," David said. "I'd have to see you get some sleep though. You need rest too."

Drake was not ready for that; his mind would not be able to steady, consumed over Rylie's fate and whether she was dead or, by some miraculous chance, alive. He closed his eyes, however, leaning his head against the window. The least he could do was fake it to provide David with some assurance, even if it was deception. He imagined Rylie would approve.

In the silence, in the ebb and flow of every thought and doubt, the words returned to David. The song began to play in his head, not only the memorized lyrics but also the chords he'd never actually had the chance to strum. It was a pleasant song, continuing for some minutes until it began to change. He enjoyed the evolving sound, a progression into something more beautiful. For the first time, David saw himself playing in front of a large crowd, many faces young and old.

*

The RV had covered a vast stretch of the city throughout the day and evening. Sam and Jensen had already filled up on gas twice. They traveled toward Highway 38 in the afternoon but were forced to turn around when they saw the mass of vehicles at the checkpoint set up in the not far distance. When night came, the two rotated on driving while the other slept. Still, there was no sign of David. It was not until an hour ago when they'd finally stopped to eat at a twenty-four-hour diner to satisfy their impatient hunger.

Sam had grown exhausted and discouraged, much quicker than his young and enduring grandson. Nonetheless, Jensen persuaded him to try once more to leave the city and survey the countryside. Sam placed himself in the driver's seat, acknowledging that Jensen had driven for three consecutive hours and could benefit from even the smallest lick of sleep, though he seemed nowhere close to resting his eyes for a second.

Sam figured the checkpoint would be set up across the 38

155

anyway, and they would be forced to turn around once again. However, with the city trailing further behind in the rearview mirror, with the lights escaping through the gap of the unfinished wall, neither Jensen nor he could yet find the distant checkpoint from earlier.

The two continued.

Sam had readily agreed to take this drive but maintained a realistic mindset. Much time had passed since they left in the morning, and although persistent when they first embarked, finding David was less guaranteed than maintaining their uninterrupted travel. It was love for his grandson that had kept Sam determined to exhaust every opportunity. But now, he was beginning to doubt the wisdom of this search and the false hope it may encourage. For a brief moment under the full weight of drowsiness, the thought came: *David's dead.*

"I'm heading back to the city, Son. I don't think they're out here." He imagined driving the unending extent of the highway if he did not speak up now.

"What? But they took down the checkpoint. We can't just turn back. They've got to be somewhere, Grandpa," Jensen said. "Department would have announced it if they'd found them. They've been too quiet all day."

"I agree they've been quiet," Sam responded delicately. "I just can't think of anywhere David could be out here. Nothing new has been broadcast. I know this is the highway they first came down, but it stretches a good distance. At this point, there's a better chance of David being in the city or headed toward another, miles away. We won't have reception for much longer out here too. If any news comes up on where he might be, we'll miss it. I know it's tough, but I think we can better help David if we go back."

Jensen kept stubbornly silent as Sam turned around for the city. Though his grandfather would sacrifice much for David, the old soul and body had its limits. Jensen gazed ahead at Bellark and its city lights putting bright freckles on the night's face. Rubbing his eyes gave him a moment to gain a reasoned thought, now unsure whether he actually wanted David in the city. It would bring the two close, true. But if David had escaped somewhere far from the Bellark CD, that would be more favorable to his survival. The predicament caused Jensen's disdain for the CD to spike, especially for Salvador Goode.

They were only a few miles from the city when the quiet, unintelligible radio muttered. "Turn it up," Sam said.

As the volume increased, so did the urgency of the voice. "It was a violent and damaging event, but the escaped Potentials, also known as the March Runaways, have been caught at the Huffman River along Highway 38. With blockades set up on both the east and west sides of the river, the Potes had nowhere to flee. The CD opened fire on the fugitives, and the driver lost control of the vehicle, crashing it through the bridge into the river. The vehicle quickly sank upon impact. While the vehicle is in the process of being towed from the water, we continue to wait on confirmation and identification of the Potential bodies. We will provide an update upon gaining new information."

Jensen punched the glove compartment, his hands and body shaking. Sam had no immediate consolation, knowing no words could take away the pain he was witnessing. Though struck with heartache, Sam could not grieve in the same manner as Jensen. There was a long drive ahead.

Sam turned off the radio as the reporter began describing each Potential. "I'm sorry, Jensen. We'll head on home."

"No." Jensen wiped his eyes. "I don't want to go home." He set his eyes to the foothills north. The city would only remind him of the loss, and the system he now loathed more than ever. Seeing the sprouting seed logo, so dominantly plastered and gloating throughout the city, would be another insult.

*

The margin for the tires was like a tightrope, the slightest of a turn sure to lead into an abyss of foliage. The moonlight had trouble through the clouds and trees, but David still could not chance the headlights. Though certain they were a safe distance from the cabin and from wherever Rylie led the CD, his

157

conditioned defensiveness would not waver. It wasn't merely paranoia, however. David refused to let Rylie's efforts be wasted due to negligence on his part, even if it meant taking extra precautions to elude.

He looked at Drake in the passenger seat. The evening's events had finally strapped him, sleep overtaking him once the adrenaline subsided. Staring to the side a moment too long, David allowed the truck to drift right, and a tree branch thudded against the window where Drake's head rested. The boy jumped upright, his eyes revealing the closest thing to genuine fear thus far.

"Sorry about that," he apologized, trying not to awaken the others in the back. "I drifted a little."

Drake signaled a thumbs-up, not yet having words as he collected himself from the sudden awakening. The thud did not awaken those jammed in the back seat, their sleep likely deeper than Drake's accidental slumber.

"We're some hours in the morning now. How does it feel to be in your Eighteenth?" David remembered the conversation with Abbi on his watch. *You've been alive.*

Drake yawned. "No different, other than feeling exhausted."

"At least you know you're safe now. Can't be taken to the contration facility again."

Drake looked at him, his long struggle for speech going unnoticed because of David's focus on the road. The words left his mouth slowly and quietly like snowfall but resounded as if they fell to the ground as hail instead. "I killed all their men," Drake said. "They'll still be after me for that."

David glanced to him but had to return his vision to the road. "What? No, I—"

"I killed them all," he cut David off. "Someone needs to answer for each one. It was me."

David was confused. "No, I killed one too. That guy in the parking lot."

"No, you didn't. Didn't you hear me? I killed them all." Drake stared firmly at David, speaking the thought that had been brewing. "Don't be stupid. It's either one of us or both of us."

158

David grasped what he was trying. "No, that's not right. That's not true. I won't let you go down like that. There were cameras."

"Yeah, and they'll show my gun sticking out the window. Not you under the car. They're gonna charge me anyway. Let's keep it to one of us, not both," he said. "Rylie made her choice. Let me make mine."

"It doesn't have to be like that," David said. "We can argue self-defense."

"As contrated Potes? Maybe you could, but you never killed that man."

"Fine. I killed the others."

Drake felt the pushback, unintimidated. "Oh yeah? Good luck arguing that with the camera footage from inside the facility. And yours was in legitimate self-defense." He grew aware of his rising voice and brought it down. "I killed one of them, even when I didn't need to. Don't make me bring up the old clerk too."

David knew Drake would likely have a rebuttal for everything. From his quick responses despite having just woken up, it was clear Drake chose this resolve before the conversation began. If there was a time to dissuade him, now was not the moment; not with the chance of the others awakening and adding too many voices to the debate. Still accepting defeat, David could not help but admire the boy with black hair. "How long have you been thinking about this?" he said, resigned to at least a temporary forfeit.

"Since tonight. I'd rather go to prison than . . ."

Drake stopped when he saw that he had lost David midsentence. Neither of them saw it coming as they turned the wind—a curtain of tree branches and leaves draped the road's passage. However, when the truck went through them, they hardly made a sound against the metal as if the rows of branches were feathers instead. After emerging, David's eyes showed more astonishment than when first plowing through the green.

Drake's attention followed David's to what lay ahead. The morning sunlight was just peeking over the mountain, faint orange and yellow fingers extending over the peaks through the clouds. The overhanging trees cleared, and the narrowed road was expanding like spilled ink on paper, revealing a landscape beyond; a lake sat adjacent to the meadow. The water's surface was dark to the naked eye, the light of dawn not yet illuminating its true color.

David's jaw hung open. He rubbed his eyes to restore the clarity the morning toil had robbed him. "Unbelievable." He leaned forward slow and delicate as if not to make the image flee, taking his eyes beyond the path well into the distance of the entire scene.

"Rylie never mentioned we'd come to this," Drake said, more curious than anything. "Where are we now?"

David let out breath to make room to speak. "I can't believe it. This is Nod Meadow." Having complete clearance of the narrow road, David parked. The current openness negated the claustrophobia he'd felt while driving. Spellbound, he exited the truck as if it was instead his own body he stepped out from.

Drake was bewildered by David's actions. Still aware of the scope and urgency of their drive, he yelled for David through the door he'd left open. "What are you doing?" Abbi, Mia, and Bobby naturally awoke from the call. "Why are we stopping?" The words were cold water to David's face.

"I know this place," he said softly as he returned to the truck. More quietly, he said again, "I know this place." The others still looked lost, especially the ones who'd just been woken up. "This is a place I come. Nod Meadow. I fished here a couple of days ago," he said turning back around."

The field was mostly the faded wintergreen, but this morning's frost topped each blade of grass under white crystal. There were a few scattered early blooms: the yarrow, lupines, and iris blooms added specs of blue, purple, white, and yellow to the tapestry. David's eyes stopped on the maple tree far in the distance at the meadow's edge. It was nearly bare, but the spring leaves were budding, soon to completely clothe the body from which they hung. David clenched his teeth and forced his sight away. Next, he saw the six fruit trees. "There might be some fruit," he announced somewhat mindlessly in an effort to give his companions some communication. "Some are dead from what I remember. Might be a little tart if there's any, but it's still something."

David's shift introduced a new person to the group. There was both a calm and mystery to the new presence as if all his typical sense of safety, urgency, and self-awareness were thrown aside, allowing for a buried aspect of him to rise.

Though the others were not quite on the same page, Drake did see an opportunity to take advantage of the meadow as David suggested. "Okay, but we need to be quick."

The sweeping chill greeted each of them with a slap, but in moments, not one shivered anymore. Bobby and Mia quickly walked behind different trees and bushes to relieve themselves. Drake and Abbi were striding slowly through the grass behind David, some of the blades reaching up as high as their calves. Their footprints over the morning frost left green stamps trailing them as they walked toward the fruit trees.

They couldn't help but receive the serenity of the meadow and the bliss of the early-morning chirping of the birds. Both Abbi and Drake steadily drifted from David and each other, meandering through the green as if they were leaves in the wind, each of them directed by a different current. The collective mindset of haste slowly disappeared from their minds like mist. Before long, Bobby and Mia were behind making more prints through the grass.

David neared one of the fruit trees. He reached forward, moving some of the branches in search. But there was no fruit to find. He looked down to the rotting base. "It's dead. It wasn't before," he said as if betrayed. He continued to study the tree and noticed the fickle leaves. "When I was here days ago, this one was alive. Some others died, but this one was alive. This one and those two." Drake and Abbi looked where David pointed. "Check the others," he said just as Mia and Bobby caught up. "Those trees should be good."

Bobby followed David to the next one. After a questioning look at David, he shot his arm through its branches, searching almost frantically for any fruit. David shook his head. "I can't believe this one's dead too." There was finally sorrow as his face went downcast.

Mia had focused on the tree furthest to the right; the second one David had pointed out. Drake walked toward her to see what had captured her attention. The base was a faint yellow-white with brown specks. With a closer look at the wilting of the branches, he called out, "I think this one's done too."

David walked over and gave it a thorough observation from base to top. "Yeah, dead or dying. I was just here the other day. I don't understand how they could all die." He plucked a frail leaf. It crumbled under a soft pressure from his fingers. "It's a shame. When I first started coming, all seven . . . I mean, all six stood healthy."

"But look." Mia pointed up to the middle of the tree where she had been staring. "There's one right there." David and Drake had to step to where she stood. From the previous angle, a small cluster of wilting leaves had covered the fruit. "How is it so big this early? And if the tree is dead, it must be dead too, right?"

"Not necessarily." David's intrigue slowed his response. "These trees can die without warning, but this apple was here when it was still alive. That is something though," he marveled. "Its tree looks unhealthier than any of the others, but this apple's looks better than even most in the spring."

"Better? You can't be serious." Mia scrunched her face. "There's no way you can eat that. The tree's dead. It probably has a disease in it or something."

Drake, the tallest of them, reached for the red fruit. "Well, if you won't eat it, I will. If I'm going to die, at least I'll die satisfied." It pulled off easily, Drake's large hand proportionate to the fruit it held. "Dessert for later." Drake received a small rise from the disgusted Mia. He handed it to Abbi, whispering, "Honestly, not a fan of apples. Just fun to be the devil's advocate here and there." He winked. "Don't worry," he said, seeing Abbi's caution. "It won't get you sick. Someone's gotta eat. At least one of us has to live, right?"

Each of them walked a separate direction to acquaint themselves with Nod. They felt the same sensory satisfaction,

162

especially Mia who had not yet expressed her passion for scenic art. She had a portfolio of her own, having begun her collection when she enrolled in free afterschool creative arts programs. No one noticed yet that she had not raised any pushback. Drake also dismissed his command to be quick. He hadn't forgotten about the need to stay alive, but he strangely and agreeably felt unable to return to the truck.

There was no recollection of the time it took to walk to the maple tree in the distance. To David's mind, he appeared there almost instantaneously after the first foot forward; the overcoming memories blotted out the other steps. Its branches and few leaves hung over him as if trying to comfort with a hug. Finally arriving to the base of the large maple, he dropped to his knees. "I'm sorry," he said, hoping his audience would somehow hear. The only person who heard, however, was Abbi, who had followed him unnoticed. She stopped where the first branches hung.

Whether Abbi was present or not would not have mattered to David. The break was impending, regardless. The memory played back vividly, the moment that at the time was pure joy. Neither he nor Olivia expected it to happen, but the romance of the day compelled them mutually. Under the maple tree, as the late summer sun fell, David and Olivia had exchanged themselves for the first time. The spontaneity and heat of the moment only heightened their passion, both foreigners in a new land of such an experience. They left the meadow that day feeling like a true man and woman together, confident that such a love and infatuation could endure forever. Nothing had ever been more profound and vexing for David. He marveled at the way a single experience could compel him to feel invincible one day and then stripped and powerless not long after.

He recalled the weeks following that summer afternoon with Olivia. A tear dripped from his eye and landed on a tree root climbing out of the grassy earth. It was the first one that broke since the incident. His fists clenched tighter, bracing himself.

It had been six months since.

Olivia met up with him in person rather than make a call.

163

David knew the situation was serious but didn't fully grasp its implications. However, as the days and weeks passed, his nights became sleepless. Her words hung over him day in and day out, a storm that would never subside or relent: *I'm pregnant.*

More tears fell from David's face, the sobbing now audible for Abbi. She took a couple of steps forward, stopping at his next broken words. "It's my fault."

"What is?" she said.

Abbi's question caught David off-guard. He turned around, making no attempt to brush the hair from his face or collect himself at all for that matter as the morning dew soaked through his flannel bottoms. There was no escaping or further keeping the truth. "I did it."

Abbi stepped toward David and slowly went to her knees to be at his level. "Did what?"

David's whole body was shaking, lips quivering from a force trying to hold back the confession. "I've done it. Contrated."

"You've contrated?" Abbi response was too quick to allow her mind to follow.

"Yeah," he said. "My own. Last summer." His unsteady voice grew more turbulent. "I told her to do it. I was scared and thought it was for the best. She didn't want to. She didn't want to do it." Abbi's few tears could not nearly match David's, but they watered the grass together. "What makes me any different from my carriers? I deserve to be here. I killed my own. I chose it for the same reasons they did. This is what I deserve."

Abbi lunged at David and wrapped her arms, squeezing his body to hers. "No. Don't you dare think like that."

"How can you even hold me right now?" David shifted to move his body away from hers, but she only pulled him tighter. His discomfort and desire to push away diminished the longer she held on. "Abbi, you're the one who believes we're alive and have always been. You shouldn't be crying with me."

"How can I not?" Abbi released David and took her head off his shoulder, meeting his reddened eyes. "David, you made a wrong decision in the past. And now you're able to see it just as that. Wrong. It takes more courage to recognize and cope with that than to keep on in denial." Abbi had to be intentional with her words, but she uttered each one with conviction. "If I can't give you compassion for that, then when can I? If someone's worth is stripped because of a mistake, then we have a world full of worthless people.

Numerous questions raced through her head, curious of what ultimately led to David's choice. None of these, however, took priority over what she felt necessary to say and be for him, knowing a hurting person does not always need to be reminded of a wound when the pain already speaks of it.

"I can't change what I did." David combed the hair from his face. "It was me who told Olivia to do it. 'There's a way to make it work,' she kept telling me. I did think about it for a little bit. Maybe I could get a job and make it happen. Then I told my carriers." David shook his head, unsure of how much blame to place on his father and mother. "Their opinion was clear from the start. To think they pulled that card too: 'You can't make a life for yourself that way. It will ruin your chances at university.' Now that I'm here . . . Maybe even for them, it would have been tough to contrate both me and my kid."

Abbi was aching. "I'm sorry," she said simply. "Olivia is her name?" The question disarmed David. "The girl."

"Umm, yeah. Olivia, or Liv." David's discomfort from the question lifted after answering. "But she still liked when I called her Olivia. I mostly used that when I said I loved her." A deep breath followed. "Wish I could go back and change it." The rest flowed out naturally, like pent-up waters able to outflow after a dam becomes displaced. The confession was laced with pain, but he was able to articulate it with a new sobriety.

The chronicle was brief but enough to allow Abbi to fill in the gaps. It was a short amount of time for two people to fall in love, Abbi thought, but then again, she had never been in love herself and had no definitive idea of what the state truly meant.

"Olivia's carriers said they would be moving to a different city. The news came during the last week in August. It devastated both of us," said David. "But we believed our love, or whatever, was strong enough to keep us together; just like any young couple

165

would think. I planned to get my driver's license at the end of the summer. The place where she was moving wasn't too far. Not too bad a drive to get there in a day." He sniffed and wiped his nose. "The night she told me she was moving was when I first said I loved her. I sometimes wonder if I would have said so soon if the move didn't happen. Young kids. We, we were emotional.

"The summer was amazing. Us together and everything about it. Novelesque, some might call it. Since secondary school, it was my first summer free of my usual cares." David nodded and almost hinted at a smile. "I didn't care, or even mind my carriers' neglect at that point. I didn't need to talk to them when I had her. First kiss, first night sneaking out of the house." He paused, wondering whether to say it or not. "First time I ever did anything, umm physical, with a girl. I thought a first kiss would be the furthest I'd ever go at this age."

David looked down, his body almost shrinking as his posture fell inward. He'd seemed pleased to share the memories for a moment, but it appeared that would be the only instance for levity. Abbi let him take a minute to stare out across the grass.

"This is where it happened. Right here," he said.

"How long did you wait to contrate?" Abbi was unsure why she asked it so plainly. David had taken another long pause, but it was not patience Abbi lacked. Perhaps speaking may have been her way to remind David she was there. Most of the time in his reminiscence, he had not even looked at her.

He looked above at the remnant of maple leaves. "Olivia was an optimist, often unreasonably hopeful. She believed we could still have a good life with a child. She even took it upon herself to look into careers for both of us that didn't require much schooling, money, and time. She knew pretty quick that I wasn't excited about it all." David finally looked to Abbi. "You want to know something too? I'm the one who always brought up that starting a family was a dream. This was before the pregnancy. It's not surprising that what I had to say did what it did.

"Nothing was the same after I asked her to keep the news from her carriers. Her attitude, her love—what was left of it—all changed. Of all the people, they of all people . . ." He shook his

166

head, condemning himself. "I had always respected her carriers for their opinions but never imagined their advocacy against the CD would even be our concern. I couldn't let her tell them, and I think that was the moment she knew." David pulled some grass from the ground. "It hurt to do. It really did. I knew it hurt her. The way she looked at me . . . Same face as yours in the facility. I never said it aloud, especially to Oliva, but that was the first moment in my life when I *truly* questioned the CD. As soon as that doubt came, I had to do everything I could to throw it away. I had to protect myself."

His voice was faint now, but Abbi could still hear, leaning forward; it was the quietest it could go before becoming a whisper. "She fell apart after leaving the facility. I tried to comfort her on the drive home, but I knew I didn't have much to give or say. I took her there without even getting my license yet. Just a permit with Jensen's truck. Pretty sure that upset her too, even though Jensen wasn't for it. Still let me borrow the truck though. 'Take me home.' It was all she had to say through the sobbing.

"I haven't seen her since." David's words cracked in a swelling throat. "I tried reaching out. Even had Jensen drive me to her house. No answer. I already knew what day she was moving and had a week to try and make amends. Not enough time, I guess. I did get one response. A text to 'move on.' But after she changed her number, I knew she wouldn't ever speak to me unless I could somehow bring our Potent— our child back. Now, she's in some other city, living a different life. I'm telling you; maybe this, me being here, is what's right."

She reached for David's hand, her eyes sure. "You wonder whether you deserve this or not? You already know my answer. You want to know how you come back from this? Amend for past mistakes or whatever you call it. Make it up to Olivia, to your child, to yourself." She rose, forcing David to stand with her grasp. "Help me. Help us. Keep us alive."

*

Abbi followed David as he walked toward the lake. He

167

did not say anything, his mind busy with reciting Abbi's last command. He did, however, keep his pace slow to signal he preferred her company. The song of the morning birds grew, the melody another addition to the meadow's sanctity. They arrived at a flat rock that found its place on the shore, which the dawn was finally able to illuminate and glisten. Abbi sat first, unaware that it was David's fishing rock. He assumed a spot next to her. Two morning doves hovered over the water. The two looked to be playing tag, one chasing the other until the roles would spontaneously switch. After a few minutes, David finally spoke. "We should probably head back."

The concept of time returned to the two, both speeding their pace after acknowledging the sun was perched well above the hilltops behind the gray. As they neared the truck, Mia was leaning on the door through the driver's window. Drake was in the driver's seat adjusting the radio, which emitted nothing but an unintelligible crackling. Mia stepped back as Drake got out of the truck to fidget with the antenna. Neither of them took notice of David's tear-stained face.

"What are you doing?" David asked.

"We almost have reception," he said, focused on the antenna. "Driving this way finally put us in reach of radio. Maybe now we can see if they're saying anything about us. We've been here too long, but before we head out, I want to get this right to keep up-to-date."

"You sure they put this kind of stuff on the radio?" Mia asked, leaning on the truck. "It's still early."

"If they put us on TV, then there's got to be some station covering it too. Shh!" Drake silenced only himself. He'd managed to work the antenna to hear a scratchy voice. "Listen, guys."

It grew louder through the speakers. "You got something," said Abbi. He tinkered with the antenna just a moment longer until the voice came to clarity. "Does anyone know radio stations? I sure as hell don't listen to the radio," Drake asked, irritated to hear a man sing a country song.

"I don't listen either. We'll have to go through each station on the road. If we get closer to the city, reception should get better too," said Abbi.

Mia slid into the passenger seat to search the radio. David and Abbi looked out at Bobby, still sifting and searching through one of the apple trees. "I'll go and get him," said David, taking two steps before Mia called out, "Someone's talking about us!"

She raised the volume. ". . . also known as the March Runaways, crashed into the Huffman River off Highway 38. While under pursuit from the CD, the hijacked vehicle crashed through the bridge into the river while under gunfire. Thus far, only one body has been identified; Potential, Rylie Banks. Tow trucks have just now arrived at the scene to haul the vehicle from the river to retrieve the remaining bodies."

Mia looked up in shock. "She's contrated." Her next words came with relief. "They think we are too."

"She's dead." Abbi's heart folded, unable to register Mia's second comment.

Drake slammed the hood of the truck with an open hand.

"She gave us time," David said before any downturned further. Abbi's command from the maple tree resounded more loudly in his head. "We need to get going while they still think we're dead. The department probably let up on their pursuit. Get in the car. I'm getting Bobby." Though resistant at first to David's immediacy, in moments, they shelved their grief.

There was an added sorrow to Mia after hearing of Rylie's fate, but the constant fear for her own life remained the main contributor to her solemnity. Much like David, she did receive some sense of security, realizing the suspended pursuit of their lives. She could not shake the thought, however, that it could be a matter of minutes before the CD discovered their deaths to be false. She looked to David making his way quickly toward Bobby, biting her lip, wishing that he would walk faster.

Abbi watched David near the trees and Bobby. *Keep us alive*, she remembered saying. David halted in the grass about thirty yards from Bobby, turning his head to the dirt road where it extended beyond the meadow. Abbi thought for a moment that he stopped from hearing her thought. Before she could question

169

that absurdity, David began sprinting toward Bobby. She turned her head to look down the road when the rumbling finally reached her ears as well.

"Get in the truck!" Drake shouted from behind, igniting the engine. Abbi was frozen, her head swiveling back and forth between David and Bobby, and the nearing threat beyond the meadow. It kicked up dirt from behind, the clustered greenery only providing a vague and incomplete image of the large beast.

David made sure not to yell Bobby's name, aware the approaching people may hear. He tackled Bobby down, which naturally brought his panic. "Shh!" David had Bobby follow his finger that pointed to the nearing vehicle. Bobby stilled, both bodies motionless in the tall grass.

Drake watched David, waiting for a cue or command. David made a shooing motion with his hand. Drake understood and quickly geared into reverse, applying as much pressure to the pedal without kicking up dirt and slid into a brushy opening next to the road. The trees and greenery provided enough camouflage while still providing some pockets for a vantage point. The three inside stared anxiously through the windshield, awaiting the unknown arrival.

Not even a blink could steal David's attention from what was coming. Bobby whispered words that David had no recollection of hearing. The behemoth finally entered the meadow and halted once it cleared the narrow road, about thirty yards from those staked out in the truck. Two people stepped out. The tall grass obstructed David's sight. He perched his head above the grass to see.

The others were focused on the new arrivals as well, having to shift their heads to different angles to navigate the limited view from the brush. Drake studied one of the individuals straying away into the meadow toward David and Bobby. Without warning, Drake opened and stepped out of the truck with the rifle. "What are you doing?" said Abbi, worried.

"One of them is walking toward them," he said. "I can take out two officers easy."

From his position, David lifted his head higher, the

170

approaching figure close enough to make out. Instinctively, David's body rose to confirm what his eyes were registering. He allowed a second's pause, then after gaining full assurance, he jumped to his feet. Bobby flinched at David's next move, already in full sprint toward the new person walking in the grass.

Abbi went to panic. "What is he doing? Drake!"

Drake rushed toward David with the rifle held to his chest, abandoning the truck and the girls.

David continued racing through the grass, invigorated as his chest expanded from overwhelm. He was not asking any questions as to how or why, only following where his body led. Some distance away, David called to the figure gazing out toward the lake.

He turned to David cautious, doubtful of what he heard.

David tried to catch his breath at the same time. "Jensen!"

He lunged at David. They wrapped each other tightly. "David! They, they said you were dead." Jensen wiped his eyes in his right jacket sleeve. "But how? How are you here?"

David's eyes were empty and could not run like Jensen's since the maple tree, yet his breathlessness was the same. "I escaped. How are you here?"

The other arrival walked to the two boys, equally speechless but able to understand the plausibility of the chance encounter. Sam blinked several times and cleared his throat, watching as his grandson clung to David. "Well," he said, a slight catch in his throat belying the jovial tone, "look who resurrected." After Jensen let go, Sam wrapped David more possessively than any hug ever before.

Drake watched the strange occurrence, slowing his jog and mindfully lowering the weapon after David and the new guest first embraced. He arrived at the scene, yet his confusion and defensiveness did not subside despite the apparent trust between David and the new strangers. He said cautiously, "I assume you guys know each other."

In similar perplexity, Abbi and Mia hurried to the field to understand the situation firsthand. Bobby felt safe to approach

171

after David waved him over.

"This is Jensen and Sam Lloyd," David said after all gathered. "Jensen, Sam . . . These are my friends who escaped with me. We probably all have many questions right now, but if there's one thing I can start us with . . . Of all people, there is no one else I trust more than each person here." That statement seemed to soften some skepticism, and heads nodded around the circle. All, except Drake's.

David explained the events that led to their arrival at Nod after their escape as quickly and succinctly as he could. Jensen and Sam were left in awe after hearing of Rylie's actions. Jensen explained how he and Sam had been searching for them the past day and night until it was the news of David's alleged death that compelled the two to Nod. "This was the only place I wanted to come," said Jensen.

Drake interrupted with a shifty body. "David, we gotta get going. It's only a matter of time before the department finds out we're still alive. We've been here too long."

Sam said, "He's right. Since you all are presumed contrated, the checkpoints on the highway have been taken down. Come with us back to the city. When they find out you're all alive, they may not suspect you went back into Bellark where their headquarters are."

"Makes sense. Let's do it." David had no hesitation.

"I know you have some good history with these guys," Drake said suspiciously, looking back and forth between Jensen and Sam. "But how do we know they won't sell us out?"

"Drake," Abbi said calmly. "They're here, aren't they?"

"Son," Sam said with a softness. "I understand why you're wary of us. You've had a lot of people after you the past couple of days. Since you were sent to the facility, you most likely didn't have many people to trust before that either. All I can give you is my word. And here it is. My word is I hate the CD. I always have. The sad thing is I was too much a coward to express that most of my life. Never even voted. I sat back passively while it continued, but then it took someone who's like one of my own." His hand had come to rest on David, gripping it as tightly as when he had hugged him. He gulped hard as if swallowing salt water, looking at the new faces. "That is why I'm here. As long as I'm around, no one will touch David without a fight. And the same goes for the rest of you all."

Drake contemplated Sam for a few seconds. *Is there any safe place or person?* Drake looked to his companions awaiting his response, their faces expressing a readiness to live, a willingness to trust the two new people. *What if they stab us in the back?* He remembered the radio report, confirming Rylie's death. He could only faintly recall the bridge's appearance before he turned up the mountain, but it was enough for him to visualize the SUV going over its edge with Rylie inside. Only her, sinking to the bottom, alone in the cold, unforgiving water. *She kept us safe. She kept us alive.* Drake raised his sight from the grass he had gotten lost in. "Well," he looked over his shoulder to the RV. "Guess we better get going." He turned to David. "We'll all be close enough together in there." He brought the rifle to his chest. "If anything unusual happens, I've at least got this."

David smirked and nodded, now able to appreciate Drake's apprehensions. There was nothing to say or disagree with. David could argue his trust for Jensen and Sam just as well as Drake could argue his skepticism. He thought he could win, in fact, especially since Drake's distrust was not enough to keep him from joining. Even so—*I'll just keep quiet and let them prove themselves.*

They transferred what little they had from the truck into the RV. It was Sam who suggested they leave the truck behind to keep their travel limited to one vehicle in case of a run in with the CD. "Better they see me driving than any of you," he added.

Even so, Mia was concerned about traveling to where the department was most concentrated, but she recognized it was better than keeping at the meadow. Bobby did not have any objection to traveling with Sam and Jensen back into Bellark, ready to go along with anything the group decided, especially if it was David's initiative. But he did not fail to ask, "Will I get to see my mom since we're going back home?" Abbi caught David's glance, just as conflicted as her own. "I don't think so," she said as they stepped into the RV.

David and Jensen were the last ones left outside, about ready to board. "I can't believe you made it this far, man," Jensen said.

"I still haven't told you how it all started at the facility."

"I think I might have an idea." David looked up at Jensen, curious about his certainty. "Let's get in the RV," said Jensen. "There's some stuff I need to catch you up on."

*

The sky's thick blanket smothered the sun, sending a meek shower for about ten minutes, though for Salvador Goode, it seemed much longer. Still, despite this morning's shadow, flashlights were not necessary as the work continued in the Huffman River. A couple of paramedics, who'd recently arrived on the scene, placed Rylie's corpse into a body bag and zipped it inside. Salvador and Luis observed the process with careful eyes. They were relieved to confirm one of the Potentials contrated after the body emerged to the surface, but Salvador's last look upon her face tainted the satisfaction. The lifeless girl seemed to appear at more peace than himself with her resting eyes. Even after Rylie disappeared behind the zipper, he could not banish her tranquility from his mind. *I've done thousands of these. She is no different.* At any rate, Salvador's stress over the remaining fugitives outweighed any sense of closure or relief he'd gained from one mere contration.

"So much time has passed, and only one body has come to the top," Salvador said, aggravated. He turned around in search, wishfully hoping to see Delaney, but he knew she was not returning.

"The rest have to be in there," said Luis. "Their seatbelts most likely held them in."

Two tow trucks were backing to the river's edge. Meanwhile, four divers were strapping on masks and oxygen tanks, preparing for the plunge. The bottom of the river was deceptively deep, its temperature making the outside feel like summer by comparison. Salvador monitored the divers' preparations, wishing they exhibit the same urgency he felt. They had already arrived twenty minutes later than expected; their reputation, however, was not on the line.

Salvador let out a grunt. "These Potes have to make everything complicated. Why couldn't they just give in and avoid such a violent end? Euthanizing is much more comfortable and humane than a gunshot or drowning in freezing water. When this is over, I'm taking a vacation as far from Bellark as I can."

"Where to?" asked Luis. "North?"

"No, too crowded."

"South?" Even Luis was capable of dishing dry humor.

Salvador shook his head but found it in himself to reciprocate the sarcasm. "Sure." It was somewhat an attempt to lift his spirit, but continuing the bit brought him no greater solace.

*

"I cannot believe it was you," Abbi said after Jensen's detailed account.

"Yeah. I didn't exactly know what I was doing. I just tinkered and beat down until something happened."

Sam navigated the RV in the descent down the mountain, having a much easier task than David did earlier since the road here was much wider. Despite the group's exhaustion, they listened avidly as Jensen recounted the night of the Closing and how all their paths came to cross.

"I can't believe you followed all that way," David said.

"You would have done the same if you were in my shoes." Jensen told the majority of the Closing night's happenings, from when he first saw David's body loaded into the CD van up until the power outage. But what he did not yet share was seeing David's carriers, their action or inaction, as David was wheeled down the driveway and into the van. "I'm just happy you're safe now."

David said, "So, it was never an accident."

Jensen shook his head. "No. The van was outside your house. It was for you. Your carriers contrated you." The retelling

175

was laced with unease, a tart aftertaste to a testimony that should be sweet. Of course, Jensen was thrilled that the miracle attempt had succeeded, but his lips were on guard, keeping something else back.

The highway came into view, the same black incision that cut through the valley to the facility and beyond. The area cleared entirely of trees as they neared the base of the mountain; only a few bushes remained. Westward toward the city, it was easy to see that the highway had no checkpoints or any traffic at all for that matter. Between them and the Huffman River lied a comfortable and substantial distance.

The RV wobbled as it turned from dirt to asphalt. Drake said to Jensen, still somewhat cautious, "So, they just gave you a slap on the wrist?"

"I guess so," Jensen said, wary of the accusative tone.

"I have a hard time believing this Goode guy would let you off that easy with community service and fines. We killed some of their guys because of the power outage. You should be behind bars, if not contrated yourself."

Abbi gripped the small table to keep her stable as the RV regained its balance. "He was never chosen for contration. They couldn't, right?"

"He does have rights, unlike us," Mia added bleakly, the only thing she'd said since boarding. The only actions of hers worth noting were her repeated trips to the restroom. It was obvious something was not sitting well in her stomach, but each person had the decency and respect to not raise the obvious questions.

David observed Jensen, waiting for an answer. He had not questioned the matter as the immediate circumstance of reunion overshadowed all else in his mind, but Drake's probing had finally piqued David's curiosity.

Jensen fidgeted nervously in his seat. It was on his lips, but it fought to keep inside. Sam watched him in the rearview mirror, understanding the hesitancy. It was the same reluctance Sam had before he disclosed the matter to his grandson. David could tell it was about to come out, but he left Jensen the moments he needed. Eventually, all took notice of Jensen's strange hesitance as if he was now on trial.

"I couldn't have had any idea," Jensen said under his breath, struggling. "Didn't believe it at first, but the more it sank, the more it seemed to make sense. Why my grandfather had to raise me. Why he had to, or else I would have been contrated." Jensen looked to David.

David sat upright. "Contrated?"

"It was my mom who wanted to keep me. Before she died."

David tried to comprehend. "Jensen, I'm sorry. That's tough. Your father was going to contrate you if Sam hadn't taken you?" Jensen nodded. David tried to help his next words following the silence. "I'm sorry, man, but I'm not sure if I'm exactly following. What does this have to do with the facility break?"

Drake stood up. "No way in hell. I don't believe it." He crouched, placing his hands on his thighs as he leaned toward Jensen. It was like a picture he'd seen before. "Same widow's peak. Think you might be taller though."

*

Luis stood on the edge of the steel beam bridge next to Salvador. "Took them long enough."

The rear of the crashed SUV emerged first as the combined strength of the two trucks hauled it out from the depths. There were multiple bullet holes in the black paint, and the two front tires were flat from the firing. The divers sat in front of their truck's heater, warming themselves with blankets after the icy plunge.

"What do we have?" Salvador yelled from the bridge. They shook their heads.

Salvador ran to the river shore. He reached for the SUV's battered front passenger door handle. Out came gallons of water, drenching his shoes. He swore but cut himself off, remembering why he'd opened the door. Frantically scanning the empty back seats, he then let out the same word, even louder as

177

his stomach shrank.

"No, no, no!" Salvador slammed the door. "Get the search back on, Adán. Every checkpoint needs to go back up immediately. I want a team of officers sent east, and another team sent to Bellark. You and I will take a group back up that mountain."

Before turning to leave, Salvador's eye caught a piece of folded paper in the mud at his feet. *Must have come out with the water.* He reached down, desperate for any lead as if it may be a stand-in for one of the Potentials. He did not bother to dry his hands as he unfolded the paper. It would not have mattered. The paper was already soaked. Most of the inked letters were illegible, almost a foreign language after the river blurred the black ink into an enigma of lost thought. Only at the end of the lost message was a faint signature, the words somewhat protected from the water as they lay in the deepest crease. While he could only read the first name and the first letter of the last, that was all he needed. He found himself straining to understand what David Kingsley had written. He gave up after a few moments, ready to drop the paper to the ground where it could be buried and lost in time just like the words on it. Another second passed. The Chief refolded the damp paper, sliding it into his back pocket.

"Did it have anything?" asked Luis.

Salvador had forgotten Luis was watching him. "Yes."

"What?"

"A name."

Salvador marched up with Luis following behind. He could not understand why he was so frustrated at not being able to read the words on the paper. *What did he say? What did he think?* His motive grew as blurred as the ink. At first, he simply wondered how the knowledge could assist the chase, but he soon found himself consumed with David Kingsley and the identity behind the note. His brain scattered further: *Did they all write one? Did Rylie Banks?*

His mind jumped to Delaney. Had it done so when he was first holding the paper at the river's edge, he would have let it drop and return to the mud. Though the note contended fiercely for his attention, if faced with a choice, he would much prefer Delaney's return rather than the paper's revelation. It did not matter, he told himself again, any thought or intention behind the note. This curiosity would not get him any closer to ending the pursuit. And yet, the note remained in his pocket as his strides quickened on the bridge.

The Chief grew less mindful of the sneers that would come with his plummeting reputation. Salvador had always managed to remain ten steps ahead of the person who was three steps ahead of everyone else, but his concern drifted from the island of self, reputation, and title. All that mattered was completing the mission and returning to Delaney. *I hope she's resting or sleeping. I hope they're safe.*

Discipline and habit had provided the foundation for all his success. He had always been committed to performing any job well, no matter the sacrifice required. He could not meditate on all his sacrifices too often though. Beyond those lied a fear of regret or self-resentment. Salvador burdened himself with the tendency to take a step back and view his life objectively. When he did so, more often than not, the lurking regrets peeked their noses through, forcing Salvador to slam shut the door of the past before they could show their faces.

He knew beyond all doubt that without leaving his son to his former father-in-law, it would have been impossible to become the Chief. Though he'd never expressed it, he was thankful that Sam Lloyd had pled and offered to raise the newborn. This allowed him to stomach the fate of his Potential, and it even allowed him to maintain the white lie to increase his hiring chances with the CD: *"I went to have my Potential contrated at two months."*

He sat in the passenger seat as Luis Adán drove. The passing trees sent him into a bit of haze, the winding and turning road much like his mind.

Since the night of the escape, Salvador had numerous opportunities to regret his decision with Jensen Lloyd, withholding the punishment that fit the crime. It was irresponsible and counterproductive, he thought. But during the incident, he'd been unable to deny the clemency that was so contrary to his policies. He had once been willing to contrate Jensen as a newborn, but in the eyes of the Seventeenth-year, Salvador saw worry, bitterness, and maybe hatred. He saw his Potential, and not for the first time. He wondered, very quietly as if he was trying to sneak a whisper past himself: *Was it guilt?*

Salvador shook his head and shot his body straight up from the slouch, taking his eyes away from the window to keep his mind from straying into the pines. *Don't think that way. He is only a Pote.*

The debacle did not stop as arms of conscience pulled him to the ground. It was not a new experience, having to search out and string together every needed rationale, logic, and narrative to overcome the *nonsense*. But the duel was prolonged like never before. He did not pay mind to how many minutes passed, but the battle drained and battered him. Nevertheless, as he always did, he broke free. *He was and is a Potential.* There was no sense of victory, however. There never was. The only reward he ever earned was a resolution that was all-too-temporary. Sometimes he maintained it for years, and sometimes for much, much less.

A figure darted to the right, dodging and winding through the trees until it scurried away from the road. Salvador followed the deer as far as he could until the land dipped for it to trot down and out of sight. He kept to the trees, appreciating the short five minutes when the light broke through the gray, going beyond itself to fight through the pines and allow the ground to take its color.

Luis felt as though he was sitting next to a different man. *Why does he look so detached? What is he staring at?* Luis had already made a subconscious initiative of distrust, sharing to another officer his recently conceived idea before they left up the mountain. It was almost inevitable that once they completed this assignment, the Chief would be under even harsher scrutiny than from the beginning of this fiasco.

Salvador paid no mind to Adán's repeated glances. *Jensen only sabotaged the facility because of opposition to the CD.* He tried displacing the contrite and farfetched motive that Luis and Delaney suggested. *Could he know one of the escapees?* The thought surfaced like goods from a sinking ship. *Not possible.* He knew well of Sam's sentiments toward the department, how he'd openly objected to Salvador's career path following the death of his daughter. A similar attitude from Jensen would be reasonable. *Nothing more than a protest.* It was almost a prayer, as Salvador was again tossed into his ruminations, thinking about the young Potential he'd created.

The door to the cabin had been left unlocked. A small force had already searched it after the Potentials escaped. The investigators reported that the teens had eaten; the food cans piled in the kitchen trash can. The family portrait hanging in the living room revealed that the property belonged to Rylie Banks' relatives. Salvador removed it from the wall, speaking quietly to himself. "Everything keeps working out for them. Did she do it on purpose." He brought the frame closer to view the freckled girl. "Did she at all expect to escape with her life?"

Luis ran through the front door, interrupting Salvador's train of thought. "Chief! A couple miles down the road, we found an unmapped road. There are tire tracks."

"Did you send anyone down already?"

"Yes, Sir," said Luis.

Salvador tossed the picture of Rylie and her family to the floor, breaking the frame and glass. "She was a decoy."

They drove through the hidden road, jetting to catch up with the first responding officers. Salvador's leg nodded impatiently as the caravan crawled along the narrow path. Neither said it to one another, but both were impressed by the strategy, and even more with Rylie's role.

"Of all those Potes, she was the only one who wasn't going to her Eighteenth. That's why she did it. Had nothing to lose," said Luis. "If only she were as clever on her Prep ESE as she was with us. But she didn't pass, and her mother thought to get the job done during our busiest month." Luis sighed. "Why didn't she just choose the Closing last month? Banks failed last year's PESE. Or even have a little more patience to wait for next month's? We would have had them all."

"Only David Drake has entered his Eighteenth year," said Salvador, seeming to dismiss Luis' previous comments. "He killed all of those facility workers. Pretty sure he got that guard outside. And there's that clerk to figure out too, so we can get him long-term."

"You fired the facility manager, correct?"

"Of course." He continued with his previous thought, "Still, even if Drake is the main threat, we cannot let any of the others reach their Eighteenth. We have until midnight."

"Sir, I have a suggestion."

Luis' tone hooked Salvador. From the sudden firmness, the Chief knew the young man had been meditating on what he was about to say. Luis glanced at Salvador, then focused again on the narrow road. His confidence did not diminish after seeing Salvador's skepticism. On the contrary, it grew.

*

"The first time I saw him in person—from what I can remember—was at the facility two nights ago. It wasn't until I gave my name when he started to act differently. I was so confused why he didn't have me put into cuffs or something worse. When we left to find you, Grandpa told me everything."

They were speechless at the bizarre news. David especially ached for his friend as Jensen struggled to find closure in the binding truth. If there were any words to console, they were unsearchable in that moment. Jensen's only counselor was the open desert he stared out into from the window.

None of the runaways, including Drake, ever questioned if Jensen was still their ally. If anything, they felt they could trust the new acquaintance all the more since he traded blood for loyalty. "Thanks for helping us out," said Drake. Jensen never looked from the glass, but he gave a single nod as he continued to bite on his lip.

"I never wanted Jensen to know of his father's, umm, my former son-in-law's life choice," Sam said from the front. "Sal wouldn't return my calls after my daughter passed, after the memorial. I had my ideas of what he was thinking. I never approved of his career route, but I'm grateful he left me with Jensen."

"I'm ashamed he's my father. But I'm not his son." Jensen arose and walked to the passenger seat next to Sam. "Looks like we all escaped him." Jensen opened the glove compartment. He almost pulled out the gun but stopped to not frighten the others. "I don't care who he is. He's not touching any of you." He closed the compartment.

They were a few miles from entering the city.

Some finally drifted to sleep, even Drake, much to the surprise of David, Mia, and Jensen who were still awake. His opinion of the new acquaintances seemed clear; Drake was unwilling to drop his guard if he perceived the slightest threat.

The RV continued through the mile-wide opening between the walls. They were erected during the secession when it appeared the South might be making an advancement; a costly, unfinished project for no real threat as it turned out.

The hulking skyscrapers seemed to loom higher than they had before the Closing. Massive, windowed bodies breathed heavily over the dwarfed RV, looking ready to devour the small piece of metal and the passengers inside. Their experience out in the desert and foothills seemed somehow outside the reality of Bellark. However, in the moment of reentering, the two worlds became stitched into one, an old cloth with a new.

Sam said, "Media and everyone else might still believe you're dead I think. Nothing on the radio and still no checkpoint here."

David and Mia were staring out the side window, and the countless building eyes stared back. The architectural achievements of the city thrust David and Mia further from any sense of ease to join the others in sleep; the grim irony of progress was haunting and mocking.

"Looks like we made it back just in time," Sam said, looking out his window to the lane going the opposite direction. Heading east was a caravan of department and police vehicles, too many to number. "Keep your heads down," he commanded David and Mia.

"What's going on?" David said.

"I'm not sure," said Sam. "Maybe they found out you're alive; it was only a matter of time. I don't think we have much to worry about either way. If that is the case, it looks like the CD called most of their forces outside the city." The brigade of vehicles jetted by and distanced itself with each second.

The trek to the edge of downtown unexpectedly went without difficulty. It was the kind of ease that unnerves, feeling as if the lurking predator quiets its steps before attacking. The RV steadied to stop at a four-way intersection. A contration facility stood on the nearest corner, the building appropriately labeled for its purpose: '*Womb and Infant,*' it read.

Sam would never forget the building, a grim reminder of the meeting place where Salvador relinquished guardianship of Jensen. He remembered the old debate, and the legislation and argument that repeated on the news for some time: *"The long-term costs of having a Potential with incalculable intelligence remains unpredictable; thus, carriers may freely contrate any Potential in the womb or as an infant."* Sam stopped working near downtown at this pivot in legislation. If eighteen years ago, infant contrations were as accessible as womb contrations today, available each day of the week rather than limited to a monthly Closing, Jensen would be dead.

"It's weird to be here," said Mia, peering broodingly at the passing traffic. "Coming back to the place that didn't want us." David was ready to respond, but Mia arose immediately, holding her stomach as she again hastened for the restroom. He first presumed it was nausea from the thought she'd shared; however, after yet another trip, he thought the canned food from the night was striking again.

Thirty minutes passed, and the roof of Glenn Haven Secondary School surfaced about two blocks ahead. David looked upon the edifice, studying it with a renewed perspective: It no longer held the same power, having already pronounced its verdict on his life. Duty fulfilled. David would not have to return, he knew, but this did not provide relief. Faces came to mind, faces from other schools, Bellark, and the country. *How many more?*

Jensen turned around from the passenger seat. "Looks like we'll be celebrating your Eighteenth here after all. Tomorrow."

David opened his mouth to speak, but Sam shushed him and turned the radio up. "I think we have something."

"We bring to you an update on the March Runaways." The speaker volume rose. "All of the Potentials, except Rylie Banks, are at large. The information previously released early this morning was incorrect. Only Rylie Banks is confirmed contrated following the wreckage on Highway 38. Again, if you are able to provide information on the whereabouts of this group, please contact the Contration Department or the police. Thank you." Abbi, Drake, and Bobby had jolted awake as if never asleep once Sam turned up the broadcast. Huddling close to the front, they looked to one another with renewed fear.

"Looks like we survived," Drake said. "Again."

Bobby stepped back from the radio. His head turned rapidly as he stared out the window, quickly recognizing the familiar city. The houses, the stores, and the parks; Bobby knew the home he believed was still his. "Will I get to see my mom?" he asked, desperation tinging his plea.

"You don't want to see her!" Mia snapped. "None of us should want to see our carriers." The recent broadcast had taken a predictable toll on the physically unwell girl. On her forehead stood beads of sweat as dark circles surrounded her blue eyes. Her hair had absorbed much of the perspiration as well, lying damply against her scalp.

Abbi's first instinct was to fend for Bobby, but Mia's appearance struck her. "Mia, oh my god. You're sweating." She walked toward her. "Let me help. Take your sweater off and let's lie you down."

Mia batted Abbi's hands away. "Stop."

"You're dripping," Abbi said. "Please, just let me feel your forehead."

Mia reluctantly allowed the gesture after Abbi's cold hand became a relief to her burning face. David had been awake all that time with Mia but was too preoccupied with the city to notice her deteriorating condition. "Well, you're definitely feverish," Abbi said. "You need to lie down and rest."

Mia soon complied with Abbi's gentle instructions, walking toward the available bed in the back. Bobby's eyes followed her as she stepped slowly with Abbi's guiding hand on her back. Confused and hurt from Mia's aggression, he was stifled, unable to speak another concern to the others. He seemed, for the first time, unsure of those around him.

*

They had combed the meadow thoroughly, from the first blade of grass to the maple tree. The footprints told of the several that had been present earlier. There was even an apple core on the ground near the trees, nourishment for one of the Potentials. The abandoned truck was empty of anything that could have provided Salvador and his team with a lead. However, there was another pair of tire tracks, no older than a few hours. They led out the road, opposite from the green-cloaked path where the CD had emerged and arrived.

"They found another ride," Salvador said aloud to himself, but Luis overheard.

"You think somebody's helping them?"

"It looks like it . . . Somehow."

"True," Luis said. "They didn't have two cars."

"They did," Salvador said, remembering Rylie. "This is their third." His disbelief grew at their maneuvering success. "These Potes are something," he admitted. It was a quick thought, but he wondered again how this might affect his position. He wished right then to forsake and abandon it all, regardless of any current criticism that existed or scrutiny that would follow. But he remembered Delaney. After, he resolved. *Finish the job. Then once this is all done . . .*

With this resolution, Salvador considered Luis Adán's proposal carefully. Luis had exhaustively researched the protocols, the national laws, and had committed relevant clauses and legislation to memory, perhaps to the same extent as the Chief. Though his strategy was unprecedented, the situation at hand might justify it. "It does not have to be permanent, but present circumstances could permit it," Luis had told Salvador to persuade. Salvador had considered it during the drive, but even if it were possible, it would undoubtedly have to be a last resort. Such an advance could have lasting effects. What starts as temporary or situational can sneakily become permanent, the Chief knew. *The very reason for our department.*

Whether the Potentials were miles out of Bellark or in another state already, Salvador worried his margin was thinning, soon to vanish entirely. His position as Chief could not survive the remaining Potentials reaching their Eighteenth; he would be terminated or forced to resign. Perhaps he could remain in a demoted department position, but now was not the time to gamble. He pictured Delaney once more, deep asleep with her hands resting atop her stomach.

Salvador came to a decision. "Tell them I'm coming on."

*

Anybody in the neighborhood would be quick to call authorities if they knew who the RV held. While most residents could find a qualm with the government, they still found it natural to trust, even praise it. If anything, the small concentration of opposition came from small university towns, these populations often consisting of those who slimly passed the ESE.

David's stomach had folded inside upon arriving to the suburban neighborhood he'd known as home just days before. It would have been his last choice for a place of sanctuary. *My carriers did this.*

Jensen and Sam knew hiding at their home would by no means be pleasant for David. But they were more certain he would shelve his conflict to take care of the others. Sam had brainstormed for any alternative while on the road but arrived at nothing; to keep on the drive when only a day or days remained for all their Eighteenth years would be a greater gamble with the

CD again taking to the streets.

David could feel as though a shadow or ghost was falling over him as he looked at each house, associating each one as his own. Every front door swallowed him and threw him inside to the dining room table where he last ate with his carriers and sister. *This isn't a family dinner,* he remembered yelling.

"This is a nice house," said Abbi as the wheels came to the driveway.

David's bitter accusations toward his mother and father stopped. Abbi's commandment broke through instead: "*Keep us alive.*" The northwest street that would eventually lead to his old home brought with it another timely reminder. *I made my decision her too.*

Jensen hopped out to open and shut the gate quickly. The others rose from their seats and helped Sam unload the RV, scurrying quickly into the garage through the back door. Sam grabbed his gun from the glove compartment, as did Jensen. The others were shocked to see that they'd each had one hidden the entire time. "You never know," Sam said. "Wait here for a sec. I have to run in and disarm our security system."

After struggling to close the stubborn side door with one hand, Jensen set his gun inside the nearby toolbox drawer. Drake almost went to help him with the unmovable door, but Jensen got it to budge and slam shut from all his strength. "It's been like this for years." He laughed the awkward looking moment off.

"Sure," said Drake.

"Come on in," Sam said, peeking his head into the garage from the inside hallway.

Jensen led the way, and the others followed inside. Not one of them, other than David, had been acquainted with such a grand house, fascinated as heads rotated all around.

"Welcome to our home," Sam said. "Make yourselves comfortable and help yourselves to food and drinks. All I have are snacks, but I'll make a food run here soon. Most importantly, stay inside. The neighbors won't take to you as warmly."

"You can really get into trouble for this," Drake said.

Sam grinned. "An old man needs to break out of the

monotony sometimes, right?"

The snacks mellowed their rumbling stomachs. Abbi and Bobby fell asleep on the living room couch. Bobby had sprawled out, and Abbi sat upright in one corner, while Drake and Mia crashed on the mattresses in the guest room. Only David and Jensen kept awake in the living room after Sam left with Jensen's truck to fill up on gas for precaution, as well as to buy take-out.

David's heart eased a bit as the minutes passed, seeming to dissociate somewhat from being so close to his home, the scene of his disillusionment. The two friends reclined in their chairs as the afternoon wore away to evening. It was reminiscent of their routine after coming home from school, though the stress of schoolwork and exams seemed laughable compared to their current predicament. David let out a large breath that was due since returning to the northwest.

"Don't want to wake them up," Jensen joked, pointing to Abbi and Bobby. "They crashed out fast."

"They need it."

"What about you?" said Jensen. "When are you gonna get some sleep?"

"When we're safe."

"David, you are safe."

"Yeah, I guess. But I think it's smart that one of us stays awake to keep alert, right?" David's glance went to Abbi. "Can't drop our guard."

Jensen saw the quick pivot of his eyes. "She's pretty. Probably made it a little easier to save her from the facility, huh?"

"I had to," said David defensively. "You would have done the same if you saw her."

"How much do you like her?"

"What?"

Jensen smirked, knowing how uncomplicated David was.

David said, "Okay, she's pretty, I'll admit . . . That's not why I saved her though. What's it all matter anyway? Right now, I more so like the idea of living."

"You pass your Eighteenth come midnight. What about then?" He figured that prying and poking might distract David while having some fun with him.

David chuckled. "I don't know, man. Can't exactly get too lost in that right now. She is cool though."

"I think she may think the same about you. There's a reason why she came running when we met up at Nod. She was quite a bit quicker than Mia. Not saying she's throwing herself at you by any means, but I wouldn't doubt if there was some interest."

David said, shrugging, "We'll see. She passes her Eighteenth last of all of us, on the Twenty-Eighth. She has to get there before anything else." David had not spoken to Jensen about Olivia's contration in some time. He wasn't sure if it was duty to himself or to his friend that prompted him. "I told her about my contration. I told her everything about Olivia."

"You told her?" Jensen could not reason it. "You barely know her, and you haven't spoken of that—"

"—in forever. I know," David said, choking up. "I know what you always thought, man. I knew you wanted me to do it different. I pretty much had to beg you to use your truck to take her."

"David." Jensen was quick to try and steady him. "What's done is done. You can't beat yourself up about that. You were afraid."

"I was," said David, looking toward the ceiling. "I was afraid. But I knew what I was doing."

Jensen could only suffer with David, unable to figure out why he was confessing this now. "This isn't doing you any good. Look at yourself. You're exhausted enough from the day. You shouldn't be consumed by this right now."

"No, no. I should." David kept his voice low. "I should, Jensen. It's why I have to keep her and all of them alive. I can't tell you exactly why or how my carriers contrated me, but if there's any way to come back from what I did, what I asked Olivia to do, it's to keep these people alive." He sat up to lean closer. "Because that's what they are. That's what my child was. That's what I am. You wonder what made me help Abbi and the others? It's that truth. She looked just like Olivia when she stepped into that facility six months ago. And through it all, I knew the truth. The voices, noise, and clamor that would try and convince me otherwise, even now, were once successful. But that girl asleep on that couch right there helped me admit and finally see what I always knew and saw.

"I'm not telling you this to sulk," David said relieved. "I'm saying this to let you know that you were right. You never said it, but you were right in what you felt. If I would have asked for your advice, we both know you would have said not to. No question. I couldn't handle that then. I can now."

Jensen could only nod. For the past six months, he'd found himself caught between his attitude toward the Contration Department and his best friend's choices. The past year was a rebuilding of a broken David following his contration. To address the matter directly then could have provoked another collapse, yanking a cloth from a set table. Almost verbatim, David had spoken the words—the realization he had wished for him but also the ideal Jensen had long found himself unable to articulate.

Jensen sat upright and said, "It takes a lot to say everything you just did. I'm proud of you, man." He was hesitant to introduce the next topic weighing on his mind. It might unearth more buried feelings on David's end, but he reassured himself that there was no time more appropriate than now, while the others still slept. It would be another brick added to a rising, swaying tower. But it was David's self-assuredness that convinced Jensen he would not collapse. "You know why you're here, don't you, David?"

He rubbed his drowsy eyes. "Yeah. I think so. Not sure how, but it didn't take me very long to figure it wasn't coincidence."

"I saw them." Jensen agonized to speak, thorns in every word that rose through his throat. "Outside your house the night you were taken. Your carriers let the CD take you. I saw them both. Your mom. She was a mess and tried to stop them, but your dad held her back. He wanted you gone."

David's eyes yielded no tears.

Jensen said, "I have my ideas, but it wasn't an accident. It

191

was that same van that picks up any other Potential."

"Job loss. Or debt," David said lifelessly. "Job loss was Drake's guess. Could have been both. Job loss to put them under the line, and debt to continue sending Penelope through school."

"That's my guess too. The only other option is some elaborate loophole. Your dad may have found some way to pull a string with the line of work he's involved . . . or was involved in."

"That wouldn't make sense." David's forehead wrinkled. "If he wanted me gone before, he wouldn't have waited for me to try and test well on the exam." David broke the blank stare, a mixture of awe and confusion. "He wanted to leave me with a chance. What kind of chance, I'm not sure. Even passing the exam with a 5 wouldn't get me any scholarships, which would have made it difficult for them to support me if their finances were on the rocks. Whatever the case, he wanted me gone. He hasn't come forward yet to get me out of this, so it's pointless to keep wondering."

Jensen could not see David's tremble in the dimming dusk light. If his rage had been audible, the cursing and judgment would have disturbed Jensen and woken all from their sleep. David was aware of his past actions, but though he'd acknowledged and pardoned himself from that guilt, he declared the verdict for his father on seemingly different grounds.

"Bastard," David uttered aloud without realizing it. Jensen listened closely, keeping his eyes on the blank television, able to make out a faint silhouette of David's reflection. He continued, but this time intending Jensen to hear. "He wanted me gone."

Jensen nodded.

"I should have seen it coming. Post-secondary school? Can't believe I thought that's what my carriers were talking about. At least there's no mystery to it all as I first thought."

"The others know, right? All of them?"

"Yeah," said David. "Took me a while to bring up at first. I was scared, you know? They got it out of me though. Drake sort of helped narrow it down. My carriers didn't want me, just like their carriers didn't want them. Just like I didn't want mine."

The last statement allowed David to reduce his father's judgment somewhat, but it was subconscious.

A loud clank from down the hall interrupted. Sam barged through the back garage door, walking down the hallway with bags full of dinner. He couldn't open the door quietly without dropping everything. Abbi and Bobby jerked awake when the door thudded against the wall. Forgetting that most were asleep, Sam announced, "Food's here!"

Drake and Mia emerged from the guest room not long after the preferred disturbance of food's arrival. Sam set out plates, cups, and napkins at the dining room table much too small to accommodate everyone comfortably. Jensen brought out a few extra chairs and jammed them in tightly. They sat shoulder to shoulder but took no mind as their gazes fixed on the food before them.

"Who's hungry?" said Sam.

"Bring it on." Bobby was eager, pulling out some chuckles from the others.

It did not take long for everyone to inhale all the greasy goodness. Jensen and Sam had not eaten since the diner last midnight, but their hunger was childlike in comparison to the others. The burger establishment offered a multitude of combinations and hearty side items. Sam seemed to have ordered it all, ranging from burger combinations to deep-fried appetizers. Mia said that she had been a vegetarian for over a year and claimed she would only eat french fries and the like, but it was only moments before she reached in the bag for a chicken sandwich. No one judged. Abbi was surprised to see Mia have such an appetite with her current fever. Her glow also returned, giving Abbi the impression of a steady recovery.

"That was so good," Mia said, satisfied.

"I guess you're feeling better. Just don't share that recipe with anyone." Sam winked.

Abbi arose. "Let us clean up for you."

"Oh no, please. You all have had a long day," Sam said.

"C'mon. Let us earn our keep," Drake said. "We've all had a long day."

The four boys cleared off and wiped down the table in a matter of minutes. Mia offered to help Abbi with the dishes, but it was still only Abbi after she disappeared to the guest room or restroom for some time. The stack of dirty dishes was not too tall, but David figured it wouldn't hurt to help.

"Go relax! You haven't even taken a nap yet," Abbi said as David grabbed a wet plate to dry with a towel.

"This is relaxing," he said. "Washing dishes is therapeutic for me. This is where a guy with dyslexia thrives."

"If you insist." She was pleased to have David's company, even hopeful Mia would not return to take his spot. Though Abbi could admit she grew more drawn to him each day, this delight was reactively unordinary.

Sam turned on a movie as Jensen brought out pillows and blankets for those sprawled on the floor. When David joined, he felt himself fading as he bundled up in a blanket. He scanned the room as if it was one final measure; Abbi, Drake, Bobby, and Mia. None of them had yet removed their guards so much as now, almost relaxed. He glanced over at Abbi and saw a quiet smile. He'd seen her smile and laugh in the SUV during their cabin watch, but this was of a different essence. With an eased heart, David closed his eyes and drifted into sleep.

Most of the others did not last too long either and went off to bed, including Sam. Nobody wanted to wake David from the deep sleep, all realizing he only got two hours at the cabin. Jensen had fallen asleep for most of the movie but woke for the end. He had seen the old western several times as it was Sam's favorite, and his fatigue added to the disinterest. Abbi managed to stay awake for the whole film. She was the type to have difficulty going to sleep at night if she napped. Despite traveling the past two days with little food and rest, her sleep pattern remained stubbornly the same. After the movie, she and Jensen continued to watch some television shows.

Jensen said from across the room, "What part of Bellark are you from?"

Abbi looked down at David to see if he would be disturbed. "Southwest," she replied, assured that the quiet conversation would add no hindrance to his rest. "Wombelle."

"Wombelle, huh? So Wombelle Secondary School. I think our school competes with yours in sports."

"They do," Abbi said. "I used to be on the soccer team. We played Glenn Haven twice a season."

"Hmm. Maybe we've seen each other in the past. I used to go to some of the soccer games. A girl I dated played. We didn't last very long, though, so I only went to a few."

"Yeah, maybe."

"David came with me a couple times. Maybe you guys saw each other." Jensen thought about it. "Ehh, never mind. I doubt it."

Abbi tried to figure out the retraction. "Why's that?"

"I don't think he would have forgotten you."

Abbi blushed. She immediately glanced over to the floor to make sure David did not hear, paranoid her reddening would be plain if he were awake. The living room lights were off, however, and the limited television light made it difficult to read facial expressions. Abbi stopped to wonder why she was so concerned. The night before, she'd openly exchanged flirting banter with him, and he had made his attraction to her clear then. Now, she felt exposed, more vulnerable as if an unbeknownst layer of her guard had been peeled back.

She played ignorant. "What do you mean?"

Jensen saw through her bluff. "What do you mean, what do I mean? All I'm saying is I don't think David would forget the face that compelled him to save a girl he didn't know."

"I was helpless, and they were going to contrate me. I know he thinks I'm pretty. He told me. Still, David would have done it for any other. It could have been Mia he saw first. It just happened to be me."

"He said you were pretty? Atta boy. But you're probably right," said Jensen. "And maybe he offered to do dishes tonight hoping to spend some extra time with Mia. A little cranky, but she's for sure a looker. Makes one wonder why he doesn't stay awake in the same room with her as she sleeps." He showed a smirk that only the dark could see.

Without a moment to process his true intent, Abbi felt a stab of jealousy. *Mia has hardly talked with him at all*, she thought. *David should not have any interest in her, even if Mia were gorgeous with her tall stature, lush hair, and sapphire blue eyes. He'd never commented on her attractiveness, and she'd never shared her dreams and aspirations with David. She's a little chubby too.* Realizing where her thoughts were sprinting, Abbi yanked them back like a barking dog on a leash.

Jensen arose. "Well, good night. I'm hittin' the sack." He was well aware of the effect his words were having, just as he intended.

"Should we wake up David so he can sleep in a bed?" Abbi said.

"I think he'll be all right. He's been out for a while. My guess is he's nice and comfortable. Anyway . . . 'Night."

Abbi tried to continue watching TV, but she couldn't refrain from looking back and forth between the screen and David. Never did she imagine herself developing any serious interest for him. She could admit to herself that he was charming in an offbeat sense in his shy awkwardness, which made him more entertaining to flirt with, but now she had to acknowledge the new attachment and possessiveness.

She rose in frustration and paced to the kitchen to get some water. Thirstier than she'd realized, she finished the beverage in seconds. Still irritated that the sleeping boy had her so distracted, she set the plastic cup down carelessly on the counter's edge. It teetered and fell to the tile floor, clanking and bopping to disrupt the house's silence. "No," Abbi whispered.

She hopped down from the counter and snatched the cup, then crouched frozen, hoping the clattering had not disturbed anyone. Her old home had thin walls, so a sound in the kitchen might travel to the furthest room if it was loud enough. Sam's house was significantly more upscale than her own, however. Those sleeping in the bedrooms were probably undisturbed, but she was not as sure of David in the living room.

"You playing an instrument in here?" David emerged into the kitchen, rubbing his eyes.

His instant, ghost-like entrance frightened her at first. "I'm sorry for waking you." She stood up with a hand on her chest.

"No, no. You didn't wake me," he said. "I actually woke up because I'm thirsty. I ate a lot of food but didn't drink much. Too much salt. I heard the commotion as I was coming here to get water."

"You think anyone else heard?"

"No way. Everyone is probably out from the long day. This house is big too. Thick walls."

"That's what I thought. About the walls." She fumbled over her words, hoping he didn't notice her nervousness. "Let me grab you some water." She gathered herself in those seconds as she turned around for a glass in the cabinet.

"Thanks."

David's calm allowed for Abbi to relax. The incident under the maple tree flashed into her mind. Next, the conversation during their evening cabin patrol resounded as well. *He's only human*, she thought, remembering David for the flawed young man he was. She looked at the digital clock above the oven. "A few more minutes. For you and Mia."

David's eyes followed hers. 11:56 p.m. "Yep. And then life begins." He caught himself. "I'm sorry. I didn't mean to say . . . I didn't want to say it like that."

Abbi handed him the glass of water she had filled. "It's okay. We have to retrain ourselves."

"Not you. Not as much, at least."

"Yes, even me. I didn't speak up until all this happened. I'll have their words and rhetoric stuck in my head for a while."

"Yeah, but still. It's different for you. Probably harder for me over the others too." David scratched his head. "When you were asleep on our way to Nod, Drake said he wanted to take the blame for shooting that one guard in the parking lot. The one I killed. He's willing to take on even more punishment to cover for me."

"He is?"

"Yeah," David said just as surprised as when Drake first

told him after fleeing the cabin. "But don't tell him I told you. I'm going to try to talk him out of it."

Abbi was still trying to come to believe it, leaning against the counter so that she and David were almost shoulder to shoulder. "I never would have thought that he . . . Wow. Even I sold him short there."

"But you still thought he deserved life as much as anybody." David shook his head. "I really am screwed up for what I believed."

"Take it easy on yourself, David," she said. "It's what you believed, but not anymore."

"What I said during our watch at the cabin got you pretty upset. Rightly so. Hasn't even been a full day since."

"Who cares if it hasn't been a full day? Yeah, I was angry. That's why I spoke up, and look where it got you. You're actually thinking now."

"I know." His voice was quiet, but its poignancy cut the silence of the kitchen. "But that doesn't change . . . my contration."

"How many times do I need to say it. That's not you anymore." She lifted David's face to meet hers. "Your child's gone, okay. A victim of a young, scared, and ignorant boy. Your responsibility, yes. Your choice to have our country as your teacher, no. We don't always get to choose which pools we're thrown in, but we do have the choice to get out." She addressed the confusion on his face. "Figure of speech. Come on, you writer." David's smirk broke through his seriousness. "You saved my life. No wrong can stop the next right."

He looked down to find Abbi's hand grasping his. "I couldn't say no again."

Abbi glanced at the clock. "Happy birthday, David." She leaned and pulled him in, resting the cool of her cheek against his neck. "You're safe now. Forever. Let's get some sleep."

David turned as she headed down the hall. "You will be too," he said louder for her to hear, losing mind of anyone asleep. The last glimpse was of curling lips, rising high enough to see even as she disappeared into the darkening hall. Once again, she looked like Olivia.

February 27th

The yolk drained from the broken egg, but the yellow seemed endless as it spread throughout the frying pan. David took the spatula over the others until the white in the pan was no more. The last egg would not seem to give way, however, no matter the pressure and force from the edge of the spatula.

"Anyone want a cup coffee?" Sam called out to those at the dining room table. He reached over David for the cupboard above and grabbed a few mugs. "Do you all drink coffee?" he said as David kept stirring the eggs.

"I can't have any. Won't be good for her." Mia faced them from her seat at the table. "I'll take some orange juice though, please," she said sweetly and grateful as if the girl from the days before was replaced by another.

"Sure thing. Anyone else want orange juice?" Bobby and Abbi took him up on the offer for the juice, but their backs were turned. Sam poured the coffee into three other mugs, the first one being for himself. "I probably shouldn't have given Jensen a sip of my coffee when he was younger, but I thought he'd hate it. Told him it would stunt his growth. Ha. That claim didn't hold up for very long."

David divided the scrambled eggs on to different plates. He did not remember giving Sam his specific request but grabbed the mug of coffee in front. It tasted different from the other times he drank; the bitterness was unusual, a similar taste as if he just bit his lip or tongue. When Mia and Abbi giggled together, he swore it was because they saw his twinging reaction to the blood-tasting coffee. He turned around, and there Mia was, laughing and more chipper than ever. It was almost unfathomable to imagine how Abbi might respond once she reached her Eighteenth. If she had been smiling this much, the joy to come would be incomparable, he thought.

David grabbed as many plates with his hands as he walked out of the kitchen for the dining room "You need a hand, David?" Jensen said, emerging from the hallway.

Knock! Knock! Knock!

The laughter and talking silenced. David never turned around to see their reactions. His sight set to the front door behind Jensen. "Stop!" David whispered out as Jensen turned and neared the door. He peeked through the door hole, turning back to David with a blank stare. "Who is it?" David asked as he walked forward for whatever reason. "Don't open it," he said, but Jensen grabbed the knob against his request. Strangely, David stopped admonishing him, walking closer with hands now empty of the breakfast plates. Jensen let go of the knob and moved out of the way as David reached his arm out.

The door wedged open as David gently pulled one inch at a time. The light creaked through first. It was golden hour, though somehow the time went beyond David. He did not stop to think about how the morning soared away, or how the sun completely overcame the clouds. These were hardly even a backdrop in his mind at this point. Her scent came through after the light. David swung the door open at once.

"I had a feeling I might find you here," said Olivia. Her back was to the light, so it was difficult to find the amber in her eyes. "I'm glad you're safe."

"How did you know where to find me?" David stepped to the foot of the door entry, in both disbelief and acceptance. "Olivia?" She looked down and hid her face. "Liv, come inside." He crouched a bit to try to find her eyes again. "Just come inside."

"You need to leave, David." She looked up, but now he had a harder time recognizing the face.

"What?"

"You're not safe."

David tried to take a step toward her, but his leg would not lift. "Olivia, I'm alive now." He was able to at least reach out a hand and put it on her shoulder. "I know you're scared, but I'm okay now. Come on in, and we can talk." She leaped from the porch into the house, and threw her arms around him, crying into his left ear. "It's okay. It' okay," he tried to console.

"I'm so sorry," she wept.

An agony came into David's right side. He looked down beneath his ribs. Olivia's hand pushed the remaining purple through the syringe and into his body. He stumbled back after she let go. No matter his efforts, he could not pull the needle from his skin as if it was a part of him. And that's what it became. The syringe turned into the color of his olive skin until it completely sunk into his side. Olivia watched him, continuing to weep as she stepped backward for the door.

David turned every which way, looking for Jensen or any of the others. The entire house was empty as darkness started to overcome the walls and suffocate any effort from the sun outside. "Olivia!" he called out one last time before she shut the door. He could no longer see himself or anything but the black collapsing around, somehow growing darker each second as if there was a black beyond black. Desperate, he reached for his side for the syringe once more. His hand found the cylinder shape, but it was inside his skin. David gave a deathly clench with his fingers and nails. He yelled louder, but not for a name or help. He clawed through, pulling away and at his skin. The warmth of his blood spread over his hand and arm as he went further into his side. With the syringe in grasp, he pulled.

A brilliant light escaped his side, the brightest he had ever seen, spilling over his entire body and illuminating the room. But it was no longer Sam's living room. Before he could make out the location and features of the mysterious place, he could no longer see again, but this time not from blindness. "David!" It was a union of a few strange voices.

"David!" he heard again, but now it was a familiar, singular calling. No matter the effort to widen his eyes, David could only see a blurred image. "Are you okay, man?"

"Turn the light off!" David said hysterically.

"There's no light on," Jensen said, aware that his friend was shaken. "Here. Take a drink of water. You're soaked in sweat."

David's clarity returned. The ambiguous shape soon took the form of his friend. He took a drink first. "Jensen, I saw her. I saw Olivia," he said, nervously scanning the room he had fallen asleep in last night.

"What happened?" he said. "It was like you were screaming for your life."

David did not know what to make of everything, how to process all of what he just the dreamt. *Or was it a nightmare?* "She said I'm not safe."

Jensen nodded, a bit unsure himself now. "After you gather yourself, come downstairs. Was going to wake you up after."

"After what?"

"It's better you just come down and see," Jensen said solemnly.

David went to the bathroom first. Everyone should be up by now, he thought, but it was only the running sink he heard in the quiet house. He lifted his shirt, looking over and feeling his unharmed and unscathed right side. A couple of times, he swore he felt the syringe, but it was just his bottom rib. David shuffled downstairs, not sure what to presume of anything at this point.

Everyone was awake and gathered, eyes glued to the TV. The volume was low, which seemed strange with such an audience. David looked at the screen and the airing news station. Abbi leaned forward at full attention, her bliss from the night before gone. The familiarity of her current expression did not bring any closure either. It was as if he were looking at her through the facility window again.

"What's going on?" he asked.

All turned toward his voice. Abbi opened her mouth but then closed it and pointed to the screen. He walked closer.

Sam pointed the remote and rewound the recorded segment from the morning. Various faces appeared on the screen. The rewinding words were inaudible, but the faces were unfortunately familiar. Sam pressed another button once it was back at the beginning. Diane Culver was the first to appear. David remembered her last national broadcast with Salvador Goode a few nights before. The introduction she gave did not steady David, though he had not expected positive tidings. "Early this morning, Chief of the Bellark CD released this statement."

David and Jensen glanced to one another. It was clear his friend had already seen what came next. The picture cut to Salvador Goode at a press conference, again wearing the same scarlet tie as in the last interview. He sat at a long table, joined by Luis Adán and other prominent officials of the Contration Department. Salvador's face had sunken since the last broadcast, cheekbones sharp enough to cut. By contrast, Luis Adán appeared rested and eager.

Salvador lifted the notes in front of him. "Three nights ago, six contrated-selected Potentials escaped from a facility outside of Bellark. During this escape, these criminals murdered four innocent facility employees and one civilian. Additionally, they've inflicted damage on state property and city infrastructures, such as the Huffman River Bridge off of Highway 38. Of the remaining Potentials, three of the five have officially entered their Eighteenth year: Mia Day, David Drake, and David Kingsley. Traditionally, this would render them alive with legal living status, and thus, no contration may be applied." Salvador looked into the camera. "However, after careful assessment of the destructive, reckless, and cruel actions of all these Potes, the government and laws of this country will no longer recognize any of these fugitives as alive with human rights or personhood.

"Carriers chose these Potentials for contration because they were predicted to jeopardize the lives of the carriers and society alike. As evident from recent events, the fugitive Potentials have proven this notion true. Therefore, this country will never

204

extend life to Mia Day, David Drake, David Kingsley, Robert Reynolds, and Abigail Rosario. With permission from the federal cabinet, the Bellark CD will pursue these individuals until all the contrations are realized. Further, anyone who assists or harbors these Potentials will be arrested and tried for criminal activity, or if necessary, incapacitated by force for retaliation against the authorities. Thank you."

The house took a different form in that moment, contracting and reshaping itself so that all felt like animals in a cage. Abbi wiped another tear from her face. Drake clenched the couch pillow in both trembling hands. Jensen stared down at the floor, looking almost guilty as if he issued Salvador Goode's verdict. Mia had the most neutral reaction, a blank and void presence as if there was no life to her, or ever had been.

The program cut back to Diane Culver. "This verdict has indeed shocked our city and the nation. Many people have already spoken out in support of Chief Goode's decision after observing the destruction and death the March Runaways have inflicted in the course of their escape. However, a small minority has voiced opposition. Some are protesting outside the Bellark headquarters downtown as we speak. To ease the nation, our president has released a statement in support of Goode.

"I quote, 'Chief Salvador Goode's decision was a difficult but necessary verdict. The Contration Department was founded to relieve our nation of exactly the destructive circumstances these escaped Potentials have created. It was created to give people a choice regarding whether to raise a Potential. As the fugitives continue in their evasion, our nation is set back to what we used to be, and what the system was designed to eradicate: instability, chaos, and the stripping of human rights, women's rights, and free will. I implore our citizens to support Chief Salvador Goode's verdict as I do,' end quote."

Sam turned off the television.

Mia said coldly, "That's it, I guess. We're all going to die."

"Don't say that," said Jensen, desperately searching for a solution in his head.

"You just heard what he said." Mia stared at a stain on the carpet. "They're not going to stop until they get all of us."

Drake spoke from where he sat. "I'm sorry, you guys." Everyone's attention went to the ashamed voice. "This is my fault. I killed all those men at the facility. The old clerk too. David shot that guy in self-defense, but I – I wanted to kill them, even if I didn't have to. Just like Goode said. This is my fault."

"It's not," David said. "They would have figured out something else to get us if they didn't use those men who died as an excuse. This is their fault, not ours, and not yours."

David's efforts of persuasion failed to ease him. Face downcast, Drake trudged away to the guest room. There was no slamming door, but a few minutes later they heard a muffled scream. The pillow over his mouth heard it in full.

"See," Mia said, now unsteady. "Even he knows it's over for us."

Abbi became impatient with her fatalism. "He's not giving up. He just needs a moment."

Mia walked away with her arms crossed, her whisper increasing in turbulence. "Should have already done it." She left down the hall as the verdict replay in her mind, over, and over.

Bobby only had one question and concern in all the unfolding hysteria. "Can you just take me back to my mom?" David saw Abbi struggle to respond, so he volunteered himself. "Sorry, Bobby. We can't. The CD isn't allowing any of us to go back to our carriers." Bobby kept silent, but began to mildly tremble where he sat, yet unbeknownst and undetected by the others.

Those left in the living room tried strategizing what to do next, but none could think of anything new from what they've suggested in the past. "Turning yourself in will do no good anyway," Sam said in reply to David's insistence. "They made you a Potential forever. Any bartering that could have ever been is off the table." Bobby's mind was far removed from the discussion as he continued to think of his mother.

Jensen spoke first after they reached the dead end. "We could go to the South," he said the proposal without enthusiasm.

David turned to Jensen, unamused at the attempt of a dry joke. Yet Jensen's enduring silence made it clear that the statement was no jest. While not convinced, David sifted through his mind carefully with the previously inconceivable. "You know what you mean when you say that?"

"Yes, I do."

"It's been years since there was anything close to resembling stability there," said Sam with the same doubt as David. "The Southerners aren't too fond of our country either."

"Not fond of us, sure. But would they kill us? There's a difference," said Jensen. "As soon as we cross the border, not even a full day's drive, we'd be out of the department's jurisdiction, and *they* are more than not fond of us."

"That's right. Our country doesn't have an alliance with the South like they do with the North," David said, starting to consider it more seriously.

"They don't have a centralized government anyway. Even if they did, their people would never negotiate with ours to send us back," said Jensen. "Who knows? If they know we're rebels, maybe that could help our cause all the more."

"I'm not sure," Abbi said unsteadily.

"I'm not either." David walked over and sat next to her on the couch. He placed a hand over her thin arm, gently closing his fingers. Her skin was cold under his. "I'm not sure about anything anymore. But I don't know if we can go where we're sure anymore. All we have left is to run where we live, even if after we get there, it doesn't last that long. That's still more a chance than what we have here."

"Yeah. I guess so," Abbi said half-heartedly, struggling to find any resolution. She wanted to say more, but whatever was behind her lips would only bring tears.

"It's one of the scariest things," said Jensen, staring at the three on the couch, Bobby on the far end. "I'm trying not to take it lightly either. I wouldn't have suggested it if there was something better. We can do this though."

David leaned forward, finally registering the implications of how Jensen had been speaking. "What do you mean *we*?"

"Exactly what you think."

David jumped to his feet. "Jensen, no. You and Sam have helped us so much, but you heard Goode. They're going to be coming for us as long as we're on the run. If it comes down to it, you could get hurt or killed."

"He's right," Sam said in an instinctive effort to protect his grandson. "You have to realize your life is in the same danger as any of theirs, possibly forever, not just these few days as we first thought."

"I know that."

David continued to implore. "Don't give up your life for us, for something that's not guaranteed. As far as the law is concerned, you've had no interaction with us and can continue with the life you've got. Do me one more favor and just stay here. Please, stay. For me."

"I'm coming with you guys," persisted Jensen, unshaken.

"Don't be stupid!" David could not hear more of it.

"I'm coming with you guys!" Jensen's feet sank deeper. "Do you know what it's like to be on my end of all of this? On the end of the guaranteed life? To see your best friend taken to be contrated as if he never was . . ." Jensen sighed to calm himself. "Yeah, I know what they say. That you aren't living. Well, I call bullshit." He let out a cynical snicker. "The number of votes that allowed this logically piss-poor system, I swear. You could not have said a word, but your existence, your presence . . . I mean, c'mon. Existence and life aren't the result of realized potential. It just is. You are. We are, just as much as anybody is." No one thought to speak in between him yet. "I'm going with you."

Neither he nor David wanted to abandon their ground, but Jensen was ready to bleed for his position. David understood the difference. Jensen's words wrapped and pulled David away from his resistance; he had to admit it would be uncharacteristic of Jensen not to make the demand. Such a personality would flesh out all the same in any other situation. Otherwise, David and the others would not have escaped the facility. David shrugged. "Alright. There's never any convincing you anyway."

"You bet there isn't." Jensen gave a sudden smirk.

"I've got some money in my savings," Sam said. "If we make it down there in one piece, it should be enough to start us off."

Though Jensen was first inclined to urge his grandfather to stay, ready to argue his reasons starting with old age, he could not in truth push back on his grandfather's request when David no longer resisted his. "Why can't you just be a normal old man?"

"Keeping up with you kids keeps me young."

"If we keep you young, what will that mean for us?" Jensen rallied it back. "If my hair turns gray early, I'll know who to blame."

It was this banter that added to David's comfort, knowing these two, together an essence of true home, were coming with him to the South. While reassured himself, David thought of Drake and Mia, who were absent. "How do you think the others are going to accept the plan?"

The two would likely express the same uncertainties about the South, but those in the living room felt certain they would climb on board after collecting themselves. Abbi said, "Well, if they have some idea we haven't thought of yet, I'll hear it. But I don't think they will, and I can see Drake jumping on board for the South. Mia on the other hand. I don't know if . . ."

Bobby rose from his seat. "I don't want to go to the South." There was a new face on him, but it was not a mask of someone else. His jaw clenched under grinding teeth.

David spoke with patience as always but exercised caution in the face of his anger. "Bobby, this is our only shot of making it. None of us truly wants to go there either, but it's all we can do at this point."

"No. No," said Bobby. "I want to go home. I don't want to be here anymore."

Abbi tried to back David and console Bobby. She placed a hand on his back, but he scooted away from her. "Take me back!"

"We can make it, Bobby." Drake emerged from the hallway, a quiet surprise. He was calm, in contrast to his reaction after the morning announcement. Drake had screamed some choice words into a pillow, which helped him arrive at the new ease. The fight had never died. "I overheard you guys talking about the South. I'm in."

Not so much his words but his presence seemed to mollify Bobby. Even David felt the contagious pull of Drake's certainty. Drake went over to Bobby and patted his back. "As long as we're together, we'll be alright." Bobby did not speak, but to everyone's relief, he gave a reluctant nod.

They discussed the plan for a few minutes. Whether or not it was just a front to encourage the others, Drake made it seem like he was doubtless about venturing into the South. "I hear it's a bit safer further south we go, as long as we hug the coast and keep going a couple days beyond the border. Safer and prettier. It's still the South though. Don't forget." He stopped to look around. "How did you guys pitch this to Mia? That could not have been an easy sell."

"I thought she went to the backroom with you?" said Abbi.

*

The window blinds remained sealed from earlier, but a bit of light crept through the edges. Salvador preferred to sleep in complete darkness, which he could only achieve in his own bedroom. But driving to his apartment in northwest Bellark would have cost time, and he knew he had to awaken early for the morning downtown press conference.

The Chief had no choice but to find his sleep in his desk chair after returning from the meadow, only to receive two meager hours. Not yet having showered before or after the conference, his odor diffused through the office. He had more pressing priorities. Desk light on and a lukewarm coffee in hand, he now scribbled his signature on various documents to finalize the verdict.

He was uncertain about entrusting the dispatch to Luis Adán, but the young officer was persistent, urging that the CD and police needed to be surveying every inch of the city, if not

210

beyond. This caused him conflict, however. For one, Luis had a capacity and drive the aging Chief now lacked. But on the other hand, Salvador was wary of Luis' eager ambition and the collateral that may come with it. *"We'll tear this city apart if it means getting them!"* Luis exclaimed to the dispatch force when leaving headquarters.

Salvador flinched and swiveled his head toward the familiar noise. Faint digital beeps emitted from the entry door. It wedged open slowly as if a wind were breaking in. Instead, it was a body that crept through. Even in short heels, her gracefulness was uncompromised, almost a glide through the slender entrance she wedged open. Delaney did not bother to look toward him; her attention focused on what lay in the corner.

"Delaney," he said, relieved and surprised.

She let out a shriek. "Sal! What are you doing here?" She put a hand to her chest to slow her breathing. "The entire department's out."

"I know. They're all searching the city." He paid no mind to the fact she'd used his entry code, which he'd told her to reserve only for emergencies. "What are you doing?"

"I left my bag here last night." She pointed to a black leather purse in the corner closest to the door. "Why aren't you out with the department?"

It was difficult to read her expression in the dim lighting. "I have duties to attend here, for now," Salvador said, reality dawning on him. "I called you so many times. I thought you were hurt. Where have you been? We had a press conference."

"Yes, I saw." Delaney turned toward him, stepping within reach of the desk light. His pungent odor became stronger with every inhale. "You told me to leave. At the bridge. You were very clear. I did not presume to believe I was required afterward."

"Delaney, c'mon. You're my Vice, and I needed you there with me at the conference."

"Did you?" She took another step closer, resting her hands on the chair opposite Salvador. "You didn't need me at the bridge after all that mess. Why shouldn't I have figured the dismissal extended through the remainder of the operation?

Someone reprimanded in such a way should not be counted worthy to stand by your side."

Salvador's intent to be apologetic was forgotten. The impromptu encounter forced the Chief to respond in his current state, famished and unfiltered. "You stepped in front of the car! That Potential must have been going a hundred, and you stepped in front of it. I still don't know what came over you."

"But I got her. I forced her off the bridge, probably saving some damage and our lives!" She made no more effort than he to maintain any self-control. She had taken time to shower and dress, yet it looked to Salvador as if she'd managed another week without a splash of water to the face. Each eye was a moon eclipsed. Their deep and strained redness competed with Salvador's, but she was at least without his stench.

"I told you to stay back. You disobeyed. You were punished. That's how it goes. You can't just go around doing what you feel is best just because you're my—"

"Your what?" Delaney snapped back. "Exactly. I'm not your wife! Call it what you want . . . Lovers or partners. It's your call, but I am not your wife. Even if I was, you couldn't respond like that just because—"

"Really? So that's what you're calling us now. You're not my wife, but you're . . ." Salvador stood up. "I can do whatever I see fit to secure our mission. That's my role. I am the Chief of this department. Not you."

She laughed mockingly. "Secured our mission? You let five Potes get away! Why didn't you even stop to think they might have split up? How much downtime did you have sitting at that bridge anyway? I bet you could have sent yourself home! Maybe then you could have taken a shower and cleaned yourself up a bit."

Salvador sat back down in his chair, closing his eyes to calm himself. *You're reacting.* The fire was stoked, much of it his own doing. And yet he still felt he was justified in many senses. *She could have died. Our Potential could have died.* But maybe he'd judged incorrectly with the extensive reprimanding.

"I'm sorry." His sincerity was authentic. "I should not

have dismissed you. It was wrong and impulsive. Yes, you disobeyed. Still, it was wrong to send you home. Both as your Chief, and as someone who loves you." Salvador walked around the desk, placing his hand on her forearm. She allowed the gesture with no flinching or resistance. "I was just scared. For you," he swallowed, "and for our child." Delaney's hands gripped the chair tightly. "Maybe you were right. It looks like working together presents its difficulties. It's been a long couple of days, but it will end soon with the verdict. Neither of us is thinking clearly. I just can't imagine. I wouldn't be able to forgive myself if anything happened to you or our chi—"

"Potential." Delaney's face looked paralyzed, yet tears slid down both cheeks. Her body pulled away from Salvador, now frantic as she scurried for the corner where her bag lay. "I need to go."

"Why? Delaney, I mean it. I'm sorry. Just stay for a minute, and we can talk. I'm not mad." Salvador would allow her to be irrational, even reckless with her words, just so long as she stayed. The tide would eventually draw back, he figured; no matter the harshness. Despite his urging, she did not turn back. Every step she drew away tugged the cord tighter around his heart, but Delaney seemed ignorant that she was its keeper.

She wiped her nose with a sleeve, shaking her head and holding her breath. "No. I can't. I'm sorry." Delaney left hurriedly. The weighted door closed just as quickly as her departure.

Salvador felt as empty and vacant as the building that he stood inside; alone, waiting to hear Delaney's steps if she were to hurry back. But that didn't happen, and the door kept shut. For a moment, Salvador wondered if she may be on the other side of the door, waiting in silence for him emerge. He wished it were true, and if it were, Salvador would have lunged to the door. But he knew the woman too well. Delaney was gone.

*

Abbi called for Mia from the living room, but there was

no answer. She looked to the others and rose. David went to follow, but she gestured him to stay.

"She might be in the bathroom. I'll go check," said Abbi. The restroom was empty, and the toilet was left open. One of the boys used it last, she understood.

Drake called from the living room, "Any luck?"

But Abbi gave no answer as she walked next to the guest room, unable to understand why she was both nervous and hesitant. The room was empty as well. Abbi almost called out for the others but grabbed the door handle for the large walk-in closet. She flicked the switch. Immediately after, the piercing echo traveled down the hall.

"Abbi?" Sam called out, concerned after hearing the familiar sound.

Abbi could hear the others arising from the living room as she ran to the garage door where the unnerving sound came. Opening the door without fear of what the mysterious clamor was, a ghostly chill swept her face. After two steps, her feet became stone. The halting of her lungs was simultaneous with the dropping clank of the gun. Though no one could hear beyond the house property, the suppressor seemed to make no difference. If the shot had never compelled the others to sprint for the garage, Abbi's scream would have. David was the first to rush in. Abbi was still frozen, giving no acknowledgment of his presence.

David checked his stride and turned his face. Quickly, he gathered the strength and forced himself to confront the sight, walking toward Mia. The gun lied on the garage floor, a foot away from her limp hand. He approached her still form and knelt for a closer look, hoping his eyes had played a trick on him. Her body sat upright against the garage door. The blood continued to drain from her ruined temple to the ground, creating a small red pool by her hip, soaking into David's flannels. Her face had a light sprinkling of residue like crimson freckles. Her blue eyes remained wide open, but even their brightness could not pass her off as alive.

"David." He turned toward Abbi's voice. She was pointing at Mia's body, but he didn't understand what she was

214

trying to communicate. "Look." She walked and knelt beside him, her hand touching where she'd pointed. David finally made the connection. Mia's hoodie lay beside her body. The urgency in Abbi's next words could not be challenged. "Get me a knife!"

David jumped to where he and Jensen stored their fishing gear after each day's catch. The utensils were stored in the lowest toolbox drawer. "How long?" It was almost a cry.

Abbi gave no response. No one and nothing else existed. Her immobilizing fear was gone. The shadow of time was looming over her, but she could pay no mind to the growing enemy. Drake came running into the garage. He took a few steps back, briefly turning away. Sam and Jensen emerged soon after with similar reactions. David took no time to explain. The three could only reason from what they saw. They oscillated between petrification, despair, and horror, but as they came to understand Abbi's meticulous movements over Mia, there was belief.

Twenty seconds passed.

Jensen stared at the gun on the floor, then glanced at the top toolbox drawer where he left it. *This is my fault. Why did I forget it there? How did she remember?* He wanted to vomit, but before he could impose more guilt upon himself, his eyes returned to Abbi and Mia's body.

Bobby entered the garage, stopping on the doormat at the sight. "What happened?" he asked shaken, but he received no answers from the silent, focused men. He walked forward to understand why Abbi was piercing Mia's stomach with a blade, but before he took another step, Sam reached out to hold him back. "I want to go home," said Bobby.

Drake pulled him back even farther. He used all his strength, grasping Bobby's arms to force his body and sight away from Mia. It was a harsh whisper, face-to-face. "Not now, Bobby! You need to go inside." One could not see Bobby's face flush through his dark skin, but his cheeks became as frigid as the garage floor. He turned around and retreated down the hall. The others paid him little mind, staunchly fixed on each of Abbi's movements and incisions.

The pool of blood expanded, well drenching Abbi's legs

where she knelt. David lifted to a crouch, his socks absorbing the heat. Abbi's sleeves were soaked as well, her hands likely to be bloodstained after. She did not have the time to sanitize or cover her skin, which she hoped would not cause any long-term damage. She was both reckless and precise, having to perform correctly but without concern for Mia's life. David thought to offer assistance, but he understood that Abbi would not hesitate to speak if she needed any. At first, he was sure she had never performed this procedure before, but her resilience to blood and her decisiveness made him doubt the presumption.

Though it seemed to last an eternity, approximately two minutes had passed from start to finish. David and the others huddled around Abbi, leaving some reasonable space. Abbi called softly, "Come on. Wake up, wake up." A pint-sized Potential nestled in her wet arms, eyes closed and body motionless. She used a dry part of her sleeve to gently wipe the newborn's face. A girl. One that too closely reminded Abbi of herself, the infant she was in photos from the past. Though younger, the hairs on the baby's brown scalp were longer than Abbi's when she was born. She patted the infant's back. "Please. It's okay. I'm here." In those seconds, no one would take a breath in case that would rob the child of hers.

"Come on, kid." Drake stepped closer, leaning over Abbi until the shadow of his head rested over the newborn. The feeblest of breaths, like the highest note of a piccolo, escaped through the infant's mouth. "My God," said Sam, stepping closer with the others. Abbi released a huge breath as the newborn's eyes met hers. They looked gray.

*

Sam drove well over the speed limit, emerging from the neighborhood and into the urban streets of northwest Bellark. This was not the time to try to remain inconspicuous. The tiny Potential curled in Jensen's arms as he sat in the passenger seat. He kept his body as still as possible, careful not to disrupt her breathing pattern. She was only slightly larger than Jensen's hand, still cloaked in faint red from her mother's blood.

The decision was one vote short of unanimous. All understood the infant would not be able to survive long if kept in their care without medical attention. They had no medical equipment, much less food or security. Sam summoned Jensen and the two departed in minutes after receiving some direction from Abigail on how to hold the baby and best ensure her stability. The others stayed at the house to tend Mia's body.

Abbi was reluctant to admit the truth, but she understood all too well that the infant would not continue to live if not immediately attended by a medical professional. It was Drake, however, who resisted, reiterating that the Potential was as good as contrated as soon as they checked her into a hospital. The reality sank each stomach; it was a difficult point to dispute. But Sam was right as well: *"It's either we turn her in now, or she dies today."* Abbi added, not quite favorably, *"Since there's no parent to sign on a contration, she can't legally be contrated until the next Closing if no one claims or adopts. That's another month."* This gave no one peace of mind, however.

Jensen was quiet for the first minutes of the drive, paranoid for the child's life in his hands as if his voice would stop her heart. He hardly seemed to notice his grandfather's sharp turns. Sam could not slow but perceived his grandson's unease. "Almost there. Thankfully no cops or department yet."

Jensen's voice shortened. "Will she die?" The infant's breathing had been steady, but her eyes opened again at the sound of the one who held her. She had not yet cried. The others interpreted her silence as a sign of strength, but it worried Abbi. She was much too fearful to pinch or make any attempt to examine the child's nervous system, however. *"Crying is a good thing."* Her words haunted Jensen, but the baby's tranquility seemed to banish the notion.

Neither Sam nor Jensen spoke of Mia. This was not from lack of empathy or devastation. The image of that girl, lifeless against the garage door, was dwarfed by the image in Jensen's arms. The determination of life simply triumphed over the finality of death.

Sam parked in the handicap spot in front of the emergency room entrance. Jensen quickly rehearsed his story, the identity to claim, and the actions to take. With no time to second-guess or revise the script, he hastened through the entrance with the newborn in arms.

Sam anxiously counted the passing minutes. A CD officer could perhaps be on duty at or near the joint delivery-contration hospital. Sam gripped the steering wheel as the truck's clock struck the ninth minute since Jensen had entered. *What if there's an officer there?* The regret was an assassin from behind. Sam had figured the most believable approach would be for Jensen to claim the newborn as his own, rush her to receive care, then leave after she was under a nurse's or doctor's supervision. This would raise the fewest suspicions from the hospital staff, even though it must be rare for someone to race in with a premature Potential. But Sam had failed to consider his recent run-in with the department.

Jensen emerged from the sliding doors, half walking, half jogging. Sam's inner dialogue ceased. His grandson jumped into the truck. "I did it." His assuredness stabilized Sam's brief turmoil.

"What'd they ask?" The tires screeched in reverse.

"The ones you suspected. My name. Where the mother is now. They were definitely confused, but they still rushed her in. After I signed some release form, a nurse asked me how far along the mother had been."

"What'd you say?"

"Far enough," Jensen said.

Sam had trouble remembering the size of Mia's stomach. Her wide, baggy hoodie would have concealed even his gut, a slow-growing belly that accumulated pounds over a stretch of time, yet it was likely still smaller than Mia's. By the time he entered the garage, Abbi had already sliced the womb, various fluids having spilled out to reduce the size. But there was no doubt for Sam in one matter; either fate could have awaited the newborn. The drawing of the two lots allowed life, but there now remained one month until the next Closing—another draw.

David and Drake lifted Mia's body onto the tarp they had grabbed from the garage rafters. They decided to bring her body with them to the South in hopes of providing a proper burial on the way. The journey would naturally take them through open coastal desert. The Lloyd property was not the appropriate place since neighboring homes rested atop a hill behind the backyard. To bury outside would risk exposure and leaving her body in the garage was undignified.

Drake continued absorbing the mess with old towels David had fetched. With the clean-up just about finished, David went to check on Abbi. The two had earlier urged her to go wash up, so she did not have to look at the sight any longer. David approached the closed guestroom door. Abbi must have just stepped out of the shower, he thought.

"Come in." Her response was quick after he knocked. She was wearing an old navy-blue shirt of Jensen's, and a pair of jeans that didn't fit tightly, but also didn't appear to belong to Sam or Jensen. Sam possessed few articles of clothing from his late wife, but he'd always kept a pair of old jeans that she'd kept from her youth. Since Abbi looked about the same size, he had laid the jeans out earlier in the morning for her without telling of the history attached.

The room had a masculine scent; Jensen's shampoo and body wash were the only options. Abbi was not picky as any aroma was better than the one filling the garage. The clean fragrance of her damp hair was a pleasant change for both her and David. Though not one to get queasy at the sight of blood, David had struggled with the tragically gory scene in the garage. In a sprinting effort, he'd made it to the trashcan, saving both him and Drake an extended clean-up. Abbi did not need to know this detail.

"How you doing?" said David.

Abbi stood beside the bed, looking out the window. "She looked like me," she said. "The baby didn't look much like Mia. I wonder who the father is or where he's at right now. Strange enough to be with Bobby."

"What do you mean?"

"I don't see many people that look like me." She continued quietly. "How many black kids are at your school?"

David struggled to recall and picture these classmates. "I can only think of one. Maybe two, but I think the other graduated last year."

"Not very many at mine either, and I'm inner city. That's why I'm always surprised to see another. Like Bobby. But seeing a baby that looks exactly how I looked is stranger."

"I'm sorry," David said, trying to track. "That's got to be tough."

Her gaze was stuck on an outside windchime, but the ring barely made it through the glass. "You know they put facilities in neighborhoods like mine first?"

"I didn't." David was slightly ashamed to admit it, looking upon the face of dejection.

"Can't blame you. I wouldn't have known either if my dad never told me. I was little, and he had a job. Probably never considered it at that time," said Abbi. "Their plan worked well; the CD got what they wanted. Sometimes I'd feel guilty for being one of the few that looked like me who got to live so long, but then I was chosen."

"But you're alive still, Abbi."

"For now. But she's dead. Mia, Rylie—They're both gone." She would not leave the still chime, waiting for the next wind to come to give it sound once more.

"They are." He could not say it numbly like her. "You saved that baby though. She's not dead."

"She will be."

David had not expected her calloused response. There was no blame or accusation to lay on Abbi, however. It was as if the purest of breezes was sent to cross through smog, clearing it out and away but having no choice in carrying its pollution for a time. David stepped next to Abbi, joining her by the window. "We can't let them get any more of us."

"I know. But what can we do? Rylie, Mia . . . "

". . . Rylie's different. She fought until the end, and for us," said David.

Abbi finally left the window and looked at him. "Mia fought until her end."

"That wasn't her end. That was their end, the CD's." He sighed, "No wonder why Mia never told us."

"Told us what? Being pregnant."

"Yeah." He crossed his arms, coming to terms himself. "She thought her life . . . wasn't. Why wouldn't she think the same for the one inside her? Her carriers, our carriers chose to contrate for the same reason. Same as me." He nodded, melancholically. "You were right about what you said at the cabin. We can't believe the system is right, or any of us have reason to do what Mia did. But we won't. We don't believe that."

A collection of steps from down the hall brought David to a stop. One by one, Drake, Sam and Jensen walked into the room from the garage. "It worked," Sam said. "They took her in. The baby's alive."

"She is?" Abbi struggled to accept the good news. "That's crazy . . . I can't believe . . ." The reluctant smile found its way as she turned back to David, recognizing the slow drift she just came back from. "Guess now I have to say that you're right."

"I'm only repeating you from earlier. You saw that baby first," said David.

The others looked at Abbi mystified, almost identifying her as the miracle itself. She finally noticed the extent of their speechlessness. "What?"

Drake said, uncertain, "Should that baby have lived?"

"It's hard to say. Yes and no," she said, remembering. "From her size, she may have been no older than thirty weeks . . . About six months. Many newborns have survived this type of birth before, but," her eyes caught the blood on Drake's sleeve, "after Mia. After she did it . . . oxygen's cut off to the baby. I had to do the c-section right away. Otherwise, a lack of oxygen can cause brain damage. I got her out in time. Thankfully. But I can't say anything about long-term effects." She continued, but none of her perplexity lessened. "It was my first time. I've just read books and watched videos. I told David. It's what I planned on going for at university."

All kept silent as Mia's image began to drape and suspend over each of them. Abbi squeezed her eyes shut and cleared her throat. "When are we leaving?"

"Gather all your stuff," said Sam. He looked to Jensen and David. "If there's anything deeply personal here, you'll want to grab those too. After some quick showers and packing, we'll leave at twelve."

Jensen had enough clothing for the other boys, especially Drake as he was closest in size. Drake walked to the living room to relay the information to Bobby and help him prepare.

Sam said, "You're all strong. Keeping your heads up like this. You should have never been in this situation. Wish I could have done more."

At a loss for words, David could not get passed his conflict with what Sam spoke. The silence dwelt longer than he would have wished, but his face lit up when he looked back to him. "You did the most. Jensen is alive because of you, Sam. He saved us all from the facility, but it all started with you."

David went to him with an embrace. Sam squeezed, pressing both his open hands over David's back as if imparting a blessing. Like a punch to his head, David imagined Sam's body as his father's. Realizing what his mind had conjured, he let go. Sam detected his obvious discomfort. "You okay, David?"

He nodded to gather himself. "Yeah." The up-and-down movement of his head was almost erratic and lasted a second too long. "I'm fine. Sorry." David's head slowed. "I, umm. For a second there, I started thinking of my——"

Drake rushed into the room. "Have you guys seen Bobby?" His steps had reverberated from down the hall well before he entered.

Jensen was the first to reply. "He's not in the living room?"

They dispersed out of the bedroom like poured grain.

"No," Drake said, pointing. "The front door's wedged open. Did anyone else go through there?" They shook their heads in a frenzy. When they returned, Sam and Jensen had come through the side garage door to check on Mia's body first. Drake pressed his hands to his forehead. "This is all my fault. I yelled at him, and now he's gone. He could have left a long time ago."

"Don't assume quite yet. Jensen's looking upstairs," Sam said calmly, making any effort to ease Drake.

Drake did not follow the group as they scurried for the second story, disappearing down the hall instead. There was not much ground to cover above, but the others still double-checked the rooms. With no luck, they hurried back downstairs.

"Drake?" David called out in the empty living room.

The front door flung open from an outside wind. Sam was sure he had shut it. In the next moment, a pick-up truck crossed their view from the door. An engine roar followed behind.

David ran a couple of steps outside. "He's leaving!"

Sam was right behind, grabbing him before he could leave the porch. "Let him go. We can't risk you being out there either! If he finds Bobby, he'll bring him back."

David could not pry or break free from Sam's arms. "What if they don't come back?"

"What if you don't come back?" Abbi grabbed his arm, and David's tunnel vision expanded to full perspective. The verdict was fixed and impartial, even for a young man seeking recompense like Drake. He, like David, was still a Potential.

*

He knew those at the house were anguished at his impulsive leave, knowing it added yet another to their burdens. But Drake did not doubt the decision to search for Bobby, despite the streets being more dangerous with the new verdict passed. All of them were almost celebrities now due to the media's efforts, their faces plastered on all the digital billboards throughout the city and broadcasted over every major national network.

The pressure sat on his shoulders, hastening the effort to find his friend before the CD or anyone supporting them. *What if he finds his mom?* It churned his stomach to imagine her calling for

Bobby's contration a second time.

After searching the neighborhood streets, he left for the nearest marketplace. Several blocks south was a plaza and shopping center, the same one Sam had fetched their dinner. It was the furthest Bobby could have wandered in the amount of time he'd had unless he'd decided to travel through the backwoods of the suburbs. *He wouldn't.* Bobby missed the home he thought was still his.

Drake wondered how long his friends would wait. It was almost noon. Every minute in the house, in their country, death inched closer. Yet each truth stood as tall as the other: There was no time to waste for the South, and Bobby must be found. He stopped biting at a fingernail as he merged into the traffic of the urban streets. A large billboard suspended above the main plaza entrance, transitioning between the faces of the March Runaways. *They'll wait for me.*

He rolled into the parking lot, driving steadily and scanning left and right. The center was full, the lunch hour having drawn a crowd. It was difficult to search for one face through all the people scurrying from their cars, entering and exiting various establishments. As he veered closer to the sidewalk, eyes began invading the driver's window. He realized if Bobby's face was known, his must be notorious from the killings. Shuffling through the glove compartment, Drake found a pair of Jensen's sunglasses under what he'd taken from the Lloyd house.

At least another ten minutes passed to complete the unsuccessful round of the large parking lot. There was a public park a mile away, Drake remembered. *Maybe he went there.* He thought Bobby might be wise enough to avoid the threatening amount of people here.

He slowed toward the main four-way stop that led to one of the exits. Some pedestrians walked in front of the truck as they crossed from one side to the other. He lowered his head to hide his face but glanced up once the people had finished crossing to the other side.

As if his foot had a spasm, Drake slammed the brake in the middle of the intersection. In front of a not too distant restaurant was a slow meandering walk, one that appeared as aimless at first glance, yet Drake knew. There was an underlying fear; a terror one fights to contain so that others may not see. At which point Bobby had figured it out, it was impossible to determine. But the quiet paranoia was there. Bobby finally knew he was a sheep among wolves, aware it was these people who mistakenly dressed one another as the opposite.

Drake ignored the first horn behind him. A second driver honked, finally grabbing hold of him. The traffic was building, and the last thing he needed was to draw attention. Drake turned right, opposite of the exit and parked the truck in the closest spot available. The concealing sunglasses allowed a quick pace to make up for lost ground. Bobby continued slowly in the opposite direction, but Drake would be able to close the distance fairly quickly. He seethed impatiently when a car went out of turn at the stop, slowing Drake from crossing right away.

He'd just taken his first step from the sidewalk onto the street when a striking blue light flicked his peripheral. Down the main street, CD and police vehicles sped closer. No siren sounded, however. *Smart move.*

Drake sprinted. He raised one of his hands in the air, hoping to grab Bobby's attention. As he waved, Drake saw a security guard parked in front of the restaurant Bobby pottered toward. The guard had a radio to his lips, speaking as he kept his eyes glued to Bobby. Drake wished he had a better defense—*I should have brought it.*

Seeking to capitalize on the distracted guard, Drake raised both his hands energetically to vie for his friend's attention. He turned once more to check on the department horde. *Maybe a minute.* Realizing the immediate adversary was the guard, Drake clapped his hands "Hey!" He called not wanting to reveal Bobby's name and identity. There were many repulsed and perplexed stares, but no person recognized the boy with black hair.

Bobby finally heard the urgent clapping in between exclamations from the familiar voice. Drake stopped in his sprint. Meeting eyes brought mutual relief. Bobby smiled, relieved to see Drake in the sea of strangers, forgetting all about his harsh words in the garage.

Drake's relief turned to urgency, gesturing Bobby to come toward him. The security guard was carefully analyzing Bobby's body shift but did not allow his eyes to leave him. Drake knew the consequences if he chose to go to him. The guard would recognize him as well, and the department would have a two-for-one if they couldn't escape. It did not matter. Drake closed the keys in his fist, ready to go toe-to-toe.

Screech!

No sirens could have alerted anyone. A caravan of department vehicles flooded in from the opposite direction. Drake had not thought to survey the other entrance. They landed in front of the restaurant, the tires screaming to form a U-shape around the terrified Potential on the sidewalk and grass. Officers leaped out. Drake's first instinct was to lunge forward, but he held still, realizing he would only jump into the same pit. *What can I do?* Dozens of officers inched closer. The black assault rifles were an unexpected sight, a closer semblance to fatality than the facility rifles. One commanded Bobby, "Freeze!"

Out of another vehicle stepped Luis Adán. He raised his handgun almost lazily. "Cooperate, and we can handle this peacefully," Luis announced to Bobby. The horde Drake first saw finally arrived, more officers along the perimeter. Many pedestrians gathered around a safe distance, surprised and captivated to see one of the runaway Potentials.

At this point, nobody would pay any mind to Drake's presence. He heard a murmur. "It's about time they got one." A boy in his Sixteenth year added, "Bad place to try and hide." A woman around the age of Fifty stood to Drake's right in a forest green plaid peacoat. She spoke as if directing the question to herself: "They aren't going to shoot him?"

Drake heard, and the image of Mia rushed through his mind, her head turned toward the red-stained garage door, the scent as fresh to him as it was then. It became natural to speak aloud as if proclaiming it would save Bobby. "No," said Drake. "It's different when you see the blood." The lady turned to him, realizing she had spoken louder than she'd thought. She nodded

226

and took an extra second to study the worried but oddly familiar face behind the sunglasses. Drake heard a small, swift breath leave her mouth. His body tightened after his brash action. Much to his shock, the woman quietly turned back toward Bobby.

Bobby's eyes enlarged as they scanned the assortment of guns pointed at him, never settling on any individual officer or weapon. Luis stepped forward with two officers. Bobby did not see the one remove handcuffs from her belt, his focus trapped on Luis' barrel.

Luis uttered something he never registered.

Listen to him, Bobby! Drake clenched the keys tightly.

The black barrel loomed closer, now just ten feet from Bobby's chest. His turn was sudden, a quick pivot toward Drake, the path decided but not a step taken. Luis' finger was a mousetrap to the trigger, the immediacy seeming to indicate a granted wish.

Drake's ears seemed to fill with white noise. None of the shrieks from the crowd nor the second gunshot took sound. His eyes, however, worked all too well as he watched Bobby's body jerk and fall to the sidewalk, chest to the sky. His body had swung from the second impact but was motionless now. Blood spread out to both sides. For a moment it looked like two red wings growing from his back. The shape was slowly lost, turning into what looked like a scarlet baptismal robe to enfold Bobby.

Drake dropped to his knees as if he felt the impact himself. The crowd gave him no attention as many eyes turned or covered from the sight. Some of the remaining stares paired with disbelief. A few appeared unaltered, yet even they had no attention to spare for the boy with black hair.

Luis looked around and said, "Citizens of Bellark: This Potential was a wanted fugitive, as has been announced and broadcasted. Many of our citizens have died because of these fugitives. This one was dangerous and could have brought harm to any of you today. Be thankful you are all safe. I gave him the option to cooperate and come with us, but as you all witnessed, he chose a different alternative. If any of you identifies another one of these fugitive Potes, be sure to act as this security guard and report it. You can save lives."

Two hands grabbed Drake's arm, a deathly clench. He flinched defensively at the lady in the peacoat. "Go," she urged quietly as she lifted him to his feet. He arose weakly as if his legs were sticks to balance stones. She pushed him with one hand while he struggled. "You need to leave now!" she said, square with his face. Drake could only respond by finally complying, lowering his head and shoving his way to emerge through the backside of the crowd. The people were distracted by the officers surrounding the dead Potential.

Drake's breaths refused to normalize, unsure whether he'd be able to catch his next. Lost in thought and continuing the fight for self-command, he bumped into a man in the intersection. His sunglasses fell and dropped to the ground. The man bent to pick them up, but his arm stopped just as he was extending them out to Drake. He analyzed the boy's face. Drake snatched the sunglasses from the man and continued for the truck. He stumbled into the driver's seat, his hand shaking so uncontrollably that it took three attempts to insert the key into the ignition. He reversed hurriedly to distance himself away from the scene.

Drake was just as much present in reflection as he was in the escape. *Why here?* Bobby was dead, but he'd never imagined such an execution. Neither had most of the witnesses, judging from their own shock. Their gasping reactions seemed to testify to something else entirely, he thought. *Maybe people just need to see it.*

He immediately doubted this however, as the other faces in the crowd returned to his mind, the very few neutral and blank at the sight. Drake's fingers were printing the steering wheel leather. *They saw and didn't feel anything.* The pedal almost touched the floor until Drake lifted his foot for the next turn. *Or did they really see?* The confusion relaxed like a boiling pot lifted from its burner.

It was rare for Drake to remember much from school, much less when he was in his Thirteenth year, but it seemed to wait for this moment: *"Evil thrives when under the guise of good. It takes various forms, shifting and changing as a tide, but doing so silently as beneath the water."* The teacher taught only part-time and mainly worked as a priest for the religion Drake had never taken to. Drake hadn't warmed up to most clergy members at private school, but this man was always kind.

The rest of the priest's parable resounded, more poignant than ever. As Drake wove through each turn for the back exit, he seemed to hear the man's voice as clearly as if he were in the passenger seat next to him:

"To try giving an evil its appropriate title, that is, evil, is the same as this. A young man lived in a village and went out with the other fishermen for the day, as was his duty. Upon nearing the lake, they noticed an unfamiliar discoloration in the water. When they stepped closer, they saw the darkening came from a fish near the surface, one they had never seen before, with scales of all different colors. Despite its beauty, the fishermen knew they had to keep the lake clean and pure. Each man first tried casting his hook and line, but the fish would not bite for anything. Then a few others sharpened and threw spears, but the fish's scales could not be pierced. The water was only growing darker with each minute, so without consulting the others, the young man stepped slowly into the water. Swift, he reached in and grabbed the fish barehanded and threw it onto the shore.

After the fish suffocated and died, the darkness cleared from the water. However, the young man looked down to find blood dripping from his fingers and palm, which had been lacerated from the fish's scales. The other fishermen told the story of the heroic young man, and the villagers celebrated him for saving the lake. But the young man's hand swelled from the deep cuts, becoming as dark as the lake had looked.

A week later, another fish of various colors hatched from an egg laid by the first, yet everyone from the village remembered the suffering young man who'd saved the lake, his entire right arm now just as dark and swollen as his hand had been that first day. The water began to turn dark just as it did the first time, but with no person willing to risk himself to the same poisoning, the new fish was allowed to swim freely. The fishermen felt ashamed for not dealing with the fish in the same way as the young man, but come the next day, they discovered the lake was neither dark nor back to its normal clear blue. Instead, it shimmered in reflection of the fish's colors: red, purple, green, white. Each person came to visit the lake in awe, intrigued by the new magical glow on the water's surface.

After, the people mocked the sick young man who'd grabbed the first fish for his short-sightedness. Not only did they allow the second fish to live, but they began to worship it. The multicolored creature became the village sigil, carved into stones and sewed into each person's clothing. A year passed, and as the story spread, peoples of neighboring villages came in droves to see with their own eyes the majesty of the fish's divine power over the glowing surface of the water. Foreigners of all kinds journeyed to the village to see, offering many gifts and riches to the village to honor the new god in the lake. Included in these gifts were various kinds of foods, drinks, herbs, and spices so that none needed to even fish from the lake for food anymore. From all the incoming wealth and people, the village expanded to a city in five years' time, thousands more offering their worship to the god of the lake.

However, in the midst of all the worship, offerings, and growth from a city hoping to become a kingdom, no person was able to see past the water's colorful glow, and they did not realize the fish had devoured all life in the lake. It grew to a grotesque size, and finally rose from the beach with thick legs, monstrous arms, and gruesome claws. It hardly looked like the same fish—no fins, scales, nor gills, but it did keep its same colors. The creature roared to let each person know it had left its lake and was coming now to take the land.

In panic, the elders came to the young man who'd grabbed and killed the first fish. He was now near death from the infection that spread from his hand throughout his body. Out of fear, no one had aided him once they judged he'd killed a fish of divine power. While the young man could not do anything himself, he was able to give the people the same wisdom he'd used to kill the first fish. 'It must go where it can't live. Take it back to the lake. It left because this is where it now breathes. Take it back and drown it.'

The young man knew the people thought he had lost his mind. 'Take half the city, and you can overpower it," he said. 'Take the rest of the city, and you can pull the creature back under the water where it will die. It must die where it comes from.' Without even thinking to mock or rebuke the seemingly insane young man, the elders and all the people fled the city, forgetting both him and the creature." Drake remembered being just as confused as the students at the time, especially with the last sentences. *"The fish swims or the hand bleeds. The creature walks or the bodies bleed."*

The lady in the peacoat came to Drake's mind. He glanced one last time into the rearview mirror as he waited for the green light, hoping maybe the woman would emerge from the crowd in her distinct apparel. Instead, he saw that the man he had bumped into had kept his position at the four-way stop, watching Drake drive away. As if suddenly deciding, the man turned and jetted toward the officers, pointing his finger toward the pickup truck.

Drake ran the red.

*

Abbi went into the kitchen to fetch another glass of water. It was her third, drinking compulsively as a way to distract herself and find something for her hands and mind. The news coverage of the search for the March Runaways continued. Every station sought to capitalize on the topic. Every time it showed Rylie or Mia's face, her anxiety yielded to grief. Every time Drake or Bobby's face was displayed, her grief to anxiety.

David sat attentively as well, wishing for but dreading any updates on his missing friends. He was the one who'd suggested that Abbi take a break from watching. Despite keeping as neutral as he could, each face—Rylie, Mia—was a splinter to his body. The woe would be greater, yet it was the portraits of Drake, Bobby, and Abbi that held him up.

After Drake left, Sam used the time to withdraw money from a nearby ATM to serve as provision for future stops and avoid traceable electronic transactions. Had he seen Drake or Bobby, he would have retrieved them. For the rest of the time, he and Jensen had been loading the RV with all the provisions for the journey. David offered to help load, but they encouraged him to keep an eye on the news. This was mostly a redirection so he would not have to help with or watch the handling of Mia's corpse.

It had been about an hour. "Where could they be?" Abbi said again.

Sam and Jensen walked in through the back door. "All loaded up," Sam said. "Whenever they get back, we'll be good to go."

"I don't understand what's taking them so long," David said. "Bobby couldn't have gotten that far."

Just as David finished, the station cut from commercial to program. A lesser-known anchor spoke into the camera. "We have received urgent news on the March Runaways. It was a critical moment for the CD's pursuit, all of which took place at Plaza Grand in northwest Bellark."

The program cut to the restaurant. Several department and police vehicles remained where they'd first parked. The reporter spoke: "It was escaped Potential, Robert Reynolds, who was walking through this parking lot when the on-duty security guard reported him. The Contration Department, along with some assistance from the city police, arrived on the scene immediately. Reynolds was surrounded and commanded to cooperate. Without hesitation, the Potential retaliated and tried to escape, which forced the departments to act decisively. Reynolds was wounded and contrated on-site as a result. It truly was an unfortunate circumstance, and a great weight and responsibility for the BCD to bear. However, lead officer Luis Adán assured us that the city can breathe a little easier knowing another dangerous Potential can no longer harm anyone."

The program returned to the anchor. She paused, putting a finger to her earpiece. "We have an incoming update. After Robert Reynolds was contrated, a pedestrian present at the scene reported the sighting of another runagate. He described him as a tall Caucasian male with black hair and a muscular build. From this description, we have reason to believe this Potential may be David Drake. The witness testified that Drake departed the plaza nervously in a gray pickup truck: model and license plate unknown. Authorities have gone in pursuit of this lead, and the CD would like to encourage all citizens to act as those who reported the sightings of Reynolds and Drake for the welfare of the city and nation. Still at large are Mia Day, David Drake, David Kingsley, and Abigail Rosario."

Everyone wanted to turn off the television or change to a different channel, but it was not an option. Numbed and beaten faces kept their eyes on the screen, determined to gather all relevant information about the event and try to guess where Drake may have headed. It seemed as if they were running scarce on grief to pay Bobby. Neither David nor Abbi could offer more than a tear or two. They were like cups repeatedly poured until there was nothing more than a drop left.

"I can't take this anymore," Abbi said.

"We'll need to leave soon," Sam added grimly, trying to keep the mission in perspective. "That place where they caught Bobby wasn't far from here. They'll be searching for Drake in this part of town, and most likely come through this neighborhood eventually."

"We have to wait for him." David turned to Sam. "If he was spotted at the plaza, that means he probably saw Bobby get . . ." He looked back to the television. "Drake knows Bobby's dead. He's gotta be headed back here now."

Sam nodded. "I hope so."

Jensen asked, "What did they even mean by 'retaliated'? They trying to say Bobby threatened them?"

"They have to sell it somehow," said Abbi. "After what Goode said this morning, it looks like they don't want to take any more chances. They know how we are. Bobby would have used every last breath to get away."

"You think they'd lie to the public?"

"Falsify information? Wouldn't surprise me," Sam answered. "They'll add some spin about how Bobby was destined for failure and milk how much a strain he was to his mother. Whatever they need for the people to understand their cause—or to not understand, I suppose."

"They killed him in public," said Jensen. "They'll need an impressive story to sell that if it was just a contration."

All three turned to David.

He hadn't even been listening, submerged in thought by a grappling agitation. It took a moment to remember. "He wanted to go to space. Bobby," he said as if starting a new conversation. "This should hurt more than it does. We have to remember him later. Whenever we can." Heads nodded, acknowledging their emotional expenditure.

"We'll be sure to mourn for Bobby, but no more of you will die." Sam arose. "If they won't hesitate, we can't either." He walked upstairs and came out minutes later with his gun in hand. In the other was the last bag he'd packed, full of ammunition. Jensen understood what the statement meant, and his assumption was validated. Sam had the others observe carefully, not thinking to ask for their consent. The procedure was simple enough from Sam's instructions. David had never formally learned how to fire a gun, though he'd done just fine with the facility rifle. Each of them held the weapon and practiced loading, unloading, and cocking.

"How many do we have?" said David.

"One other." Sam arose and went to the garage, disheartened at the thought of having to clean the blood from the forgotten gun. Not seeing it on the floor where Mia's body had been, he assumed it had fallen behind or under the workbench. Placing one hand on the bench, Sam went creakily to his knees to search.

*

The buildings rose higher with every mile, but the tallest in the distance seemed forever under construction, tirelessly climbing each day in its effort for the heavens. Drake drove quickly but was careful not to exceed the speed limit. The sirens had eventually gone from faint to silent, but he was still uncertain how much distance he'd put between himself and the CD.

"Why did you have to leave the house?" Drake said. Anger mixed with guilt. *If only I never . . .* Nonetheless, the Contration Department was still accountable, and the instinct for vengeance ruled his every movement and choice for a time. *I was the one who killed your men.* He slapped the dashboard.

Drake could not in goodwill return to the house where the others waited. It was too great of a risk to lead the department to their location and ruin the plan. It was his decision to leave the house in search of Bobby. It was he who rebuked him in the garage. It was he who murdered the men at the contration facility and gas station. Drake well understood his role in all that had passed. While he helped lead the others out of the facility, the killings made him the scapegoat for the CD's hostility. If the nation sought their deaths because it believed them a threat, then he alone would give them reason to hold that truth.

Drake's passion was a festering combination of hate and love. *You can't just keep killing us.* He reached over to the glove compartment and pulled out the blood spotted gun he had seized when the others searched for Bobby at the house. Mia had pulled the trigger, but it was the department's finger over hers. At the time, grabbing the weapon from the garage was just a precaution, but Drake would now show the CD and the nation who the real threat was. His only concern was what David, Abbi, Jensen, and Sam might think of him after.

It's for them.

*

The face was unscathed, the dark skin full in unfading color. Asleep, one might think. But that presumption faded with the lifting of the cloth that concealed the rest of Robert Reynolds' body. Salvador held one hand over his nose as he raised the covering to inspect the contrated Potential. He removed his hand from his nose and placed it on Bobby's forehead. It still had some warmth.

Had he only accompanied Luis after the morning conference, Salvador believed the outcome might have been different, panned out more appropriately. When the call about Robert Reynolds' whereabouts came, he knew Luis Adán had the closer location. Salvador had assumed the appropriate action to take would be intuitive; it hadn't even crossed his mind to specify that the Potential *must* be taken into custody first.

"Not as clean as we would have liked," Luis said behind Salvador while he looked over the body. "But we got him."

Salvador's first instinct was to come down on Luis, but nothing would come from that reaction. Nothing productive. Such words of rebuke would not bring the other Potentials into their grasp, and they would not absorb the blood either. And the reality stood: A Potential was contrated. However, even with the assurance that the mission was advanced, Salvador could not brush off the feeling. "Next time, just apprehend and bring them to a facility."

Luis perceived his dissatisfaction. "What for? We got him."

"We could have interrogated him. To find the others." The response hinted of restraint, the words slower than how Salvador usually spoke. "And we don't contrate this way. It shouldn't look like this."

Luis breathed deeply but kept it quiet lest the Chief hear his impatience. "Yes, Sir. You're correct about the interrogation. I should have been more thoughtful."

Luis and Salvador closed the contration van doors for another officer to drive the body to a facility. The Chief figured it best to return to headquarters as the search for David Drake had been fruitless. Authorities swept all of northwest Bellark as they spoke. The police department dogs even hunted beyond the streets into the backwoods of the suburbs, the most likely direction anyone would flee. If they had not found him yet, then the report from the witness was likely false. The search in northwest Bellark would continue, but much of the CD would regroup at headquarters.

On the drive to the plaza, Salvador had given Delaney multiple calls, extending every effort to will her back into the mission. It was a means for restitution, but more crucially, he needed the Vice for all she was capable. Indeed, *she* would never have opened fire on the Potential. Perhaps she would have even been able to articulate to Luis more eloquently why one must be contrated in a facility. Entertaining the thought earlier, he could not confidently dismiss Adán while the other Potentials were still on the loose. He'd already made the mistake of relinquishing a skilled officer, but keeping Luis in a position of authority begged for Delaney's sure hand all the more.

The pedestrians never took their attention off the Chief from the moment he arrived at the plaza. They may as well have been the eyes of the world, every person over a magnifying glass he was trapped beneath. He could not figure what the gazes meant for some time, his confusion matching theirs.

They don't know. It seemed to come from the air; Salvador had no idea what inspired his realization.

The people were unsure what to think of what had just occurred, what to think of the Chief, and what to think of the CD itself; its rightness had seemed clear for so long. They had been instructed to paint black in one place and white in another. But for the first time for many at the plaza, the two spilled over their established borders, mixing into a gray that began to drown all who stood within.

*

Sam told the others about the missing gun. Though not first assumed, the discussion eventually left little doubt that Drake had taken it. He would not go out into the city unarmed, not without the ability to defend himself or Bobby. At first, they were reassured to know he had protection as they waited for his return. However, this confidence dropped with the sun as the afternoon strained forward.

"He should be here by now. Somethings off," said Jensen in the living room with the others.

"What if he doesn't want to come back?" Sam replied. "He was spotted at the plaza. If he came here and the CD somehow managed to follow him, we would all be in trouble."

Abbi said, "If he didn't come back, you're saying it'd be to protect us?"

"Maybe. I don't know where that boy is or what he plans on doing. What I do know is that it's been well over an hour since, and he's not here. He has my gun, so he has some protection if he were to go on his own." Sam turned to David. "We'll wait a little while longer. If Drake doesn't come back, we'll have to leave."

Though David would wait through the night, he knew the lives of Sam, Jensen, or Abbi were equally at risk. If the CD found one, it found all. *At least Drake's still alive.* David knew the media would not waste a second to broadcast Drake's death or apprehension. The CD fought to rally their supporters around the cause of the pursuit, and more importantly, they needed to restrain those who opposed that morning's verdict. The more Potentials contrated, the quieter those voices would become. At least, that was the hope.

Abbi switched between every news program, leading with any seemingly relevant information. Much airtime dedicated coverage to an opposition group standing outside the Bellark CD headquarters. They chanted with picket signs and posters, demanding the living and legal status of the teens who had reached their Eighteenth year. Some went further by requesting a pardon for Abigail Rosario, who had not even reached her Eighteenth. Most interesting was an interview with three fervent radicals who went so far as to denounce the CD altogether, hard-pressing the viewers to abolish the system entirely.

Abbi patted David on the shoulder. He did not remember drifting asleep, feeling like he was attentive to the to the news the moment before. It was just the two of them in the living room, but she had nothing to say behind the sunken frown, only a finger pointing to the TV. David had to blink a few times to clear his vision. *Why is he on there?*

The segment had transitioned into an exclusive interview the station had managed to obtain. There had already been multiple interviews all day with physiologists and philosophers to discuss the merits of the system: choice, the greater good, even women's rights, which was one of the arguments of old. However, the one ready to begin was the first interview of its kind since the March Runaways had escaped.

The man dressed for a typical workday in dark jeans and a brown polo. While Diane Culver was confident and composed as always, the man slumped and continually shifted in his seat. He looked around the interview set-up as if it were a waiting room for a surgical procedure. Interestingly, though he usually had a good read on the man, David's perception prevented him from noticing these details of the man's body language.

Diane Culver looked to the camera. "Hello, Bellark. We are pleased to announce that we have gained an exclusive interview with Braham Kingsley, former carrier of the escaped

Potential, David Kingsley."

The resemblance struck Abbi. She had never met or seen any picture of David's father, but their relationship was certain. David's brow furrowed as he leaned closer, not for lack of having glasses. The picture was close and clear. She watched David carefully as if her leaving him would unbind and set him loose. David had experienced waves of anger at various times since the escape, but this was different. It was the same glare that Drake had when murdering those men at the facility. If not hatred, it was something close.

A new fear took her, one entirely different from the kind she'd felt at the cabin after David said she deserved to live over the others; that was rooted in his ignorance and guilt. In a matter of moments, however, she saw David completely forsaken and replaced, or better yet, possessed. Even under justified grief, David had never entirely relinquished hope. But this new being had no good will, no compassion, no love.

"Thank you for joining us, Mr. Kingsley," said Diane. "We have you here today to discuss your position on the Contration Department. Given the actions of the March Runaways and the CD's pursuit, we'd like to hear your thoughts. There is a lot of dialogue surrounding this situation. Obviously, you chose to contrate a Potential of your household, who is now one of the fugitives. What we would like to know is why you made the decision."

David's father sipped from the mug on the table separating his chair from Diane's. "Yes. Umm, well," he said shakily. It was not stage fright, however. Rather, it was like a foreign language with which he was not well acquainted. "My wife and I never originally planned to contrate him. I don't think it's necessarily anyone's original plan."

It was like taking the knife in David's back and carving it up his spine. Only, David did not fall into paralysis as the action should accomplish. Every sense heightened as if the knife was instead a key opening a locked door inside himself that he never knew existed. David distinguished his own contration from his father's as far as east was from the west. He felt righteous, even blameless in that moment.

David's father continued. "It was when I lost my job a few years back when things got tough on my family. I jumped from part-time job to part-time job, which helped offset some bills for a few years." Abbi had never seen someone so unsure as he stopped to rub his eyes. "But our oldest daughter was going off to university. Even with all her scholarships, we had to help out a bit. That made finances even tighter. Our income had already fallen below the line."

David did not even flinch. He did not once question the authenticity of the claim. *Makes perfect sense . . . now.* It was more than reasonable why his carriers sold one of their three cars a year ago, why they had not replaced furniture in some time, why his father and mother stopped flying out of the country for their anniversaries. *But he just had to keep the house.*

Jensen and Sam had emerged in the living room after making one last circuit of the house. They stood quiet and unnoticed, watching David, discretely studying his responses as they glanced back and forth from him to the television.

"Was David aware of your financial crisis?" Diane asked.

"He was not. I don't think so, at least. He never said anything." Braham took another unsteady drink. "We thought it would be best to keep it from him. We wanted to leave him a last chance to score well on the ESE without giving him an added stress."

"It was to protect him?"

"Yes," said David's father. "It's never plan A to have to contrate any Potential, so with David, I suppose keeping it from him would bring a little less worry to his last years." The statement had a solemnity woven in. "As I said, we still wanted to leave him with some opportunity if he passed his exam. Maybe a small university would have accepted him. He wouldn't get any scholarships, but he could make it through with loans. But he didn't pass, and we were faced with a tough choice." He tried to take a drink from the now-empty mug. "It was just the most reasonable thing to do."

Diane nodded. "Yes, Yes. And as we can see, he is

240

continuing to jeopardize our society even now. He and the others have caused quite some problems for Bellark. I'd say he's a pretty dangerous individual."

"Well, no," his father said in mild disagreement. "He was never an angry kid. Gosh, I doubt he would have any bad intentions at all. Probably the others who've caused most of the havoc."

"Thank you for joining us, Mr. Kingsley," Diane cut him off briskly. "As you have heard, these decisions to contrate a Potential are not always easy. However, the decision never fails in its reason when considering all risks. We only hope the CD stops these Potes, so our citizens may have peace of mind as they go about their lives, without having to worry about the threat they pose."

David's father looked like he had just been robbed. During Culver's concluding statement, just before the scene cut, David looked past his father's confusion and pain, just as he had overlooked it from the beginning. There was no grand conspiracy, no mistake as David yearned to believe. It was a simple conclusion: *I qualified, and they didn't want me.*

Sam rested a hand on his shoulder. "I'm so sorry, David."

"Don't be," he said with a hostile bite. "I'd rather be here than live another day in that man's house." He moved so that Sam's hand fell off his shoulder. "Probably kill me in my sleep if he had the chance."

Jensen was not surprised at his devastation, but the extremity of David's begrudging nature disarmed him. The next words would be a gamble he knew. "David. He didn't want to do it."

The sentence snapped David's head to him. He sprang to his feet. "He didn't want to do it? Did you not hear him?"

"I heard him," Jensen said.

"Then what the hell are you saying?" David was in his face now. Abbi was terrified. Even Sam was unsettled, without a gauge to predict the outcome. "Huh? I don't know what you think you heard! It's not only what he wanted. It's what he needed. I

241

was too stupid, and Penelope needed to go to college."

Jensen lifted his hands in front of his chest as a treaty. "I know, David. I know. Please just listen."

"Then why would you say that? No, seriously. You want me to listen? Okay, go ahead. Please. Please, tell me how after both you and I, and all of us heard him . . . Tell me he had his arm put behind his back! Better yet, tell me it was my mom who forced him." He pushed Jensen. "Not all of us can ace exams and be good at everything like you, okay? Maybe that's why it's so hard for you to believe. I'm not you, Jensen! Not everyone is you. If we were, then the CD wouldn't exist, and all this shit wouldn't have happened!"

Jensen was careful not to react. The only productive response was to duck from the fury rather than match it. "Did you see his face?" He now stood some feet away from David.

"Huh?"

"His face, David. His face, his body language. Remember and think about it. It sounded like most of those sentences were scripted, or at the least, forced."

David shook his head violently. "No, no. I don't believe that for a second. You're trying to tell me he never wanted to have the contration, and all that on TV was a forced act? Bet they even paid him a nice dollar for that. No, I don't buy it." His rage almost transferred to tears, but he continued to fight to keep the wrath kindled rather than let it wash out. "You're my best friend. How can you say that? How can you say he never wanted me contrated?"

"Because you never wanted to kill yours!" He saw David gulp. "You contrated your child, but you never wanted to! You did the exact same thing as your dad. You justified, you lied to yourself, and you forced a girl to make a decision she never wanted," said Jensen. "Sure, maybe your dad's hardness grew thicker than yours ever could, but don't you ever think yours didn't come from the same place. I love you and you know I'll go to war for you. But I won't let you lie to yourself. If you continue hating him, then make sure to hate yourself." He did not remember walking back toward David, but his hands were gripping his friend's arms by this time. "Neither of those needs to be true though."

David gave no response, not even a movement. His eyes remained fastened on Jensen's hands for almost a minute. There was a thin layer over his eyes that seemed unable to break or recede, a cascade frozen in time. He removed himself from Jensen's loosening grasp. He walked to the kitchen, ignoring Abbi and Sam until his back was to them. The rage did not leave, but it also could not find his father like before, nor could it consume himself as Jensen suggested. He stretched his arms out and placed his hands on the refrigerator to keep from fainting.

*

The rumbling traffic bounced and echoed through the streets and buildings of downtown Bellark. The area never rested, but the late afternoon offered the peak of congestion. The people ending their day shifts and the people arriving for dinner transformed the streets into a thronging ant farm.

The street in front of the CD headquarters was especially crowded, more than usual. The resilient protesters raised picket signs and shouted synchronous chants: "Mercy for the runagates!" and "Let them live! Let them live!" Several news vans were parked out front, each station and reporter staked out in anticipation. The impending encounter between the department leads and the group of protesters would pay dividends for every media source.

Half a block away on the opposite side of the street was parked a pickup truck, intentionally positioned to face away from the headquarters entrance. Drake watched the protesters and the reporters through the left side mirror. It had taken him over an hour to reach downtown through rush hour traffic. He'd been surprised to find such a close parking spot unoccupied. It was too perfect, he thought. Drake was not typically one to believe in destiny, but the favorable conditions seemed to confirm the decision. He held the gun, thinking of his friends. *Please, don't wait.*

Drake did not have to wait long. When he saw the

department SUV driving his direction, he ducked his head to prevent the seed logo from seeing him. It was as if the one Rylie had crashed into the river had resurrected and found a new driver. Behind the SUV followed two police car escorts. After the vehicles parked directly in front of the headquarters building, the police officers were the first to step out. They pushed back the protesting crowd and news reporters to allow a clear passage for the Chief to enter the building.

The door opened, and out stepped Salvador Goode and Luis Adán. Bobby's body would have seemed alive in comparison to the Chief, his skin paler and eyes darker than the morning conference. Then he looked to Luis Adán; a shorter height, but his straight-backed stature and neatly slicked hair could deceive one into thinking it was he in charge. *It won't be him.* Drake opened the door.

*

A reporter said into the camera, "I'm standing outside the BCD headquarters, and Chief Salvador Goode has just arrived. We will see if he has any comments about the continuing search for the at-large March Runaways, as well as the debate that has followed his verdict from this morning. Declaring these teens as irrevocable Potentials has certainly spiked controversy."

Salvador stepped onto the sidewalk with Adán and some officers following. Each reporter with a cameraman closed in on the Chief while the protesters shouted from the police perimeter. "Killer!" One of the radicals shouted. In moments, reporters assailed Salvador and his officers from all sides as protesters fought to add their voice.

"Chief Goode!" The reporter stuck a microphone as close to Salvador's mouth as possible. "Do you have any information on where the other Potes might be?"

Some of the officers attempted to block the reporters, but Salvador stopped and turned to one of the cameras. The protesters, the citizens of Bellark, and the people of the nation had to see that he had dominion. He needed to persuade, not necessarily the protesters, but the simple working-class viewer that there was no doubt regarding his morning declaration.

Seeing Salvador's new posture, another reporter jumped in. "Do you believe any of our citizens are assisting the March Runaways in their evasion?"

Salvador forced his certainty to the camera. "We are working very hard to apprehend the Potentials. Thankfully, we are making progress. We apprehended one of them today, and we'll capture the rest soon enough. This search will end, and a situation like this will never happen again."

"Chief, is there reason to believe other citizens are helping the fugitives?" repeated the second reporter.

"A thorough pursuit of the remaining Potentials is underway as we speak." He moved his head back from the intrusive mic. "While we have not discovered anyone to be assisting them, it is not improbable. The citizens of Bellark have been incredibly helpful in our search, and we encourage such assistance from everybody to bring this situation to an end."

"We have not heard from you since you revoked the chance for these Potentials to become living." The reporter had to squeeze through the others. "Many are speculating whether the Bellark CD can justly contrate these Potentials even with this verdict."

"The law allows it," he said directly. "I can only make my decision on that basis."

Another reporter cut in. "Chief Goode! There have been doubts of Robert Reynolds' contration this afternoon. Should contrations only be completed at facilities?"

The crowd was pressing in closer, giving the police officers difficulty in holding the set U-shape boundary. Luis turned to the Chief and said, "We need to get inside. This may get out of control." Goode glanced at the restlessly fierce crowd, provoking his combativeness rather than his forfeit. He shook his head at Adán's request.

Salvador put his hands up defensively. "Okay, one question at a time. As I stated, these Potentials have only affirmed why their carriers selected contration in the first place. They have

245

brought chaos to not only their carriers but now to the society on a larger scale. Is this not why we designed our system? They have demonstrated their lack of capability to benefit their carriers and society, and should—" He stopped as soon as he felt the pressure to his head.

"Step back!" shouted the boy with black hair, holding the gun to Salvador. He was surprised not one police officer had thought to patrol the rear next to the SUV. Drake jumped out from behind after stealthily creeping alongside the other parked cars; every distracted officer held back the pressing crowd.

All scattered from the scene immediately, the chants turning to gasps as the protesters fled. The reporters were right behind them, except one cameraman who took cover behind a van some yards away. He pointed his camera toward the Chief and the Potential. Luis and four police officers quickly drew their weapons.

"Lower your guns!" Drake said to Salvador, knowing there was no turning back, "Tell them to lower their guns now!"

"Put them down!" ordered Salvador; he was wide awake.

Luis was the last one to lower his weapon, almost testing whether the boy with black hair would pull the trigger. The thought was brief. It might make the entire ordeal easier, and Salvador could even go down as a martyr after Luis avenged the Chief and contrated the Potential. But when he caught another glimpse of Salvador's fear, Luis could not help his concern for the man who'd groomed him the past several years.

The boy slowly walked backward with Salvador to the parked SUV to cover his back from any threat he could not see. Drake glanced left and saw the lingering cameraman peeking the camera past the rear of a nearby van.

"Put the gun down," Adán said, "or this won't end well for you."

Drake shouted, "Why? This is what you want, right? Isn't this helping prove your point?"

"What are you talking about, kid?" Salvador said cautiously.

"I'm the very reason why your department exists!" He

was almost manic, but there was a composure that kept it impassioned instead. "This is what keeps you all your jobs! Me and the other Potes who have burdened you all. Our carriers had it right, huh? It's a shame you couldn't get us back at the facility. Now a good man has to die today! Me, I'm bad. A bad man indeed." A chuckle left Drake. "Man? Can I even say that? No. As long as I breathe, I'm only a contration gone wrong, a Potential forever. A liability because I killed *all* your people. Don't forget that old man at the gas station too. I wanted to see a helpless man suffer. That's right. I killed them all!" He glanced at the camera once more. "I didn't even have the heart to free the other Potes at the facility. That obstruction was committed by another one of us. Isn't that something, though? He put his *life* . . . on the line to save some other Potentials. Or how about Rylie? Bet she pissed you all off. She tricked your entire department. At least you got the pleasure of seeing her body in that river.

"Did you like that?" Drake speared the question at Adán, who was carefully watching his every action. "It wasn't enough though, was it? You had to get Bobby too. The kid who wouldn't hurt a fly, but god forbid his mom has to keep caring for that retard. Luis, right?" Their stares were locked. "You got him before he did something *really* dangerous."

"You're right," Adán shouted back. "You're only proving us right. All the world is watching you." He pointed at the cameraman focused on the scene.

"But I find something ironic!" Drake seemed to let the comment go over his head. "I didn't want to help the other 'March Runaways,' as you all call us. Catchy name. Though it doesn't matter much anymore. That month won't be saving us." The disingenuous laugh faded again. "I only cared about saving my own skin. I could have done it too. I could have gone on my own, but I let one free. And then that guy went all Johnny-hero. Annoyed the hell out of me to herd all of them." Drake clenched the tie around Salvador's neck. "But down the line, it was those Potentials who kept me alive. Hate to admit it, but I don't think I woulda made it this far without them. For the first time, I saw somebody, a few somebodies, give a damn about me. Fortunately for you, some died doing so."

Salvador Goode was dreadfully sure of the boy's intent. Delaney kept flashing in his mind. He begged, "Let me go. Please, don't make this mistake."

"The friends who died didn't kill anybody. Same as the ones who are still alive," Drake said. "I'm the bad one! I'm the one who has the gun to your Chief's head. If I were contrated, this wouldn't be happening. This right here was my destiny." His hand moved suddenly, pulling the scarlet tie so that it was nearly horizontal. "Back to why I'm here. Like I said. A good man has to die today."

The gunshot roared down the streets, overcoming any traffic clamor. The Chief fell forward, collapsing to his knees first. The officers had their clear shot and opened fire. The black-haired hit the ground, bullets sunken into every inch of his body. It would be difficult to say which one pierced first. To the naked eye, all nine seemed to enter at once. However, Luis Adán would bet his life he'd fired first, accounting for the gap in the middle of David Drake's forehead.

Luis walked toward the Potential. He saw the blood pulse to the top of the small forehead gash like a newly dug spring. "You okay?" he asked without turning away from the contrated body.

The Chief could not have registered or remembered Luis' question. He frantically felt around his body, particularly his chest to search for a wound where the gun had fired; instead, the only damage he found was the severed half a tie around his neck. The hairs on his neck rose like trained soldiers. Face a ghost, Salvador turned to inspect Drake's body, still holding the other half of the scarlet tie.

"Chief?" Luis turned to him. "Are you hurt?"

Every bit of Salvador's attention focused on the cloth in the boy's hand. Luis came and shook him. "What?" Salvador said, snapping back to reality. Luis had never seen this expression come from the Chief before. It was more than just fear. Never had he seen such desperation.

Stern and frantic, Salvador demanded, "What happened?

Did he miss?"

"He was crazy," said Luis. "You heard how he was talking. Sounded like he was losing his mind. Just feel fortunate that he buckled like that."

Salvador was not satisfied. He stared at the corpse of the boy with black hair. Another one contrated, but no relief gained. Instead, Salvador's vexation grew every time he glanced at the cloth in the Potential's hand. He disagreed with Luis. The boy had not sounded crazy. In fact, it was his precision of thought that brought Salvador to vomit on the sidewalk.

*

David had expected Drake to pull the trigger at any moment. Yet he kept speaking, at moments seeming to ramble. When he looked into the camera, it was clear that he had sought from the start to be heard by an audience. David tried at first to deny it, but deep down he understood, just as well as Drake, that death was certain as soon as the gun went to the Chief. David's immediate assumption seemed reasonable: If Goode died, then perhaps they could travel to the South safely.

When the first gunshot blew through the television's speakers, all believed he had finished the Chief. Subsequent shots followed just as any viewer would have expected, and Drake lay on the sidewalk. No one in the house, likely no viewer anywhere, expected Salvador to move again. But the cameraman zoomed in on Drake's hand, clenching a portion of the scarlet tie.

The program replayed the clip several times over. In a fluid motion, Drake lowered the gun from Salvador and shot it through the tie instead. He dropped the gun and with both hands ripped the fabric from the hole it had left. The abruption sent Salvador to his knees. The cable network could not continue to review David Drake's graphic end following the live feed. After the anchor confirmed the contration, not even Sam could fight the tears, the first he had shed over the recent deaths.

David's confusion dominated anything else. He had to leave, locking himself in the room before Abbi could go to him.

"Give him a moment," Jensen said. Surprisingly relieved to see Salvador survive the scene, Jensen could not maintain this attitude after Drake's contration was confirmed. Pretty quickly, he understood what the boy accomplished. It was not clear when Drake first grappled with the Chief; however, it only took a few minutes after the first shot. But this was a realization David would have to arrive in solitude, where the internal grappling ensued.

Sunset was near, but it may as well have already set as if the clouded sky ushered in the night an hour early. There was no discussion of Drake's death, what it all meant or how it could have gone differently. There was no speaking at all, only bodies rising to pursue a fate more promising than the one reserved for Rylie, Mia, Bobby, and Drake.

Abbi looked at the different water glasses left atop the coffee table, unsure which had belonged to her fallen friends, but picturing the memory of everyone sitting and drinking together the night before.

"Jensen," Sam said in the silence. "Go get David. We have to get going now."

"You sure?"

"We don't have time to stay here. He can take whatever time he needs on the way."

"I'm okay." David's voice came from down the hall. He appeared before the three. "Let's get going." It was like he'd just received a full night's sleep. However, there was no time to ask how he'd acquired the newfound tranquil state.

The impending darkness would benefit them in their travels. Waiting throughout the day may have worked out to their advantage after all. The department was like a fox chasing a mouse but forgetting the nest it had fled. If Drake and Bobby had never left, the CD would have been more likely to locate the group in the daylight, whether on the road or in the house. Though they'd gained that benefit, any of them would have rewritten Drake's or Bobby's fate to leave for the South alive and together.

Most of the clouds retreated after the sun officially dropped below the horizon, humbly stepping down for the next act. Outside, Abbi was reaching through the RV storage hatch, spraying some of Sam's wife's perfume over the tarp covering Mia. The brisk of the night would slow decay, but Abbi felt it would be an honorable gesture to add the feminine aroma.

David stood at the front of the RV, letting the breeze kiss his face. Though the temperature was dropping for the night, the wind did not bring with it discomfort, and David had been indoors for so long that day. The winter air seemed to patter his cheeks like a light rain; not invasive, but enough to awaken.

Abbi said, "How you doing?"

David turned to her. "I think I have a better idea."

"Drake did a brave thing," she said. "You know that now, right?"

"Three days ago, he would have shot Goode right then and there."

"That was then."

"It was," said David. "Drake showed they were wrong about him, wrong about the whole system. Most won't understand that though."

"Does it still give you some peace?"

"Not enough to make it easier to accept, but yeah. They took his life. They would have taken it even if Drake didn't have the gun. They killed him, but he put them in checkmate. The whole nation saw him pass up on the opportunity to kill the man who wanted his life."

Abbi heard the remaining doubt. "So, why are you still troubled?"

His mind returned to the same train of thought as when he locked himself in the room. The confusion and turmoil were not so much about why Drake allowed the Chief to live. He reckoned that quickly enough after leaving to the guestroom.

"David?" she said more insistently.

His breath was noticeably visible in the last tithe of twilight. He looked to Abbi sincerely. "I can't go with you guys."

Her heart skipped. "What? What do you mean?"

"I need to stay here."

"What?" she asked, dumbfounded. "We're leaving right

251

now."

"Drake said we were the ones who changed him. That's why he did what he did. That's why he's dead and Goode's still living. But he's done something that I haven't."

"What's that?"

"It was like a pardoning," he said. "Since this whole thing happened, once I understood it was their choice to have me contrated, I viewed my carriers as worthless. No, I saw them as less than human. Jensen called me a hypocrite, and he was right."

"David . . ." Abbi searched.

"I need to talk to them."

"Who?" Inside she knew, but it seemed beyond reason.

"Who else?"

"You mean in person?" Abbi tried grasping the realism of the suggestion. "How?"

"I guess I'll just go to the only place I know where to find them. I'll walk to my house."

"What are you going to say?"

"I'll have to figure it out."

"I understand you want to talk to them, or whatever," she said. "But they might not be sorry. You can forgive them without seeing them. They made the decision, remember? What if they call the department on you?"

"I don't expect them to be sorry. I'm sure Drake most definitely knew after he spared Goode, he was going down anyway." He maintained confidence. "I just have to."

A soft cry left her. "David, please don't. I don't want you to go." She lunged to embrace him. "You're all I have. You, Jensen, and Sam are all that I have now."

He held on, her head resting on his chest just under his chin. "I don't want to go either. This isn't what I ever wanted. What I want is a new beginning. Leaving you, leaving Jensen and Sam is not what I want. But if I don't, if I don't see my carriers, I'll be trapped in some way—" the thought did not come until then, "—and so will they."

With David's chin resting atop her head, Olivia came to his mind, yet Abigail was not at all overshadowed; it was she in his

252

arms. Neither her hair nor its scent was anything close to Olivia's, but David would not have wanted it to be. The two young women had a unique beauty to themselves, and David felt no need to try and conjure Abbi into someone she was not.

Abbi sniffled and shifted her head as she wiped her tears on the new white T-shirt he grabbed from Jensen's closet.

"Go and get out of this country and never come back," he said to her. "You need to do it for all of us: Bobby, Drake, Rylie, and Mia. You'll be in good hands with Jensen and Sam. Show the world they were wrong about you, about all of us, about anyone who has ever been contrated. Show them I was wrong."

Abbi lifted her head. "I hope to see you after."

"Me too."

"After you talk with them, maybe we can figure out a way to contact one another? You can meet up with us somehow."

"That would be nice," he said.

Her request was lofty, but perhaps reconciliation was possible. Abbi knew that David would have to leave his carriers' house safely for it to be true, but she was not willing to relinquish all belief.

Jensen emerged from the side garage door. "You guys ready?"

David responded, still looking at her, "Let's get you all loaded up."

Jensen shut the door as Sam walked out. "How do you think they'll take it?" said Abbi

"They'll understand." David watched the two. "In time."

Both Jensen and Sam lost the knocking sense of urgency they had all afternoon right after David opened his mouth. Time was no matter in the minutes he shared with Jensen what he just spoke with Abbi. Jensen vehemently appealed to his friend to abandon the newfound desire, "David, you do not need to do this. You shouldn't! We need you. Abbi needs you just as much as you think your carriers do."

Jensen's plea moved David, but he stood firm. "It's more than even what Abbi needs. It's about what they need, what I need. Trust me. I think it sounds insane too, but I wouldn't do it if

I didn't have to. I, we, have an opportunity to do good for more than just her now."

Well, what about what I want, what I need? Jensen wanted to say it, but David's sullen confidence finally restrained him from voicing and continuing the case.

For David, it seemed an insult to abandon the two who had already protected his life with theirs and were ready to keep doing so all the same. But it was this loyalty that seemed to grant them the salvation he knew his carriers were without. "I wouldn't do it if I didn't have to," David repeated, tears prickling his eyes.

Jensen could not doubt the difficulty in his decision, finally able to acknowledge he could not in love or fairness continue to press David to remain. "Just be safe." Jensen pulled him in for a hug. "We'll see you soon."

David glanced at Abbi, who watched the two friends. "Take good care of her."

"We will," said Jensen, letting go of David and turning to Abbi. "I swear it." He looked back to David. "When you join back up with us, you're buying me a beer."

David grinned. "Oh yeah. At Eighteen we can do that in the South, huh?"

"There, we're considered adults at Eighteen. But here, that's when life starts." He rolled his eyes.

"You've got yourself a deal." The optimism was a bit forged, but David had to do anything he could to reassure him.

Unlike Jensen, Sam did not argue with David. The man immediately understood the unalterable conviction. The straining courage to David's words was the same kind that finally compelled him to help David and the others. Sam embraced David for a great deal longer than Jensen or Abbi had. He allowed himself to hope David would rejoin them in the South, but he wanted to savor the moment just in case. "Do what you have to do, then get back to us."

"I'll do my best."

Sam walked in to start the RV. Jensen gave David one last hug and followed. Abbi remained several feet away from David as they stood beside the RV. Even under the evening sky,

254

David could see new tears building. She went to cross her arms until David grabbed her hands.

"I'm sorry that I might not be with you on your Eighteenth," he said. "One more day, or just a few hours, really."

"Do these dates even matter anymore?" She shook her head. "Funny enough, I was born on the Twenty-Ninth of a leap year. For legal purposes, they rounded down. Technically, I'm still not Eighteen tomorrow."

"Wow. A leap year kid? But you're right. What they say doesn't matter anymore."

Abbi lifted her head to find David's eyes. "It's hard."

"What is?"

Her voice shyly undressed itself. "Accepting the fact that my little girl fantasy of a happily-ever-after might not come true. It makes sense though."

"What does?" he said.

"Before we can ever fantasize, we need to have a reality, something real to start with."

There was no restraint. David leaned and brought his lips to hers. Her head lifted on its own as he gently placed his hands on the bottom of her cheeks, lining each of his ring fingers with her smooth jaw. Their lips quietly left each other seconds after.

Abbi walked up the steps into the RV as her blushing cheeks returned to their light brown. She could not foresee what the future held, but though she desired nothing more than to see David again, she rested assured that they exchanged all necessary words and gestures.

David opened the side gate for them to back out. The three peered out of the front window. They waved, as did he.

There was no remnant of the twilight, the hands of night entirely folding over the retreated sun. David looked one last time at the Lloyd house. All the lights were turned off, even the porch light they had long kept on through the evenings.

He looked up the street toward his own home, unable to keep out the uncertainty, not for his life, whether he was to live or die after meeting his carriers. Rather, his stomach knotted at the thought of his carriers seeing a Potential. *Son*, he thought. *That's all*

I want. He started up the street, also wondering if he might see any of his old neighbors on the way.

*

Salvador stared down from his office window, unblinking from his bird's-eye view. Seven stories below outside the entrance were the protesters, shouting atop the pavement where the boy with black hair had been contrated. The first two buttons of his shirt were left undone after he removed the remainder of his tie. It was clenched in his hand, absorbing every bit of sweat that left his palm. Though his sight was above the people, it was not they he saw. His memory had sifted them away, his mind instead projecting the earlier event. The gunshot was as loud in his head as it was when it actually fired.

A knock came on his office door, yet he heard nothing.

"Salvador." It was the only voice that would have been able to snatch him. Not as eager as he may have been in the morning, he turned nonetheless. He felt neither relief nor resentment. He may have been able to feel one, or perhaps both, but right now his mind was a cup and his current trauma a running faucet over it; any other feeling that might try to fill it would be washed out in a brief moment before he could even identify what it was. "I'm glad to see you're okay," Delaney said. "I thought he was going to kill you."

He took several seconds. "He didn't."

Delaney presumed correctly that the event would have left him shaken. His posture was like a statue and his voice just as lifeless. She wanted to provide a comfort or warming, but her feet would not move from in front of his desk. She could not find words to say either, though she felt more compelled to speak now that Salvador had ignored her calls for the past hour.

After a minute's silence, Salvador turned back to the window. "Is that what it takes? I must have a gun to my head for you to show? You also bought his bluff. He wasn't going to kill me." He closed the window blinds. "I guess what's done is done." He walked toward Delaney, some shred of humanity returning to

256

his voice as it released distress. "He should have killed me. He should have. At least then we could have gone down one for one." The statue demeanor broke in an instant. "Now we're just going to keep pursuing the others because it's what needs to be done." He opened his hand and hung the tie in front of Delaney. "This should have been my head. Does he really want me to kill those other kids so bad?"

Salvador sat on his desk, rubbing his hands over his eye sockets. "They shot him. They shot him like it was target practice. Nine times! And Adán got him right between his eyes. Where were you? He should have been apprehended and taken into custody. I needed you. For god's sake, now we have a mob right outside our doors. Should have been me. A bullet sounds much better than this migraine that won't go away. Fired it right in front of my face."

"Don't say that." Delaney quivered, only able to put a hand on Salvador's shoulder. Her other arm crossed over her stomach. "They contrated him because they could. That Potential was contrated because it was someone else's decision. We're just the hands to make it happen, whether in a facility or, though less ideal, the streets. Doesn't matter. The vote's the vote. All those people outside—their voices are loud only to compensate for how few people there really are."

"To hell with the vote. I should have just let them pass Eighteen and issue a trial as living beings. I'm sure they would have accepted any jail time over death." He braced his hands on the desk as he leaned forward. "What if I did now? Withdraw the verdict and offer the Potentials a trial."

Delaney said nothing, but he was not asking her, she knew. It was a conversation with himself, his words back and forth, hot and cold as he tried to find some assurance within himself.

He paced to the window and peeled back a blind for another look. "No. Wouldn't do anything. Then the other side will crucify me. What's done is done. We just need to get the rest out of the way and finished. Another one's dead, so we're that much closer." He returned to his chair to draw up a plan,

257

scribbling neurotically. "I'm done after this, Delaney. I can't stay with the department any longer if I'm not fired first. I don't care about any of it anymore. Let them decide what they want after this. What matters is I'm still here, by some insanity or miracle . . . And you're here with me. If you want to stay with the department, I completely understand. It'll still be good money. Stability for us to start our family. I know you're still hesitant about marriage—" He would have continued if not for her cry. Salvador glanced up from his papers. "What's wrong?"

It was beyond her strength to withhold. In her was remorse, but she could not pin it where it ought to hang. For certain, her love for Salvador heightened the grief, but she was unsure if that was the only reason. She resisted.

"Delaney, sweetheart."

His tenderness was like a choking, forcing the words upward. "I had it contrated," she said, hardly audible. There was no going back, and ambiguity would only drag him through the thorn bush more slowly. "I contrated our Potential. Early this morning, I contrated it at a nearby facility. That's when I saw you in here this morning. I came back to the office right after I did it." She held her hand under her nose to stop the dripping. Salvador showed no inclination to interrupt, a corpse of a face as her audience. "I'm sorry. I was angry. I was angry after you sent me home. I got scared it would only get worse. If you stripped me of respect then, what else would come when the Potential grew? I know I probably jumped to crazy conclusions of how it would pan out, and I know you were under a lot of pressure. I'm sorry. I was just scared."

Salvador stood, expression returning, but not its better side; darkness animated every facial movement. "You were scared? That's what you were. Because I dismissed you. You were scared and you contrated our baby?"

She shook her head, sending some tears to the carpet. "I'm sorry, Salvador. I really am. I would take it back if I could. Talk to you first. But you can't keep saying that."

"What?" he lashed. "Can't say what?"

"It was a Potential. I messed up. I went behind your back

out of spite. But it was a *Potential*. Please stop calling it that."

"You're going to come in here, tell me you had a contration without telling me—after I was held at gunpoint hours ago—and correct me for calling the Potential, which you killed, a *baby*?" His voice escalated to a height never before climbed. "Delaney! This is the third time! Can't I make a mistake, without having to worry if you'll steal the one damn thing that I want? You think what gets me out of bed in the morning is my duty to the department or this country? The hell with both of them!" It was the first time she saw him cry, the tears few but the grief in each one worth a thousand. "Why did you have to take it away? Not even a second thought. The only child I'm a father to, I can't even . . ." The pivot was quick and seamless. Delaney did not think twice to consider his unfinished statement, preoccupied with rationalizing a response. "You can't just have a contration without telling me."

"How could you say that? No. Of course, you would!" She did not hesitate to match him. "Easy for you to say when being pregnant never gets you dismissed from your job. You have no place to speak into what I do with it at all. We're not married, and on top of it, it's my body! I wish you could get pregnant so you can do whatever it is you want. Then it doesn't depend on the compromise of my career. It would be perfect since you hate the department so much anyway!" She gained a breath, "A family was your desire, but did you ever stop to ask me mine? No, you just assumed I bought into yours as if I couldn't think up a future myself? Yeah, I know. I didn't speak against it whenever you imagined this life, but that's because you put so much goddamn pressure on it! But of course I want to be a part of your future." Some loose strands of hair fell over her forehead. "It's confusing, I know. I don't know. I just don't know how I want it to look, Sal."

It was not conscious, the progressive muting of her voice. *It's my body.* The words were like arsenic to his soul, refusing to accept or attempt to digest even another ounce. "You're done here," he said. "You're done here at Bellark CD."

"Oh what, now you're going to fire me because I won't bend to your every wish and desire?"

He looked at her with as much sincerity as he could salvage. "Please, leave. I'll give you whatever recommendation you need. I'll report irreconcilable differences, even confess my feelings for you to the higher-ups. A conflict of interest won't blemish your résumé. Only mine. I'm letting you go only from Bellark. There are plenty of other departments that will hire you without a second thought. Please, leave."

Her defense dropped, and she leaned on his desk as her hands gripped the wood desperately. "Wait, Salvador. You're not serious."

"I am."

"Sal?" It was a dance of belief and doubt. "No. You can't just say that. Wait a second. Can we just keep talking for a minute?"

"We've talked for several."

"You can't just do this. We're stronger than this!" It was a frantic effort. "Our relationship is more than just a Potential. It's you and me. That's how it started; that's how we fell in love. Please don't throw it away over this. I have to mean more than for you to go and flippantly say that! You can't trust yourself right now. You're exhausted, you have a migraine, and yes, my decision hurt you. For god's sake, you had a gun held to you! I'm sorry. It was wrong for me to get the contration without telling you. That's why I apologized. What is our love if it quits after veering off-road? It has always gotten us back on course. It can again."

"It can."

She relaxed, lifting her hands from the desk and bringing them to her hips for an easier breath. "Exactly. If we continue to move forward and understand each other—"

"No." The interruption was quick but sorrowful. "No. We could pick up the pieces. We could get back on course as you said. But that's not what I want. It's not a road I want to travel. Not with you. Not anymore." The word crushed any effort to continue. Had it not been so firm, she may have persisted. "I don't want either of us to hurt one another anymore. Leave, please. For both of us."

Her exit was a silent one. She mustered her remaining composure so that her walk through the department halls would go unnoticed. Even in heartbreak, she would not allow another to see her in such a vulnerable state, a wound so wide and deep that she had no awareness yet of its full dimension.

There was probably a more delicate or balanced approach to have articulated his final thoughts, but trying to speak of his reasoning would not have lessened the pain for either of them. It was strange to relinquish responsibility for Delaney's feelings, but Salvador finally resolved that obligation should no longer be his. The resolution still did not bring comfort to his despair, but better that than for his heart to take another stab; Delaney's contration was the last it could take.

*

Luis rushed into the room, the door still unlocked after Delaney's departure. He said fervently, "Sir, we received a call from a resident in northwest Bellark. She claims to have seen David Kingsley walking through a neighborhood a few miles away from where we apprehended Robert Reynolds." He never saw Salvador still hadn't opened his eyes yet with his chair turned toward the window. "Sir?"

"You mean, contrated him?" Delaney had left an hour ago, and he found his only place of solace was behind his eyelids. It was a light enough slumber to hear Luis enter and find his wits quickly. "No need to use that language here. I'm not the public," he said, lifting his eyes and rotating the chair.

Luis nodded impatiently, wishing only to deliver the news. "Our men investigated the claim and discovered the neighborhood matches David Kingsley's original address."

"Really?" Salvador's attention was captivated now. "Have you sent officers over?"

"Yes, Sir. Right before I came in here."

Salvador jumped out of his chair. "Well, let's go."

Luis remained still while Salvador buttoned his shirt and put his jacket on. He knew his Chief's request, but Luis did not want to withhold any vital information. He, more than any other officer, more than Delaney, had observed the Chief's progressive loss of composure and judgment. He glanced at Salvador's right hand, finding the divided tie still in its grip. "We looked further into this neighborhood," Luis said, knowing this was the moment he needed to assert himself most. "Jensen Lloyd, the Potential who shut off the power at the facility, lives a couple of blocks away from the Kingsley residence."

Salvador turned as he put on his jacket. "Were they friends?" he asked directly, cautious to monitor his tone.

"There is strong reason to believe so. Same age, same school. It may have been why he sabotaged the facility power. He could have helped or still be helping the escaped Potes. It would seem highly unlikely that they would hide at Kingsley's house, seeing it was his carriers who contrated him."

"Yes, that makes sense," Salvador said, collected.

Luis was surprised not to see a negative reaction, wondering if his Chief was perhaps regaining his sense as lead. Yet he did not return his complete trust to him. There was only one more piece of information Luis had to announce. "I told our men to take out Lloyd, and anyone else found assisting the Potentials if they demonstrate resistance."

"What?" Salvador said. "Why? I never gave an order."

"Sir, if he is helping the Potes, he needs to be shot, contrated if necessary." Any confidence he may have begun to regain in Salvador had washed away. Luis could see the Chief's composure vanish before him. "You said it on television this morning in the verdict. The one you decided on."

Salvador strode to the door, avoiding contact with Luis. "You are correct. Let's go."

Luis did not follow immediately. For the entirety of his career in the Contration Department, Luis Adán had gladly taken orders from Salvador, capitalizing on every moment to learn from his esteemed mentor. Now, he decided with much hesitation, but he needed to see the resolution through—every escaped Potential must be contrated. The cost of peace, stability, and choice would be worthwhile. Luis was not certain of Salvador's hindrance, but the Chief's hesitances would no longer be his to bear.

*

As usual, the front porch and front lawn were barren of light. David began to wonder if perhaps the porch lights were never replaced to cut the electricity bill. The cynicism naturally festered. *If he got rid of me, why not electricity too?* He silenced his ill thoughts, realizing where they would drag him. Anxious as ever, David knocked. While he waited, he searched for what he would say. The doubt soon came when he could not figure where to start. *Why am I here?* "No," he said to himself.

One minute passed. David knocked again, louder. Another minute, yet no one answered. The house was vacant. It was unusual for them to be out on weeknights, especially with Penelope away for university, his carriers long having a clear calendar from the sports she used to play in secondary school. David wondered if it was perhaps a sign. If it was fate not to have the encounter, then maybe it was sensible to leave. Arriving at his childhood home could qualify as a symbolic act for what he first intended, but as much as David rationalized it, he found himself unmoving.

How long can I wait out here? He remembered the neighbor that had seen him after she got out of her car, though David did not recognize her. *Maybe she's new to the neighborhood.* It was a block away, and his worry had left after she calmly walked from her car into the house. *But I need to get inside before someone else sees me.*

Hopping the fence was easy enough, though he scanned behind first to make sure there were no passing cars. The key in the backyard was still where he remembered it, next to the patio door under its rock. Walking back toward the front door, he glanced up at his carriers' window as he winced at the memory of his carriers discussing his failing exam score.

The house was pitch black when he stepped inside. His carriers must have been away for most of the day. Otherwise, at least one light would have shone indoors for when they returned. David flicked the main living room switch. "Hello?" No answer.

He scanned the new portraits on the walls, replacing the dismantled family of four; a family of three now as if that was the only one that ever existed. His mind spun and body swayed, figuring it was likely his mother who'd replaced the photos.

He grabbed one of the frames and sat on the couch before he completely lost his balance. The photo of his carriers and sister at a neighborhood park was hypnotizing. Penelope was in her Seventh year in the photo, and David in his Fifth. Though out of frame, he could imagine himself smiling on the jungle gym, just as his mother, father, and sister did for the camera. *"No one plans for a contration."* He could hear his father's words from the interview.

The empty house finally made sense. *That's why they aren't here.* Realizing his carriers must have committed to a downtown studio for the interview, David figured he might have more time alone at his old home than expected.

He walked upstairs, keeping a hand on the stair rail in case his faintness should return. Upon entering his old room, he saw his desk completely cleared, other than a few pens in a jar. On the carpeted floor were a box, a bed frame, and a stripped mattress. His glasses were nowhere in sight as he looked where his missing nightstand would sit. *I can see well enough. I have for days now.* He hoped his guitar was at least donated to someone rather than trashed. David's passion was worth more than waste.

He leaned down and opened the box. On top of his books and other belongings was a photograph. He and Jensen were lifting their fish from a catch at Nod. It was in October during their Sixteenth year. David was holding up three fish in each hand; no mystery why he looked so satisfied. Jensen's eyes did not meet the camera as they fastened on the favorable amount of fish David lifted in triumph. Sam had gone out with them that autumn day to capture the photograph.

David stood up suddenly, folding the photograph and sliding it into his back pocket. Angst growing, he looked around his room as if he was trying to find something concealed. Seizing the box and grabbing an old notebook from it, he tore out a couple of blank pages and went to his almost vacant desk.

Grabbing a pen, he looked into the air to gather his thoughts. It would not be like the last, he knew. Not a song. He already had that with him forever. Finally, he stopped twirling the pen in his hand and pressed the tip to the blank paper.

For the next thirty minutes, David wrote. It came naturally, like shouting atop a winter mountain peak, unaware how long or far the avalanche would descend. He did not contemplate whether he would see his carriers or not that evening. He never considered whether he would reunite with his friends in the near future. He did not have any presumption about whether he was to live or die. All he felt confident of were the memories, dreams, and woes culminating, stretching each fiber of himself.

As soon as he signed his name at the bottom, the silence in the house was interrupted by an all-too-familiar sound. The garage door was opening, sending a mild vibration through the house. Leaving the papers on his desk, he cautiously flicked the light off and walked out into the hall. The back door opened, and he could hear an intense conversation underway.

"You need to calm down," David's father said.

David's mother followed him in. The argument had begun before they arrived. David leaned against a wall, staying hidden.

"No, I don't!" Her voice was worried, unlike his father's harshness. "I don't want to see David die on the streets like those other boys!"

His father appeared in David's field of view. Stopping in his tracks and turning to his wife, he said, "He made his choice. We aren't responsible if that happens."

"He didn't make that choice. We did!"

David's father erupted. "That is enough of that! We did what was best—for him, for us. You're looking at this the wrong way."

"Oh, and doing the interview was 'for him,' huh?" His mother looked to the tile floor. "He was our son."

"That lady irritated me with her questions and judgments as well, but the station gave us more than they originally promised for doing the interview today rather than tomorrow. That gives us an even larger buffer if I don't land the new job next week," he said, attempting to persuade. "I wish it hadn't happened—for his sake, too—but it did. You think I haven't lost any sleep? We did what we had to do."

David's mother glanced up, unconvinced. She opened her mouth to reply until a picture frame lying on the glass table stole her attention. She walked over.

"What is it?" he asked.

"Did you leave the lights on before we left?"

"I don't know. I can't remember," he said impatiently. "What's the matter?"

She turned to look at the front door. "I think someone was in here. The door's unlocked."

Suddenly comprehending, David's father turned his head every direction to gain a sense of security. He looked up the stairs and peered over to what he could see on the second floor. The darkness helped David remain out of sight. To his surprise, his father did not come up to investigate.

"If there was someone here, they're most likely gone now," he said, walking to the kitchen. "I'll call the police."

David walked down the stairs, one step creeping behind the other to keep him unnoticed. His mother studied the framed photograph of her husband, her daughter, and herself at the park. A tear tumbled down her face onto the glass covering. She wiped another with her sweater sleeve and set the frame face down.

"That was a fun day."

She turned around, startled by the familiar voice. Upon seeing her son, she grew lightheaded, the dizziness keeping a response. David's father could not hear over his phone conversation in the kitchen.

"I was in my Fifth year," said David. "We used to go to that park every week when Penelope and I were little."

"David?" She was stunned, struggling to get the words out of her mouth. "Wha . . . What are you doing here?"

"I had to see you. I wanted to talk."

Her disbelief did not wane as the ceiling light reflected off the accumulating layer of tears. She went to speak again but stopped at seeing her son step closer.

His father's voice rose as he walked toward the living room. "Yes, we are all right," he said into the telephone. "My address is—" He came to an abrupt stop as if the vocal cords ripped from his throat. His vision froze when meeting the eyes, the same as his. "David? What are you doing here?"

*

Salvador and Luis were not far from reaching the neighborhood. They had originally planned to investigate Sam Lloyd's property, believing David and the other fugitives were most likely there. The caller who'd reported David Kingsley's whereabouts lived only a block up the street. Salvador had resisted beginning with the Lloyd residence, but he could not voice his disapproval, knowing Adán's suspicion had heightened. But from what Salvador was overhearing, it appeared there would be a rerouting.

"He's at his own house?" Luis Adán demanded of the person on the other end of the phone. "We'll have our men positioned. We aren't too far behind."

Salvador had another itching concern. "What do you have for me, Adán? Is Kingsley alone?" He tried his best to keep the question strictly matter-of-fact.

"Braham Kingsley, former carrier of David Kingsley, just called the police to report a possible burglary. When they asked for his address, all that he said was 'David? What are you doing here?' As if talking to someone else. Then he hung up."

"Hmm. I doubt any of the others would go with him. It seems, if Kingsley is actually in fact there, then he has felt some imperative to see his carriers. But why?"

"He's probably so far gone by now. Survival mode, doing whatever he can. Probably trying to beg his carriers to take him back or help him. Silly, really. Our men are headed there now. We'll soon discover the truth if he's there."

Salvador nodded, trying to regain confidence. He found

himself trying to jump into David's head, curious about his ambiguous intentions for confronting his carriers. But more pressing, he wanted every bit of information about his relationship to Jensen Lloyd. "I want them to take David Kingsley into custody, wherever and whenever we locate him."

Luis looked to his Chief, disappointed. "The orders I already gave were to take him out on sight; the same orders you gave the department this morning."

"I'm giving you new orders." Salvador glared at Luis. "Do not contrate him or any other Potentials. I want Kingsley taken into custody so we can question him further."

Luis said, raising his voice, "Sir, he is a fugitive. He is legally dead on paper. Every second he remains alive undermines the entire system. When they remain alive, we chance a repetition of what happened to you downtown. Where is this coming from?"

Goode did not have an answer for Luis or himself. He was not thinking as thoroughly as usual; otherwise, he would have had a rebuttal ready. Yet while he could not answer, his mind was not blank. On the contrary, the Chief's head was at its busiest. Salvador did not entirely understand his overwhelming desire to again see Jensen, nor could he recognize that it arose following his last exchange with Delaney. "Do not ask why," Salvador spat. "I gave you my orders. Now contact whoever is in command of that dispatch and give him my orders."

Bitterly, Luis took out his phone. "We have new orders," he said. "Do not contrate Kingsley or any Potes who might be with him. Chief Goode wants them arrested and taken into custody."

"Thank you."

Luis did not respond, an invisible hand over his mouth to fight back his aggravation. He lowered the phone and glanced down at the phone screen, forcibly remembering what meant most to him. His belief in the Contration Department sustained him each day and motivated him to be a part of the positive difference happening in the nation, especially since experiencing the backlash firsthand when the system went manipulated or unadhered. Every escaped Potential might as well have had been his brother.

Luis slid his phone in his pocket, sure. Salvador had no doubt that he had issued the order, just as the young officer had complied with every command he'd given since the day Luis joined the department. He relied upon Luis' obedience as if he'd entrusted the task to himself, which is why it would never have occurred to Salvador that there was never a voice on the other end of the phone.

*

They stared at one another. Father and son. David's mother glanced back and forth between the two. Her husband's body squirmed and spoke a defensiveness that required no words to understand. David's apparent neutrality further provoked him. "Why are you here?"

"Hello," said David.

"You have no business here," his father said. "The CD and police are after your life."

The last word almost nudged an inappropriate reply, but David held his tongue. Otherwise, his composure might disappear. He never expected to receive a warm welcome from his father, but David did not anticipate the nuance of how his father spoke either. He felt like a stray dog, but his father had no intention of providing refuge for even a moment.

"You leave now and your mother and I will never speak of seeing you."

"My mother?" David finally blurted, seeing the irony in the statement. "But I wanted to talk."

His father realized his poor word choice. "You have no reason to be angry."

"Who said I was angry?" The comment was deathly quiet. His tone remained the same, but it was merely a paper mask over a stoking fire on the verge of being consumed. His premeditated intent was to approach the dialogue with his carriers in a levelheaded fashion. However, this desire grew less realistic with every word his father uttered.

"I never wanted to lose my job, David! You weren't supposed to wake up. You weren't supposed to ever know anything or feel any pain. We were taking care of you."

"Just like you're taking care of Penelope?"

"Don't. Don't go there. You have no right."

David said, "She's brilliant. And she's beautiful."

"David. Please . . ." his mother said, putting her hands over her mouth.

His father said, "Don't be upset that she's alive. Penelope had nothing to do with our decision."

"I have no reason to be. She has a lot to offer. That's one gifted girl, one worth keeping." David's strike was a ghostly lash, unforeseen but surely felt as it whipped its target.

"Then what are you doing here?" said his father.

"You need to leave somewhere safe, please," his mother added frightened. "I don't want to see you shot to death on the streets and your body broadcast all over the news!"

David's father shook his head. "You were just a . . ."

". . . a Potential?" His façade dropped like lightning, quick and aggressive, set to strike down the tallest object in the same manner. "Yeah, that's what they keep saying. Because I didn't fully develop until what? One day ago? Tell me this . . . Do you feel like you're finally talking to a person because that clock hit twelve last night? What if we were having this conversation at 11:59 yesterday? Quite the mind boggler, huh? That's okay though. No need for you to have to think critically. The CD did it for you already. Because of them, you're still speaking to a Pote, a Potential forever. But wait. The official, *complete development* is when I'm Twenty-Five, right? What'd they do? Average that out from a handful of brains? Too bad they couldn't get any of us kids to fight their wars if they didn't choose Eighteen. Makes sense though. Bending the rules a bit if it helps your team." His father crossed his arms as his mother's jaw steadily dropped, but these perturbed reactions did not compel David to restrain his tirade. "Even if I did manage to pass Twenty-Five, they would think of something else after. I know it. Another new *logic* to redefine completion and person. The average doses of meds a person is

270

dependent on, maybe? I can imagine it now: 'A dependent person is no person at all.' Ha. You'd be in trouble, Mom. Have to give up at least one bottle of your pills, for sure. But depressed and alive is still better, right?" He turned her way, a calm returning. "Maybe my development would still have a ways to go, but I like to believe I'd have some life to me . . . Some life in me."

His father hurdled to speak. "David. I'm . . . I." He looked down to the tile again, shaking his head. "It's part of our law. This is our society. I—for god's sake, you had your own contration! You should know the difficulty, just as much as you should know why you did it in the first place."

It was exactly what David needed to hear to step back from his anger once more and remember his purpose. He closed his mouth to keep back the next fire he was readying to spew. "You're right." Even his father heard the genuine humility. "I had a contration too," said David softly. "I know I've already said a lot, but believe it or not, I didn't come here to say any of that." He had to remember Drake, the strength it took to tear the tie instead. "Dad. Mom." He wanted to look away from them, but it would only take away the truth of it. "I forgive you."

Their eyes widened together as if cued.

Keeping his eyes locked to theirs was like holding a beam of steel over his back. But as seconds passed, as David glanced back and forth between the two of them, the weight lightened. His mother abandoned all resistance, eyes now flooding. David gulped, realizing he had tears also. He turned to his father. Though his were dry, his attention was undivided, second-guessing whether he'd heard his son right.

David stepped toward him. "Dad."

He took a step back as if threatened. "David. If you leave now, your mother and I will never speak of seeing you. You can survive."

"I don't care about surviving." David continued toward his father. "I've already lived. All I need is for you to know that I—"

Crash!

A thunderous roar filled the house. Broken glass from the

271

kitchen window cascaded onto and off the counter. David's father threw his body over his wife's, both of them falling to the floor. Still lying on the ground, they turned to look at their son.

"David!" his mother yelled, mortified at the way he gasped for air. He held the left side of his stomach as blood seeped through his hands and soaked his white T-shirt.

The front door kicked open, armed CD and police officers rushing in. They surrounded the injured body like horse flies ready to devour more. The officers raised their weapons. "Stop!" she cried out, throwing her body over her son's. More officers funneled into the house.

"Ma'am, you need to move!" commanded one. "This Pote is a threat to your safety."

Salvador Goode emerged through the front door with Luis Adán two steps behind. They'd arrived moments after the shooter fired the bullet from his position in the backyard. The Chief stepped closer, looking over the bleeding boy. David's hand pressed over his wound as his mother hovered over him, ready to go to death if another officer threatened her son. Salvador turned to all the officers. "What's gone on here?" he shouted, irate. "I gave orders not to shoot him! Who shot him?"

A nearby officer answered, "Sir, we had orders to take him out. We were waiting for a clear shot and more opportune time, but he started approaching this gentleman." He pointed to David's father. "We had to take the Potential out to ensure his safety."

Salvador immediately realized the insubordination that had taken place. He grabbed Luis by the jacket and slammed him against the wall. "What have you done? Leave, now!"

Disgruntled, yet satisfied to discover David's suffering state, Luis said, "Yes, Sir." The other officers took note of the odd confidence he marched out with. For Luis, Salvador's reprimand had lost all credibility before he even spoke the dismissal. It was mercy that disqualified his Chief, the pity and horror in his eyes when beholding the wounded body of a mere, lifeless Potential.

Salvador watched Luis to ensure he left the house. "Were there any others here?" His concern for Jensen returned to his mind. "Any others killed?"

"No, Chief," said the same officer. "Just him."

Salvador neared David. His mother helped David sit up and lean his body against the staircase wall. She had removed her sweater and pressed it to the wound. David's olive skin had become white.

David struggled to lift his head. "My pocket. On the right." With fading strength, David leaned leftward to expose his right back pocket. Salvador understood, reaching into the jeans and pulling out a photograph. He could not remove his eyes from Jensen, a careful study of his eyes, face, body. At first glance, Salvador thought it was himself in his youth.

"He helped you?" he asked David. "He's your friend."

David nodded, slow of breath. "He saved me. Like a brother."

Salvador reached for his own back pocket, the thought striking him for the first time since he slid in the paper beside the Huffman River. He opened it in front of David, the black ink now dry but forever obscured and washed from the water. "You wrote this."

David nodded. "A song."

"What did it say? What were you saying?

"You can't know," said David.

Salvador wanted to press him, but he knew David's life was growing short. There was a frustrating yet unalterable truth to what he said. It was David's fate that blurred the words, never to be known; the song never had a true beginning, had never been sung. Salvador folded the paper and placed it in David's open hand.

An officer approached Salvador urgently. "Sir, we just received intelligence telling of an RV heading south out of Bellark. A security camera at a gas station captured the identity of the driver; Samuel Lloyd. He's the grandfather of Jensen Lloyd, both now presumed to have assisted the Potes."

Salvador turned to David. "Okay." He studied the bleeding boy and thought on his son's efforts. "Get men ready to go." He knelt next to David. His mother kept by his side, pressing

273

the sweater against his wound, but by this time it had absorbed all it could. Her reddened hand blended into the wool.

"They're going to come for him too." The pain and limited breath only allowed David a whisper. Salvador leaned in closer. "He's your son." His mouth was to Salvador's ear.

Salvador rose tall, no longer possessing the lifeless body he walked in with. It was as if he was taking the life David was slowly losing, or giving.

"David, I'm sorry," his mother said, burying her head in his chest. "I'm so sorry." David closed his grip over the piece of paper and wrapped an arm around his mother.

His father had been watching the scene from where he first collapsed after the gunshot. Any inclination to speak or act was beyond him as if his tongue was cut and his legs severed. He watched his son bleed as his wife embraced the product of their intimacy. The thought crossed his mind several times, to make an effort toward David. But he reasoned through what it would mean, how he would view David if he heeded the desire.

"A vehicle is ready to take you to a helicopter, Sir," said the officer. He glanced down at the Potential. "He'll die, but it'll take some minutes, maybe longer if he's resilient. Would you like me to contrate him?"

Salvador was aware that the other officers had observed his every move since he dismissed Luis. "No." He removed his gun from its holster. David nodded in approval, knowing well that the officers needed to witness their Chief act as so.

Alarmed by the weapon, David's mother immediately raised her arm in front of him. "No!" But David placed his hand atop hers. She was grievously troubled, but after looking into his dimming eyes, she lowered her arm with her son's.

With a final strength, David called out, "You didn't know, Dad. You do now."

The statement felt like a hand punching through his father's chest, reaching to grip his heart. It was a paradox, one of pain and assurance. At first, Braham Kingsley thought the hand closed with intent to crumble and flatten. Then he looked to meet David's suffering, welcoming eyes just before they shut. "Son." It was the only word he could utter.

Salvador knew remorse would likely haunt him until his last day. But his duty remained. Those in the department would continue to follow and obey, and only the Chief could pursue Jensen Lloyd, Samuel Lloyd, and whoever was with them. He kept his body in front of the other officers lest they see his trembling hand.

David's mother turned away.

"I know," David said. "It's different when you see the blood." He coughed for air. "He'll forgive you, too . . . Jensen." Salvador finally understood David was speaking to him.

David's last thought was not of Jensen or Sam, hoping they would make it out of harm's way. It was not of Abigail either, the last of his new friends. Nor was he lost in thinking of his carriers; he'd said and done everything necessary for all their sakes.

It was Olivia who came to his mind, remembering their moment under the maple tree. It was interesting, returning to the memory that would later add to David's greatest despair, but this was not his focus. Rather, it was the actual moment that came back. Each of his senses remembered—her touch, her breath, the uniting sensation with each passing second that their gaze remained unbroken—provoking a quickened beat to his fading heart. It was a good thing, he believed, the bringing together of two.

Yet he would trade everything from that moment for her grief to turn to joy, if any of hers still existed; not to wipe clean the past, per se, though he knew if it were possible, her later sufferings would never exist. But that was unchangeable, and without their shared experience, his growing yearning and compassion might not be near what it was now. There was, however, something David felt he had some measure of say in. He felt almost unworthy to be *its* recipient—peace. Now, if at all possible, he wished to exchange his current solace for her sorrow. The gunshot did not allow him to understand the final prayer, other than that it added to his peace.

February 28th

Not one cloud gathered in the sky, letting the blue spread and overlay in its entirety. It was the brightest sunrise of the year so that a quick glance was like a minute stare with the sun. Perhaps the day would even bring warmth.

Jensen had driven for the South for a short while during the night. After they'd left the city and the cameras scattered throughout, Sam insisted he would drive through the border so that his grandson might finally sleep; Jensen's eyes and mind had protested rest, unable to release the thought of David for even a minute.

Despite losing radio reception after drifting from Bellark, the uninterrupted travel allowed a substantial distance from the city. A two-lane highway lined the coastal desert, but unlike the highway that ran east from Bellark, there were no mountains in sight, only the ocean to the west. The moisture in the air naturally yielded some surrounding plant life, mostly scattered bushes and short trees.

With the gas gauge slightly above half a tank, there remained enough fuel to cross the border, now less than an hour away. The last stop where they refilled was at the remote beach town out of Bellark's jurisdiction. There existed a few of these autonomous populations that Bellark hoped to annex in time, but neither of the two beach townsfolk paid the RV any mind, especially since it was in the early a.m.

"It's about time," Jensen said, leaning over the dash to look on the east horizon. "Was beginning to wonder if we'd see any real sunlight at all this year."

"In March, all grays open," said Abbi, awakening from the fold-out bed behind. "Didn't ever imagine . . ."

"What's that?" Sam kept his eyes forward.

"The sun will burn it all eventually," she said through a yawn. "At least that's what my dad would say whenever I got sad as a kid. The clouds would annoy all around, even if I saw just one. Could be seasonal depression or something. 'It'll all be gone by March,' he'd say. Every year I remember to watch and see if he's right. This year, I thought the gray might win . . . until today. A day to spare."

"Your dad said that?" said Jensen.

"Yeah. Looks like he was right about that much."

Sam said, "We pick and choose which wisdom we like."

"What?" asked Abbi.

"Let me put it another way. Hmm. Tell me to stop if it gets too personal," Sam said, finding Abbi in the rearview. "Take your dad for instance. Sounds like he was a smart guy in some respect, who most likely said or did some good things."

"He did know a lot," she admitted reluctantly, trying to detach from her former trust in her father. Abbi looked out the side window again almost hopeful for it to now be false, yet she failed to see any remnant of gray. "Smarter than most."

"I'm sure he was, but here's the thing. Anyone can be bright, but wits in one thing can only get you so far."

Jensen turned after hearing Abbi's sudden rise from the fold-out. "Grandpa. Let's not talk about this."

"No, it's okay," Abbi said. "I think I know what you're trying to say, Sam." She kept a hand to the RV counter and cabinets as she stepped to the front. "It's the reason why I'm here."

"Unfortunately, yes," said Sam. "What does the master roadbuilder, who's never seen the ocean, know what to say or how to direct the seafarer?"

"Hmm," pondered Jensen. "So, the master is just as

much a fool?"

"Only if he allows himself to be," said Sam. "Anyone has the choice stay a learner, which of course is work, but the title of master has its comforts to go with its ego."

"You're right. 'Great is the temptation to claim ignorance to none after knowing just one; but worse is the temptation to act and live on the knowledge never had,'" said Abbi, bringing her shirt to wipe her glossing eyes. "My dad said it like that. Pretty close to how you put it."

"And that's the tragic irony of it all." Sam watched Abbi leave the scant view he had from the rearview. "What he said isn't any less true, but neither is your father's wrong any less foolish."

Sam pulled off the side of the highway. Not only was the heat festering in the lower storage, but the border patrol would likely search the RV for any illegal or suspect belongings. He and Jensen grabbed the shovels they'd brought to dig a large enough ditch. Abbi was the one who'd suggested providing Mia with the burial sooner than later, solely out of respect without thinking about the laws of the South; transporting a dead body was impermissible.

Jensen and Sam placed Mia in the resting place and buried her inside the tarp. They could not bring that item either, a sure stench to marinate beneath if not removed. All three stood over the mound of the young girl, but only Sam spoke. It was a generic eulogy with not much elaboration, but still enough to bring value to their short-lived experiences together. Abbi placed some flowers she'd pulled from Sam's side yard onto the mound. The simple words had finally formed, a comfort Abbi hoped Mia would somehow hear. "We saved her. She made it."

*

Two helicopters hovered above the coastal highway. From their view, the rising sun sent its light to skip atop the endless blue ocean sheet. Salvador Goode sat in one of the helicopters, never taking his sight away from the highway and beyond. Three other officers, including the pilot, accompanied

278

him. Another four officers followed in the helicopter behind as a caravan of two ground vehicles trailed some distance further.

The Chief had to immediately fashion a strategy after receiving word that the RV stopped for gas at a station on the edge of Bellark. He did his best to delay the pursuit as long as possible, requiring a thorough background check of both Samuel and Jensen Lloyd to confirm any relationship with the escaped Potentials. Of course, as he expected, numerous reports, testimonies, and classroom video confirmation revealed that the two boys, Jensen Lloyd and David Kingsley, were far beyond mere acquaintances and the grandfather often gave the two rides to school in the past. Even though he no longer had Luis Adán to subvert him, Salvador could only exhaust so many hours of delay before he risked his removal.

"You have until noon." The president went out of her way to call him personally. Salvador did not give much thought to what the specifics of the instruction, or better yet, what the threat meant precisely.

Their plan was obvious to Salvador and the accompanying officers. One balked, "What do they think is going to happen for them in the South?" Their perception compelled the Chief's decision to assign a small-scale operation to locate and engage. He made sure to keep most of the CD forces close to the city for "alternative Pote activity."

"How far are we from the border?" the Chief asked.

The pilot officer responded, "About thirty minutes. Let's hope they didn't make it across already."

"Let's hope so." The Chief could not allow his relief to be detected. If those in the RV managed to cross the border into the South, he could forfeit. There was never an invitation for diplomacy, let alone a welcome from the South. Their loss in the secession left them a bitter taste, one that could not wash out as it did for the North.

Salvador pondered what would become of his life when he returned to Bellark. Certainly, officials would inevitably remove him from his position. When the president had to apologize to the nation on behalf of the Bellark CD, as she had an hour ago, the writing was on the wall. This did not devastate Salvador as it would have even the day before. The department no longer carried for him the promise he'd once thought it held. He was far beyond the delusion that he was contributing to some social, moral, or economic good. More importantly, Delaney, who'd fed Salvador's perpetual denial of his intuition, no longer awaited him. It was love lost for truth gained.

He then wondered if love could even be authentic without truth, if their relationship had ever had truth in it at all. For a brief moment, he doubted whether he genuinely loved Delaney. He found himself redefining the term, the standard for it, what qualifies it, what trials authenticate it, and so on. But it was the internal void that gave him his real answer, that if he were to have a look inside himself, his eyes would go lost wandering in the recently formed abyss. There was his answer: he could not deny being in love with Delaney, but that heart's devastation was no longer hers to fill.

If they did make it across, Salvador did not plan to venture into the South to search for Jensen and Sam. Even if he could guarantee a reunion with them, his shame would forestall such a meeting. The current search only granted Salvador the appropriate means to protect the two, along with any others in their company. After the pursuit ended and his removal as Chief, he could not justify searching for them, assuming the two would have no desire to see their mutual deserter.

"There it is!" the pilot said. "That looks like our RV." The announcement shattered Salvador's thoughts like a rock thrown into a mirror he had gazed into for too long.

"Fly ahead." Salvador had to improvise immediately. "We'll set up a checkpoint and see if it's them." He had to keep their numbers limited. "Tell the other chopper to hang back in case the RV decides to turn around."

*

The three lifted their heads at once. Above was a dicing in the air. Abbi looked out the window to see the helicopter flying

280

directly over. They were less than four miles from the border, and on the southern horizon was a dark speck, slowly enlarging into what they hoped was the border station. "Is that them? The CD?" Jensen asked worriedly as Sam accelerated.

"They flew on ahead." Sam watched the helicopter as it hovered beyond. "I don't know. It could be a border patrol chopper."

Jensen asked, "Ours or theirs?"

"We stopped putting up our own border security more than ten years ago after that law. No need to since the Southerners stick out if they try to migrate to one of our cities. They stopped crossing when we stopped hiring to put it simply."

"Well, will they even let us cross?" Abbi said. "Are we just going to try and pass through the station?"

"That's the plan," Sam answered. "We shouldn't be given too much trouble. They may not be too fond of our people, but if they can understand why we need to bring you over, I think we should have some success. 'The enemy of my enemy is my friend,' right?"

Beyond was the border station, now clearly identifiable. It was the only structure in sight. Sam was not as confident as he pretended about the helicopter. It had flown from the north. True, their nation was not as strict concerning the border, their government likely to remain ignorant whether a Southern helicopter flew one or ten miles from the line. But at the same time, the department was still in pursuit. It was the behavior of this specific helicopter that remained out of character, however, and Sam believed the CD wouldn't even let them go another inch.

The helicopter began to descend. Abbi and Jensen noted the activity with less calm than Sam, both swallowing their breath. A cloud of sand climbed into the air from its landing site about a mile down, the distance closing with each turn of the wheels. Sam had no choice but to press forward, certain that if it were the department, turning around would lead to no better outcome.

Salvador had forgotten what checkpoint resources a helicopter had, compared to the department's ground vehicles. The officers placed down a spiked roadblock, metal barbs spiraling across the black asphalt. He'd never directly ordered for that direction, but the procedure was standard protocol. While he could not instruct them to do otherwise, he did, however, have some alternatives to limit the pressure.

He spoke into his radio to the lead officer from the other helicopter, several miles behind. "We're all set up down here. Remain at your post until I give further instructions. If any cars come our way, stop them and alert me. Over."

*

The sergeant on the other end of the radio stood a few yards away from the other three accompanying him. Their helicopter had landed a few yards off the highway. So far, the lead had complied with everything the Chief had demanded. "Chief Goode wants us to remain here until he gives further instruction," he said, walking toward the other officers. "We are to stop any incoming traffic, and I will notify the Chief."

They nodded in submission, except one. The outlier kept hidden his dissatisfaction from the orders since he'd vehemently disapproved of how the Chief commanded the current operation. If it were up to him, he would have focused all the CD's forces on the suspected RV, not keep the majority in Bellark. He rejected the Chief's decision so stubbornly that he'd boarded the helicopter without orders. He was no officer at all in fact, having just lost his position the night before. It was no arduous task for Luis Adán to persuade the sergeant to let him board, seeing that the nature of his dismissal was not made public yet, only the spreading knowledge of his altercation with Salvador.

"He wants us to just wait here, while only four officers confront the Potes?" Luis' displeasure leaked out. "Not to mention, the Potentials are pretty much right beside the border."

"Those are our orders, Adán," the sergeant said. "You

shouldn't want to upset the Chief again."

Luis admitted of he and the Chief's "disagreement," which helped account for why they split for this operation. He added another clever arc, claiming that the Chief gave him a temporary demotion to basic officer until he could regain trust. Had it not been for the mission's urgency, the lead would have investigated the matter further. To Luis' satisfaction, the sergeant was so preoccupied with following orders that he had not exhibited the slightest hint of suspicion.

Luis stared down the highway. "I'll take up a post on the side of the road to halt any coming vehicles."

The sergeant was pleased to see his sudden compliance.

Luis walked to the shoulder with his standard-issue rifle. He peered north up the highway, anxiously anticipating a first sighting. It was commonplace for black-market traders to make exchanges with Southerners at the border, and though the trekking CD caravan closed the buffer distance the Chief set out to create, Luis bet on a trader to appear first.

He wished he had urged the caravan to depart for the border well before Salvador gave the order. It was simple enough to deduce the Chief's intention to stall reinforcements. Luis sent a text message to the caravan, to the person he knew was not driving. More than a vehicle, he would need a defense, a crucial witness to verify the Chief's threatening decisions. It was a bold decision to call upon the one who might understand Salvador's unraveling best.

*

"No." Jensen saw the spiked chain first.

The helicopter sat beside the highway. They couldn't yet tell whether the four figures belonged to the border patrol, the Contration Department, or the police. Sam continued driving nonetheless. If he did attempt to turn around, the helicopter would have no difficulty in catching up. "Abbi," Sam said. "Hide in the back. Go under the master bed."

"Why?" she asked. "Is it the CD?"

283

"Most likely." Jensen leaned over the dashboard.

"Let's not take the chance." Sam opened up the glove compartment and pulled out the gun. "Take this. Just in case. Go in the back now. Don't wait if you think you need to use it."

Abbi hurried to the back bedroom and took cover under the bed. She lay with her belly on the floor, aiming the weapon in front of her face. Her concern grew, but not for her life. Abbi thought that if the helicopter and men belonged to the Contration Department, then David's life might be in jeopardy, or worse. She entertained the possibility of his death but abandoned it quick. The only reality she could bear was that of David being taken into custody if the department did find him.

"Can you see if it's the department?" Sam asked Jensen. "Are you able to see Salvador Goode or anyone else from the CD?"

Jensen squinted at the checkpoint about fifty yards away. "They're armed, Grandpa. Each one has a gun."

"Department or police?"

"I think CD." He turned to his grandfather. "Who would we rather have it be?"

Sam understood his conflict. "I don't know."

As they neared, the pulses of the three played like a drum line. Jensen kept his eyes fixed on the men standing beside the highway. Sam briefly explained to him their cover story, though he would be the one to tell it. "If they try to talk to you, you can say you're my grandson. I'm a trader, and you just came with me for the day. Just don't let your name slip."

Abbi lay still, unsure of the object in her grasp. The RV slowed to stop twenty-five yards from the spiked chain. "It's him," Jensen said, spotting the face of the Chief. "It's the CD. And Salvador."

Goode watched the slowing vehicle. He had not yet decided his plan of action, unable to predict how he or the others would react after the first exchange. Salvador had not seen his former father-in-law since he gave up Jensen and questioned whether he could maintain his Chief's composure while ensuring the obedience of the other officers. "They're stopping," he announced. "I want you two to stand in position here." He pointed to the pilot, the shortest officer; one witness was critical. "I want you to come with me to search."

Sam rolled down his window. Jensen had grabbed a pillow, putting it over his lap to cover the other gun. Sam managed to remain steady as he met the eyes of the Chief, coming to a greater ease as he studied the man. *He looks sad. He looks . . . guilty.*

Jensen sat forward, understanding the leverage he held. He took a deep breath to reinforce the belief. The Chief had broken protocol to release him the night of the facility break. Thus, there was no reason for him to later disclose his relationship to Jensen. More confident now, he glanced at his father. It was a power play of sorts, to let the Chief know he did not fear him. Yet while he meant to intimidate, Jensen found his aggression put at bay. That night at the facility, he'd seen confusion. Now, Jensen saw something he did not before. Before him was a new face, one drawn with shame. The lines were shaded to bring form and dimension to the previously obscure mystery of the Chief of Bellark.

Salvador was about to speak, but his radio sounded, "Chief, we have a vehicle coming our way."

He grabbed the radio. "Bring it to a stop. No one comes through here." He turned the volume all the way down and attached the radio back on his belt, looking north to ensure there was no one coming. Salvador could tell Sam was analyzing his every move, trying to understand the mysterious behavior. The nearby officers waited, ready for orders.

"What can I do for you?" Sam said, holding out his license.

Salvador took the card from Sam's hand. "As you may have heard, some Potes escaped from a facility a few days ago. We have reason to believe they are headed this way. We're going to have to search your vehicle. I assume you are a trader for the black-market but do not worry. If that is the case, we aren't the police."

Sam nodded, trying to follow the unspoken hint.

285

Salvador drew his gun and led the small officer to the RV's side entrance. Jensen grasped his gun tightly under the pillow. Sam turned around to watch, hoping Abbi would remain undiscovered.

"Keep an eye on them," Salvador ordered the officer as they stepped inside. "I'll search the back."

"Hands on the wheel and dash," the officer commanded the two. Reluctantly, Jensen released the hidden gun and complied.

Salvador stepped toward the rear. He glanced behind to make sure his officer's attention was on the front. After clearing the bathroom, Abbi saw his black shoes near. Her body kept still, but the gun in her hands shook. Keeping her breathing quiet was like trying to trap smoke from rising. However, she felt if anything exposed her, it would be the heartbeat that pounded the floor beneath her.

Abbi could only move her head to follow his feet. The Chief knew he had to search under the bed after clearing the right and left sides, but was fearful, remembering how resourceful his former father in law was. If there were anybody beneath, Salvador was certain she or he would not be helpless.

Swiftly, he bent his head down from the left side. Frightened, Abbi went to point her gun at the Chief through the narrow gap but stopped as soon as she registered his hand gesture. Salvador held his index finger to his lips. It took her a moment to comprehend. Caught between incredulity and relief, she kept the gun forward instead.

"Okay, we're all clear in here," Salvador announced, walking back to the front. "Okay, Mr. Jared Wilborne." He handed Sam back his license. "I would say turn around, but I am not the police. I do have to at least say you endanger yourself trading with the Southerners. Especially with your, your . . ."

"My grandson," Sam said.

Salvador could only see the side of Jensen's face. "Yes. Your grandson." He turned to his officer. "We're all done here."

Sam gave the Chief a nod. He returned the gesture but found himself uncertain on what to do or say to Jensen, if anything; he was not positioning himself like Sam for acknowledgment. Despite Salvador's efforts to help them, Jensen's could not quite wipe clean his dusted, bitter lens. Even so, Salvador leaned forward to his son, "Good luck."

Upon hearing, Abbi released a breath. She leaned her head down and closed her eyes, taking one hand from the gun to wipe the sweat from her forehead. The weight of the weapon was too much for her clammy hand; the clanking traveled to the front. Alarmed, Abbi fumbled to pick the gun back up from the floor.

Sam, Jensen, and Salvador froze at the unexpected noise, as did the short officer. Just as he was about to take his final step outside, the man turned. The officer looked to the Chief for direction, noticing a greater alarm on him. Salvador gave a head nod for permission. The officer brought his rifle to his shoulder, taking aim and stepping toward the bedroom.

While Sam watched the officer, Jensen reached for the gun under his pillow. Before Jensen could lift to shoot, however, Salvador Goode had raised his own.

He fired.

Salvador looked out the windshield to expectedly see the other two officers sprinting to the side entrance. "Stay here," he said, shutting the door behind.

If Jensen still harbored any doubt, it had disappeared in an instant. Salvador Goode was no longer the Chief who issued yesterday's verdict. Jensen looked intently from the window, watching Goode appeal to the two officers, both clearly unnerved. Though the window was rolled up, he could hear their intense, muffled conversation.

"It was a Potential," he said. "I got her. The accomplices are being cuffed inside." Salvador tried to dissuade them, but the officers' skepticism remained. Stepping aside, he permitted them to proceed through. When both passed Salvador, he raised his weapon. "Put your guns down!" The two froze and cautiously turned to Salvador, perplexed by the command. He shouted, "Now! Put your weapons down, or I will shoot."

Reluctantly, they set them to the ground.

"Lie down. Hands on the ground!" Salvador kicked away

the two rifles under the RV. Maintaining aim, Salvador signaled to Jensen; he rolled down his window, understanding the urgency. "Pull the chain off the road," he said. Jensen jumped out and ran forth, leaving the gun under his pillow on the passenger seat.

Abbi had rushed from under the bed, jumping over the dead officer. She and Sam looked through the door Jensen left open, listening for Salvador's direction as Jensen ran for the chain.

"Wrap the body in a sheet. We have to toss it if you're going to cross the border." Sam and Abbi scurried to the back without hesitation.

Instinctively, Salvador turned to check on Jensen.

One of the officers capitalized on the Chief's vulnerability, jumping up from the ground. It took a moment for Salvador to register that he was falling to the pavement, but adrenaline kicked in to help him wrestle the officer on top of him. The gun flew out of his hand skipping a couple of feet from the brawl. The other officer darted for the rifles under the RV.

Jensen turned around at once from the commotion. His feet seemed to have decided on their own as he left the chain and sprinted back.

Salvador received a few strikes to the face. Finally, he managed to land a punch strong enough to blow the man back and remove some of the weight pinning his torso. Salvador reached for his nearby handgun, but his fingers scrabbled vainly on the asphalt inches from it. The officer was recoiling from the strike but reached for the gun himself once he saw where Salvador's eyes were searching. Understanding his new enemy had the same ambition, Salvador renewed his efforts, feeling as though he was granted an extra inch of arm. He seized the weapon an instant before, like one snake beating out another for a single prey. He fired into the officer's chest.

After rolling the body off of his, he moved to rise. "Freeze! Drop the gun!" Salvador heard. The third officer stood next to the RV with his regained rifle. Salvador dropped the gun.

Jensen slowed just as he closed in.

A quieter gunshot sang through the desert air. Salvador thought he was dead until he opened his eyes to find himself standing unscathed. Jensen turned in confusion. The rifle lay next to the third officer's body. Sam was leaning out of the passenger door, gun in hand. The old man did not take his eyes off the still body, ready to fire again at any sign of movement. Before any could speak or decide what to do next, all attention diverted to another unexpected sighting. Up the highway approached a vehicle at a soaring speed.

"We've got a car coming!" Salvador shouted. "Get in! You all have to get going."

Jensen said worriedly, "What about that chain?"

"You'll have to drive around it," said Salvador. "This RV can take the sand for a short while. It'll be quicker." He looked up the highway again. "I'll slow down whoever's coming."

Jensen remained frozen in place. His mind hurdled around the idea of leaving Salvador behind. But then he remembered Abbi and the promise he'd made to David.

"Get in, Jensen," Salvador repeated. "I'll tell whoever it is to turn around. Just get on the other side." Salvador walked out toward the nearing car and secured his gun in its holster to make the scene appear under control. He held up his badge until the sedan finally slowed.

Despite all reasoning, Jensen could not enter the RV. His promise to David regarding Abbi took a back seat with Salvador's life in danger. It was as if he'd discovered another oath he never knew he'd made.

"Jensen, get in!" Sam implored as he dragged the officer's body out of the RV.

"But we don't even know who's in that car," he said, shifting away from the entrance. "Let's just wait it out. If he needs our help, we'll be here."

Sam shook his head, knowing there was no convincing his grandson otherwise. Jensen gestured for the gun Abbi held, reaching for it through the passenger window. She handed it to him without question. Jensen walked to the rear, keeping a close eye on Salvador and the sedan. Sam rushed to the driver side for the quick escape, keeping his sight to the side mirror that aligned with Salvador's path. Abbi hustled to the rear window, peeking past the curtain.

Still holding up his badge, Salvador stepped closer to the car as it slowed to a stop. The sun pasted a glare on the windshield, preventing him from identifying the driver or any passengers. However, the driver reached an arm out of the window and gave a wave of acknowledgment.

Salvador began to speak as the driver neared. "I apologize, sir, but we had a checkpoint set up a couple miles back." He was almost to the window. "There's an investigation underway." Salvador stopped at what pointed between his eyes.

Luis Adán kept one hand on the wheel while maintaining his aim. It was a simple request to acquire the car from the trader. The officers at the opposite checkpoint were too cautious to leave their post and pursue Luis, who blatantly disobeyed orders; they simply presumed the Chief would discipline him instead. Luis stared at Salvador severely, a glare of betrayal at discovering the extent to which his former Chief had gone to keep the Potentials safe. "Put your weapon on the ground," he said. "If you do anything suspicious, I'll end it right here."

Salvador kept silent but followed the directions.

"Turn around and walk away from the car slowly."

Jensen's stomach plummeted as he watched Salvador lower his weapon. His concern became panic when Luis Adán stepped out of the car with a gun pointed to the back of Salvador's head.

Sam and Abbi watched fearfully. They could all perceive an element of heightened conflict, recognizing Luis to be one of Salvador's usual accompanying officers. Luis led Salvador to the RV, his eyes darting around to analyze the scene.

"Get inside, Jensen!" Sam yelled.

"No. We have to help him!" Jensen took his aim. Luis walked directly behind Salvador, provoking Jensen's uncertainty in his marksman skills. He lowered his weapon, not wanting to risk hitting Salvador.

"Leave!" Salvador shouted.

Luis said quickly, "No! Put your gun on the ground and stay there!"

Jensen would not heed Salvador's command. He stepped backed up a few steps and set down his gun.

Sam was gravely troubled as his concern was for his grandson's life, not Salvador's. However, he was presented with no alternative other than to intervene on Jensen's behalf. Quickly tucking his handgun in the back of his pants, Sam stepped from the driver's seat and hopped out of the RV side entrance, taking as many steps forward.

"No! Nobody moves anymore!" Luis said, on guard to see Sam's sudden appearance and nearing behind Jensen. When Luis finally approached the rear with Salvador in front, he looked to the dead officers. "I don't know what the hell is going on, but it ends here. All of you will talk!"

Abbi could hear everything from the bedroom, but she wanted to be close enough to help. Stealthy and quiet, she tiptoed to the side door. She kept her hand on the doorknob, waiting for any signal that would require her.

Luis dug the barrel into Salvador's head. "Why are these men dead?"

Jensen jumped in defense. "I shot them."

Luis gave a sinister smirk. "Did you? All of these trained officers." He took a step back from Salvador. Without warning, he lowered his aim and shot, lodging a bullet into Salvador's left calf. He released an agonizing yelp and dropped to his knees, unable to support his weight. The blood dripped down the left pant leg over his shoe. "Do not lie to me!" Luis no longer made any attempt to maintain composure. He looked at Jensen and Sam. "You have given us quite the odyssey already. And just who are you two? I know the kid's got to be more than just a crazy who messed with our facility."

Sam looked at Salvador where he knelt in torment, knowing that lying was not an option. "I'm this boy's grandfather."

Luis received a measure of satisfaction. The decision to shoot the Chief was proving fruitful. However, he realized there was a matter that should take precedence. "Who else is in the RV? Any of the criminal Potes?"

Abbi opened the door immediately. She did not want to give Sam or Jensen the opportunity to cover for her, having no intention of letting either of them get shot, even if they were willing. She stepped out with her hands raised, hoping her compliance would appease the unpredictable man.

"Abigail Rosario," Luis said, pleased. "There you are! We've been looking everywhere for you." His smiled vanished. "Where's the other one? Mia Day. Bring her out."

Jensen said, "She's dead. Killed herself yesterday. You can find her buried in the desert some miles back."

Jensen's malice did not seem a bluff, but Luis did not take pleasure in the rebellious attitude either. "Well, I'm glad she saved us some extra work." Luis scanned the three. "So this is everybody? The March Runaway and company." Believing that Abbi was, in fact, the last Potential, Luis focused on Jensen and Sam. "Back to my original question. Who are you two, *really*? Or let me ask this first . . ." He leaned into Salvador's ear, watching the others. "Why is my Chief helping you escape?"

Salvador kept silent, choosing death over exposing his relationship to Jensen, and he certainly did not want to grant Luis any more leverage. Adán dug the gun further into the Chief's scalp. "Well, I guess it has to be this way," said Luis.

"Stop!" said Jensen. "I'm his son!"

Luis lifted his finger as his animosity evolved into perplexity in an instant. He looked again at Salvador and laughed abruptly after a few moments. "He's your son, Chief? You're his father?"

"Yes," said Salvador, disappointed that Jensen had made himself vulnerable, yet there was also pride in the confession.

"I can't believe . . ." Luis' squinting in the sun added to his discomfort. "Now that is just somethin'."

"Shouldn't it have been obvious?" said Jensen, lifting his head high. "Our story was set before."

"What are you saying?" Luis asked dumbfoundedly, to which Jensen kept silent and unsure himself of what he spoke. "Well, it all makes sense now," Luis went on, his lips next to Salvador's ear. "Why you let him go from the facility. Why you wanted to take him into custody rather than do what we had to do. The guys back at the department are not going to believe this." He paused, remembering. "Wait a second. You told me you had your Potential contrated way back when."

Salvador said through a heavy breath, "I almost did. I wanted to."

Luis glanced down at Salvador, disgusted. "You never deserved your position. But you know what? I'm pretty sure that after today, I'm going to see a promotion." He pushed the barrel deeper.

Abbi stepped forward. "Just let us go! We're almost out of the country. Let us go, and you won't ever have to see us again. You can get his position, and we'll be gone forever."

"Let you go?" Luis said. "You know how much I've had to go through to get all of you? I'm not going to stop just when I have you all right here on a silver platter."

Salvador looked to his son, remembering the day some eighteen years ago. "I was wrong, Jensen," he said. "It's why your mother never wanted to contrate you, even though the tests predicted what would happen; but not contrating you then doesn't make me a hero now. I would have done it anyway if it weren't for your grandfather." His wounded leg throbbed, reminding Salvador that Adán did not intend to stop there. "After your mother died, I was angry that you lived and not her. I convinced myself I could have no part in your life because it would only remind me of the one I lost. As I look at you now, many years later, I know more than ever that I was wrong. I see you, and I see me when I see you. I wish it didn't have to come to that for me to get it, but it did. It did, and I'm so sorry for that. I'm sorry for everything."

Jensen listened. He showed neither pleasure nor anger, but rather a searching confusion for an emotion he was not well acquainted.

Luis did not think to interrupt Salvador's profession. He listened instead, interested to learn why the Chief had forsaken his career and life for this Potential. Salvador said, "I spoke to your friend, David. David Kingsley"

Abbi's head lifted, her heart booming. She was ready to cling to any word that would support her hope. Perhaps by some miracle, David was already secure in the South. If Salvador was helping them, maybe he had already helped him.

Jensen, on the other hand, was weighing all possible realities. "Is he alive?"

"No," Salvador said regretfully. "He died last night."

Abbi put her hands over her mouth to keep her breath. Jensen turned around to her. She waited for his reaction, but the one she expected did not show. He only looked at her, nodding his head for some reason, and then turned back to Salvador. At first confused that he hardly even flinched, she quickly understood: *He has no choice.* There was no time to drown in the sea of tragedy. Following his example, Abbi again clawed and reached for the surface. As tempting as it was to surrender to the mourning, she straightened her body tall, remembering not only David, but also Drake, Bobby, Mia, and Rylie.

Jensen focused on Salvador, knowing there was more to be said about David. If he had allowed himself, he would have experienced pain similar to Abbi's, maybe worse. However, that would have to take place later. He fought back the tears, but there was just enough for the wet glass shield over his eyes.

Luis' radio sounded, "Adán, we have arrived to your post. Where are you? Chief Goode is unresponsive. Is everything okay? We heard gun—" He silenced the radio before the voice could continue.

Salvador spoke low for Luis. "I don't want to be seen like this." This was the only mutual understanding Luis could afford him. It was almost sympathy, though his wryness undermined it. "I'll tell them all after. Believe it or not, I don't want you to be seen like this, Chief," said Luis. The others barely noticed this exchange, still stricken by the news of David.

Luis snapped back to Jensen and Abbi in their effort to recover strength. It was clear they had a fondness for David Kingsley. But even Luis could see that, though the news caused a gaping pain, their wounds seemed to tend to themselves. He glanced at Sam to see if the man had similar sentiments. *The old man keeps his calm. He's seen death before.* No tears fled Sam's eyes, but his devastation was great under the silence.

Salvador said, "I tried stopping our men, but I couldn't. I spoke to David right before he passed." He saw no reason to speak of his specific role. It would likely make no sense, an immediate cry of betrayal to know it was he who ended David's life. Perhaps they would learn later from the media, but Salvador could not throw them off balance yet again, not when they needed readiness for what he was devising.

Jensen swallowed. "What'd he say?"

"He said you were his brother. I'm sorry, Son."

It was too much for Jensen after hearing it. *Son.* He repeated it in his head, slowly parting with the resentment he befriended for so long. "I . . . I forgive you." He managed to get the words out, though his tongue kept trying to recoil.

Luis decided it was time to rein in everything. The exchange was causing him to grow quite unsettled, which tightened his trigger finger. "Okay, that's enough. Be thankful I allowed you two to make peace. If there is another side, you two just might see each other there."

Salvador glanced at the gun Jensen had set on the ground. He looked to him to make sure Jensen still maintained his attention. With a slight head gesture, Salvador managed to direct Jensen's attention to the weapon, while the other barrel ground into his scalp.

At once, with all the agility and strength he had reserved, Salvador ducked his head to remove the pressure. In the same motion, he turned and, with both hands, shoved Luis' arms upward to further remove the aim from his body. Luis fired; he missed, just as Salvador had planned. Using the power in his one healthy leg, Salvador sprang.

Jensen reached for his gun dartingly, but before he could grab it, the roar overcame the air. Jensen saw Salvador's body go limp and fall on Luis. Scrambling to secure himself, Adán pushed Salvador's body off and away. Yet Luis' quickness was not enough to keep the next bullet from his chest. Luis' body spun, dropping to the pavement on his stomach. Jensen stood, smoke leaving the end of his gun.

Jensen ran to his father, seeing some movement as he neared. "Salvador!" The man's breath was slow from the new wound in his lower abdomen. Jensen knelt beside his injured body, lifting Salvador and pulling him to lean against the back corner of the RV.

"This one's pretty bad," Salvador panted, grateful to see Jensen unharmed. The gap near his side would afford some minutes of life, but the Chief knew it was over. In any other scenario, the agony would have been the most terrible, but the physical pain could not compete against the relief.

Sam ran up. "We have to get him inside and get moving if he's to get any help. There may be medical care in the South." He shouted to Abbi, "Get the RV started! I'll grab something to help slow the bleeding."

She leaped inside for the driver's seat. Sam arose to grab the first aid kit, a few steps behind Abbi. He'd reached the entrance when suddenly he felt as though a Goliath had struck a finger through his leg. The stab happened with an eruption, immediately followed by a second. He fell forward into the RV, his head crashing into the edge of the table just inside. His gray hair was like water for red ink as the blood spread above his right ear.

"Grandpa!" Jensen called in horror.

Even Salvador's peace seemed to flee at that moment. He and Jensen looked to Luis as he had one hand pressing the piercing below his collarbone; in his other, he held the aim. Luis' grin was not one of benevolence, rather, an unquenchable rage stoked by vendetta.

Jensen frantically tried to reach for his gun by his side but stopped once Salvador coughed. Salvador fought to move as if to lunge toward Luis, but Jensen gripped him tightly. He was first lost on Jensen's passivity, but his son's resolution seemed to enfold Salvador as well, his body soon returning to the slow fade.

Abbi called from the driver's seat, "Sam!" He lay on the floor, his hamstring wound exposed. It was almost impossible to determine exactly where the second shot pierced, but a tiny pool formed on the floor from the right side of his head. It flowed quickly, added to by the split above his right eye from colliding with the table. "Sam!" she cried again. Her eyes may have never left him had his arm not moved, followed by a mighty effort to speak. "Drive," he said heavily, almost wheezily. "Drive."

"Abbi! Leave now!" Jensen yelled, able at the moment to recall the last promise he made to David. She had not crossed the border, but the oath felt fulfilled; his belief in her deliverance to come was just as strong as that day's sun.

Screech!

No one had seen it approach from up the road, distracted by the struggle. But the aggravated tires seized all attention, even Luis', who had not realized the silencing of his radio would lead to such. From a CD truck exited Delaney Abbot, alone. At first, she merely stared in shock at the asphalt scattered with bodies. "Abbot! She's inside! The Potential's in the RV!" Luis screamed, ravenous.

Abbi looked out the right side-view mirror, but the new arrival was not in view. Instead, she saw Jensen leaning against the back tire, supporting the Chief's head on his shoulder. She kept her foot off the gas. "Jensen!"

Luis' impatience did not lessen as Delaney slowed in her walk, and only grew shorter once her heels stopped beating the asphalt. "What are you waiting for?" Luis barked as she beheld Salvador.

"Abbi, get out of here!" said Jensen.

"That's enough from you!" Luis fired.

"No!" Salvador shrieked, his tongue finally released. In that instant, Delaney's unexpected appearance became irrelevant. When he first saw her, Salvador wondered if it was his blood loss that made him project some hallucination. This mattered no longer, however. Salvador's eyes fixed on the head of his son, his hands over the lingering warmth of Jensen's face. The head slowly slumped to his father's chest as he let the weight have its way. "You killed him," he said, his voice almost vanishing. "You killed my son."

"No," Luis said. "I didn't." He aimed at Salvador,

remembering all the frustration and every grudge he'd ever held against his mother, father, and brother, all of whom tried to deprive him of what he deserved, all of whom tried to take his life.

The scent of gunpowder and smoke rose to fill the open coastal skies. The salted ocean breeze sent it east along with the rest. Delaney tried to assemble the pieces, bring about some conclusion, no, even one logical thought. She found herself short of breath at the sight of Salvador, and ever more confused at the Potential who rested against his chest, their blood mixing and spreading across the asphalt. It was not an answer she first sought, however. Answers were not even a thought when Luis Adán had his gun to Salvador. Regardless of any conspiracy or coup Luis had attempted to accuse Salvador of, even if she believed it, the outcome would have remained the same; any person who would seek to take Salvador's life would, in turn, lose theirs.

It was that moment when Salvador was able to confirm that Delaney was no figment of his imagination. She kept her gun over Luis if he were to chance resurrect, but there was little comfort from the sight of the dead young officer. Salvador's end was written whether Adán was able to have fired or not. Only now, he had to wait to fade from this life as Jensen's skin went cold. "This is my son." They were the last words he could speak to comfort himself and provide Delaney the closest thing to a parting gift he could offer.

She rushed to Salvador, coming into Abbi's view through the side mirror as she lifted his head to hers. Yet no amount of calling his name elicited a response. "Sal!"

Abbi watched and waited for any movement from either Salvador or Jensen, but there was nothing but shrieks from the woman. Abbi turned to the back. "Sam," she said, trembling in her seat. There was a slight rising and setting of his body, a breath of a breath still inside him. Abbi went back into the mirror to see again if any of the Vice's pleas had brought back the Chief.

It was a whip of a head turn as if Delaney could feel Abbi's gaze. The mirror seemed about to crack if the stare-down went unbroken. Abbi needed no other prompting to finally accelerate. She was unsure whether she was the recipient of the

Vice's hostility or its creator, but the truth of it did not matter.

Delaney struggled to her feet, stumbling to the department truck to contrate the escaping Potential.

*

David's mother found no rest during the night. She checked into a local motel after the CD ordered her and her husband to vacate their home, only to wrestle between the unfamiliar sheets and thin pillows. The department needed to assess, investigate, and sanitize the scene before the Kingsley's could return to their home. The Contration Department was fairly swift and thorough, however, promising the house to be ready by morning.

She hadn't heard from her husband all night. He'd abandoned his cell phone when he made a frantic exit from the house after Salvador Goode finished David. She thought he had left to find Penelope, but leaving soon after, she drove past a local bar near the plaza and spotted her husband's car. She kept driving as her resentment evolved into a vicious creature she had never known.

Upon returning to the house this morning, she entered through the garage door and scurried upstairs while keeping a hand to shield her eyes. She would not spend a second, even look in the direction of the living room; a sequence of the night before would surely replay. The box was upstairs, and nothing else would have convinced her to return, seeking any reminder or token of David. Just one thing, she ordered herself, and then she would leave.

She walked toward the cardboard box in the center of the carpet. Glancing at David's desk, however, she spotted sheets of paper with a pen resting next to them. The papers had not been there on her last visit the day before, she knew. *He was here.* Fear of what she might read almost kept her from reaching, but whatever he might have said, she felt she might deserve every word. She read the letter several times over, and over, her fear leaving some time ago.

Dear Mom,

I managed to make it into the house, as you can tell. I've never heard it so silent or come to it so dark before. Probably why my thoughts are louder than ever and why I needed to tear this paper out in the first place. I'm writing in case I never see you or Dad again. I hope that I do, but you never know. You two may be out all night, maybe for days, and I'm not sure how long I can stay.

I've had a lot of time to reflect on my life the past few days. And I think I've got it, or at least have a good idea. The reason you had me contrated. At the root, I know you two didn't do it out of malice; it was simply your attempt to prevent and preserve. To prevent me from experiencing a hindered life, and to preserve yours. Nonetheless, though I understand, I do have other thoughts on the matter.

I'll begin by asking, what is a fruitful life, a life of promise? Is it having complete assurance that hardships will not come your way, or if they do, they can be handled with ease? I believe this is the life most seek. The one you two sought, the one I sought with Olivia. It is the life that every person in our country strives for, indoctrinated to believe that existence is for striving, striving is for wealth, wealth is for comfort, and comfort is the epitome of fulfillment. Any obstacle that might break this linear sequence must be inherently bad. Right? Sounds like it has some truth to it, at least on paper. I'm sorry. Honestly, no pun intended, but I'm writing with ink.

Anyway. I now believe that it is the absence of comfort that gives life a full, complete color. In a sense, when trial comes, one's existence is granted a stage for the rest to watch and understand, any audience brought to awe once there is victory. Many of my friends I have traveled with the past days have proven this to be true, taking the stage of adversity for something

300

greater. Sounds honorable, even glamorous to hear when people step into the role of hardship. But all too often, the glamor fades when we're asked to take the stage next. This is because, of course, it interrupts the sacred progression of the "life of promise." Otherwise, each person would be lining up, fighting to steal the next suffering from one another.

  In most cases, trial will bring despairs with it, muzzling the will of any person until they quit. Even so, if there is despair to come, does this mean one ought to run away from difficulty? Yes, there is no longer hardship, but you must be just as certain there is neither joy in overcoming. What would any achievement be worth if the pressure were removed? No one beholds a tower without knowing it was gravity the builders had to overcome, while at the same time knowing that gravity can crumble it back down if the right brick is pulled.

  I hope to survive beyond tonight, for many years to come. But I have to admit . . . I would not have much direction if I were to go on living. I'd most likely end up at many forks, all paths having some uncertainty. I think that's okay though, keeping satisfied with the simple pleasures of relationships, love, and the beat of my heart.

  I wonder if I had written this letter yesterday whether you would read it as legitimate? (Sorry for the quick subject change, but as you can imagine, I have a lot on my mind). What's a letter authored by a Potential in his Seventeenth year? What's a song sung by a child in her Fourth? Is the kicking in the womb a dance, or is it all only a stage in the Potential's development?

  In those few extra days of life I received, something happened to me, in me. At first, after learning you two chose me for contration, I never wanted to see you again. I admit I even said some hateful things. Then I examined my feelings, with a push from a few others. After seeing that boy with black hair get killed on television (one who took the stage quite literally), I eventually decided. Though I was probably the last of us Potes to

301

come to this, I wondered how I could claim to value life so much if I couldn't give it back to those it is hardest? There is life in words, depending on what they carry.

Why should I be the only one who receives the opportunity of redemption? I can't even imagine what I would begin to feel if Olivia forgave me. She may already have. I don't know. I can only wish. But that's exactly why I write tonight, in this very home the two of you raised me in. To put it simply, I write to let you and Dad know I forgive each of you. You may not want it or think you need it, but I offer it nonetheless. If I do not see you two tonight, I hope the letter finds a place somewhere in your hearts. Someday. And when it does, I hope it remains there forever.

With love,
David

After yet another read, David's mother broke. She had already wept the night before, but this was a new kind of emptying. The solace may have been the greatest to ever overcome her. She looked up at the ceiling, but the vision of her heart went beyond the physical structure. Reaching her arm straight into the air, she opened her hand. It would not close entirely, however, as though her fingers were interlocked.

*

Abbi believed she had created a safe distance by the time the Vice entered the truck to give chase. The woman possessed the quicker vehicle, but Abbi already had the pedal to the floor. The turn of events birthed in her new courage, Abbi coming to understand that she was last of them. Besides Sam lying limp on the floor, there was no one else for her to protect or be protected by. Her only obligation was to cross into the South, and perhaps the Southern patrollers might render Sam aid, she hoped.

Abbi turned off-road to dodge the spiked chain. The RV leaned over precariously as she angled off the pavement. Heart in throat, she tilted her body to the left, pressing her upper arm hard against the door as if her paltry weight would keep the vehicle from rolling over. Her teeth clacked together as she sped over ripples in the sand, finally returning to the pavement.

Delaney made ground swiftly. She steered her vehicle off the road to avoid the chain and rejoined the pavement much more efficiently than Abbi, aided by the truck's large tires and suspension. Before long, she was only a few car lengths behind. Not even she could understand where her resolve came from, why now more than ever she was determined to prevent this Potential's success.

She first pinned responsibility on Abbi for Salvador's death. To a degree, it was true, but Delaney quickly reasoned it was Luis' hand to execute. Despite so, there remained a stronger motivation that fueled her relentless pursuit. In a sense, she felt compelled to correct Salvador's wrongs and avenge him from the lie that hijacked his actions. Yet she could not maintain that falsehood within herself. Salvador had changed and that was the truth. There was no convincing herself that he'd been manipulated; blinded perhaps, but he made his choice. If Abbi were to now survive and escape to the South, Salvador's idea of the unfolding narrative might find a higher ground to stand and shout its truth. *She cannot be alive. She must not live.* It sounded contradictory even in Delaney's head, but she could not sort it out in that moment.

Abbi repeatedly glanced into her rear and side mirrors, panicked to find the Vice approaching so quickly, but she had reached her top speed. In moments, Delaney had brought the truck parallel, next turning the steering wheel to give the RV its first dents and scratches.

Abbi struggled to maintain control of the behemoth and keep it straight as the hope of crossing the border seemed to shrink. The bumps grew more aggressive, pounding the door and nearly clipping Abbi's side mirror off. The Vice would not even allow a breath's space between the two vehicles. Steadily, the RV veered against the stronger engine and durability of the CD truck. Its left-hand wheels ran off the pavement, meeting the sand in turbulence. Abbi glanced ahead at the unobstructed view of the border station and the fence lining the sand. It rested on a flat, a hundred-yard space between the rolling dunes.

There was at least another half a mile to go. Desperate, Abbi turned off the pavement, and soon enough the wheels were spitting up sand. It seemed like the only option, lest the RV topple over the asphalt to its destruction.

Delaney remained on the road, confident as she waited for Abigail to return to the highway. Yet that certainty became alarm as the Pote continued, weaving and bumping through the sands. The direction was not aimless as the zig-zagging first suggested as Abbi continued southeast, away from the highway and station, but toward the border fence nonetheless. Delaney jerked the steering wheel and veered off, following the dust cloud trail into the dunes.

Both battled opposition from the unwelcoming sand. The ditches and holes were unpredictable, yet each of them managed to keep moving. Abbi could no longer see the border station through the dust fog and rising and falling hills. Second-guessing her decision, Abbi worried she might be straying too far from the station.

THUMP.

The thud from the rear caused Abbi to jolt forward, smashing her head against the steering wheel. Delaney accelerated into the rear again, adjusting the steering wheel slightly left and then slightly right. The RV was beginning to wobble and sway.

Abbi was untrained, but she gripped the steering wheel and turned to counteract the Vice's attempts. The physics and persistence of Delaney's aggressions were becoming more difficult to thwart. In desperation, Abbi slammed the brakes, skidding and almost tipping over in the unstable sand. It would have if the truck did not collide into the opposite end to bring the RV back to four tires.

CLASH!

The collision was a belting from two monsters, the metal indentations a war horn of their own like. Delaney tried regaining control in her already-battered state, but her efforts went unanswered. The truck flipped and was soon horizontal, flinging first into the air as if kicked like a can to then violently tumble through the sands.

Abbi struggled to maintain control of the RV as it skidded. Despite her best efforts, the vehicle was brought to wrecking halt, plunging into a hidden sunken ditch just wide enough to swallow the mouth. Abbi's body jolted forward, her head again thudding against the steering wheel, but this time splitting her forehead after the airbag failed to deploy. The seatbelt protected most of her body, but it did not protect from the strike. Her vision blurred. Dizzy, she wasn't sure when or even if she would awake if blacking out came to pass. *Maybe this is it.* There was a resignation that persuaded her to close her eyes.

"Abbi," he said her name faintly.

She lifted her eyes just before they shut. With a hand pressed to her forehead, she turned her ear to the voice.

"Abbi."

She unbuckled her seat belt and turned. Sam lay on the floor, now behind the front seats; the RV's sudden and violent halt had sent his body forward. From his appearance, it was difficult to tell if he'd gained another injury since the first ones. It was a horrifying sight, looking as if a bite was taken from the top of his right ear, yet she was reassured to know he was not shot in the head as she'd first presumed. Sam kept his right eye closed, a vain effort to protect it from the perpetual red spill from his contact with the table.

She said, astonished, "Sam? You're alive."

"Not for long. I can't move, and I'm still bleeding."

His response seemed to resuscitate her. Her head was an accelerated clock hand, circling and searching every which way to find anything in the RV and think of some way to help him. "Where's the first aid?" She rose from her seat, pushing herself up with her right hand while keeping pressure to her forehead with the left. The out of place rib finally sent its pain, dragging a yelping groan from her lips.

In their debilitated states, Sam understood their chances were drastically unbalanced. "You need to leave. You need to run and get out of this country right now."

"What? I can't just leave you."

"No." Sam breathed hard. "You will leave me. I'm not going to make it. You can't either if you try to help me. Go."

"No! It's just a gunshot to your leg."

"Yes, but my body has already lost too much. Just look at my face." He coughed from the straining. "Please, Abbi."

She nodded, panicking, trying to trust his words. Sam spoke as if his death was inevitable, but she could not quite understand. *It's just a leg wound and a couple gashes. But maybe he's too old.* Her knowledge of medicine and anatomy was still limited, but she felt she knew enough to treat him. *If I can take that baby out of Mia, I can stop his bleeding.*

"Go, Abbi." Sam knew she was thinking of a way to bring him. "You can't help me. Please, leave. Even if you could, I can't move, and there's no way you can help me in your condition. Don't waste your efforts on a fading life when you can keep your own."

She bit her lip, frustrated and saddened. "Thank you for everything."

"It was a privilege." He collected every bit of faith he had—*Abbi will live.* It was why he lied to her, a deception she may later discover after crossing to the South. There was no better way to ensure her survival. A man who could not walk, let alone crawl, would only be a hindrance. He'd hoped the brutality of the wreck would end his life, but though untouched, he was certain of the extent of his injuries. At first, he was worried Abigail would call his bluff, but her injuries and confusion thankfully allowed him to pass it by her.

In minutes, maybe an hour, Sam knew the lurking Contration Department would apprehend the wounded man in the totaled RV. They would soon assess his nonfatal injuries to begin the incarceration. By then, he hoped Abbi would be well across the border. The idea of her on the other side brought him a consolation for the impending fire he would face. He could already imagine himself before the court and authorities, forced to answer for his crimes. He would confess it all, confident. Whatever punishment or ridicule awaited, it was his to own.

Finally, Sam closed his eyes to sell his deceit. He could not see Abbi move, but he heard a struggle to open the door. Relieved, he began rehearsing what he would say for the future.

Abbi leaned her body against the exterior to keep on her feet as the sunlight began to warm and dry the blood on her forehead. She kept one hand against the RV, balance slowly returning. Thin smoke from the engine rose and diffused in the air. The battle became uphill as she climbed from the ditch, collapsing to her knees against the formidable incline. Abbi thought of all her friends who had died: The remembrance of their efforts, their sacrifice, and their love lifted her from the sand pit. The crawl became a stand, the stand a walk. She looked behind to see what became of the woman in the truck. *Is it just me?* In another moment, Abbi was to a limping jog, holding her side to keep the displaced rib from pushing against her skin.

From the new vantage point, she could see it. Fifty yards away awaited the South. Abbi turned once more to discern her adversary's whereabouts. Another cloud of smoke lifted to the sky. She could not see the truck, but the distance was enough. This smoke was darker, thick as ink. Abbi figured the Vice must be in similar shape as the truck.

She hoped for it to be true, but her heart dropped as the woman appeared, struggling to the top of a dune; the Vice had a limp of her own. At what point Delaney had escaped the truck was a mystery, but her distance from the wreckage made it apparent she was well enough to keep chase.

Abbi held her ribcage as the sprint toward the fence aggravated the pain. She made no effort to fight her cries escaping through gritted teeth. West of her, on the other side of the chain-link fence, a white truck dartingly accelerated—a patrol from the South. Desperate, she raised her other arm to grab the driver's attention.

Abbi put every bit of her dwindling strength into the next step, not once looking back to see if the Vice had caught up to her; not a moment or breath could be sacrificed that might instead help take her to the border. Even if she did turn around, the rolling dunes could hide Delaney. It was an up-and-down, exasperating fight as the softness of the sand seemed to grip and yank on Abbi's feet, but she received some reassurance knowing it must be the same for the woman after her.

Her feet lifted from the swallowing grain and turned after emerging atop the last dune before the fence. The Southern patrol was closer than she'd hoped, the white truck showing some greater haste itself, zooming past each post that supported the fence.

The hellish run seemed unending. She glanced left and right, east and west; the chain-link fence rose north on each side. She presumed the station sat an extra half-mile north where the highway passed through, to then recognize that fate had sent her to the lowest point of the border, the center of a converging V.

That fact was irrelevant now as the fence was just yards away. Abbi was readying to climb and throw herself over to meet the patrol just seconds away. She jumped onto the fence, screaming to resist the pain in her side. "Help!" she yelled, hoping a Southerner would emerge from the white truck to grab and lift her weakened body. Abbi's fingers clenched the metal; it was the last of her strength.

"Get down right now." The voice Abbi had hoped not to hear called from behind, but it was not what she expected. Abbi gambled for an immediate gunshot instead if the moment came, but the command was a bullet in its own right.

Time felt almost frozen, proceeding slowly as a yawn. The Southern truck had skidded to a stop, and out emerged two men. One was lanky and of fair skin; the close semblance made her think for a moment he was her father. The other had skin like Abbi's, highlighting his white teeth as his mouth dropped for a moment at understanding the scene. Both wore sunglasses, but neither of their horror could hide behind that black. They looked to the woman behind the injured girl and immediately raised their weapons.

"Get down right now, or I will shoot you," Delaney said, seeming to ignore the Southerners.

One of Abbi's fingers slipped away from the chain-link. "Help." The cry was more for the men to know whose side to take. They stepped forward, one lowering his weapon while the other kept his on the Vice. The first continued toward the fence, extending a hand to reach over for Abbi.

"No, no, no!" Delaney shouted rapidly. "This is our nation's fugitive. You have no business here." The Southerner maintained his contempt by continuing forward with a derisive frown. "Stop!" Delaney would not waver either, taking extra steps forward and planting her feet into the sand. "If you take one more step, I'll shoot her right here." The new command halted him. He looked to his comrade, both frustrated. The one signaled the other to lower the weapon.

Delaney said, "Down now, Abigail. They can't do anything from the other side. It's you and me." Wailing inside, Abbi struggled down, but once she returned to the sand, there was an unexpected intermission. She was unsure if Delaney's hesitancy was because of pain or delirium, but, exhausted herself, Abbi could not figure it out.

Abbi caught her breath and adjusted to the silence, taking the opportunity to analyze her captor. Delaney had also received a forehead wound, a gash that staggered above her left eyebrow. The blood had seeped over Delaney's eye and down her cheek like mascara in the rain. Her left hand palmed her right collarbone as well. Abbi wondered if the Vice had broken anything, yet whatever injury, it wasn't enough to stop her. Delaney gripped the gun with a steady hand.

"Are you going to kill me here?"

"I'd prefer not to." Delaney's heaving was quieting. "But it doesn't look like you're in a condition to make it back. You may just want it to end here yourself."

The two men began to understand their place in the situation set before them. It was a fight they wished to make their own, but the young girl was inside. It was a miserable predicament, cornered and having no option but to wait, praying for a miracle, or perhaps, a prompting. Still, both considered how they would act if the woman were unarmed.

Abbi interrupted the silence again. "Why are you taking so long?" She perceived the resistance. "I'm so close, aren't I?" Abbi looked over her shoulder past the two men, allowing herself to get a glimpse of the South. There were no buildings or signs of human life from what she could see, but the barren openness seemed to beckon her. "You can let me go. I can tell you don't want to do this."

Delaney would not have been aware of her hesitancy had Abbi not spoken. About a minute had passed while she was preoccupied with the memory of her and Salvador back in his office when she confessed her contration. To contrate Abigail would prove that her only wrong was deceiving Salvador, she thought. *Nothing more.* Now, the longer she looked upon the girl, it was as if Salvador's last desire was becoming her own.

"It's not about want. This is duty. This is law," said Delaney. The long pause didn't allow her to find the words she hoped, but then again, she could never find them before. "You were chosen for contration."

"If it were about want, then what would you want?"

"What do you mean?"

Abbi put a hand over her eyes to shield the sun. "You said it's not what you want. I'm asking what is it that you do want."

"It's irrelevant what I want," said Delaney. "That's why I said it's not about that."

Abbi's broken rib had oddly stopped throbbing. "Well, I know what it is."

"You don't know anything about me," said Delaney sharply. "How can you begin to know what I want?"

"It's simple," she said, unblinking. "You want what I want, what we all want. I saw you. After Goode died. I saw the anger from the way you looked at me as if I had shot him." She brushed back some hair the breeze had blown astray. "But you don't seem angry anymore. That seems to have passed. Now, you're confused and sad. I'm guessing you loved him, or something close to it. It was taken away from you, a hope, a life with a man you cared deeply for."

Delaney shook her head as if Abbi's words were debris falling into her hair. "Why are you even bringing this up? What my relationship was to Sal doesn't matter. What I feel doesn't matter. All that's important is following through with orders and our law."

"If you loved him, why would you go against him and his dying actions?" she said, ignoring Delaney's rhetoric. "He was trying to help us, you know? You didn't have to chase me. You could still be holding his body right now like you should be. Instead, you have a gun pointed at a girl just trying to move one step south."

"You need to shut your mouth."

"What would he think if he were still alive?"

"If you don't shut up . . ." Delaney's voice climbed.

"Why can't you just walk away?"

"Because I can't! If I do, you're alive!" Delaney searched for her composure but could not rid the growing lump inching up her neck. "Don't you get it? I've been doing this close to ten years. Do you have any idea how many contrations I'm responsible for? For god's sake," her voice became a shiver, "I've contrated my own with the man who lies dead up that highway. More than once. And before I met Sal," Delaney swallowed, "I, I wasn't happy to contrate the first. But I was alone, and I was young. The sleepless nights weren't nearly as terrible as the dread of having to rise out of bed each morning, unsure if I'd be able to feed just myself. So don't think that I've ever been happy to do it."

Abbi closed her eyes, trying to reimagine all just shared. "How far along were you? The first time."

"Does it matter?" Delaney shook her head. "He was a Potential."

"A boy? Did you ever pick a name?"

"No." It looked as if Delaney's eyes were dams, flexing and pressing against all that it held behind. "I couldn't."

"Why not?"

"Don't play dumb. You're clever. Your questions show that," Delaney said with some assuredness to her dry words. "I can't let you cross for the same reason."

The two Southerners tried to piece the conversation together. They were unsure whether the officer in her current condition would ever shoot since she had stalled for so long already. If they could see Abbi's face, perhaps they would be eased by her calm, and more, they too might have had sympathy for the woman just as Abbi did.

"You would have to confess it, admit to all of it." Abbi's tread became more delicate. "I can't imagine how difficult that would be. To tear down a belief you'd built up and leaned against for so many years, especially through the doubt."

"Don't go putting words in my mouth. I never said I doubted."

"Then why are there tears in your eyes? They haven't fallen, but I see them."

"You have no grounds to be asking these questions!" Delaney lifted her arm away from her collarbone to wipe the wound above her eye. There exposed was a red stain on her shoulder, maybe from glass, Abbi thought. "This is the way it all works, how society stays afloat—more than that, how it thrives. Try imagining that nation of old again, a nation stripped of choice, when someone is restricted from living out their life fully because of a Pote like yourself. We're not just out to contrate for fun. No one said this was a fun business. We do it—"

"—for the greater good, for economic welfare, for the virtue of choice. I know. I was educated in our country." Abbi said, circling back, "But still. Why do you fight back tears as if you don't believe your own words?" From the inner corner of Delaney's eye, Abbi saw a red droplet descend her nose; it must have sneaked past her hand when she went to wipe. The droplet suspended, not quite dense enough for gravity to pull it to the earth. "It's different talking with me, huh? Always easier when there's no seeing, no hearing, no speaking."

The two men behind Abbi flinched when they saw

Delaney's gun twitch.

Abbi never moved a muscle. *It almost slipped.*

Delaney's other hand came to support the weapon. If numbness had a voice, it spoke then. "Always has been easier that way. This will be difficult, but it's the only way to have it all make sense. I'm sorry. I am. But I have to do this."

All of Abbi's confusion dispelled after the Vice answered. Even in all their contradictions, each of Delaney's actions and words strangely made sense. Perhaps if swapped in shoes and life circumstances, Abigail would respond similarly. She turned around, releasing all fear as well as control. All was on the table now, nothing left to dissuade or persuade since the Vice had conceded her beliefs. For Abbi to continue appealing for life was like endlessly swimming upriver against a mountain with no peak.

Delaney noticed the sudden shift in her posture. It was not that the girl was unconcerned for her life, but there remained a resolute calm. Abbi looked over her shoulder to the South; it was as if she were dreaming. Delaney grew even more unsettled, glancing to the two Southerners behind. Before the exchange, she would not have questioned the passivity of the two men, who now watched solemnly with their weapons down. They were merely observers, free to assess and judge, but knowing well any decision or intervention was neither in their control nor was it their right.

"If you do, be ready. It won't be like the other ones," said Abbi, looking past the gun into the petrified eyes.

Delaney was readying to speak her last in the exchange, but her mouth trapped shut as the girl's stare blew down the door and stepped inside her soul; and now, Abbi knew everything in it.

"It's different when you see the blood." The girl sat in the sand and leaned against the fence. Tucking her knees to chest, she wrapped her arms around her legs, raising her face to the blue that had been hidden for too long.

March 1st

The room was congested of bodies so that the muggy warmth was no better than the outside cold as the men awaited one type of news or the other at the joint delivery-contration hospital. They occupied the few rows of chairs, an empty seat here and there to space out a few. There was a strict policy excluding them from the delivery rooms, in case the woman decided differently.

There was only one in the waiting room with an outlying motive, who had earlier stumbled in as if his arrival were a mistake. On his breath was a residual aroma of alcohol; the front desk worker and those sitting beside him knew that best. Had it been several hours before, he might still have been intoxicated. It was reasonable for the receptionist to assume it so, especially hearing the shakiness in his alcohol-scented breath and witnessing his clumsy entry.

Despite so, Braham Kingsley had never felt more sober. He'd sought to ensure it in the pivotal moment after the story of the final March Runaway broadcasted over the dive bar television; it was his second night there. Having already guzzled three cocktails and four whiskey shots before the broadcast, he barged into the restroom and lodged two fingers down his throat before the liquor could take effect and drown him for yet another night.

His tripping entrance into the joint hospital was not from

314

drunkenness, but from an unfamiliar urgency, one he'd lacked for some time. He had a keen awareness, completely clear in thought unlike many inside the hospital, all drifting through the fog of passivity as if they instead forced back too many drinks. The faces that would leave were neutral, for the less-composed, grievous, and for the few, happy.

Twice a year at most, a person would arrive to make the same request Braham Kingsley did. The Potentials already selected for contration within the womb could not be requested; only those on contration row. The list for adoption was often short, and with the recent Closing, there was only one Potential available on the online listing.

"Mr. Kingsley," the front desk woman announced. It had been almost an hour wait, but his eyes glued to the television screen. The story of the final March Runaway was inescapable, no matter which television channel it seemed. "Mr. Kingsley," the woman said again. Braham was next to the speakers, and the anchor spoke loudly as he condemned the accomplice Samuel Lloyd, speculating on the nature of his crimes and the well-deserved trial to come.

Braham was committed to learn how the CD and police would move forward with Sam's prosecution, but even this matter was not as urgent. He rose from his chair, catching many confused glances. Not one person was able to accurately guess his business, and most grew more uncomfortable to watch him fidget in his seat. His response was only natural, however, when certainty steadily suffocates doubt, when the one giant pushes the other back. The woman slid the paper in front of him; a series of words, clauses, and legalities. At the bottom was the blank line awaiting a signature.

"You sure your wife is okay with this?" The woman was hesitant for him. "If this is your first Pote, know it'll be some work, especially with this one. Came in a couple days ago after some kid dropped her off. Don't know why they did a home birth if the plan was to bring her here. Can't imagine the pain and the mess. Almost died when it came here, but now it's healthy enough, somehow."

"A couple days ago?" He looked up from the blank signature line. "Can I see her?" The information was never listed online as he checked.

"Sure. Don't know why you didn't ask before. Figures you should at least have a look first." She chuckled. "Who buys a car without a test drive, right?"

The receptionist escorted Braham through a hall, only a few rooms from the front. The room could have been green or blue depending on the lighting. In the center stood a lone, crib-like casing, a glass oval over the sleeping infant. It appeared the case was designed to shield a larger body.

He walked closer, coming to hover above the pint-sized girl who had tubes attached to her mouth and nose, presumably for oxygen or other necessary nutrients. Three pounds was much tinier than he'd imagined. He leaned closer, his eyes an inch away from the glass, but quiet to avoid disturbing her sleep. The memory returned: David hadn't cried after the birth, and the doctor was forced to prick his skin to confirm a healthy nervous system. After the tears, however, David had drifted to the same heavenly state in which the baby girl now slept.

He recalled every provision Penelope and David required as they aged, counting the cost if was truly possible. The online description had not included the premature Potential's extensive degree of dependency. He wondered if it was a blatant lie to label the infant 'healthy.' *Why am I here? This was a mistake.* He slid both hands into his back pockets to dry his hands.

Paper rustled under his right.

The compensation check he received from the network interview had never left his pocket since he left the studio before he saw his son die. It was a generous donation, one that could sustain him and his wife and support Penelope at university for several years, all without finding a new job. But the benefits of the check would eventually run out. He shook his head at the realization. Far be it from him to prolong a Potential's existence only to have it come to an end if he could not provide for his current family. *Is this selfish of me? She's not David. Give her mercy and leave.*

The doubt had returned as a flood, overwhelming the certainty of the moment before. The man who entered the facility had remolded again into a warped image of the sure self he arrived as. It was not a regression into the old self, however. The old self would not be straining to remain on his feet while grief climbed atop his shoulders; the former would never have felt the need to come to this hospital in any case.

Braham slid the check back into his pocket, disappointed with himself but somewhat reassured by the new justification. He gave one last look at the sleeping infant, a respect he felt obligated to extend to the child that would soon depart from this life, perhaps to see his son. It was ironic, even for him he knew, to wish that the carriers had chosen to keep and raise her. *What made them make their choice?*

The baby lifted her eyes.

Braham's body went still, watching her curious eyes wander about the room. She closed them for a high-pitched yawn, opening them again until they met the man who stood above her. He printed his hand on the oval glass, leaning forward to confirm his wonderment. He brought the document out of his other pocket, rereading the description to understand if he was the one mistaken: *Female. 3 Lbs. 8 oz. Premature, 26-29 Weeks. Healthy. Eyes: Gray.*

The girl looked upon him, from his head to his waist, the extent to which she could see. Her peering was like a deep cleansing rather than an observation. In an instant, all of Braham's doubt diminished to nonexistence like water under the sun. He was slow to sign the document, rattled by the weight, the full measure of his humanity as well as hers. The only question left in his mind was wondering at which point her eyes had turned blue.

The End

Made in the USA
San Bernardino, CA
29 March 2019